STAR TREK®

COUNTDOWN

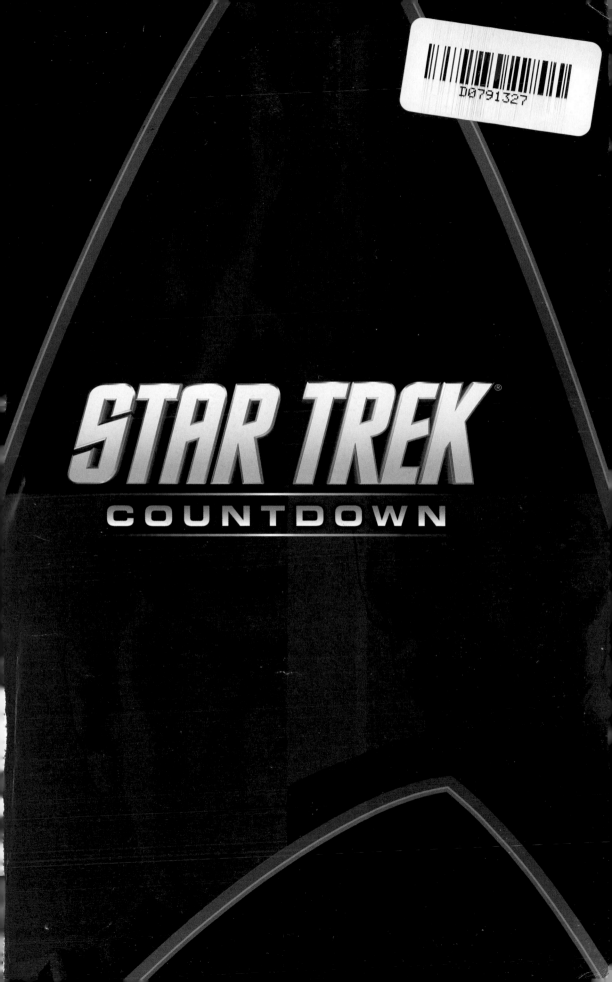

STAR TREK
COUNTDOWN

STORY
ROBERTO ORCI & ALEX KURTZMAN

WRITERS
MIKE JOHNSON & TIM JONES

ARTIST
DAVID MESSINA

COLOR ART
GIOVANNA NIRO

ADDITIONAL COLORS
DAVID MESSINA AND PAOLO MADDALENI

COLOR CONSULTANT
ILARIA TRAVERSI

LETTERERS
CHRIS MOWRY, ROBERT ROBBINS, AND NEIL UYETAKE

CREATIVE CONSULTANT
DAVID BARONOFF

ORIGINAL SERIES EDITORS
ANDY SCHMIDT AND SCOTT DUNBIER

COLLECTION EDITOR
JUSTIN EISINGER

COLLECTION DESIGNER
NEIL UYETAKE

IDW Publishing
Operations:
Ted Adams, Chief Executive Officer
Greg Goldstein, Chief Operating Officer
Matthew Ruzicka, CPA, Chief Financial Officer
Alan Payne, VP of Sales
Lorelei Bunjes, Dir. of Digital Services
AnnaMaria White, Marketing & PR Manager
Marci Hubbard, Executive Assistant
Alonzo Simon, Shipping Manager

Editorial:
Chris Ryall, Publisher/Editor-in-Chief
Scott Dunbier, Editor, Special Projects
Andy Schmidt, Senior Editor
Justin Eisinger, Editor
Kris Oprisko, Editor/Foreign Lic.
Denton J. Tipton, Editor
Tom Waltz, Editor
Mariah Huehner, Associate Editor

Design:
Robbie Robbins, EVP/Sr. Graphic Artist
Ben Templesmith, Artist/Designer
Neil Uyetake, Art Director
Chris Mowry, Graphic Artist
Amauri Osorio, Graphic Artist
Gilberto Lazcano, Production Assistant

www.IDWPUBLISHING.com
ISBN: 978-1-60010-420-6   12 11 10 09   2 3 4 5

STAR TREK created by Gene Roddenberry
Special Thanks to Risa Kessler and John Van Citters at CBS Consumer Products, JJ Abrams and Bryan Burk at Bad Robot Productions, Mandy Safavi, Ben Kim, Pete Chiarelli, Kim Cavyan, Steven Puri and Rafael Ruthchild at K/O Productions, and Elena Casagrande, Rick Sternbach and Scott Tipton for their invaluable assistance. Additionally, David Messina would like to thank his girlfriend Sara for all her love and support.

Originally published as STAR TREK: COUNTDOWN Issues #1–4.

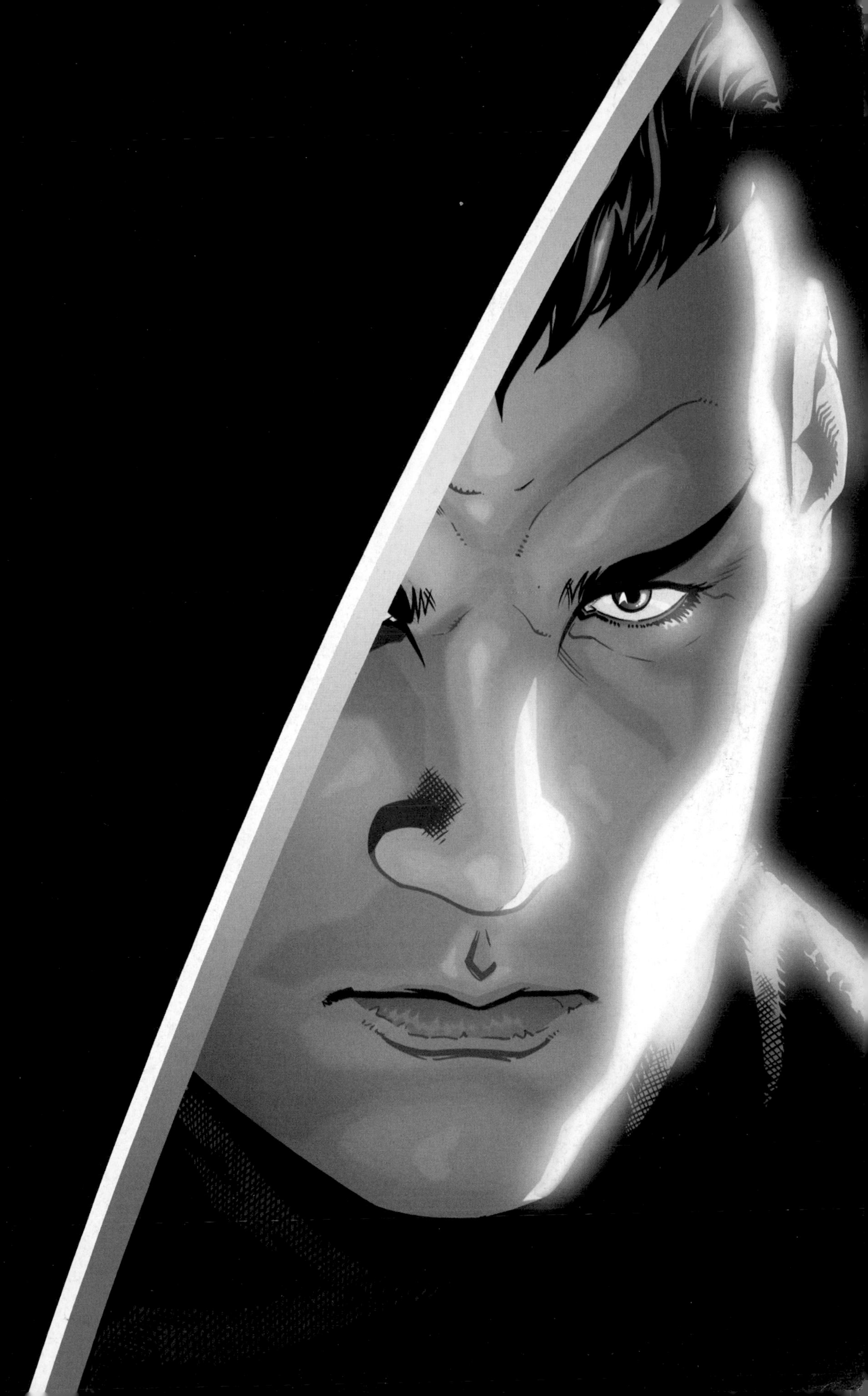

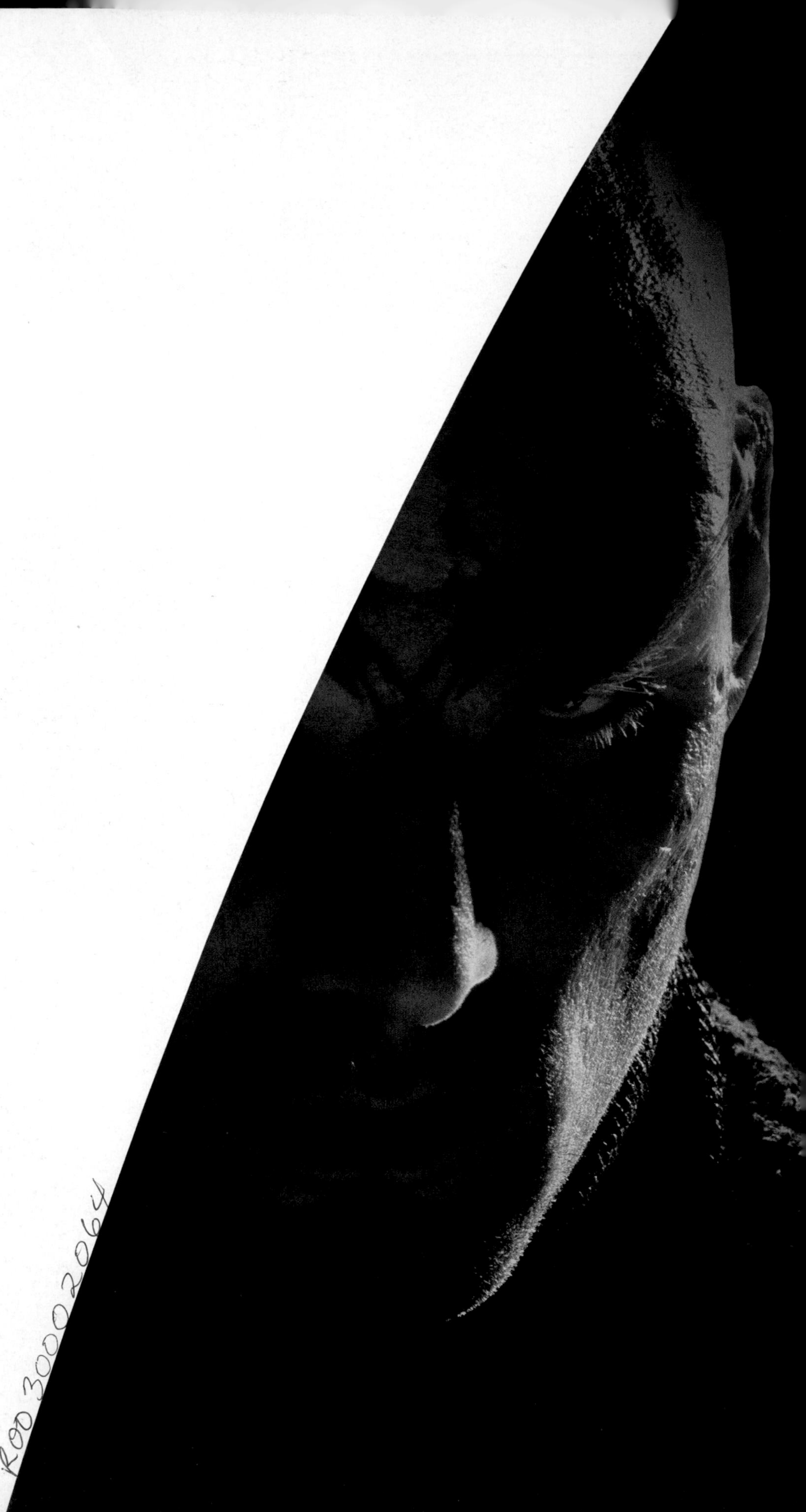

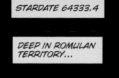

STARDATE 64333.4

DEEP IN ROMULAN
TERRITORY...

WHERE ONLY A FEW HAVE
GONE BEFORE...

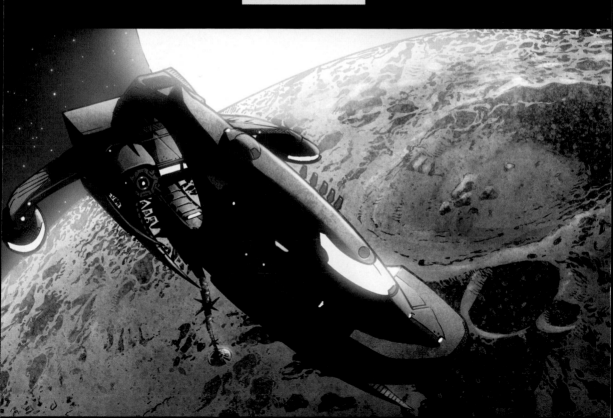

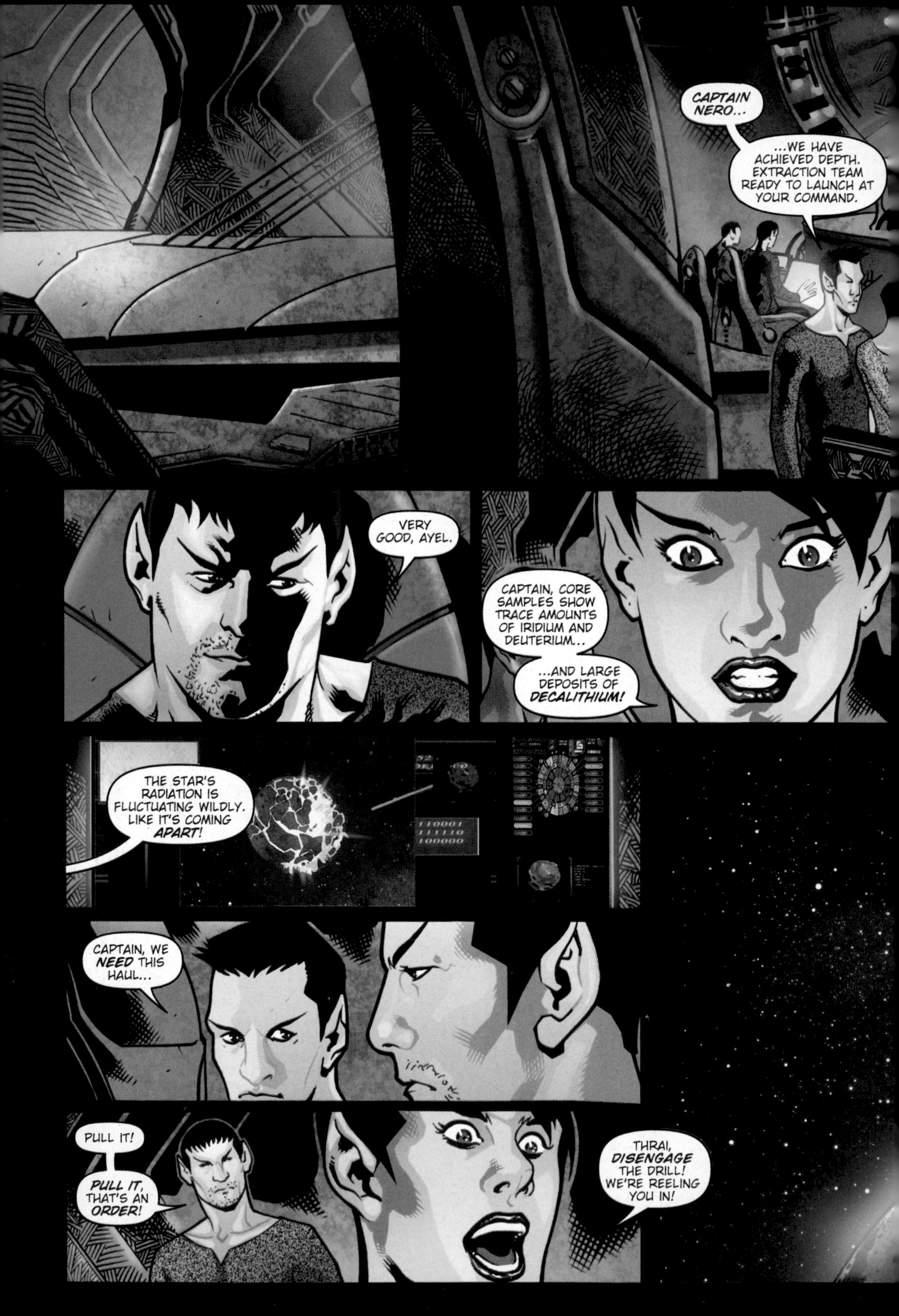

CAPTAIN NERO...
...WE HAVE ACHIEVED DEPTH. EXTRACTION TEAM READY TO LAUNCH AT YOUR COMMAND.
VERY GOOD, AYEL.
CAPTAIN, CORE SAMPLES SHOW TRACE AMOUNTS OF IRIDIUM AND DEUTERIUM...
...AND LARGE DEPOSITS OF DECALITHIUM!
THE STAR'S RADIATION IS FLUCTUATING WILDLY. LIKE IT'S COMING APART!
CAPTAIN, WE NEED THIS HAUL...
PULL IT!
PULL IT, THAT'S AN ORDER!
THRAI, DISENGAGE THE DRILL! WE'RE REELING YOU IN!

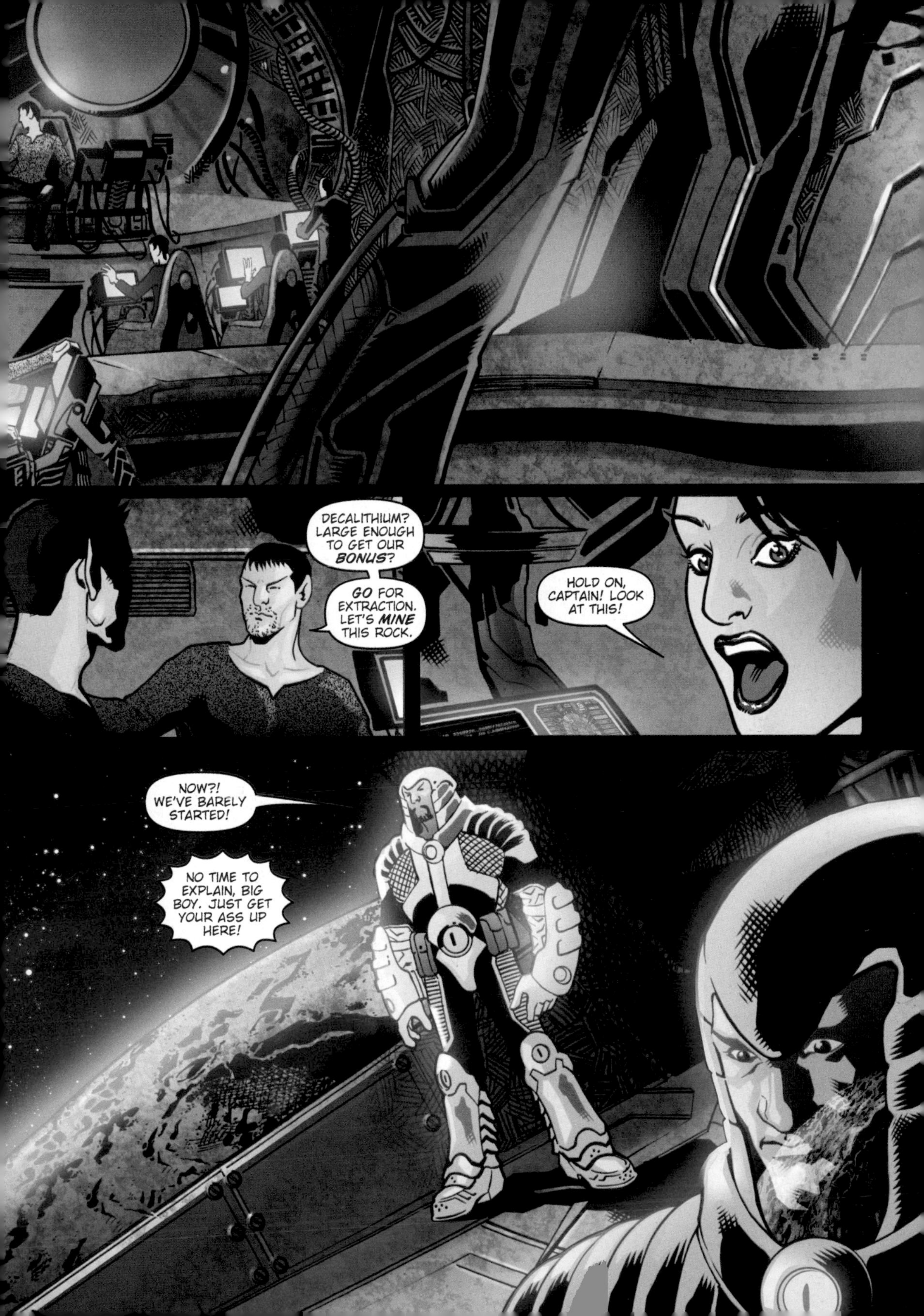
DECALITHIUM? LARGE ENOUGH TO GET OUR BONUS?
GO FOR EXTRACTION. LET'S MINE THIS ROCK.
HOLD ON, CAPTAIN! LOOK AT THIS!
NOW?! WE'VE BARELY STARTED!
NO TIME TO EXPLAIN, BIG BOY. JUST GET YOUR ASS UP HERE!

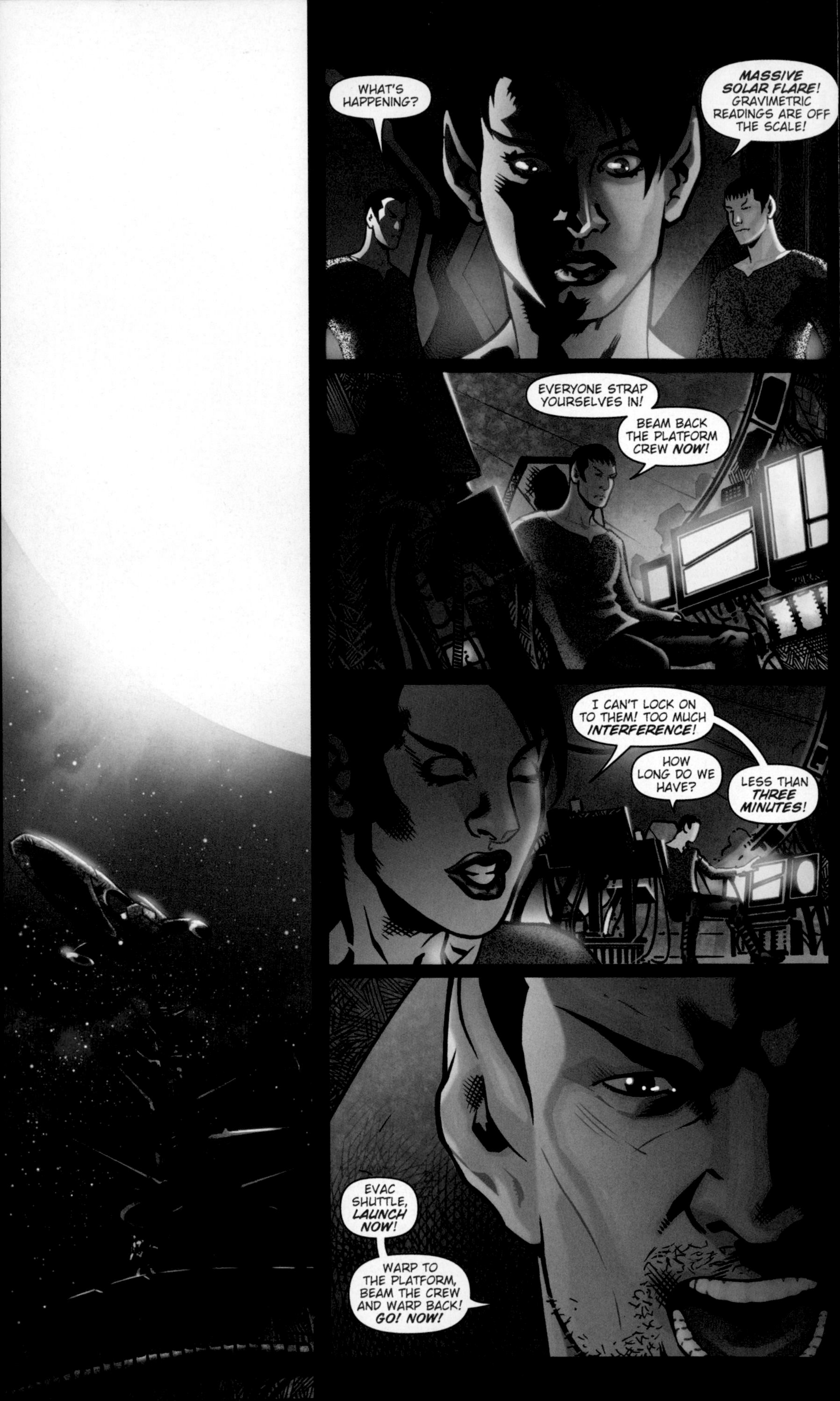

WHAT'S HAPPENING?
MASSIVE SOLAR FLARE! GRAVIMETRIC READINGS ARE OFF THE SCALE!
EVERYONE STRAP YOURSELVES IN!
BEAM BACK THE PLATFORM CREW NOW!
I CAN'T LOCK ON TO THEM! TOO MUCH INTERFERENCE!
HOW LONG DO WE HAVE?
LESS THAN THREE MINUTES!
EVAC SHUTTLE, LAUNCH NOW!
WARP TO THE PLATFORM, BEAM THE CREW AND WARP BACK! GO! NOW!

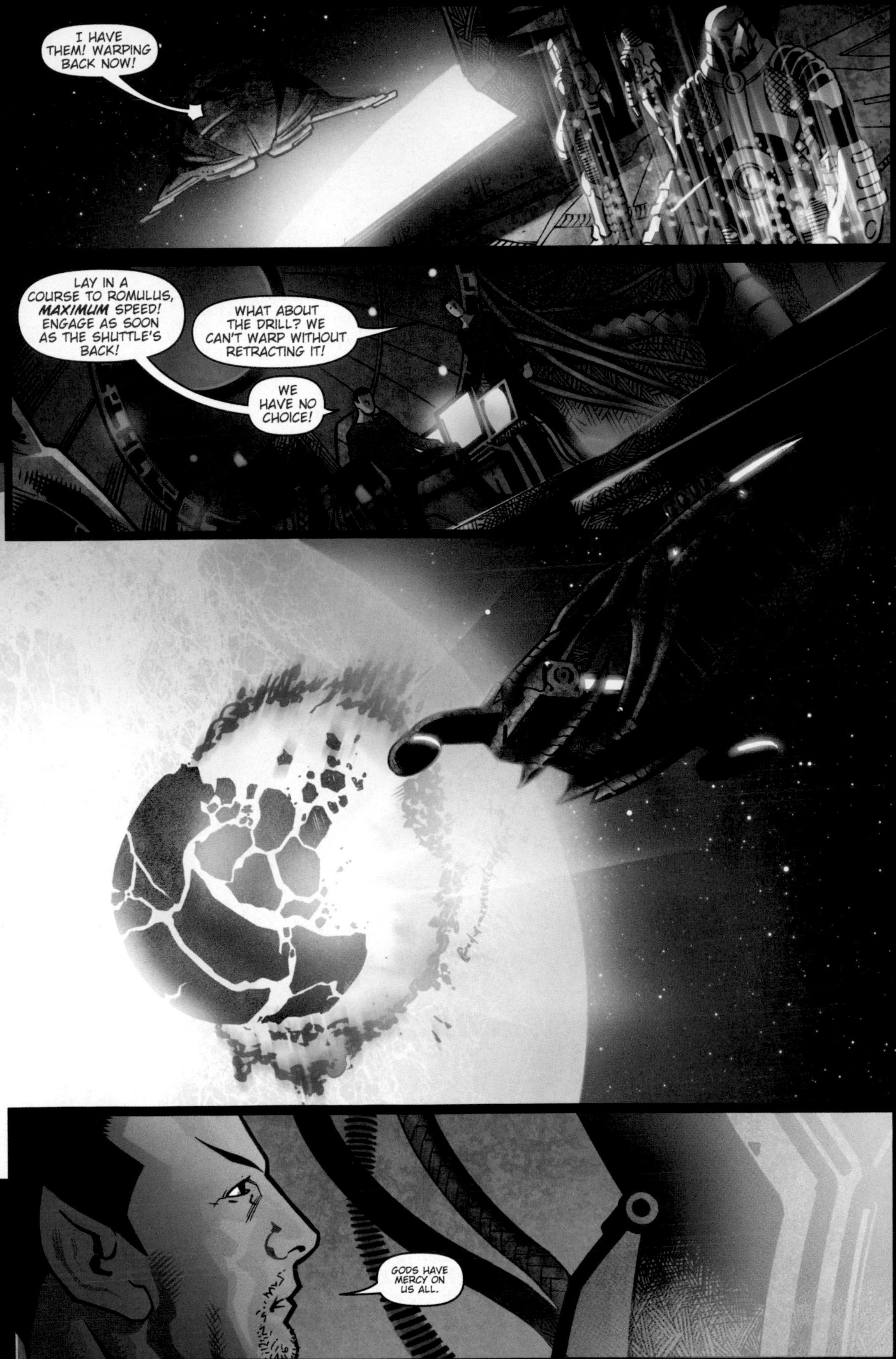
I HAVE THEM! WARPING BACK NOW!
LAY IN A COURSE TO ROMULUS, *MAXIMUM* SPEED! ENGAGE AS SOON AS THE SHUTTLE'S BACK!
WHAT ABOUT THE DRILL? WE CAN'T WARP WITHOUT RETRACTING IT!
WE HAVE NO CHOICE!
GODS HAVE MERCY ON US ALL.

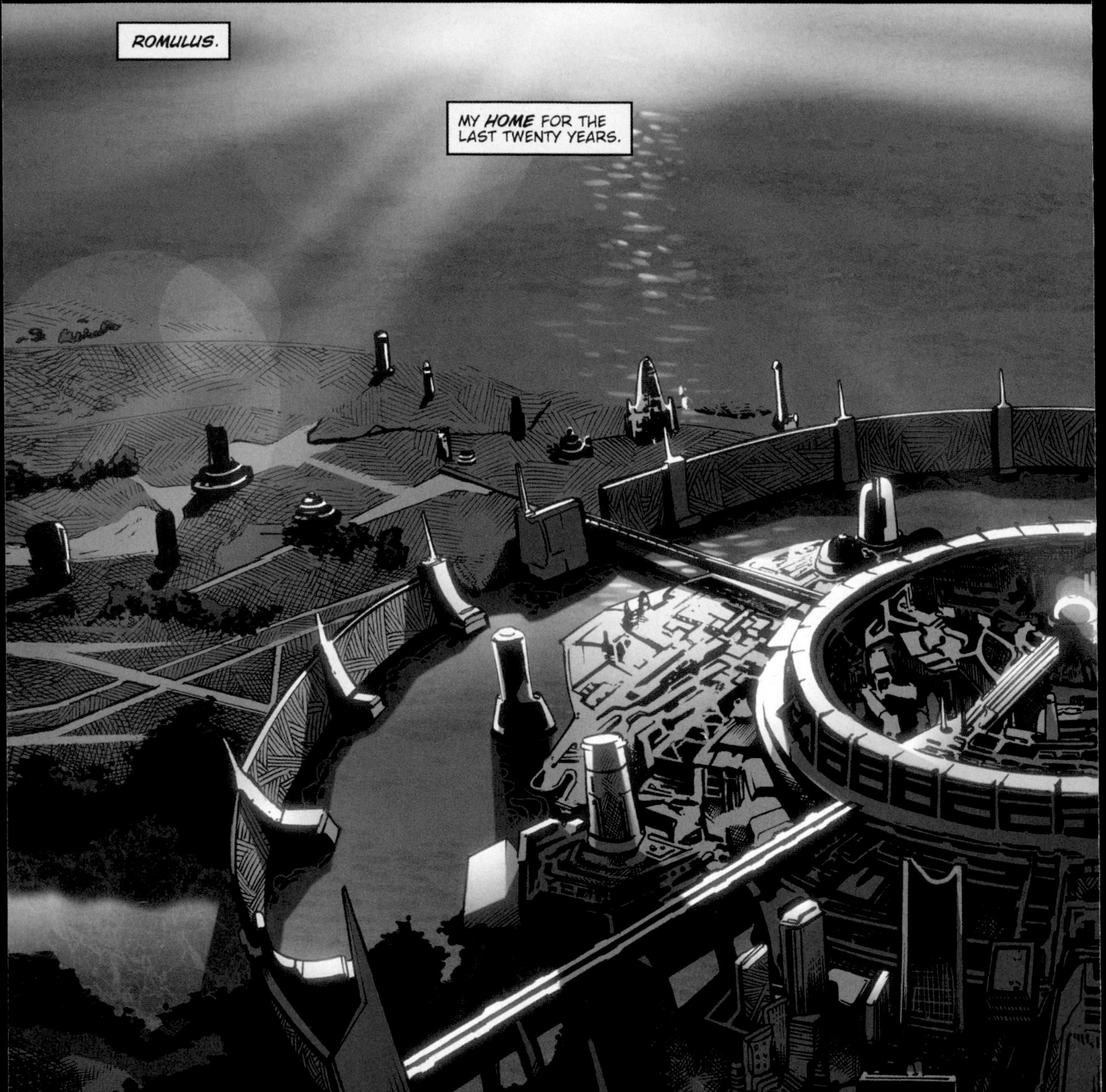
ROMULUS.
MY HOME FOR THE LAST TWENTY YEARS.

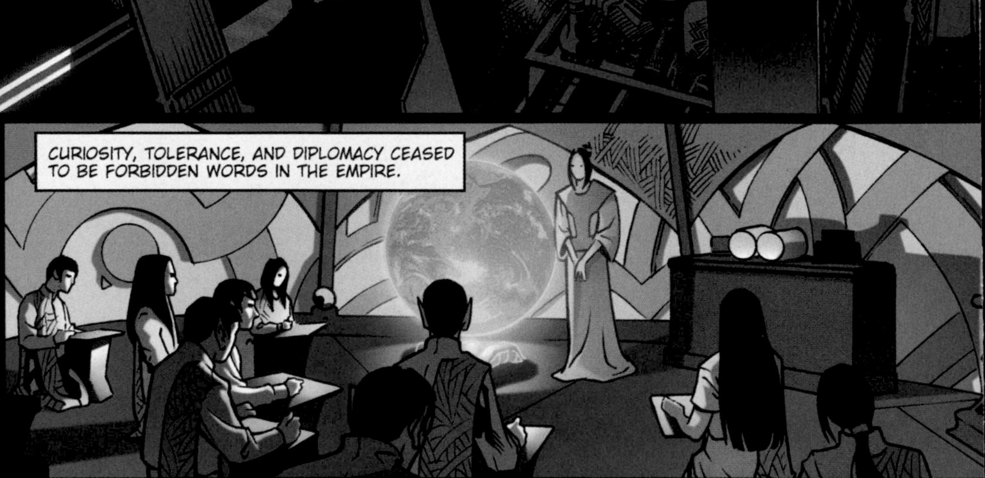
CURIOSITY, TOLERANCE, AND DIPLOMACY CEASED TO BE FORBIDDEN WORDS IN THE EMPIRE.

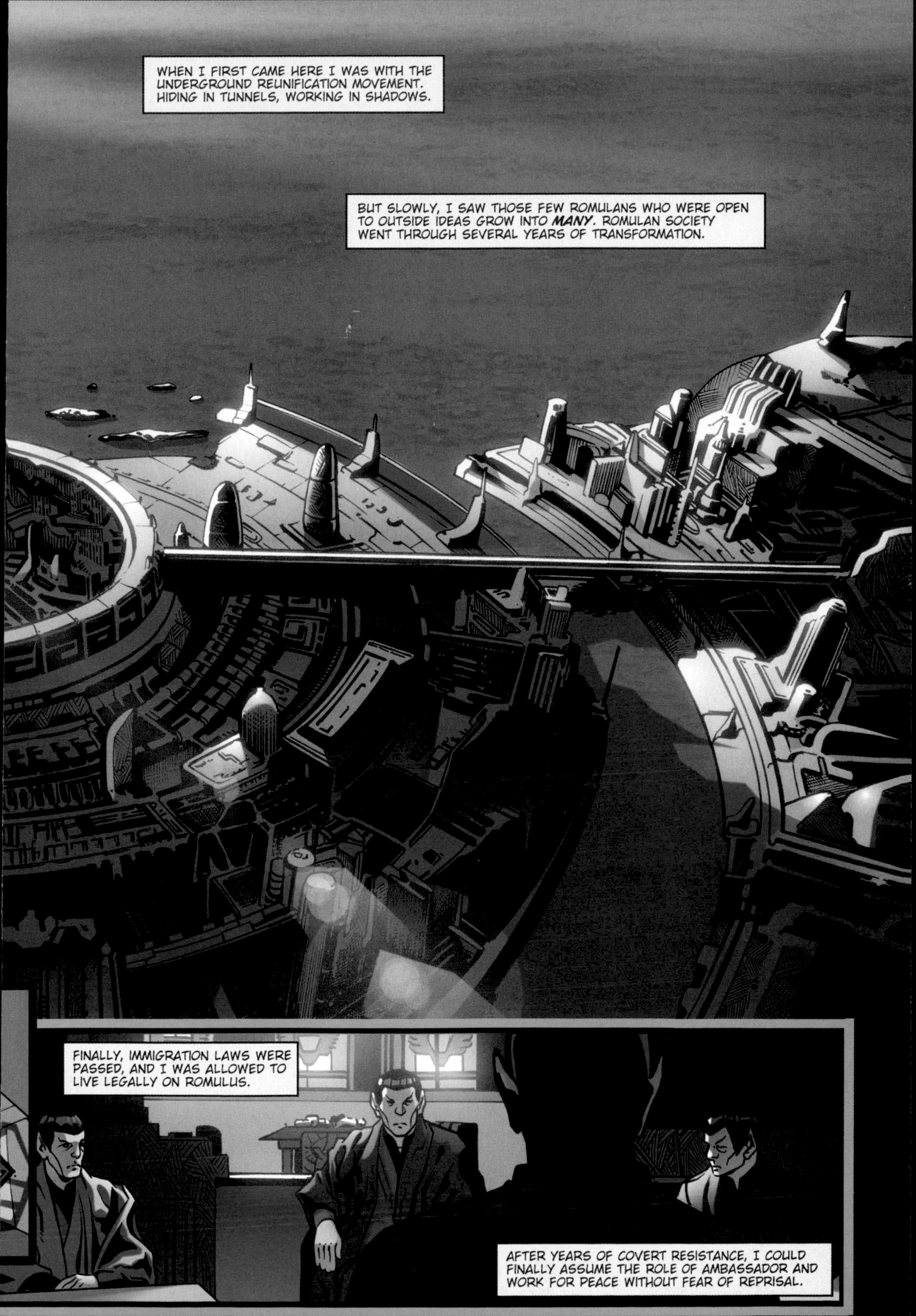
WHEN I FIRST CAME HERE I WAS WITH THE UNDERGROUND REUNIFICATION MOVEMENT. HIDING IN TUNNELS, WORKING IN SHADOWS.
BUT SLOWLY, I SAW THOSE FEW ROMULANS WHO WERE OPEN TO OUTSIDE IDEAS GROW INTO ***MANY***. ROMULAN SOCIETY WENT THROUGH SEVERAL YEARS OF TRANSFORMATION.
FINALLY, IMMIGRATION LAWS WERE PASSED, AND I WAS ALLOWED TO LIVE LEGALLY ON ROMULUS.
AFTER YEARS OF COVERT RESISTANCE, I COULD FINALLY ASSUME THE ROLE OF AMBASSADOR AND WORK FOR PEACE WITHOUT FEAR OF REPRISAL.

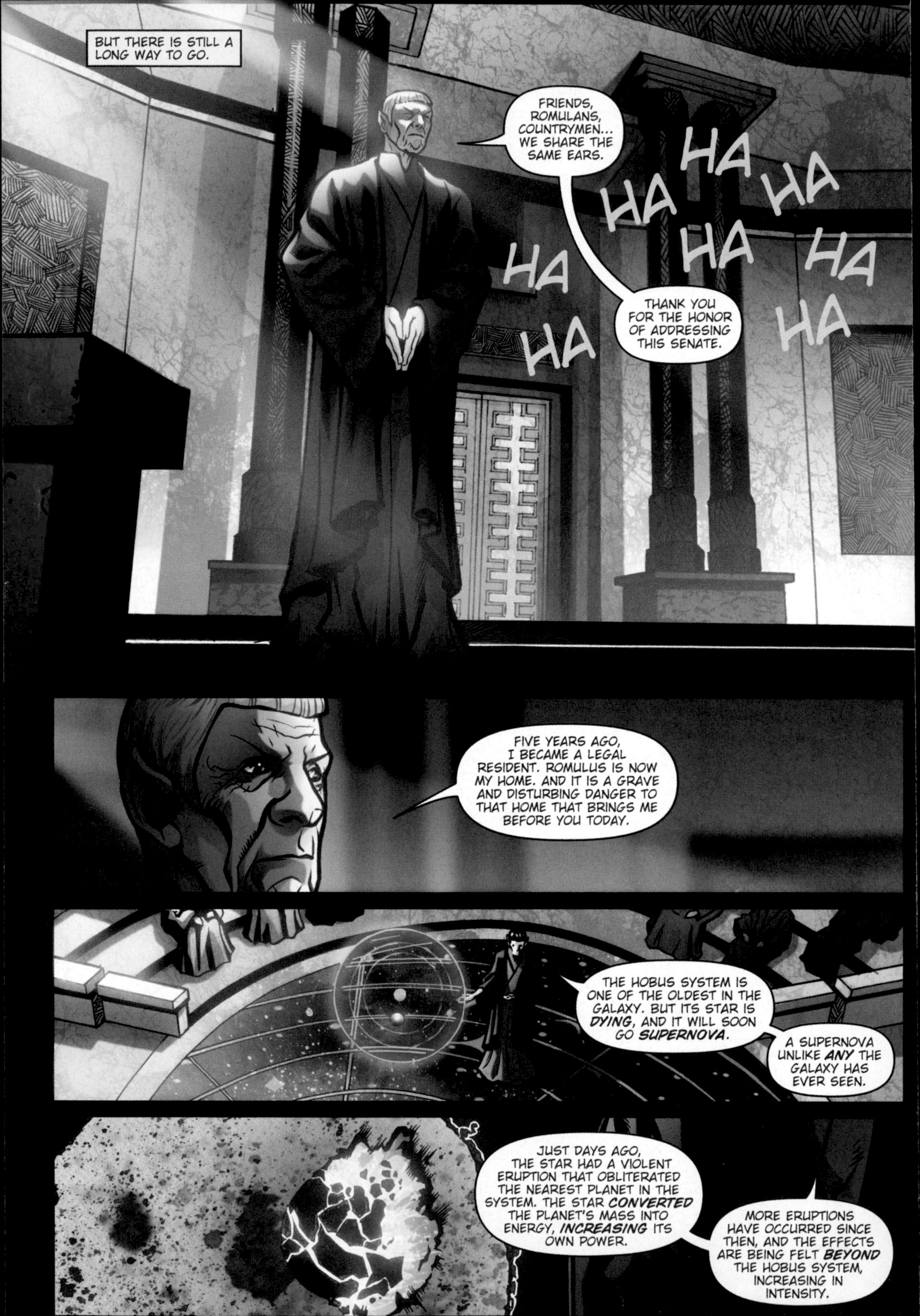
BUT THERE IS STILL A LONG WAY TO GO.
FRIENDS, ROMULANS, COUNTRYMEN... WE SHARE THE SAME EARS.
HA HA HA HA HA HA HA HA HA
THANK YOU FOR THE HONOR OF ADDRESSING THIS SENATE.
FIVE YEARS AGO, I BECAME A LEGAL RESIDENT. ROMULUS IS NOW MY HOME. AND IT IS A GRAVE AND DISTURBING DANGER TO THAT HOME THAT BRINGS ME BEFORE YOU TODAY.
THE HOBUS SYSTEM IS ONE OF THE OLDEST IN THE GALAXY. BUT ITS STAR IS ***DYING***, AND IT WILL SOON GO ***SUPERNOVA***.
A SUPERNOVA UNLIKE ***ANY*** THE GALAXY HAS EVER SEEN.
JUST DAYS AGO, THE STAR HAD A VIOLENT ERUPTION THAT OBLITERATED THE NEAREST PLANET IN THE SYSTEM. THE STAR ***CONVERTED*** THE PLANET'S MASS INTO ENERGY, ***INCREASING*** ITS OWN POWER.
MORE ERUPTIONS HAVE OCCURRED SINCE THEN, AND THE EFFECTS ARE BEING FELT ***BEYOND*** THE HOBUS SYSTEM, INCREASING IN INTENSITY.

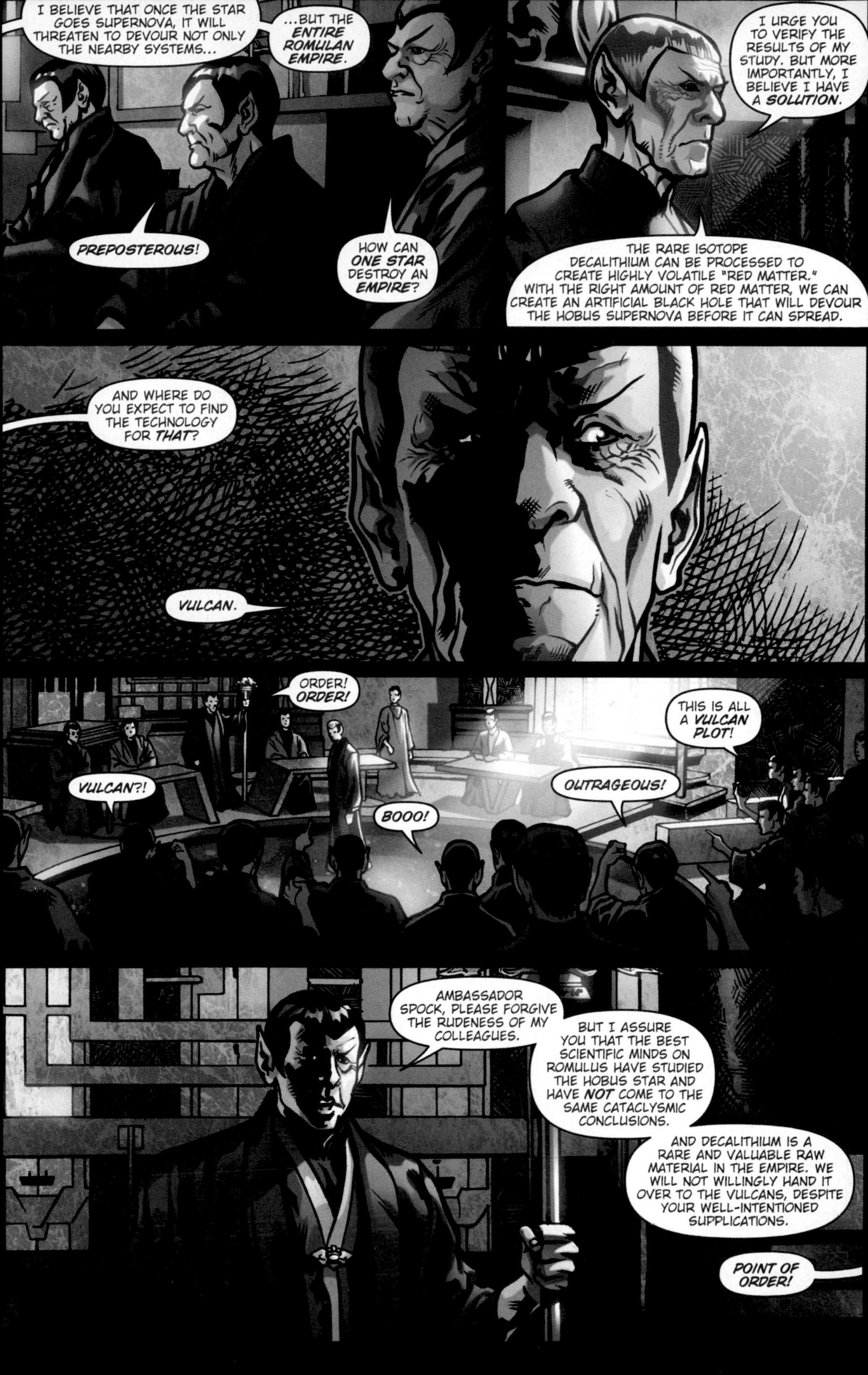
I BELIEVE THAT ONCE THE STAR GOES SUPERNOVA, IT WILL THREATEN TO DEVOUR NOT ONLY THE NEARBY SYSTEMS...
...BUT THE ENTIRE ROMULAN EMPIRE.
PREPOSTEROUS!
HOW CAN ONE STAR DESTROY AN EMPIRE?
I URGE YOU TO VERIFY THE RESULTS OF MY STUDY. BUT MORE IMPORTANTLY, I BELIEVE I HAVE A SOLUTION.
THE RARE ISOTOPE DECALITHIUM CAN BE PROCESSED TO CREATE HIGHLY VOLATILE "RED MATTER." WITH THE RIGHT AMOUNT OF RED MATTER, WE CAN CREATE AN ARTIFICIAL BLACK HOLE THAT WILL DEVOUR THE HOBUS SUPERNOVA BEFORE IT CAN SPREAD.
AND WHERE DO YOU EXPECT TO FIND THE TECHNOLOGY FOR THAT?
VULCAN.
ORDER! ORDER!
THIS IS ALL A VULCAN PLOT!
VULCAN?!
OUTRAGEOUS!
BOOO!
AMBASSADOR SPOCK, PLEASE FORGIVE THE RUDENESS OF MY COLLEAGUES.
BUT I ASSURE YOU THAT THE BEST SCIENTIFIC MINDS ON ROMULUS HAVE STUDIED THE HOBUS STAR AND HAVE NOT COME TO THE SAME CATACLYSMIC CONCLUSIONS.
AND DECALITHIUM IS A RARE AND VALUABLE RAW MATERIAL IN THE EMPIRE. WE WILL NOT WILLINGLY HAND IT OVER TO THE VULCANS, DESPITE YOUR WELL-INTENTIONED SUPPLICATIONS.
POINT OF ORDER!

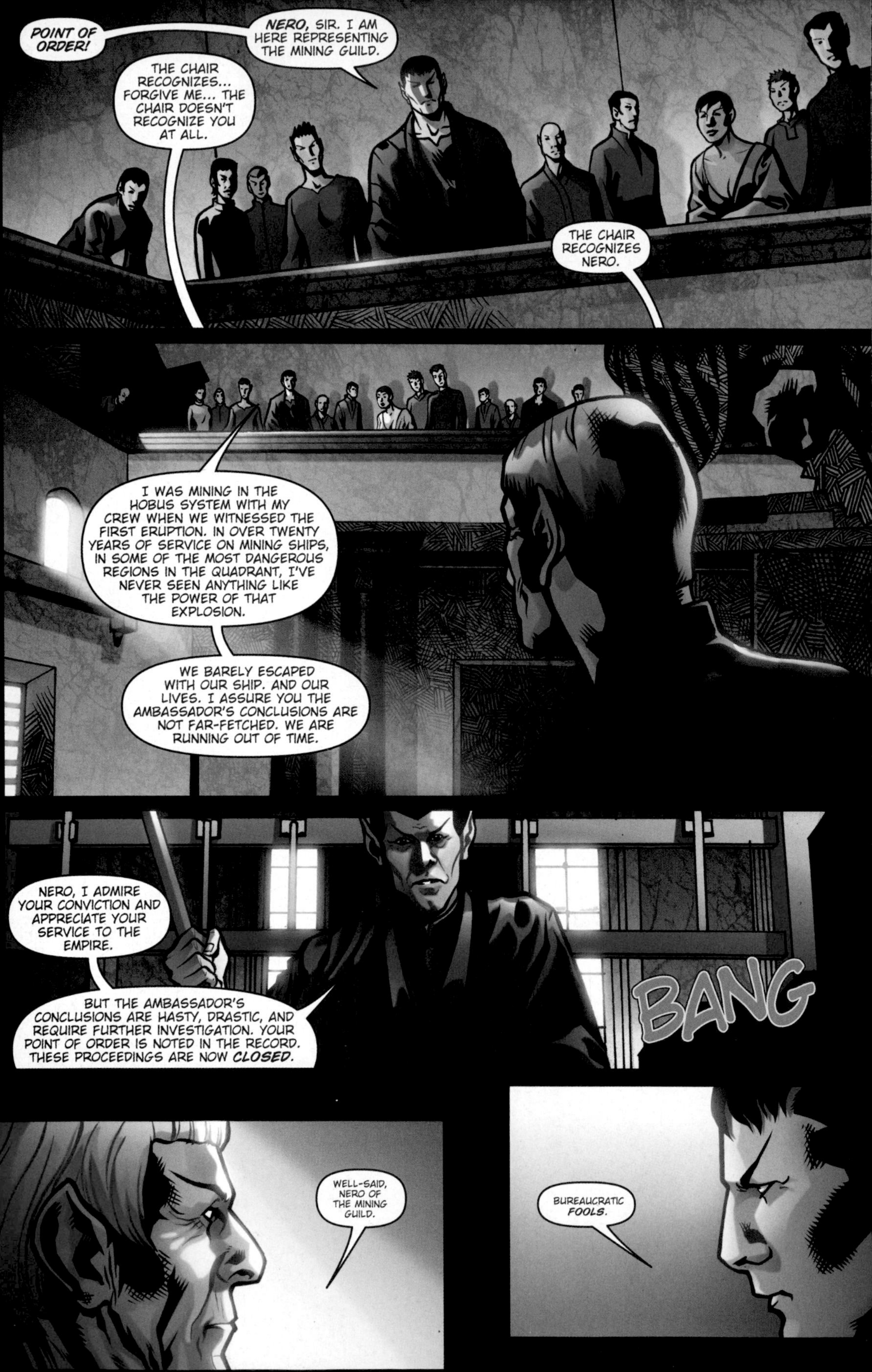
POINT OF ORDER!
NERO, SIR. I AM HERE REPRESENTING THE MINING GUILD.
THE CHAIR RECOGNIZES... FORGIVE ME... THE CHAIR DOESN'T RECOGNIZE YOU AT ALL.
THE CHAIR RECOGNIZES NERO.
I WAS MINING IN THE HOBUS SYSTEM WITH MY CREW WHEN WE WITNESSED THE FIRST ERUPTION. IN OVER TWENTY YEARS OF SERVICE ON MINING SHIPS, IN SOME OF THE MOST DANGEROUS REGIONS IN THE QUADRANT, I'VE NEVER SEEN ANYTHING LIKE THE POWER OF THAT EXPLOSION.
WE BARELY ESCAPED WITH OUR SHIP. AND OUR LIVES. I ASSURE YOU THE AMBASSADOR'S CONCLUSIONS ARE NOT FAR-FETCHED. WE ARE RUNNING OUT OF TIME.
NERO, I ADMIRE YOUR CONVICTION AND APPRECIATE YOUR SERVICE TO THE EMPIRE.
BUT THE AMBASSADOR'S CONCLUSIONS ARE HASTY, DRASTIC, AND REQUIRE FURTHER INVESTIGATION. YOUR POINT OF ORDER IS NOTED IN THE RECORD. THESE PROCEEDINGS ARE NOW CLOSED.
BANG
WELL-SAID, NERO OF THE MINING GUILD.
BUREAUCRATIC FOOLS.

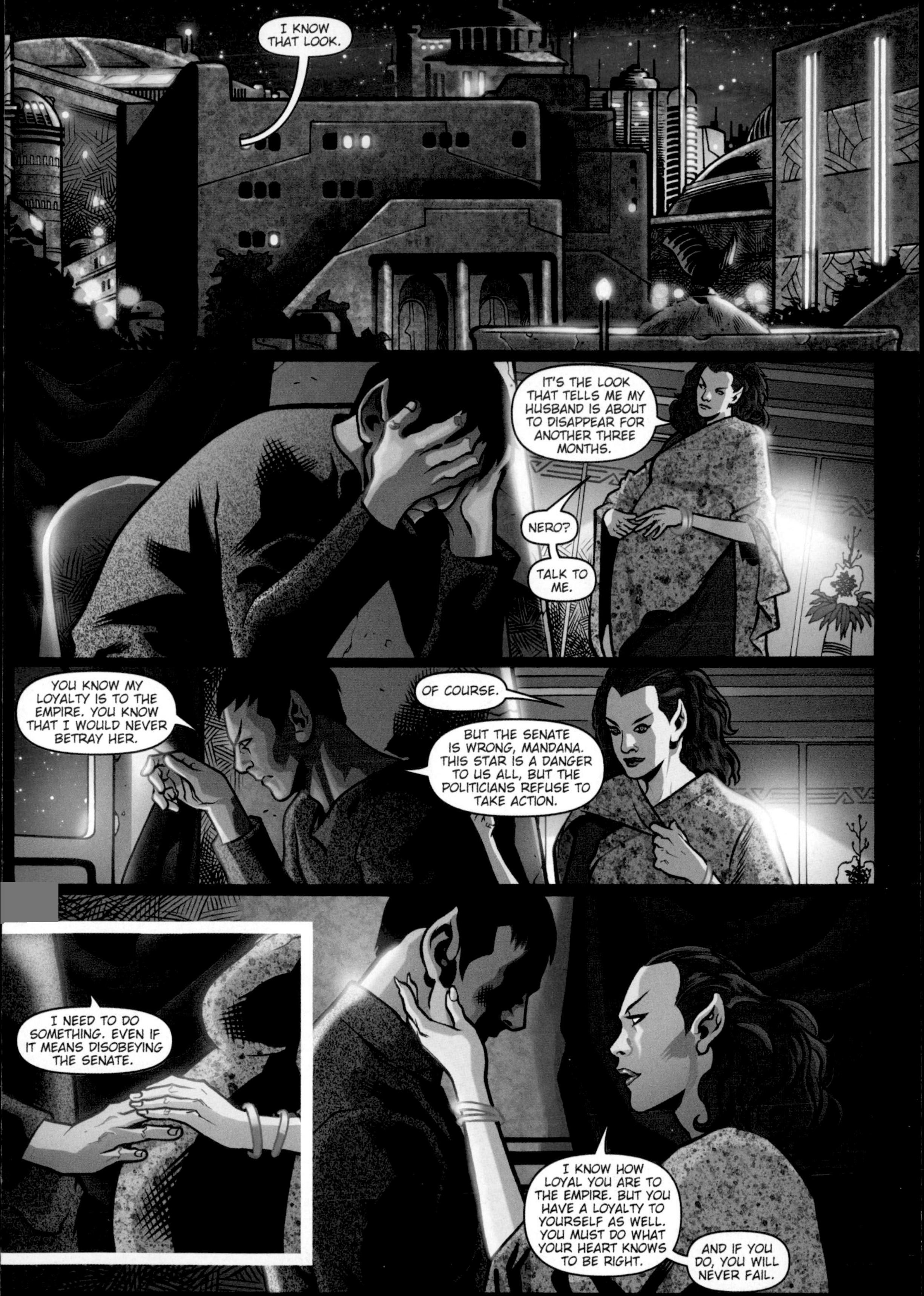
I KNOW THAT LOOK.
IT'S THE LOOK THAT TELLS ME MY HUSBAND IS ABOUT TO DISAPPEAR FOR ANOTHER THREE MONTHS.
NERO?
TALK TO ME.
YOU KNOW MY LOYALTY IS TO THE EMPIRE. YOU KNOW THAT I WOULD NEVER BETRAY HER.
OF COURSE.
BUT THE SENATE IS WRONG, MANDANA. THIS STAR IS A DANGER TO US ALL, BUT THE POLITICIANS REFUSE TO TAKE ACTION.
I NEED TO DO SOMETHING. EVEN IF IT MEANS DISOBEYING THE SENATE.
I KNOW HOW LOYAL YOU ARE TO THE EMPIRE. BUT YOU HAVE A LOYALTY TO YOURSELF AS WELL. YOU MUST DO WHAT YOUR HEART KNOWS TO BE RIGHT.
AND IF YOU DO, YOU WILL NEVER FAIL.

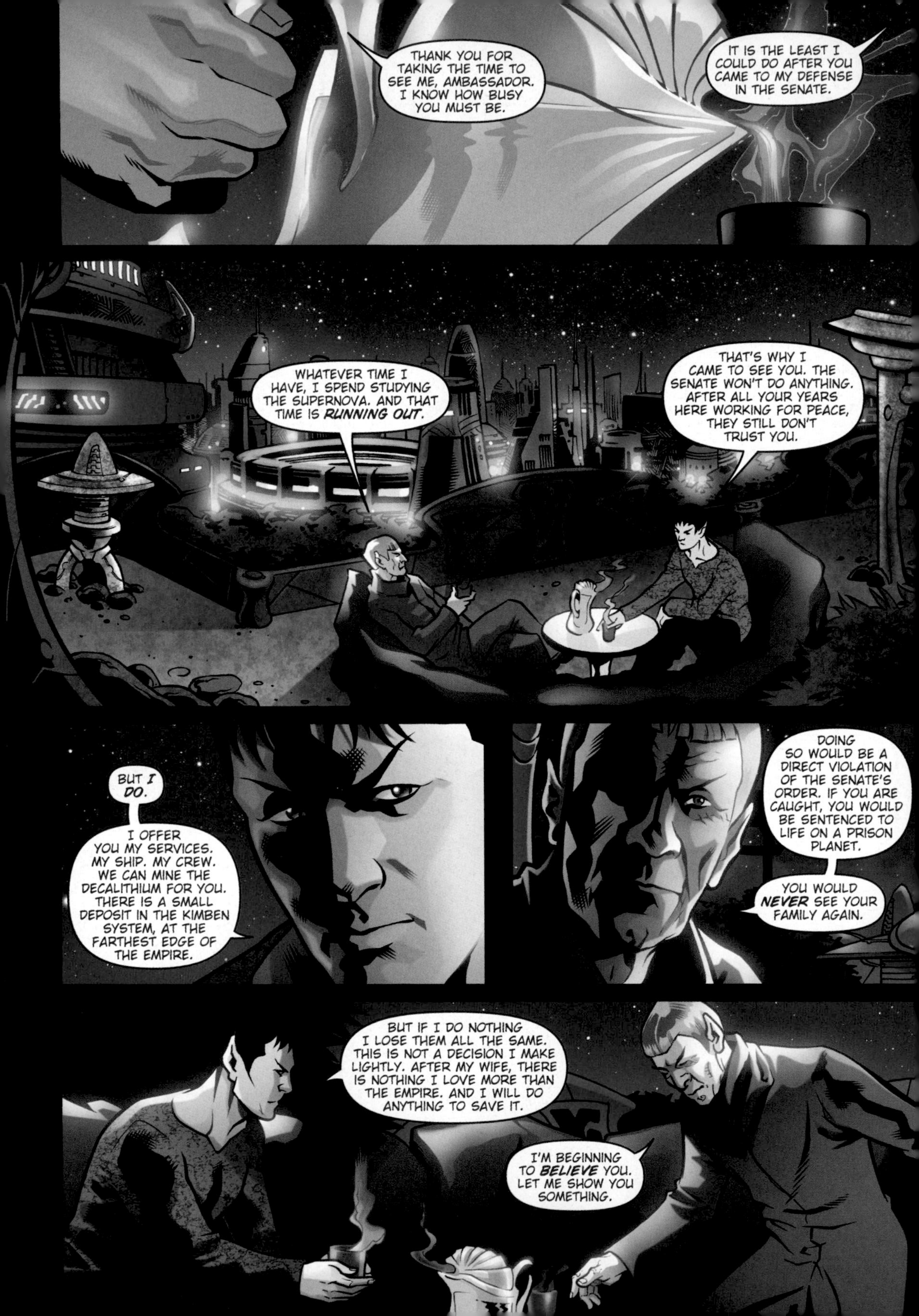
THANK YOU FOR TAKING THE TIME TO SEE ME, AMBASSADOR. I KNOW HOW BUSY YOU MUST BE.
IT IS THE LEAST I COULD DO AFTER YOU CAME TO MY DEFENSE IN THE SENATE.
WHATEVER TIME I HAVE, I SPEND STUDYING THE SUPERNOVA. AND THAT TIME IS *RUNNING OUT*.
THAT'S WHY I CAME TO SEE YOU. THE SENATE WON'T DO ANYTHING. AFTER ALL YOUR YEARS HERE WORKING FOR PEACE, THEY STILL DON'T TRUST YOU.
BUT *I DO*.
I OFFER YOU MY SERVICES. MY SHIP. MY CREW. WE CAN MINE THE DECALITHIUM FOR YOU. THERE IS A SMALL DEPOSIT IN THE KIMBEN SYSTEM, AT THE FARTHEST EDGE OF THE EMPIRE.
DOING SO WOULD BE A DIRECT VIOLATION OF THE SENATE'S ORDER. IF YOU ARE CAUGHT, YOU WOULD BE SENTENCED TO LIFE ON A PRISON PLANET.
YOU WOULD *NEVER* SEE YOUR FAMILY AGAIN.
BUT IF I DO NOTHING I LOSE THEM ALL THE SAME. THIS IS NOT A DECISION I MAKE LIGHTLY. AFTER MY WIFE, THERE IS NOTHING I LOVE MORE THAN THE EMPIRE. AND I WILL DO ANYTHING TO SAVE IT.
I'M BEGINNING TO *BELIEVE* YOU. LET ME SHOW YOU SOMETHING.

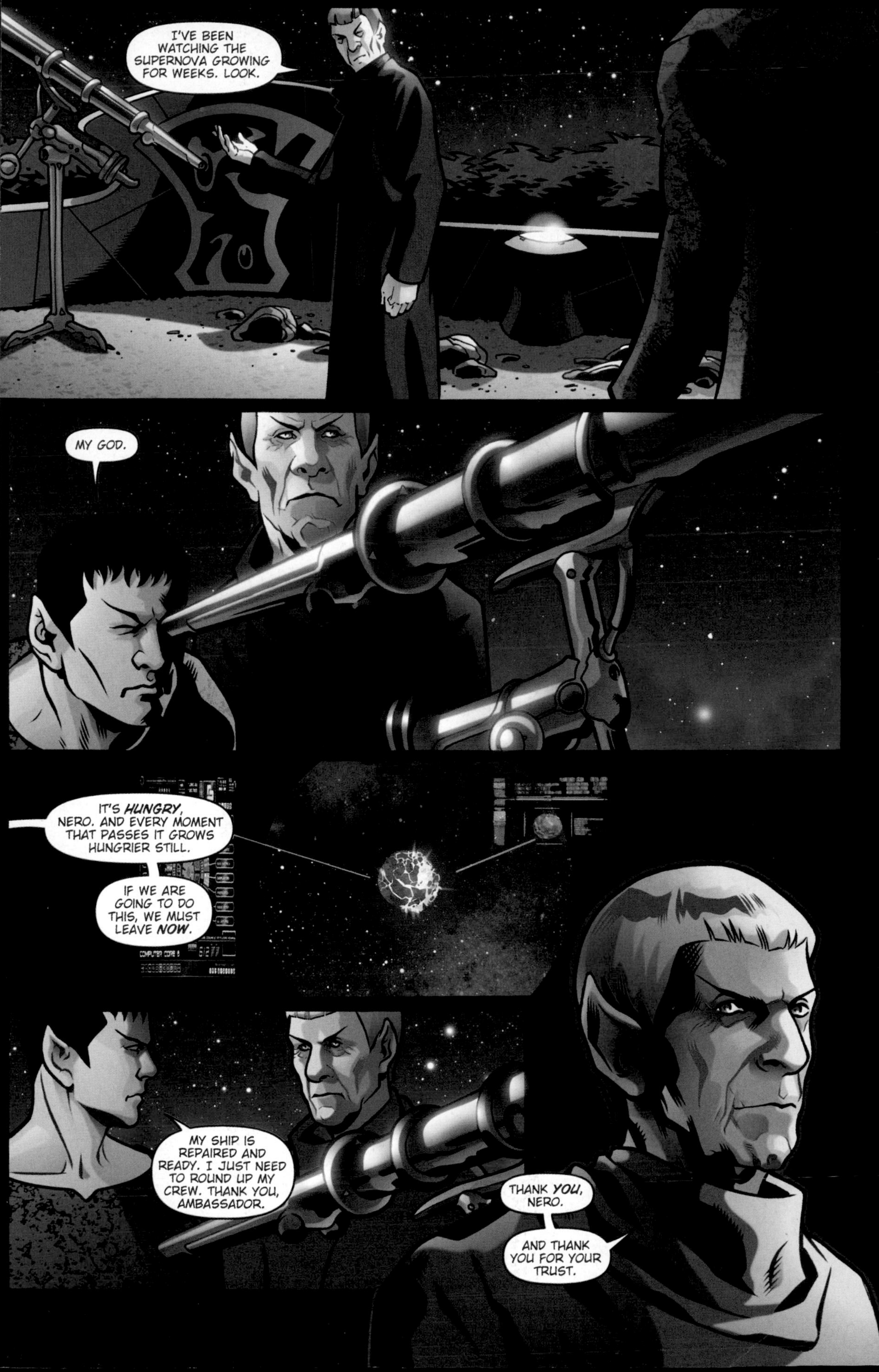
I'VE BEEN WATCHING THE SUPERNOVA GROWING FOR WEEKS. LOOK.
MY GOD.
IT'S *HUNGRY*, NERO. AND EVERY MOMENT THAT PASSES IT GROWS HUNGRIER STILL.
IF WE ARE GOING TO DO THIS, WE MUST LEAVE *NOW*.
COMPUTER CORE 8
MY SHIP IS REPAIRED AND READY. I JUST NEED TO ROUND UP MY CREW. THANK YOU, AMBASSADOR.
THANK *YOU*, NERO.
AND THANK YOU FOR YOUR TRUST.

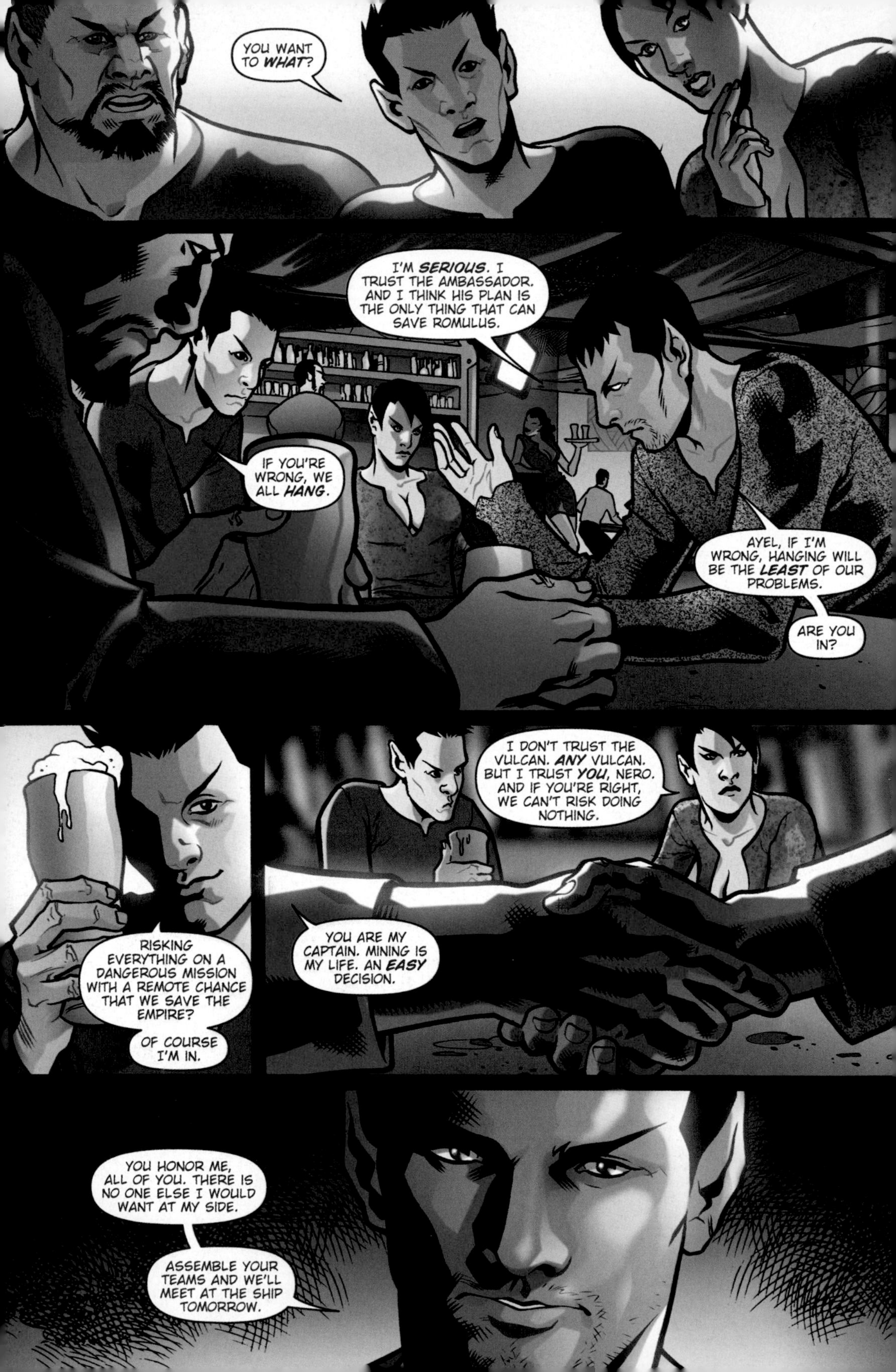
YOU WANT TO *WHAT*?
I'M *SERIOUS*. I TRUST THE AMBASSADOR. AND I THINK HIS PLAN IS THE ONLY THING THAT CAN SAVE ROMULUS.
IF YOU'RE WRONG, WE ALL *HANG*.
AYEL, IF I'M WRONG, HANGING WILL BE THE *LEAST* OF OUR PROBLEMS.
ARE YOU IN?
RISKING EVERYTHING ON A DANGEROUS MISSION WITH A REMOTE CHANCE THAT WE SAVE THE EMPIRE?
OF COURSE I'M IN.
I DON'T TRUST THE VULCAN. *ANY* VULCAN. BUT I TRUST *YOU*, NERO. AND IF YOU'RE RIGHT, WE CAN'T RISK DOING NOTHING.
YOU ARE MY CAPTAIN. MINING IS MY LIFE. AN *EASY* DECISION.
YOU HONOR ME, ALL OF YOU. THERE IS NO ONE ELSE I WOULD WANT AT MY SIDE.
ASSEMBLE YOUR TEAMS AND WE'LL MEET AT THE SHIP TOMORROW.

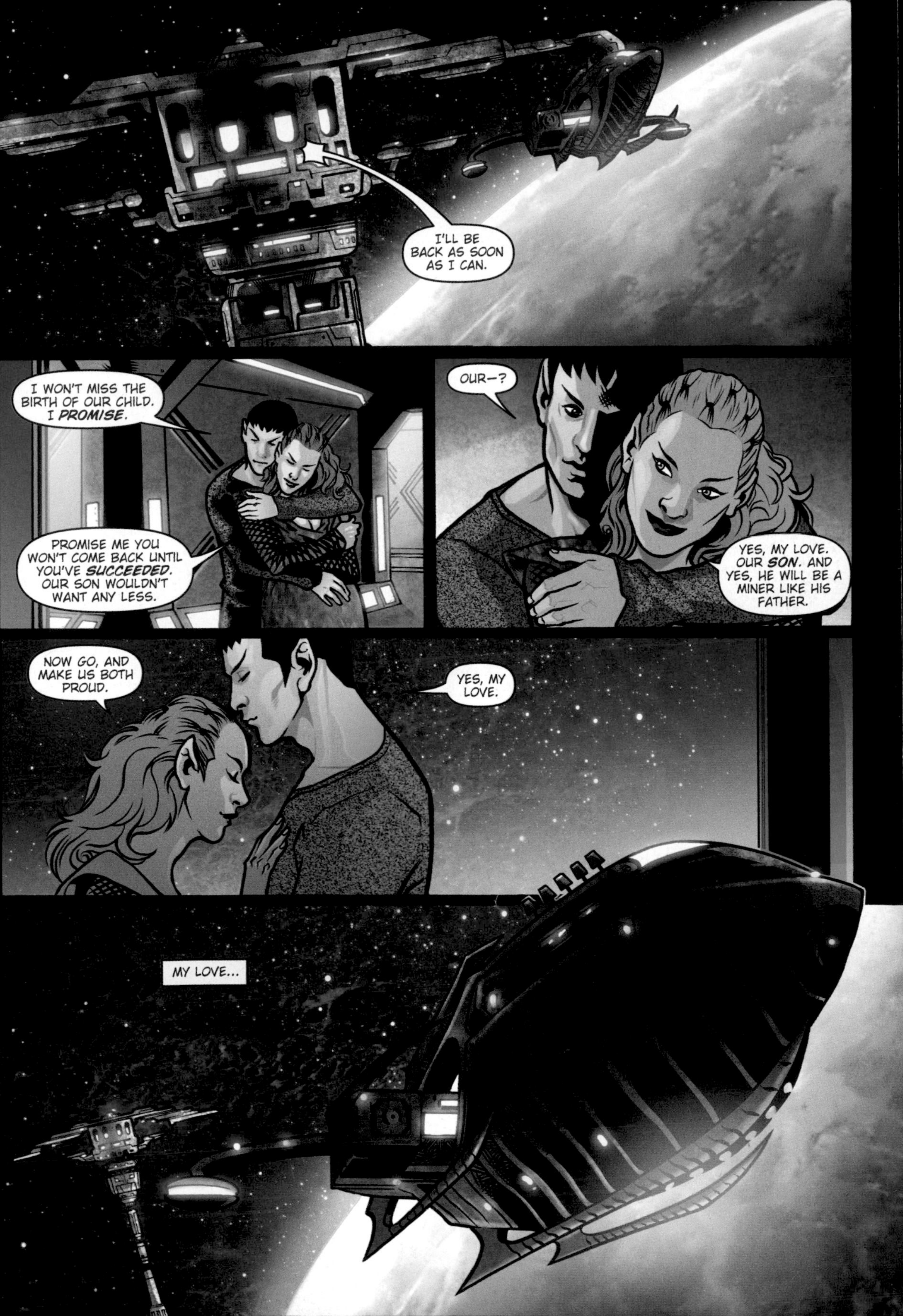
I'LL BE BACK AS SOON AS I CAN.
I WON'T MISS THE BIRTH OF OUR CHILD. I PROMISE.
PROMISE ME YOU WON'T COME BACK UNTIL YOU'VE SUCCEEDED. OUR SON WOULDN'T WANT ANY LESS.
OUR—?
YES, MY LOVE. OUR SON. AND YES, HE WILL BE A MINER LIKE HIS FATHER.
NOW GO, AND MAKE US BOTH PROUD.
YES, MY LOVE.
MY LOVE...

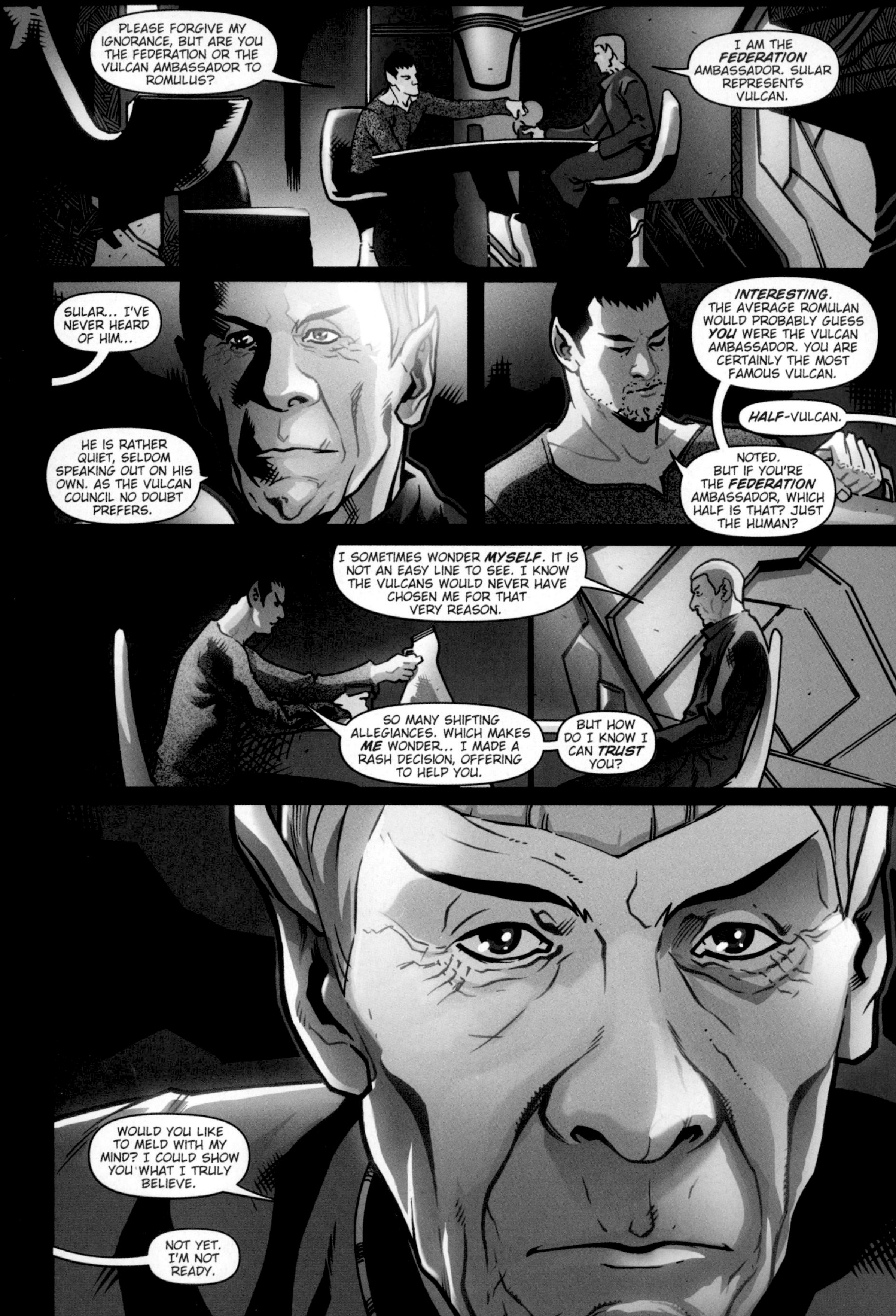
PLEASE FORGIVE MY IGNORANCE, BUT ARE YOU THE FEDERATION OR THE VULCAN AMBASSADOR TO ROMULUS?
I AM THE *FEDERATION* AMBASSADOR. SULAR REPRESENTS VULCAN.
SULAR... I'VE NEVER HEARD OF HIM...
HE IS RATHER QUIET, SELDOM SPEAKING OUT ON HIS OWN. AS THE VULCAN COUNCIL NO DOUBT PREFERS.
INTERESTING. THE AVERAGE ROMULAN WOULD PROBABLY GUESS *YOU* WERE THE VULCAN AMBASSADOR. YOU ARE CERTAINLY THE MOST FAMOUS VULCAN.
HALF-VULCAN.
NOTED. BUT IF YOU'RE THE *FEDERATION* AMBASSADOR, WHICH HALF IS THAT? JUST THE HUMAN?
I SOMETIMES WONDER *MYSELF*. IT IS NOT AN EASY LINE TO SEE. I KNOW THE VULCANS WOULD NEVER HAVE CHOSEN ME FOR THAT VERY REASON.
SO MANY SHIFTING ALLEGIANCES. WHICH MAKES *ME* WONDER... I MADE A RASH DECISION, OFFERING TO HELP YOU.
BUT HOW DO I KNOW I CAN *TRUST* YOU?
WOULD YOU LIKE TO MELD WITH MY MIND? I COULD SHOW YOU WHAT I TRULY BELIEVE.
NOT YET. I'M NOT READY.

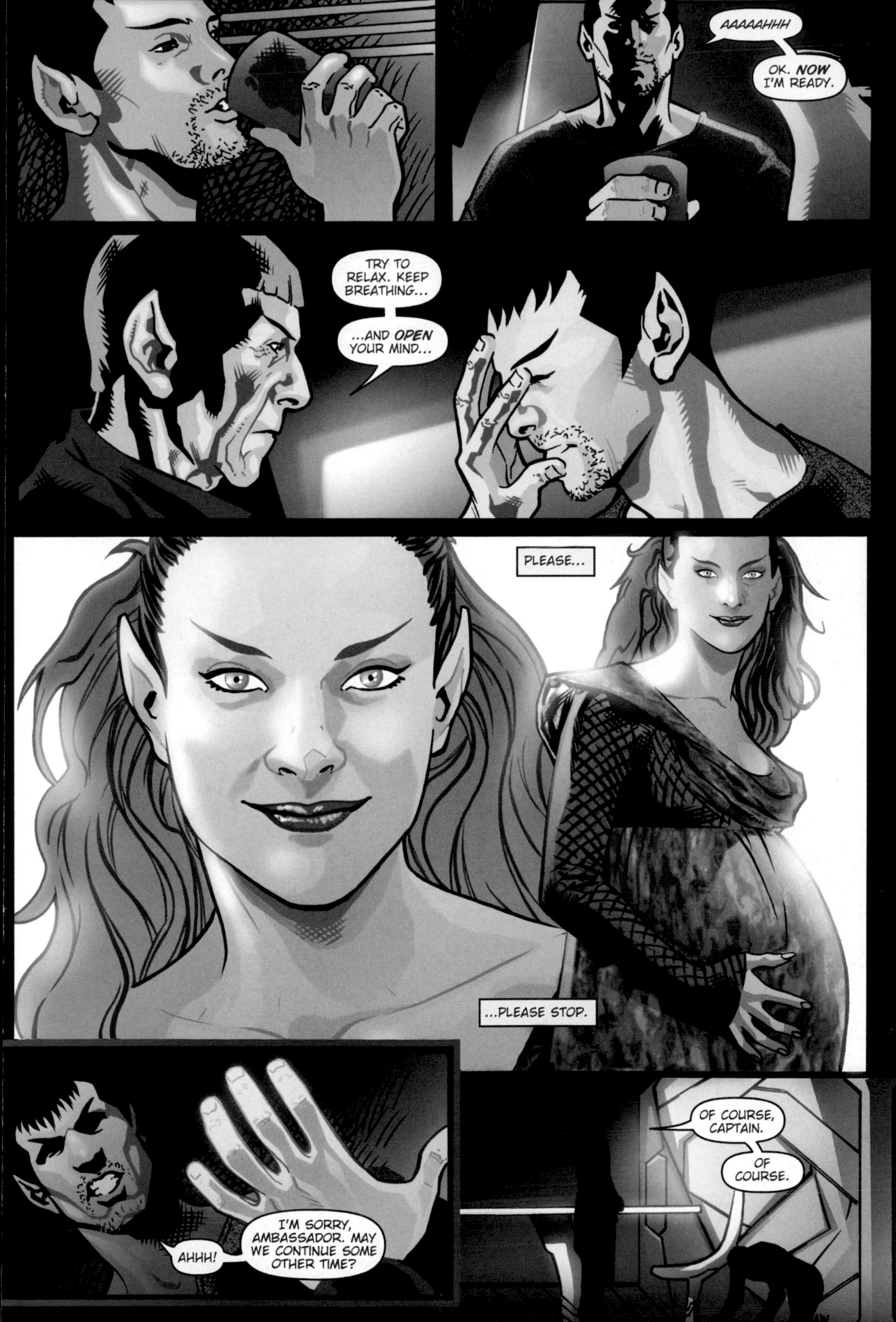
AAAAAHHH
OK. NOW I'M READY.
TRY TO RELAX. KEEP BREATHING...
...AND OPEN YOUR MIND...
PLEASE...
...PLEASE STOP.
AHHH!
I'M SORRY, AMBASSADOR. MAY WE CONTINUE SOME OTHER TIME?
OF COURSE, CAPTAIN.
OF COURSE.

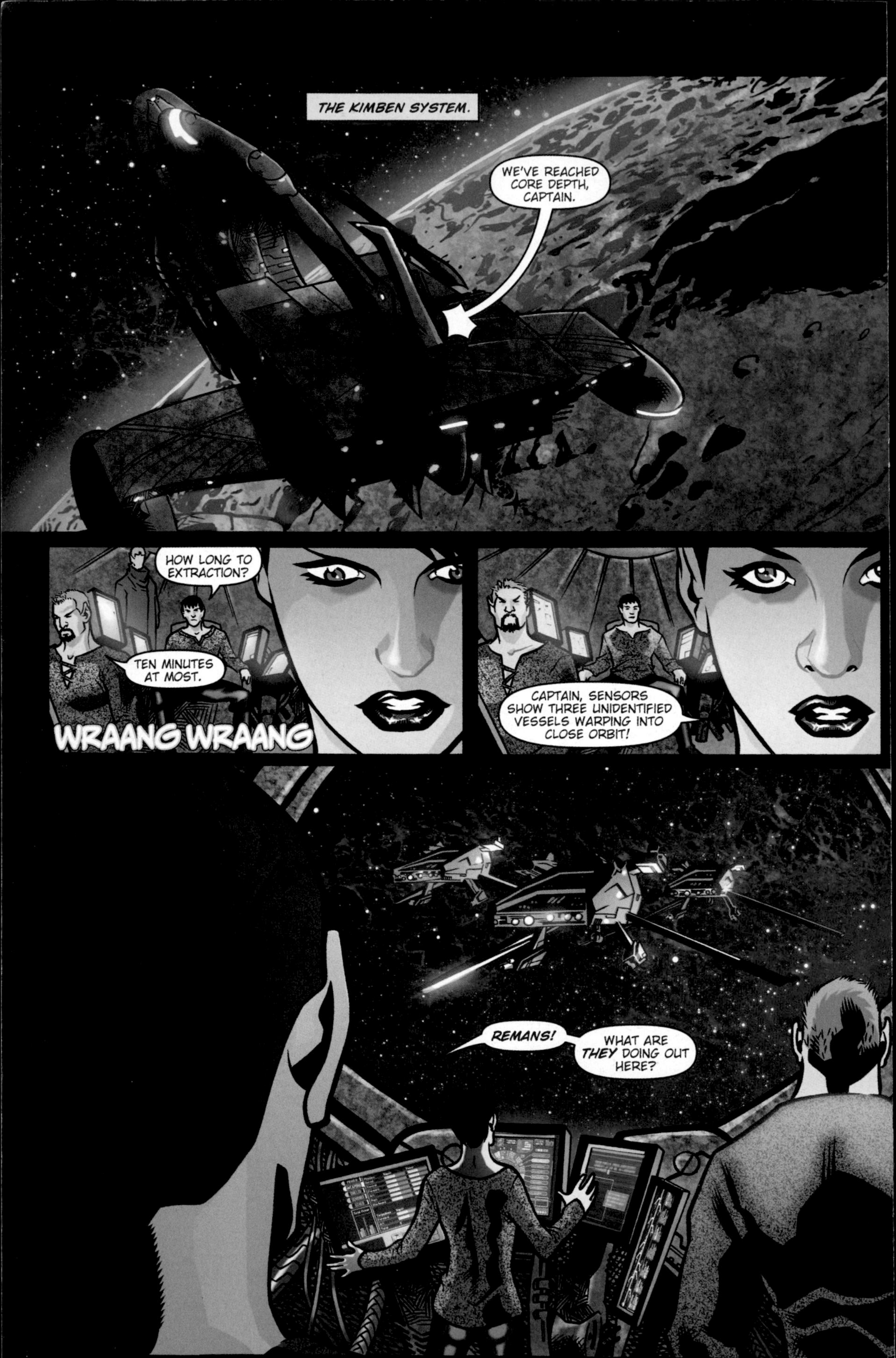
THE KIMBEN SYSTEM.
WE'VE REACHED CORE DEPTH, CAPTAIN.
HOW LONG TO EXTRACTION?
TEN MINUTES AT MOST.
WRAANG WRAANG
CAPTAIN, SENSORS SHOW THREE UNIDENTIFIED VESSELS WARPING INTO CLOSE ORBIT!
REMANS!
WHAT ARE THEY DOING OUT HERE?

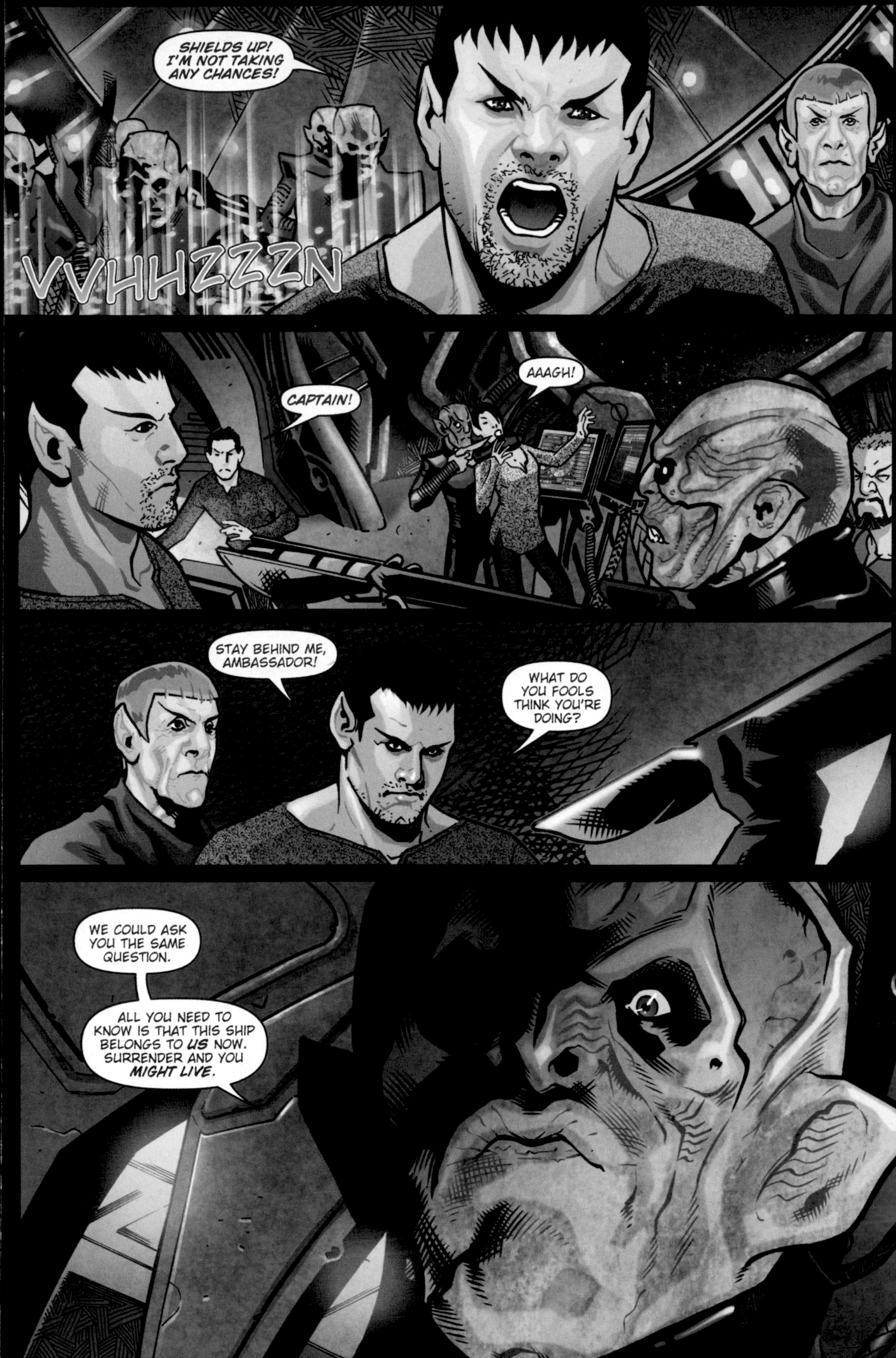
SHIELDS UP! I'M NOT TAKING ANY CHANCES!
VVHHZZZN
CAPTAIN!
AAAGH!
STAY BEHIND ME, AMBASSADOR!
WHAT DO YOU FOOLS THINK YOU'RE DOING?
WE COULD ASK YOU THE SAME QUESTION.
ALL YOU NEED TO KNOW IS THAT THIS SHIP BELONGS TO US NOW. SURRENDER AND YOU MIGHT LIVE.

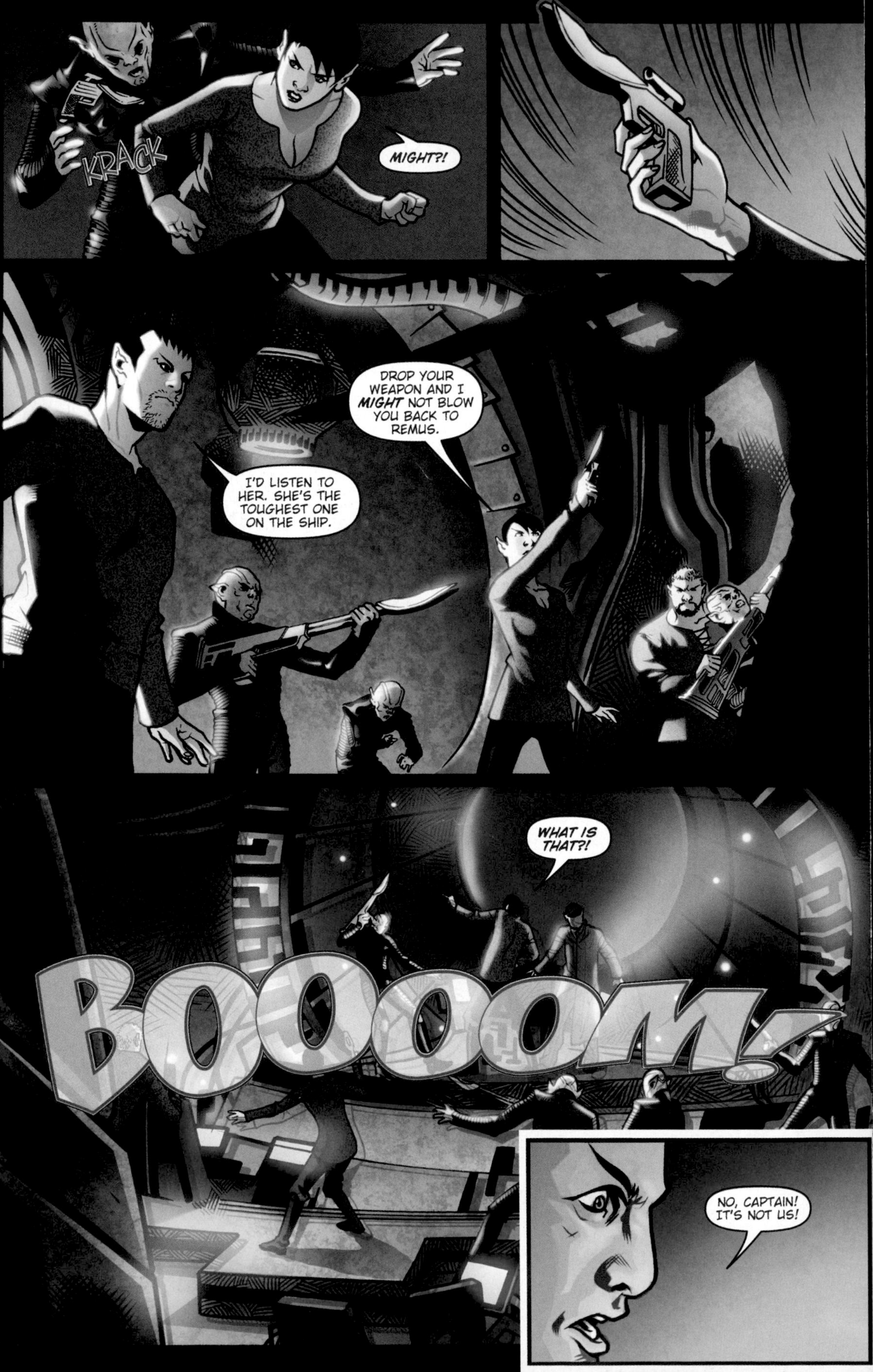
KRACK
MIGHT?!
DROP YOUR WEAPON AND I MIGHT NOT BLOW YOU BACK TO REMUS.
I'D LISTEN TO HER. SHE'S THE TOUGHEST ONE ON THE SHIP.
WHAT IS THAT?!
BOOOOM!
NO, CAPTAIN! IT'S NOT US!

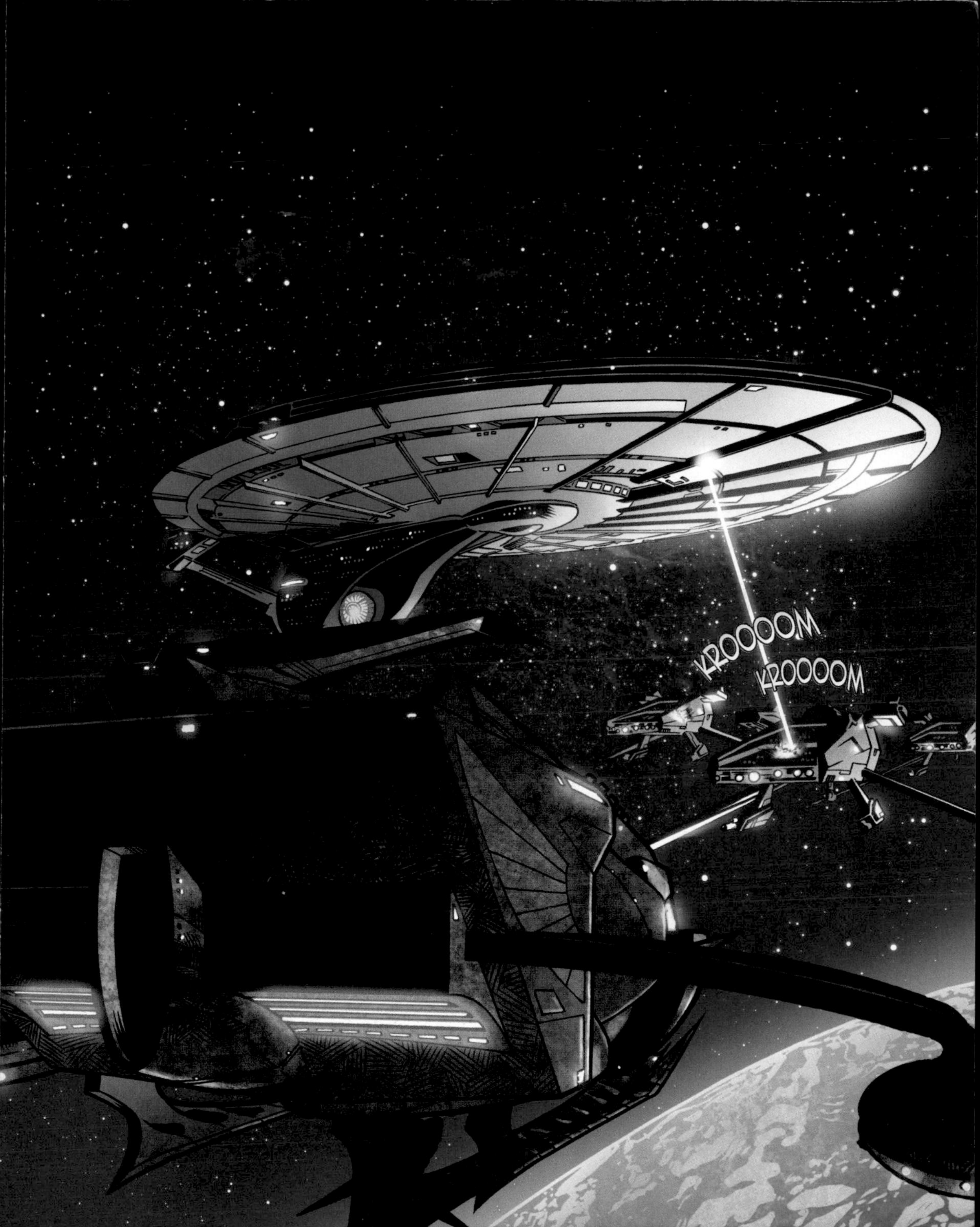
KROOOOM
KROOOOM

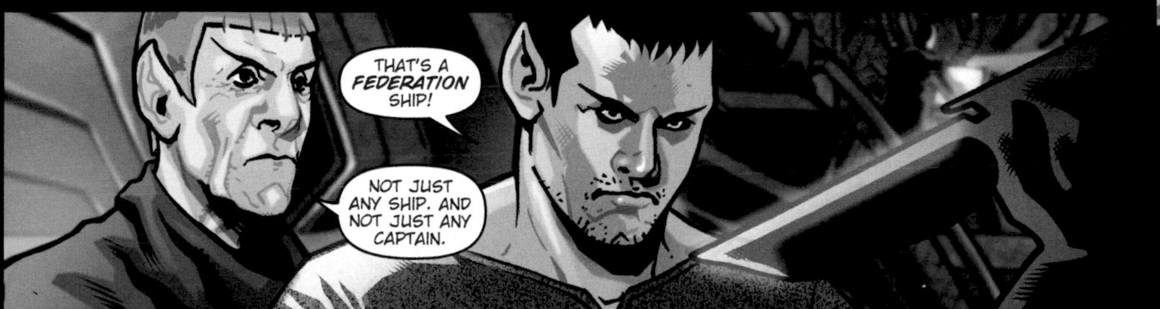
THAT'S A *FEDERATION* SHIP!
NOT JUST ANY SHIP. AND NOT JUST ANY CAPTAIN.

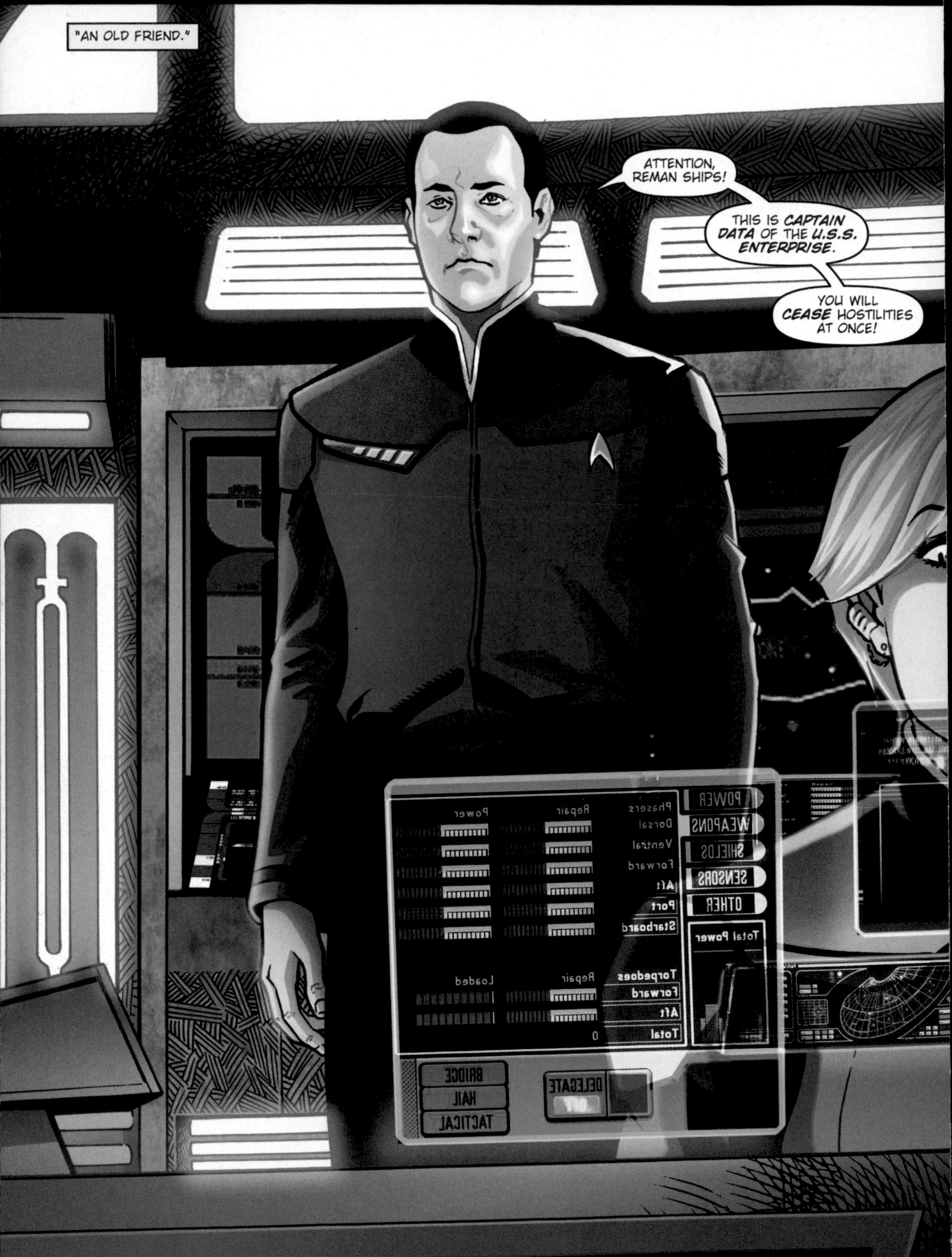
"AN OLD FRIEND."
ATTENTION, REMAN SHIPS!
THIS IS CAPTAIN DATA OF THE U.S.S. ENTERPRISE.
YOU WILL CEASE HOSTILITIES AT ONCE!

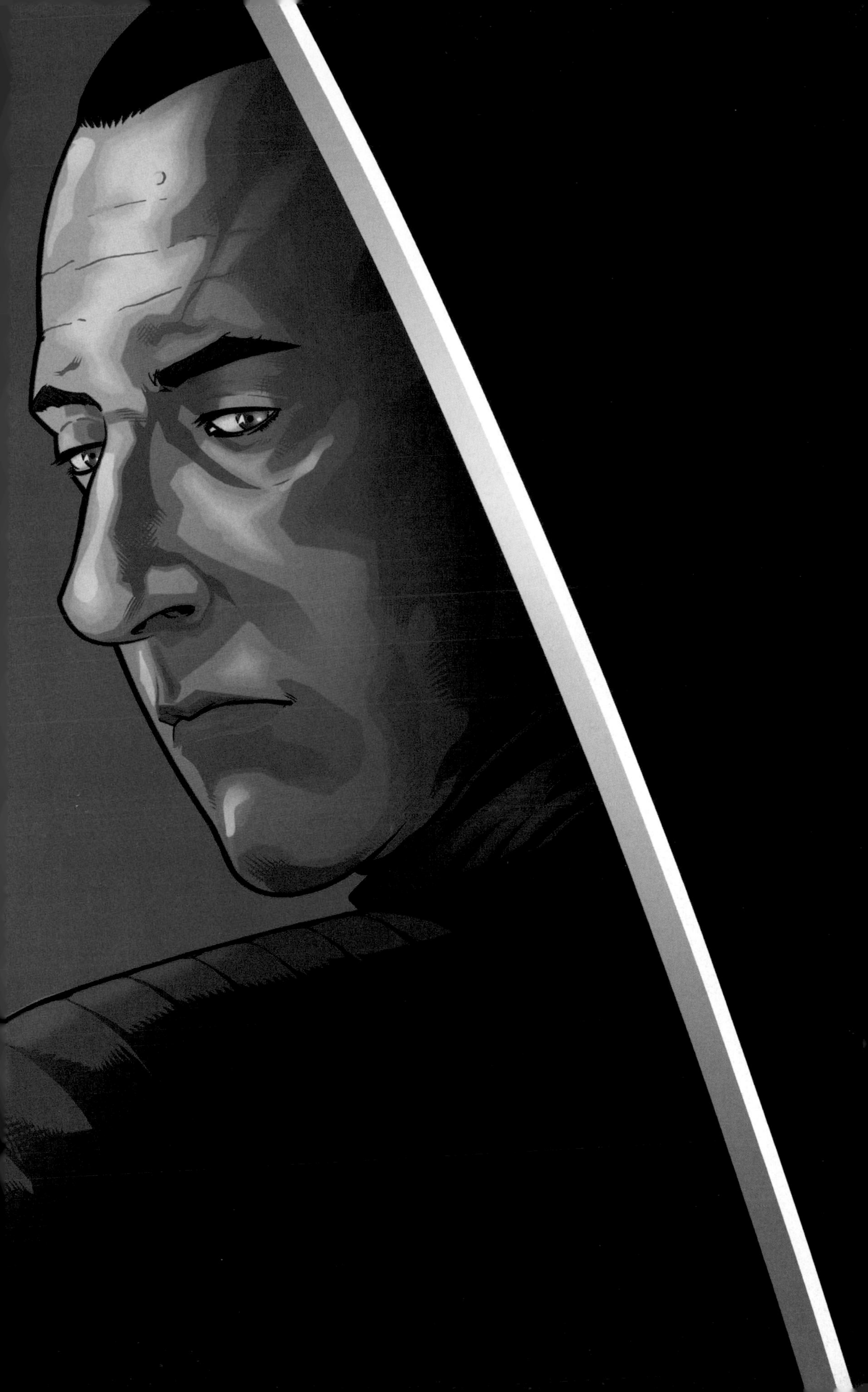

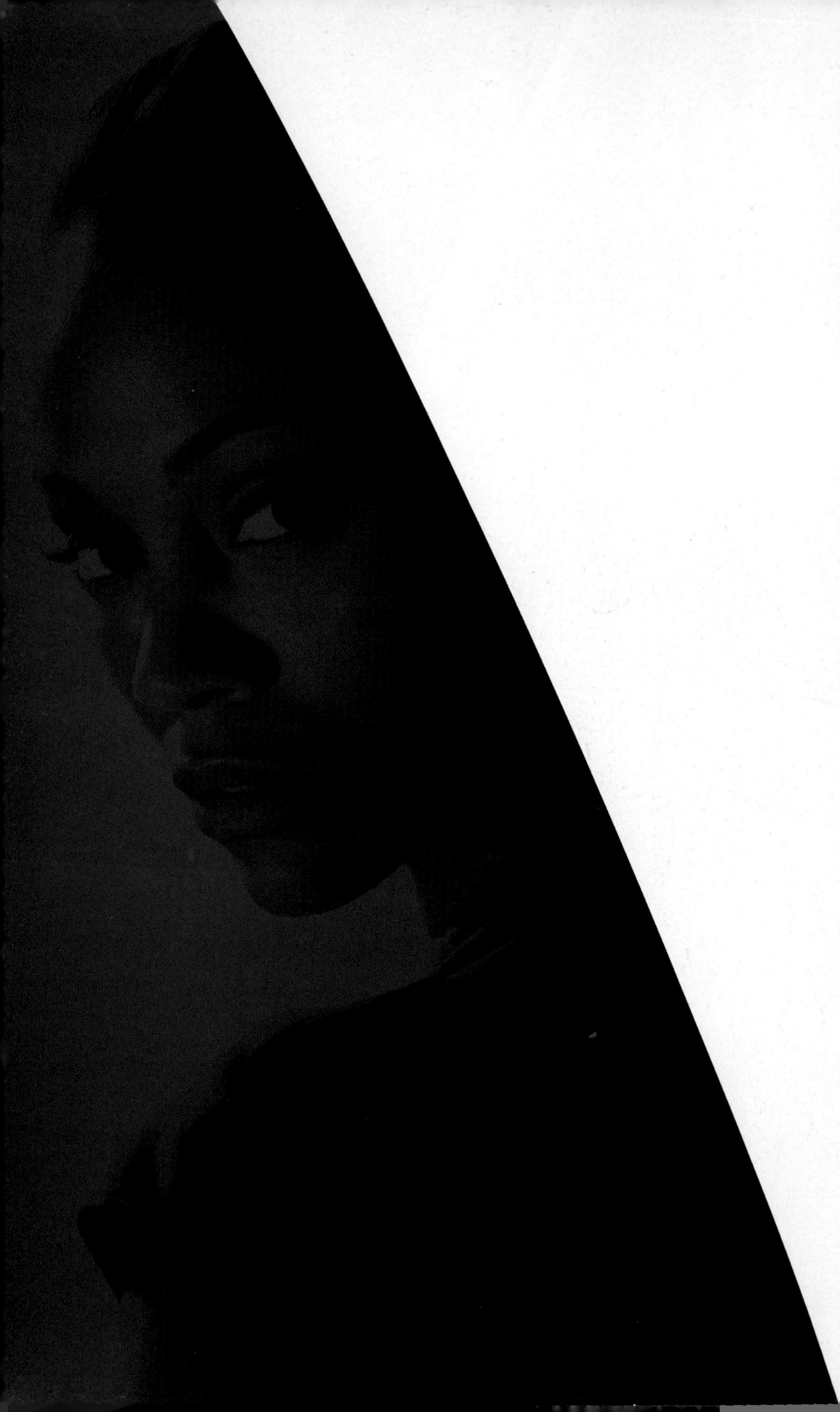

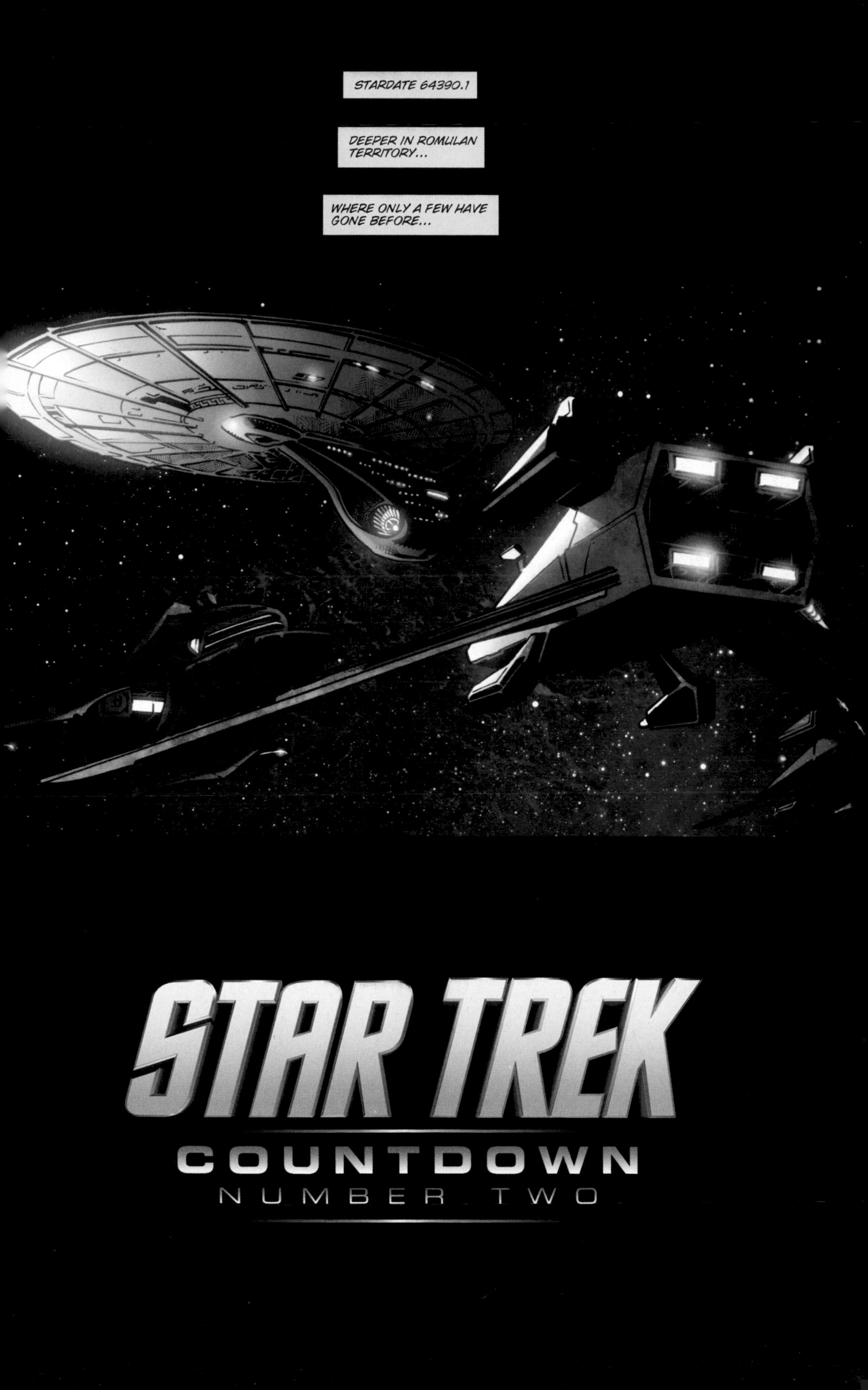
STARDATE 64390.1
DEEPER IN ROMULAN TERRITORY...
WHERE ONLY A FEW HAVE GONE BEFORE...
STAR TREK
COUNTDOWN
NUMBER TWO

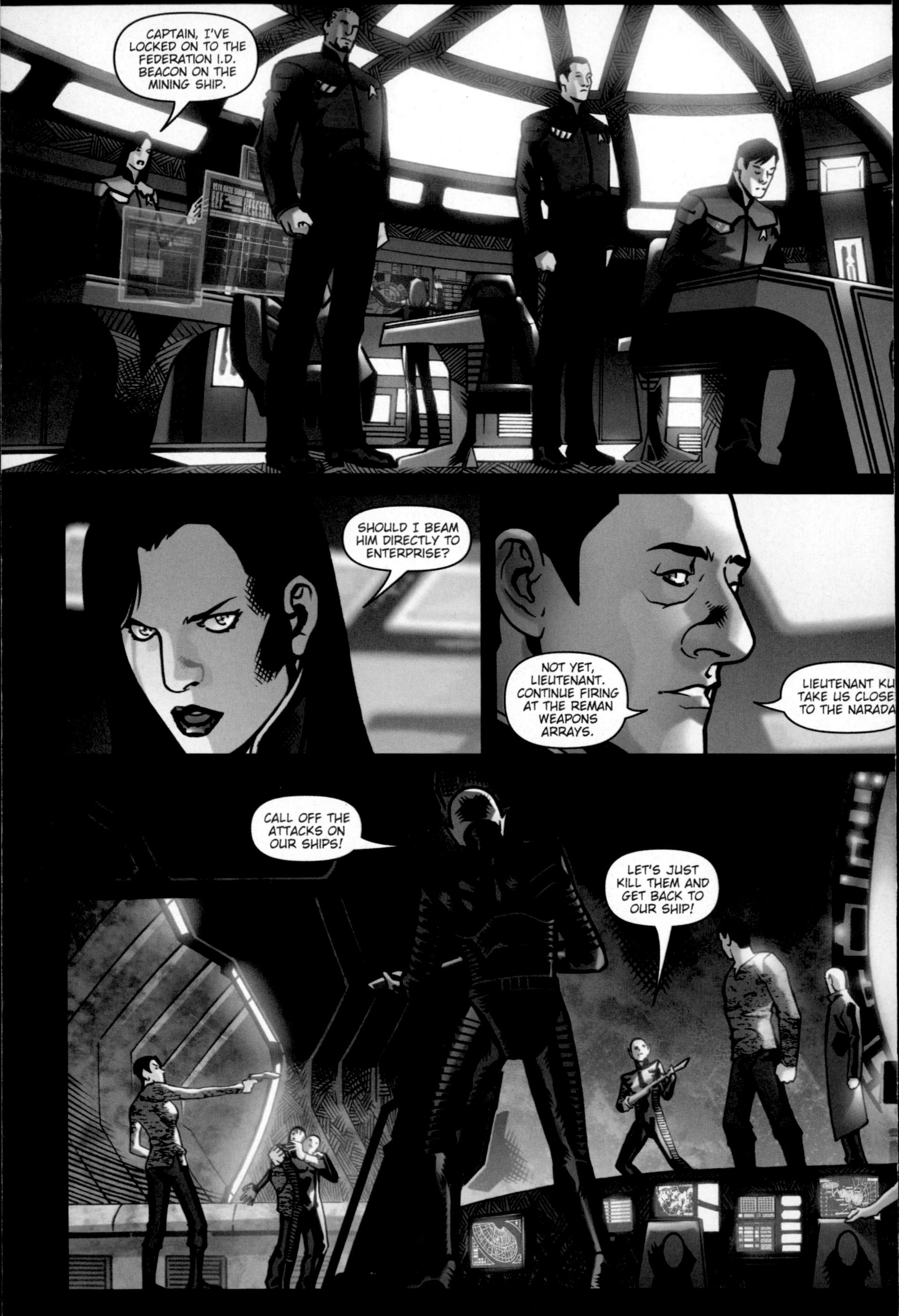
CAPTAIN, I'VE LOCKED ON TO THE FEDERATION I.D. BEACON ON THE MINING SHIP.
SHOULD I BEAM HIM DIRECTLY TO ENTERPRISE?
NOT YET, LIEUTENANT. CONTINUE FIRING AT THE REMAN WEAPONS ARRAYS.
LIEUTENANT KU TAKE US CLOSE TO THE NARADA
CALL OFF THE ATTACKS ON OUR SHIPS!
LET'S JUST KILL THEM AND GET BACK TO OUR SHIP!

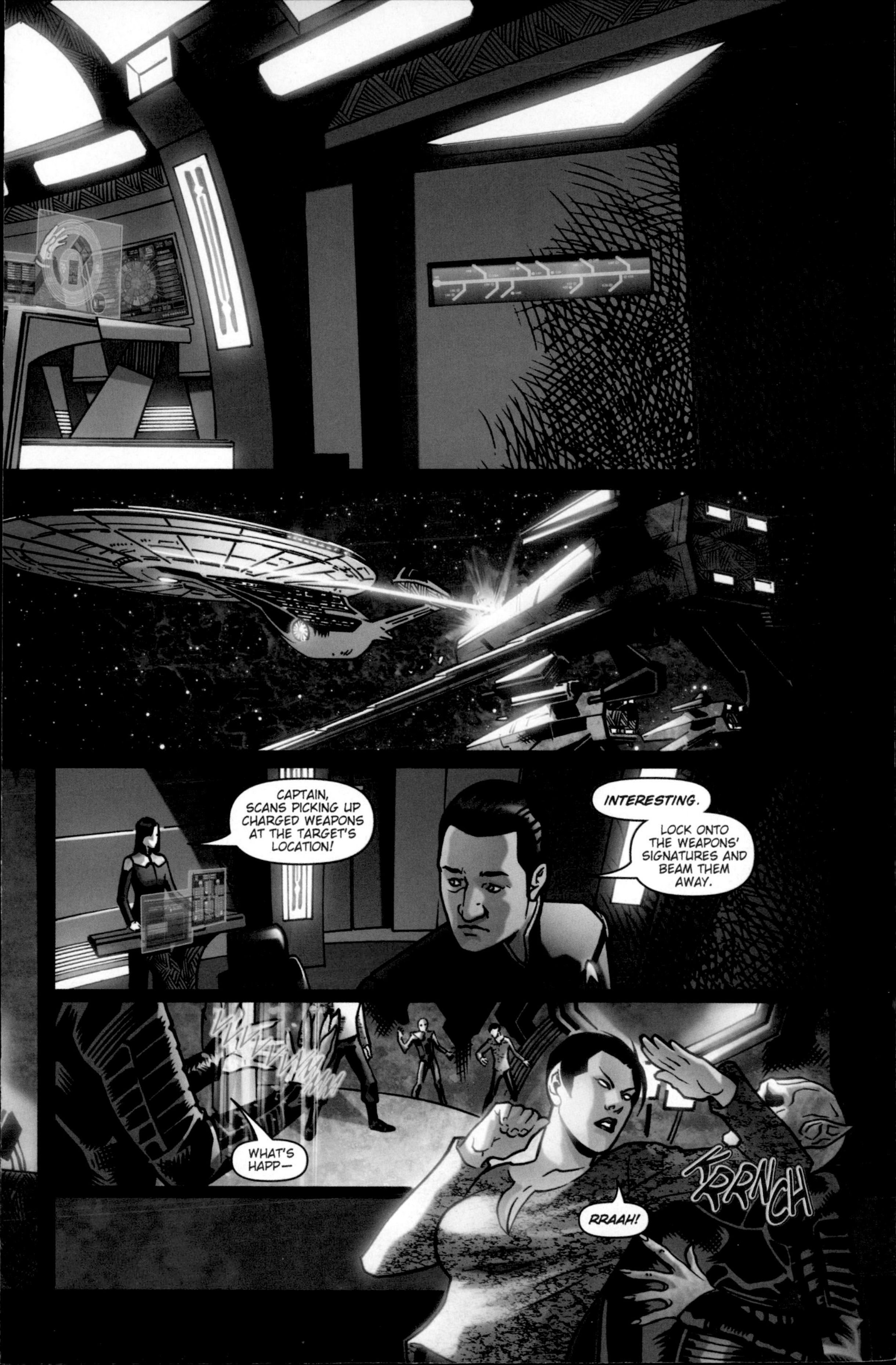
CAPTAIN, SCANS PICKING UP CHARGED WEAPONS AT THE TARGET'S LOCATION!
INTERESTING.
LOCK ONTO THE WEAPONS' SIGNATURES AND BEAM THEM AWAY.
WHAT'S HAPP—
KRRNCH
RRAAH!

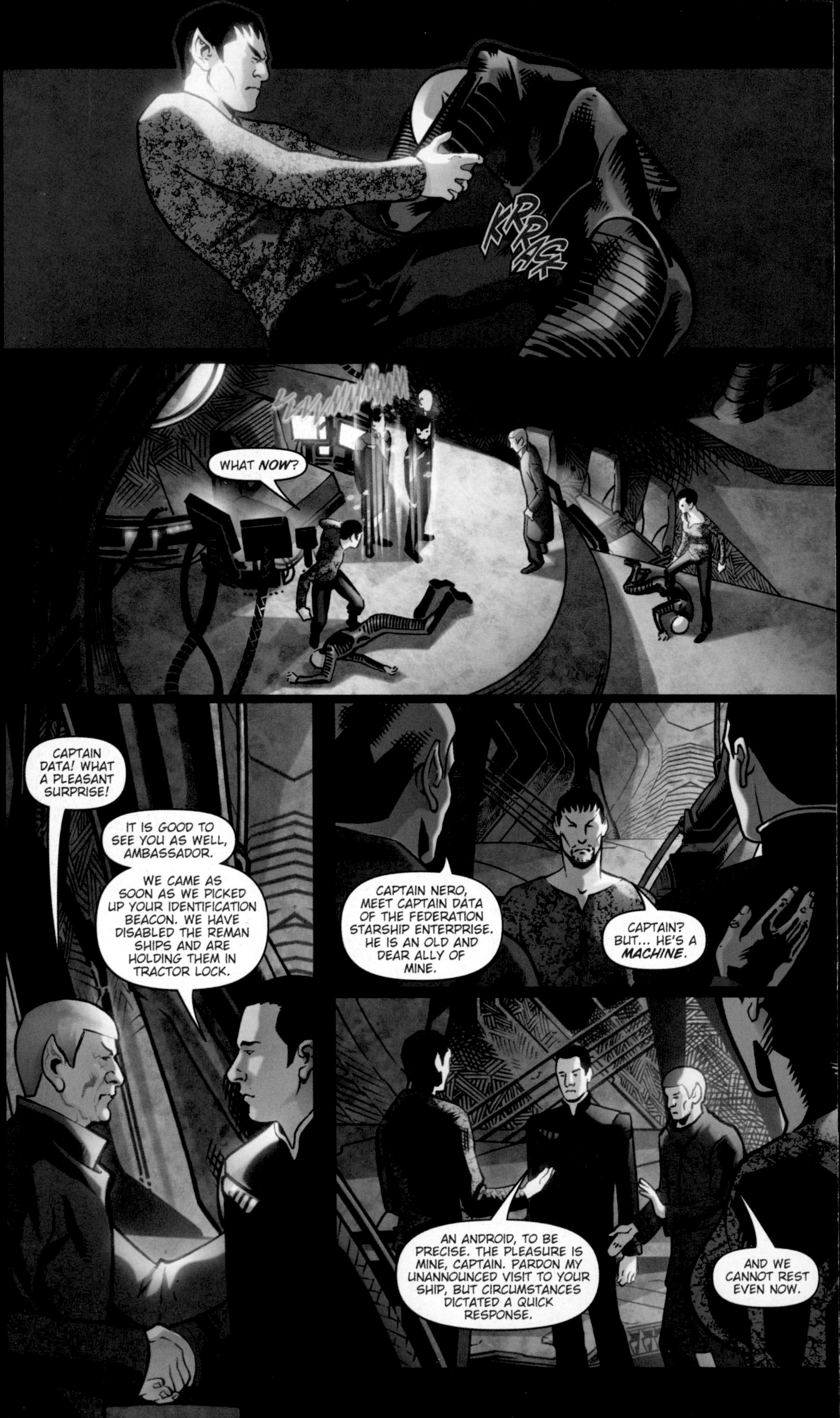
KRRAK
WHAT NOW?
CAPTAIN DATA! WHAT A PLEASANT SURPRISE!
IT IS GOOD TO SEE YOU AS WELL, AMBASSADOR.
WE CAME AS SOON AS WE PICKED UP YOUR IDENTIFICATION BEACON. WE HAVE DISABLED THE REMAN SHIPS AND ARE HOLDING THEM IN TRACTOR LOCK.
CAPTAIN NERO, MEET CAPTAIN DATA OF THE FEDERATION STARSHIP ENTERPRISE. HE IS AN OLD AND DEAR ALLY OF MINE.
CAPTAIN? BUT... HE'S A MACHINE.
AN ANDROID, TO BE PRECISE. THE PLEASURE IS MINE, CAPTAIN. PARDON MY UNANNOUNCED VISIT TO YOUR SHIP, BUT CIRCUMSTANCES DICTATED A QUICK RESPONSE.
AND WE CANNOT REST EVEN NOW.

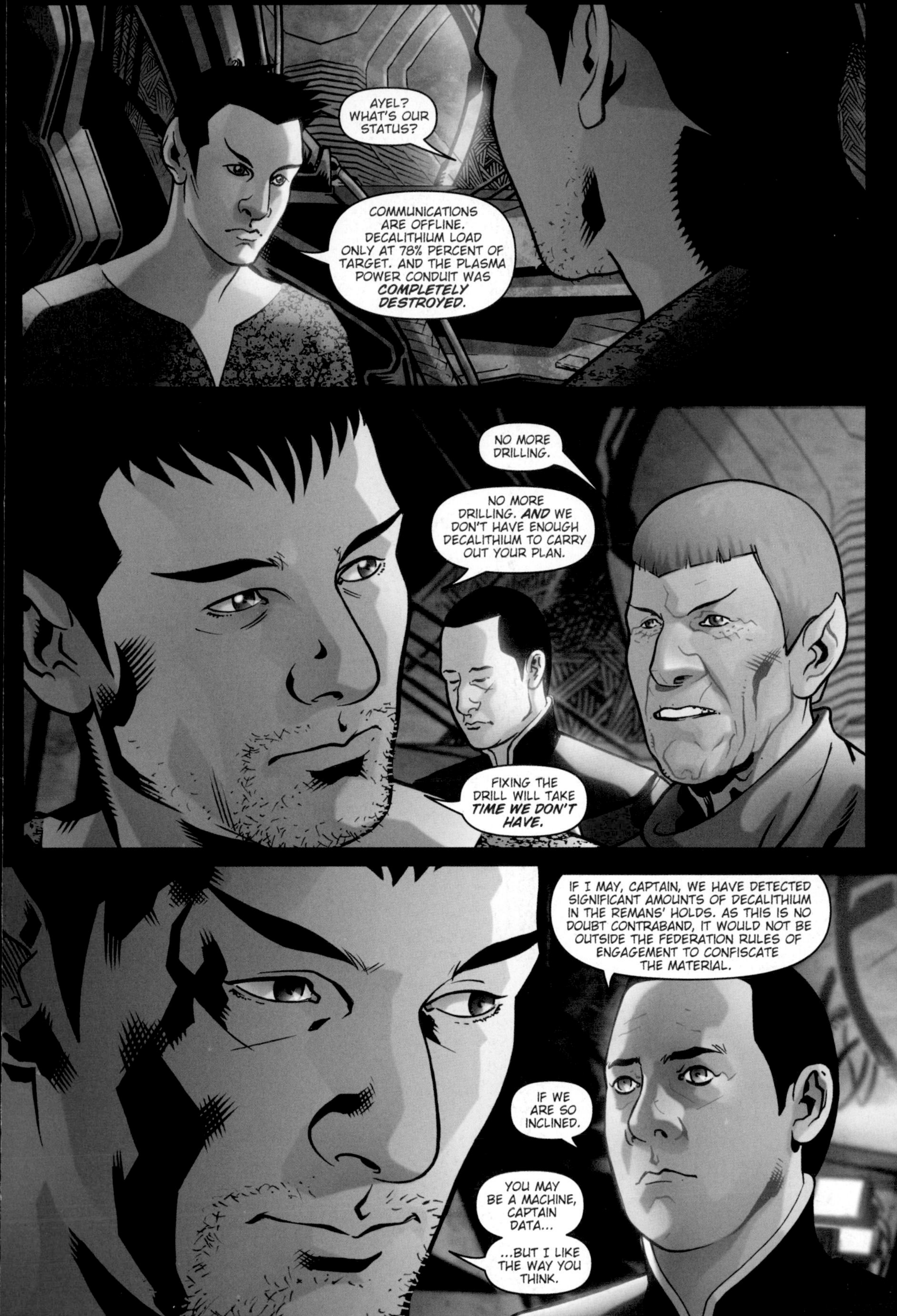
AYEL? WHAT'S OUR STATUS?
COMMUNICATIONS ARE OFFLINE. DECALITHIUM LOAD ONLY AT 78% PERCENT OF TARGET. AND THE PLASMA POWER CONDUIT WAS ***COMPLETELY DESTROYED.***
NO MORE DRILLING.
NO MORE DRILLING. ***AND*** WE DON'T HAVE ENOUGH DECALITHIUM TO CARRY OUT YOUR PLAN.
FIXING THE DRILL WILL TAKE ***TIME WE DON'T HAVE.***
IF I MAY, CAPTAIN, WE HAVE DETECTED SIGNIFICANT AMOUNTS OF DECALITHIUM IN THE REMANS' HOLDS. AS THIS IS NO DOUBT CONTRABAND, IT WOULD NOT BE OUTSIDE THE FEDERATION RULES OF ENGAGEMENT TO CONFISCATE THE MATERIAL.
IF WE ARE SO INCLINED.
YOU MAY BE A MACHINE, CAPTAIN DATA...
...BUT I LIKE THE WAY YOU THINK.

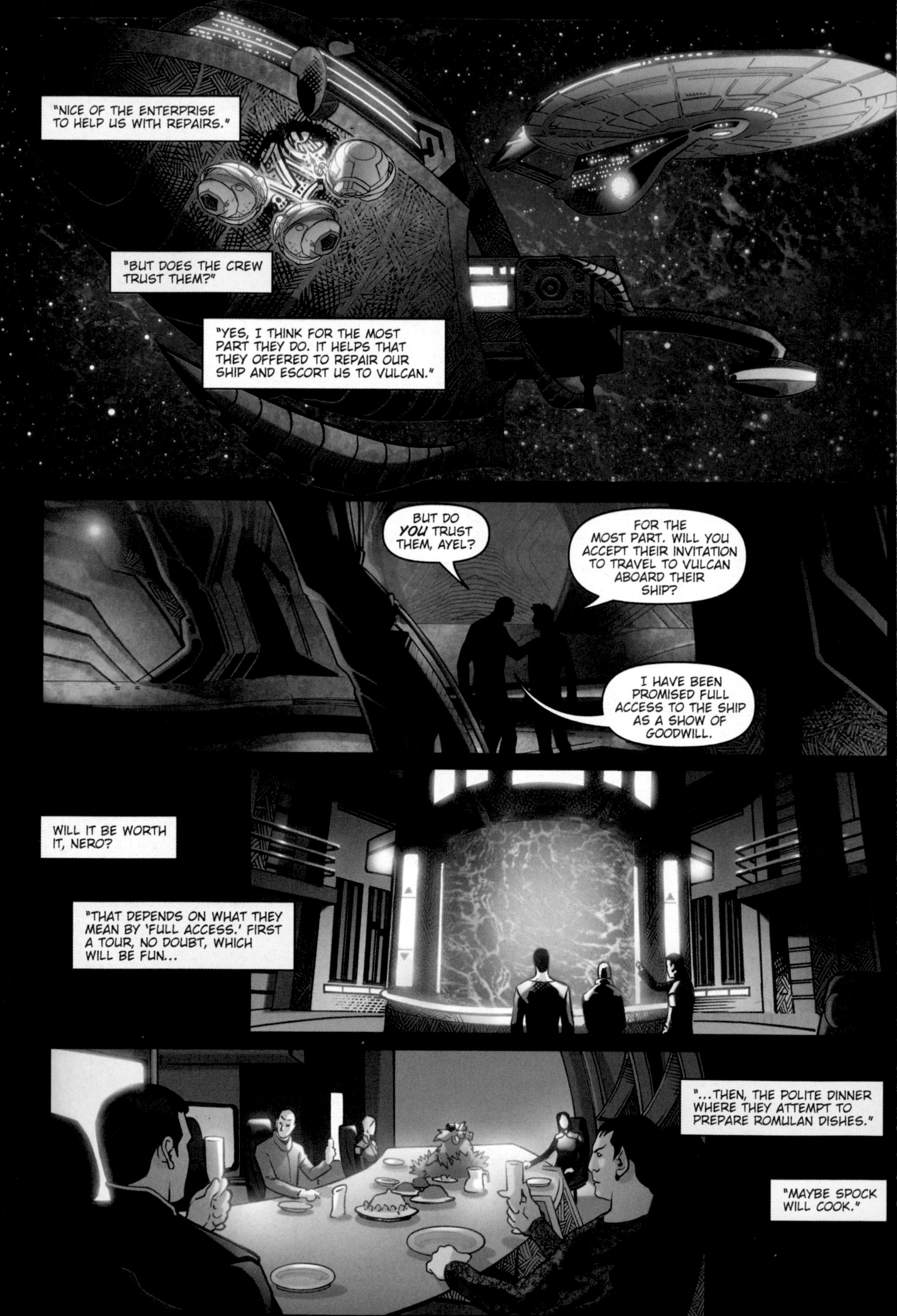
"NICE OF THE ENTERPRISE TO HELP US WITH REPAIRS."
"BUT DOES THE CREW TRUST THEM?"
"YES, I THINK FOR THE MOST PART THEY DO. IT HELPS THAT THEY OFFERED TO REPAIR OUR SHIP AND ESCORT US TO VULCAN."
BUT DO *YOU* TRUST THEM, AYEL?
FOR THE MOST PART. WILL YOU ACCEPT THEIR INVITATION TO TRAVEL TO VULCAN ABOARD THEIR SHIP?
I HAVE BEEN PROMISED FULL ACCESS TO THE SHIP AS A SHOW OF GOODWILL.
WILL IT BE WORTH IT, NERO?
"THAT DEPENDS ON WHAT THEY MEAN BY 'FULL ACCESS.' FIRST A TOUR, NO DOUBT, WHICH WILL BE FUN...
"...THEN, THE POLITE DINNER WHERE THEY ATTEMPT TO PREPARE ROMULAN DISHES."
"MAYBE SPOCK WILL COOK."

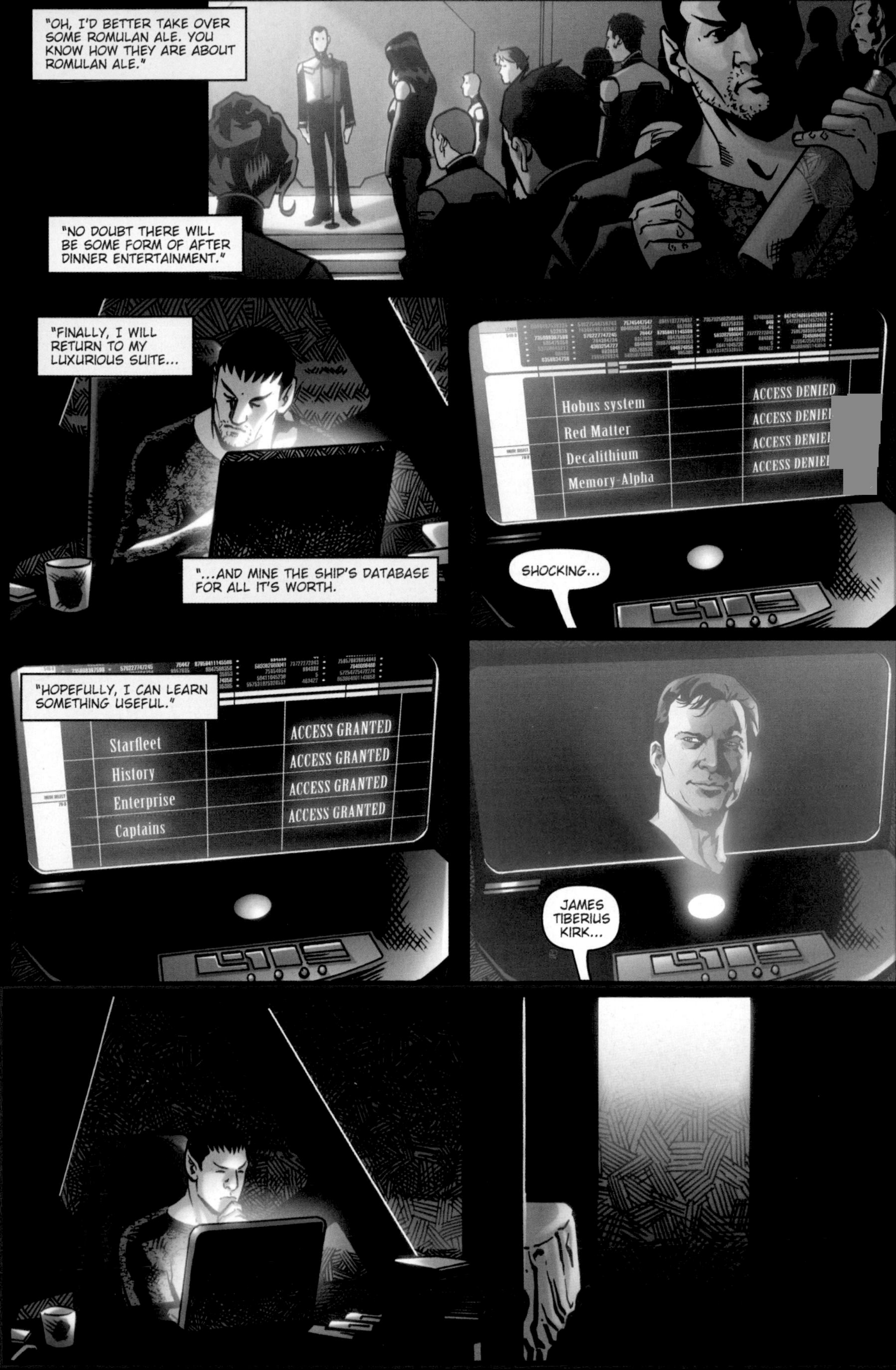
"OH, I'D BETTER TAKE OVER SOME ROMULAN ALE. YOU KNOW HOW THEY ARE ABOUT ROMULAN ALE."
"NO DOUBT THERE WILL BE SOME FORM OF AFTER DINNER ENTERTAINMENT."
"FINALLY, I WILL RETURN TO MY LUXURIOUS SUITE...
"...AND MINE THE SHIP'S DATABASE FOR ALL IT'S WORTH.
Hobus system
Red Matter
Decalithium
Memory-Alpha
ACCESS DENIED
SHOCKING...
"HOPEFULLY, I CAN LEARN SOMETHING USEFUL."
Starfleet
History
Enterprise
Captains
ACCESS GRANTED
ACCESS GRANTED
ACCESS GRANTED
ACCESS GRANTED
JAMES TIBERIUS KIRK...

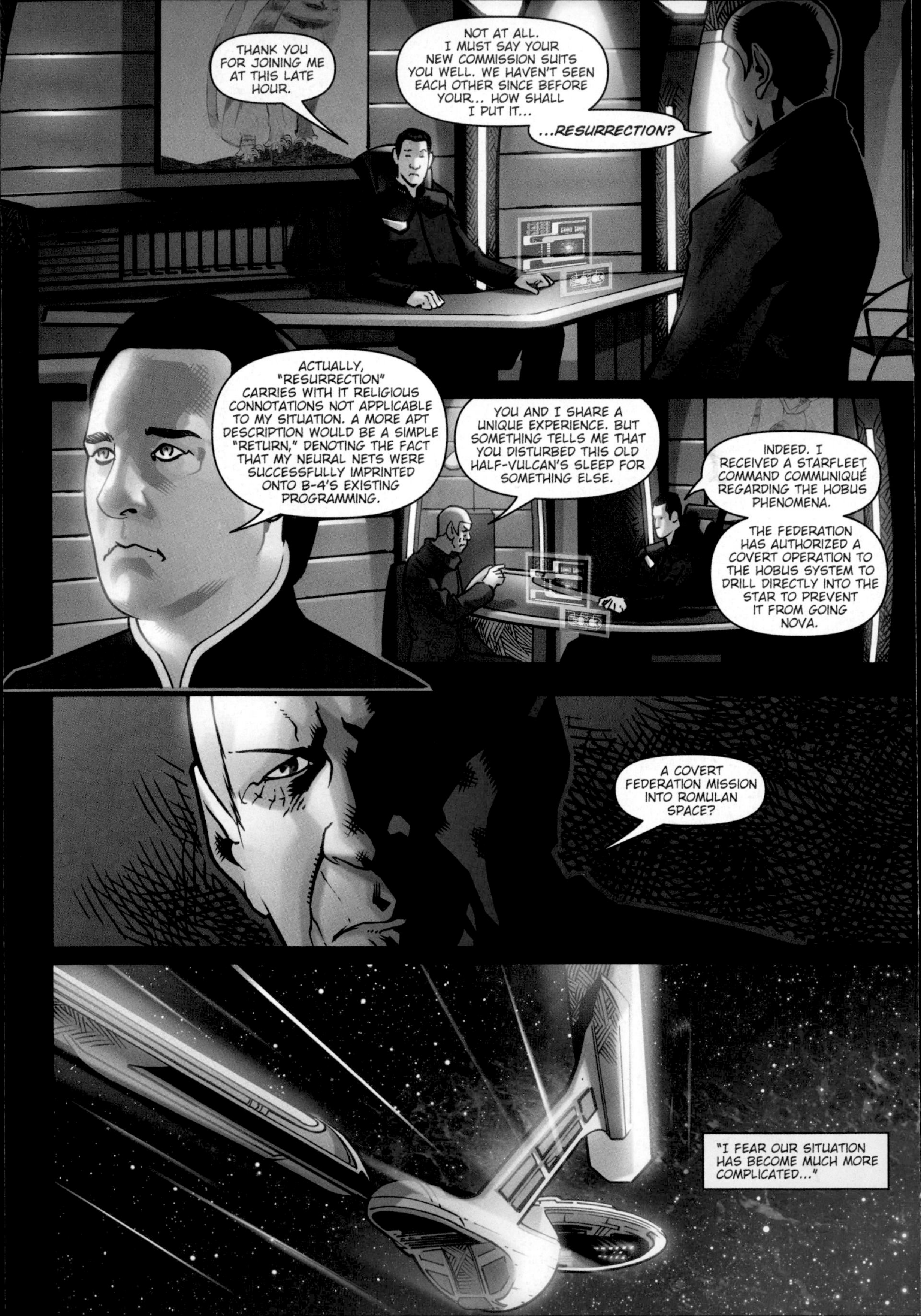

THANK YOU FOR JOINING ME AT THIS LATE HOUR.
NOT AT ALL. I MUST SAY YOUR NEW COMMISSION SUITS YOU WELL. WE HAVEN'T SEEN EACH OTHER SINCE BEFORE YOUR... HOW SHALL I PUT IT...
...RESURRECTION?
ACTUALLY, "RESURRECTION" CARRIES WITH IT RELIGIOUS CONNOTATIONS NOT APPLICABLE TO MY SITUATION. A MORE APT DESCRIPTION WOULD BE A SIMPLE "RETURN," DENOTING THE FACT THAT MY NEURAL NETS WERE SUCCESSFULLY IMPRINTED ONTO B-4'S EXISTING PROGRAMMING.
YOU AND I SHARE A UNIQUE EXPERIENCE. BUT SOMETHING TELLS ME THAT YOU DISTURBED THIS OLD HALF-VULCAN'S SLEEP FOR SOMETHING ELSE.
INDEED. I RECEIVED A STARFLEET COMMAND COMMUNIQUÉ REGARDING THE HOBUS PHENOMENA.
THE FEDERATION HAS AUTHORIZED A COVERT OPERATION TO THE HOBUS SYSTEM TO DRILL DIRECTLY INTO THE STAR TO PREVENT IT FROM GOING NOVA.
A COVERT FEDERATION MISSION INTO ROMULAN SPACE?
"I FEAR OUR SITUATION HAS BECOME MUCH MORE COMPLICATED..."

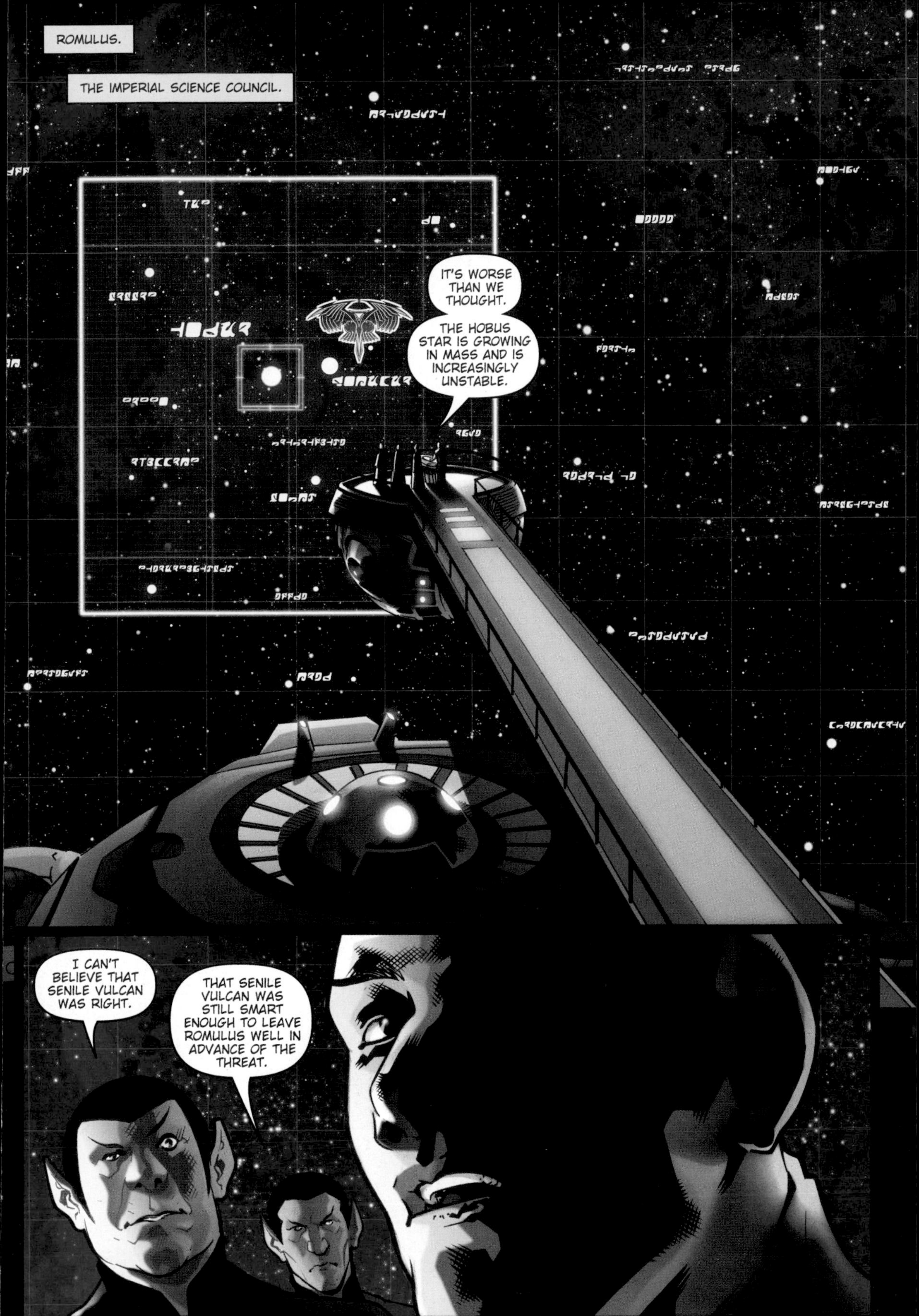
ROMULUS.
THE IMPERIAL SCIENCE COUNCIL.
IT'S WORSE THAN WE THOUGHT.
THE HOBUS STAR IS GROWING IN MASS AND IS INCREASINGLY UNSTABLE.
I CAN'T BELIEVE THAT SENILE VULCAN WAS RIGHT.
THAT SENILE VULCAN WAS STILL SMART ENOUGH TO LEAVE ROMULUS WELL IN ADVANCE OF THE THREAT.

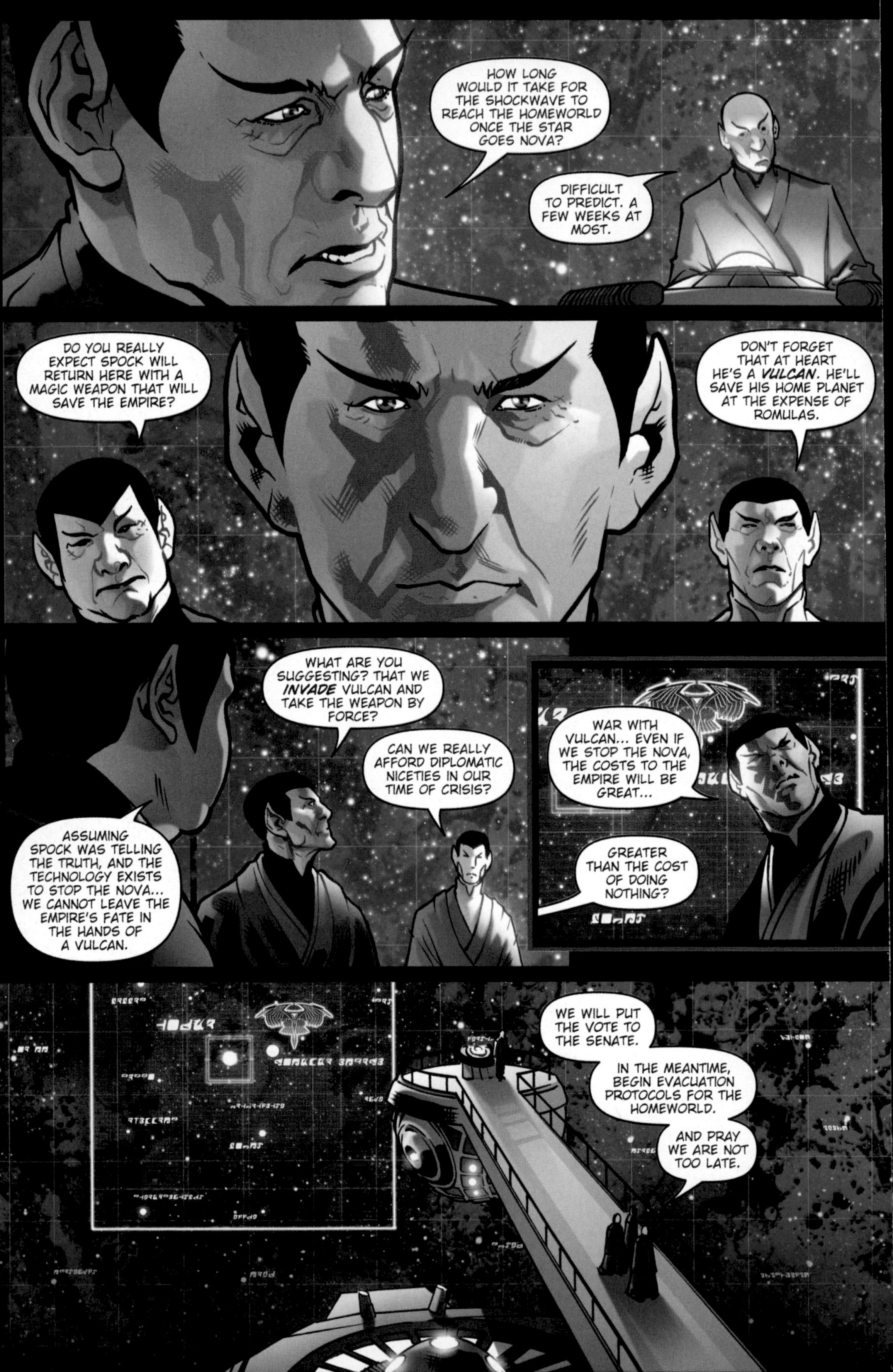
HOW LONG WOULD IT TAKE FOR THE SHOCKWAVE TO REACH THE HOMEWORLD ONCE THE STAR GOES NOVA?
DIFFICULT TO PREDICT. A FEW WEEKS AT MOST.
DO YOU REALLY EXPECT SPOCK WILL RETURN HERE WITH A MAGIC WEAPON THAT WILL SAVE THE EMPIRE?
DON'T FORGET THAT AT HEART HE'S A VULCAN. HE'LL SAVE HIS HOME PLANET AT THE EXPENSE OF ROMULAS.
ASSUMING SPOCK WAS TELLING THE TRUTH, AND THE TECHNOLOGY EXISTS TO STOP THE NOVA... WE CANNOT LEAVE THE EMPIRE'S FATE IN THE HANDS OF A VULCAN.
WHAT ARE YOU SUGGESTING? THAT WE INVADE VULCAN AND TAKE THE WEAPON BY FORCE?
CAN WE REALLY AFFORD DIPLOMATIC NICETIES IN OUR TIME OF CRISIS?
WAR WITH VULCAN... EVEN IF WE STOP THE NOVA, THE COSTS TO THE EMPIRE WILL BE GREAT...
GREATER THAN THE COST OF DOING NOTHING?
WE WILL PUT THE VOTE TO THE SENATE.
IN THE MEANTIME, BEGIN EVACUATION PROTOCOLS FOR THE HOMEWORLD.
AND PRAY WE ARE NOT TOO LATE.

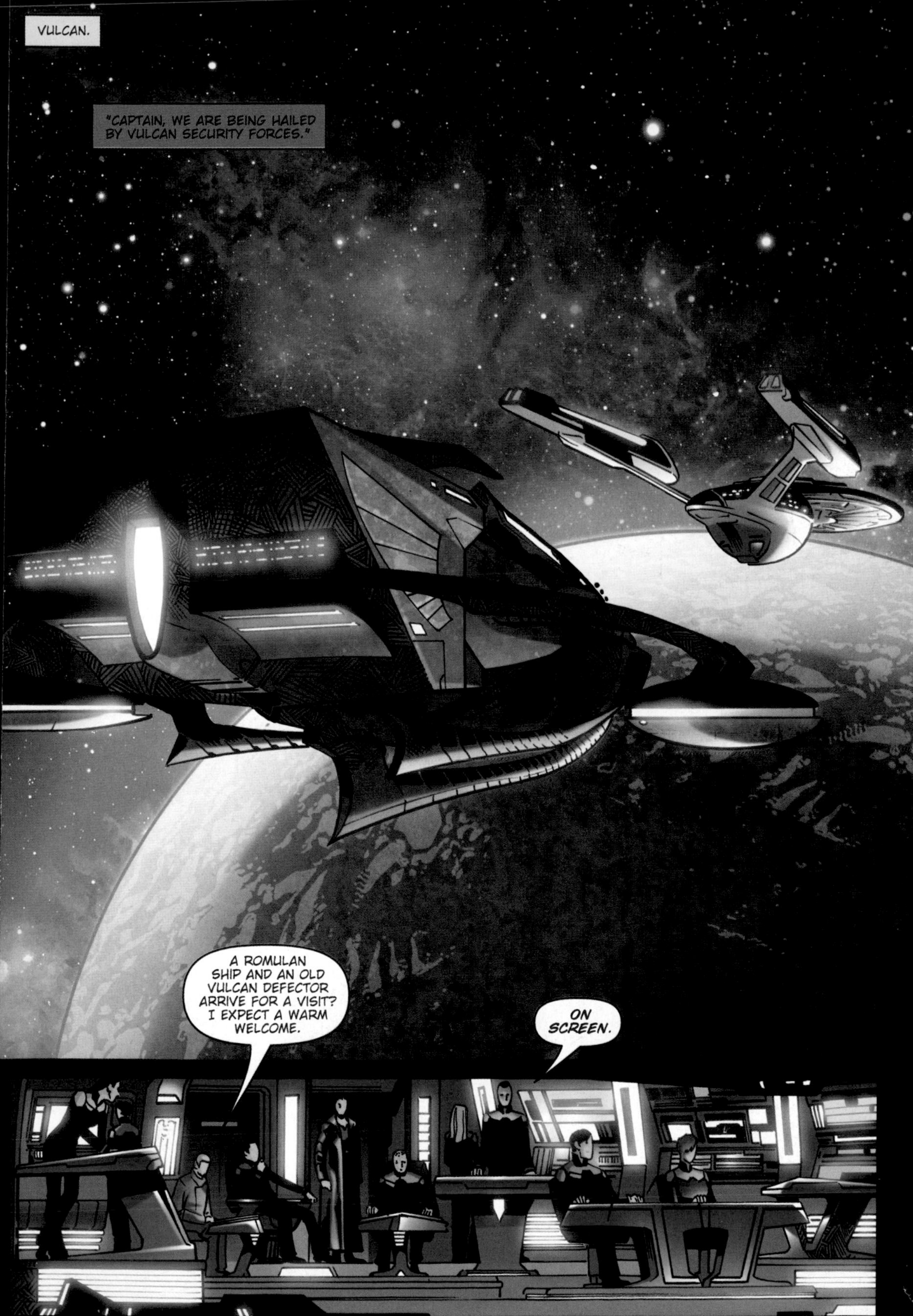

VULCAN.
"CAPTAIN, WE ARE BEING HAILED BY VULCAN SECURITY FORCES."
A ROMULAN SHIP AND AN OLD VULCAN DEFECTOR ARRIVE FOR A VISIT? I EXPECT A WARM WELCOME.
ON SCREEN.

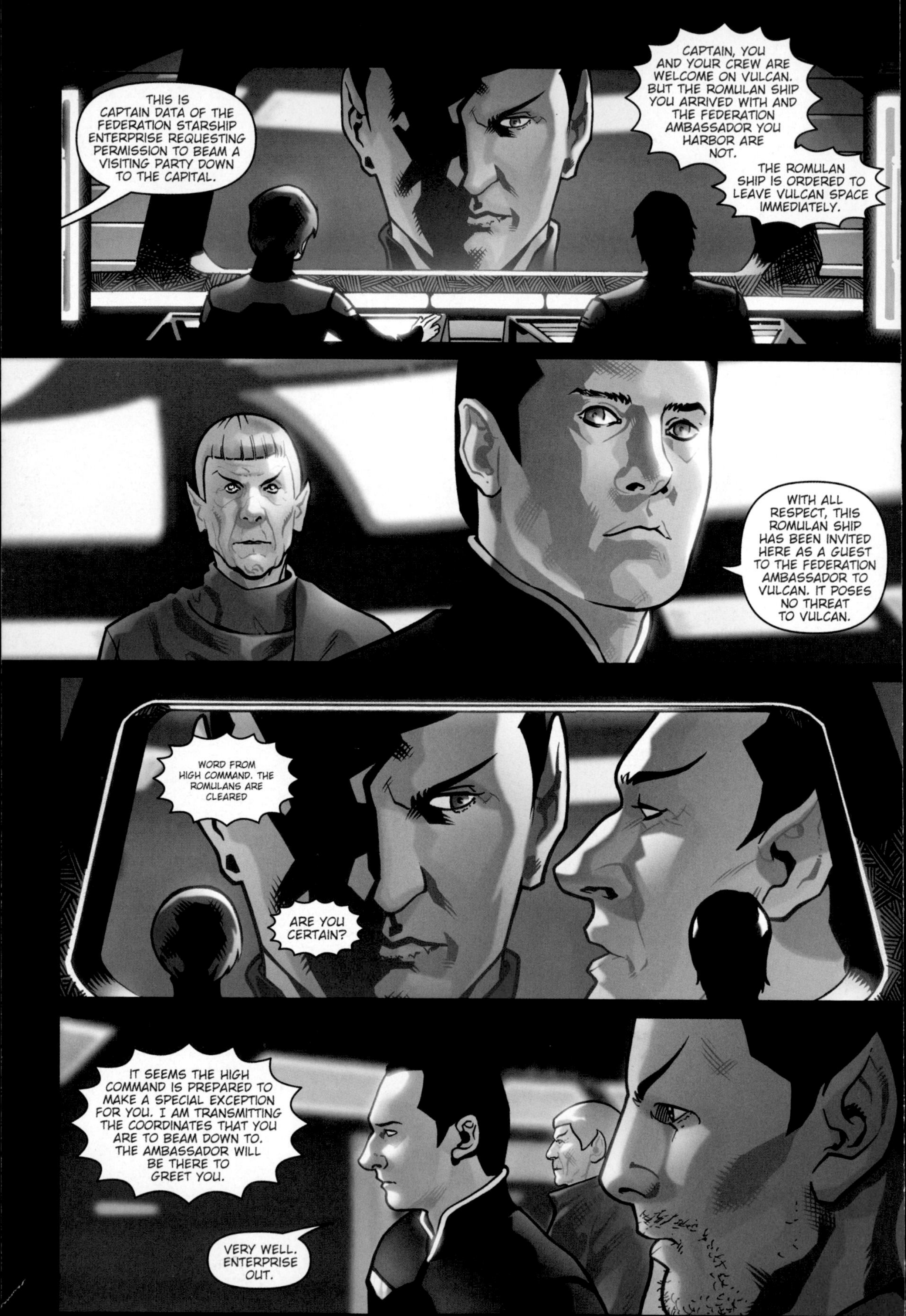
THIS IS CAPTAIN DATA OF THE FEDERATION STARSHIP ENTERPRISE REQUESTING PERMISSION TO BEAM A VISITING PARTY DOWN TO THE CAPITAL.
CAPTAIN, YOU AND YOUR CREW ARE WELCOME ON VULCAN. BUT THE ROMULAN SHIP YOU ARRIVED WITH AND THE FEDERATION AMBASSADOR YOU HARBOR ARE NOT.
THE ROMULAN SHIP IS ORDERED TO LEAVE VULCAN SPACE IMMEDIATELY.
WITH ALL RESPECT, THIS ROMULAN SHIP HAS BEEN INVITED HERE AS A GUEST TO THE FEDERATION AMBASSADOR TO VULCAN. IT POSES NO THREAT TO VULCAN.
WORD FROM HIGH COMMAND. THE ROMULANS ARE CLEARED
ARE YOU CERTAIN?
IT SEEMS THE HIGH COMMAND IS PREPARED TO MAKE A SPECIAL EXCEPTION FOR YOU. I AM TRANSMITTING THE COORDINATES THAT YOU ARE TO BEAM DOWN TO. THE AMBASSADOR WILL BE THERE TO GREET YOU.
VERY WELL. ENTERPRISE OUT.

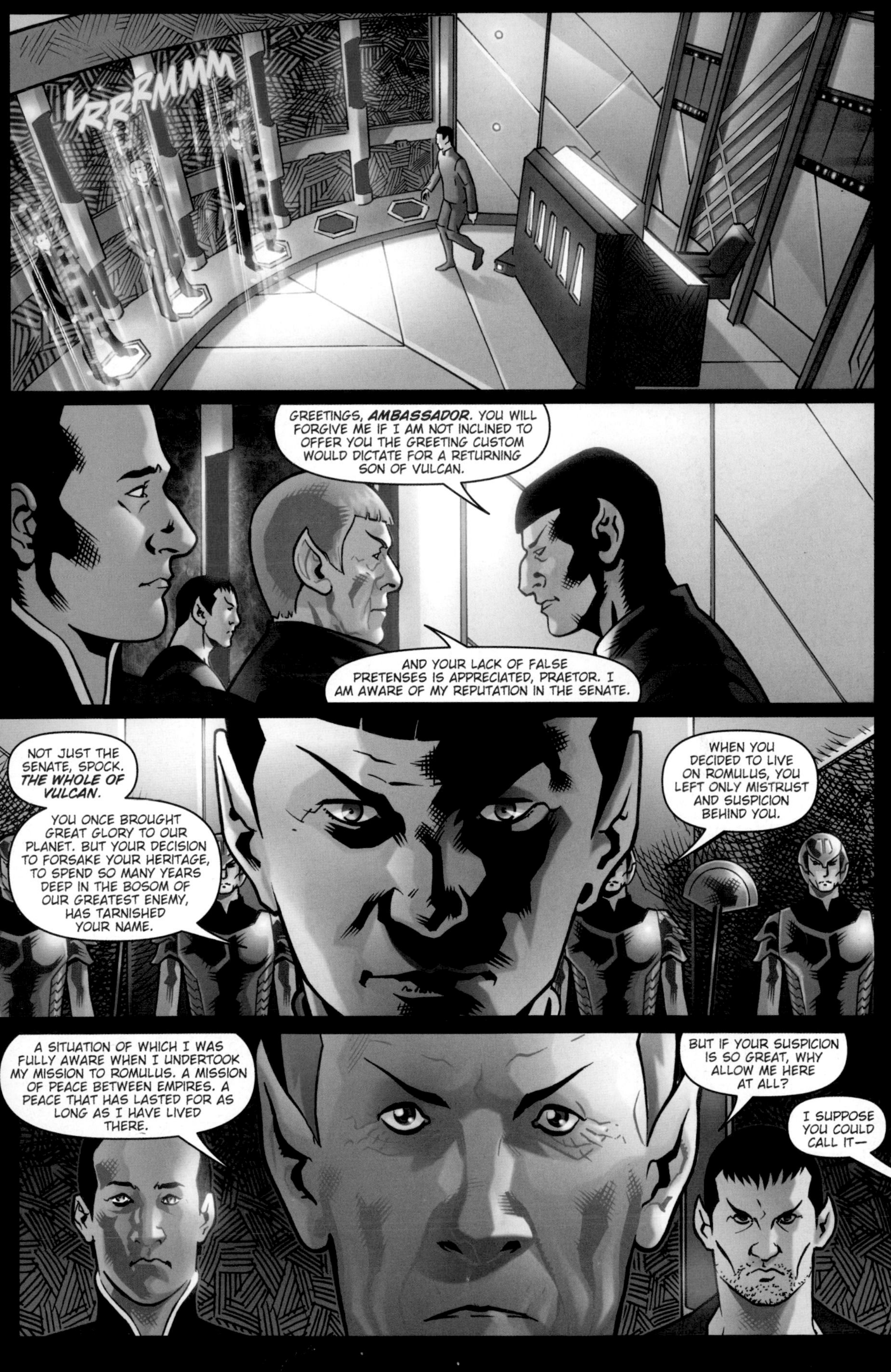
VRRRMMM
GREETINGS, ***AMBASSADOR.*** YOU WILL FORGIVE ME IF I AM NOT INCLINED TO OFFER YOU THE GREETING CUSTOM WOULD DICTATE FOR A RETURNING SON OF VULCAN.
AND YOUR LACK OF FALSE PRETENSES IS APPRECIATED, PRAETOR. I AM AWARE OF MY REPUTATION IN THE SENATE.
NOT JUST THE SENATE, SPOCK. ***THE WHOLE OF VULCAN.***
YOU ONCE BROUGHT GREAT GLORY TO OUR PLANET. BUT YOUR DECISION TO FORSAKE YOUR HERITAGE, TO SPEND SO MANY YEARS DEEP IN THE BOSOM OF OUR GREATEST ENEMY, HAS TARNISHED YOUR NAME.
WHEN YOU DECIDED TO LIVE ON ROMULUS, YOU LEFT ONLY MISTRUST AND SUSPICION BEHIND YOU.
A SITUATION OF WHICH I WAS FULLY AWARE WHEN I UNDERTOOK MY MISSION TO ROMULUS. A MISSION OF PEACE BETWEEN EMPIRES. A PEACE THAT HAS LASTED FOR AS LONG AS I HAVE LIVED THERE.
BUT IF YOUR SUSPICION IS SO GREAT, WHY ALLOW ME HERE AT ALL?
I SUPPOSE YOU COULD CALL IT—

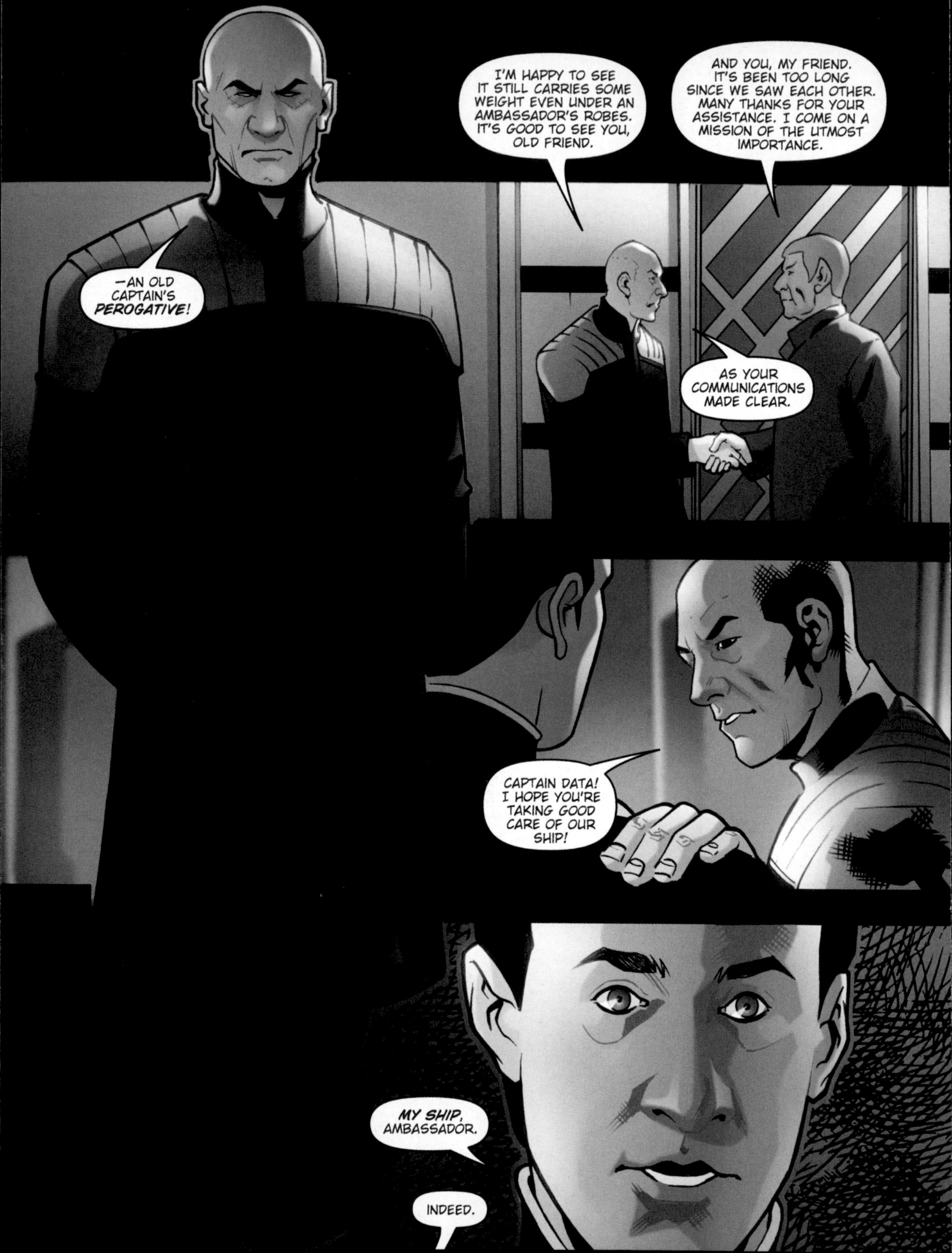
—AN OLD CAPTAIN'S *PEROGATIVE!*
I'M HAPPY TO SEE IT STILL CARRIES SOME WEIGHT EVEN UNDER AN AMBASSADOR'S ROBES. IT'S GOOD TO SEE YOU, OLD FRIEND.
AND YOU, MY FRIEND. IT'S BEEN TOO LONG SINCE WE SAW EACH OTHER. MANY THANKS FOR YOUR ASSISTANCE. I COME ON A MISSION OF THE UTMOST IMPORTANCE.
AS YOUR COMMUNICATIONS MADE CLEAR.
CAPTAIN DATA! I HOPE YOU'RE TAKING GOOD CARE OF OUR SHIP!
MY SHIP, AMBASSADOR.
INDEED.

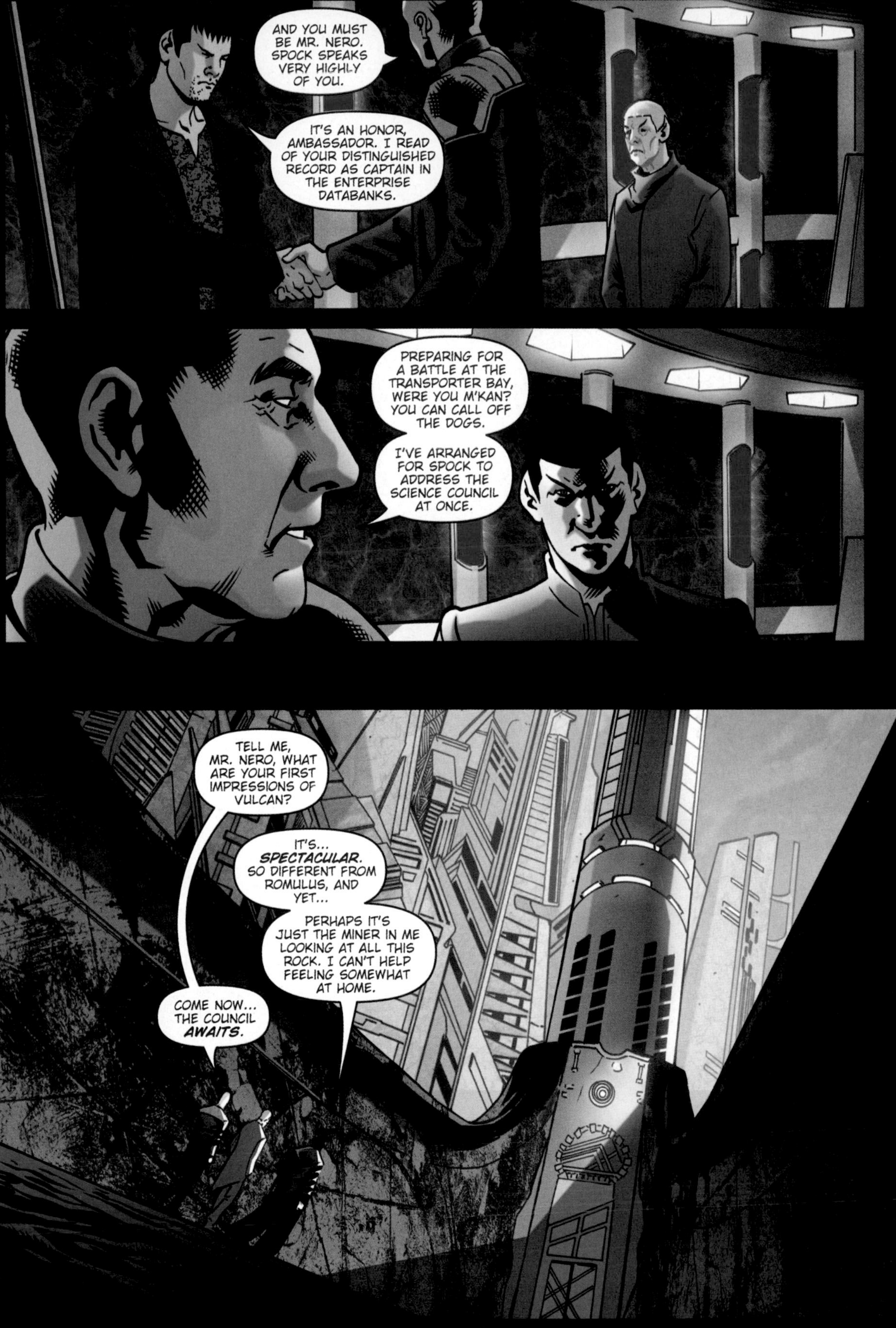
AND YOU MUST BE MR. NERO. SPOCK SPEAKS VERY HIGHLY OF YOU.
IT'S AN HONOR, AMBASSADOR. I READ OF YOUR DISTINGUISHED RECORD AS CAPTAIN IN THE ENTERPRISE DATABANKS.
PREPARING FOR A BATTLE AT THE TRANSPORTER BAY, WERE YOU M'KAN? YOU CAN CALL OFF THE DOGS.
I'VE ARRANGED FOR SPOCK TO ADDRESS THE SCIENCE COUNCIL AT ONCE.
TELL ME, MR. NERO, WHAT ARE YOUR FIRST IMPRESSIONS OF VULCAN?
IT'S... SPECTACULAR. SO DIFFERENT FROM ROMULUS, AND YET...
PERHAPS IT'S JUST THE MINER IN ME LOOKING AT ALL THIS ROCK. I CAN'T HELP FEELING SOMEWHAT AT HOME.
COME NOW... THE COUNCIL AWAITS.

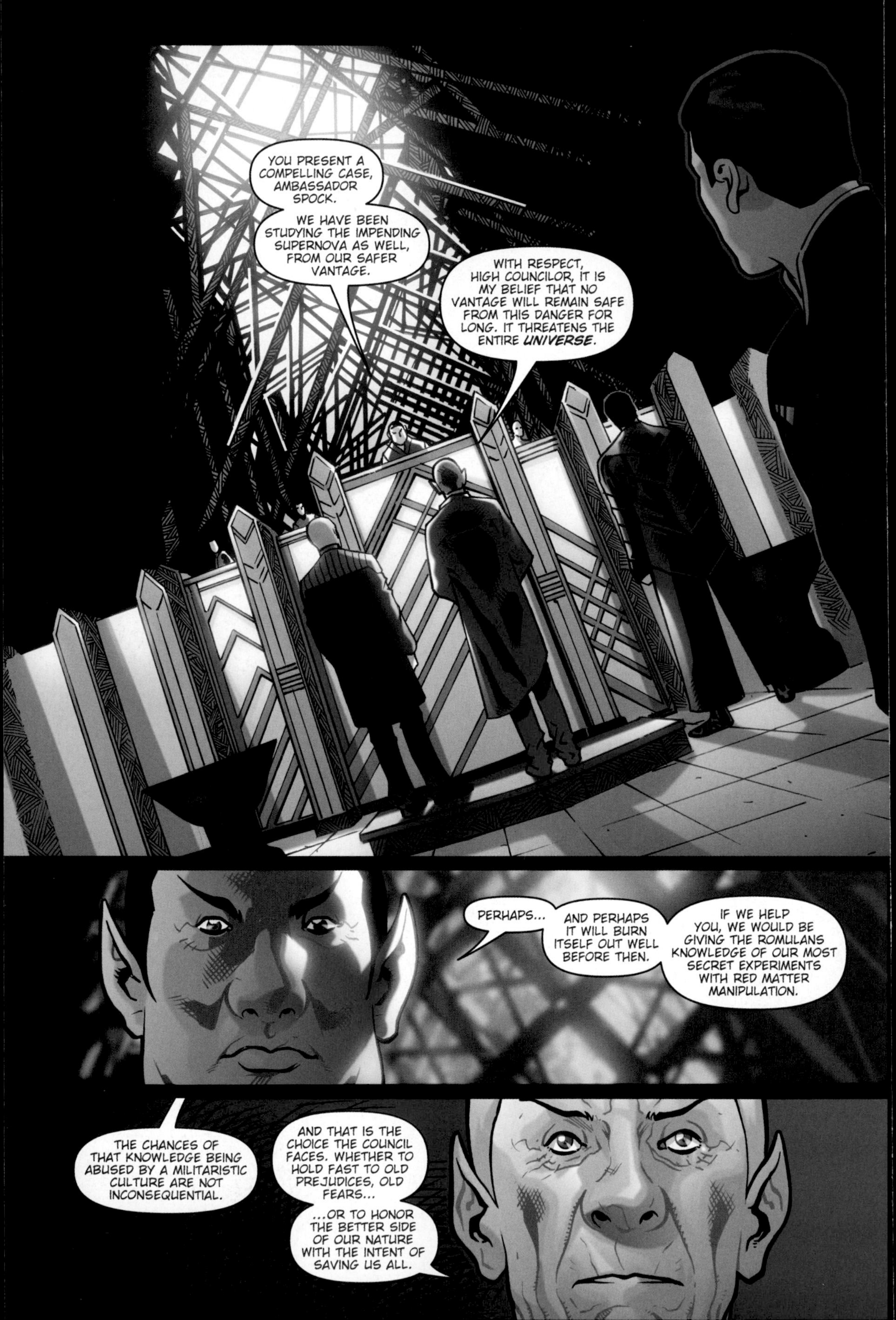
YOU PRESENT A COMPELLING CASE, AMBASSADOR SPOCK.
WE HAVE BEEN STUDYING THE IMPENDING SUPERNOVA AS WELL, FROM OUR SAFER VANTAGE.
WITH RESPECT, HIGH COUNCILOR, IT IS MY BELIEF THAT NO VANTAGE WILL REMAIN SAFE FROM THIS DANGER FOR LONG. IT THREATENS THE ENTIRE *UNIVERSE*.
PERHAPS...
AND PERHAPS IT WILL BURN ITSELF OUT WELL BEFORE THEN.
IF WE HELP YOU, WE WOULD BE GIVING THE ROMULANS KNOWLEDGE OF OUR MOST SECRET EXPERIMENTS WITH RED MATTER MANIPULATION.
THE CHANCES OF THAT KNOWLEDGE BEING ABUSED BY A MILITARISTIC CULTURE ARE NOT INCONSEQUENTIAL.
AND THAT IS THE CHOICE THE COUNCIL FACES. WHETHER TO HOLD FAST TO OLD PREJUDICES, OLD FEARS...
...OR TO HONOR THE BETTER SIDE OF OUR NATURE WITH THE INTENT OF SAVING US ALL.

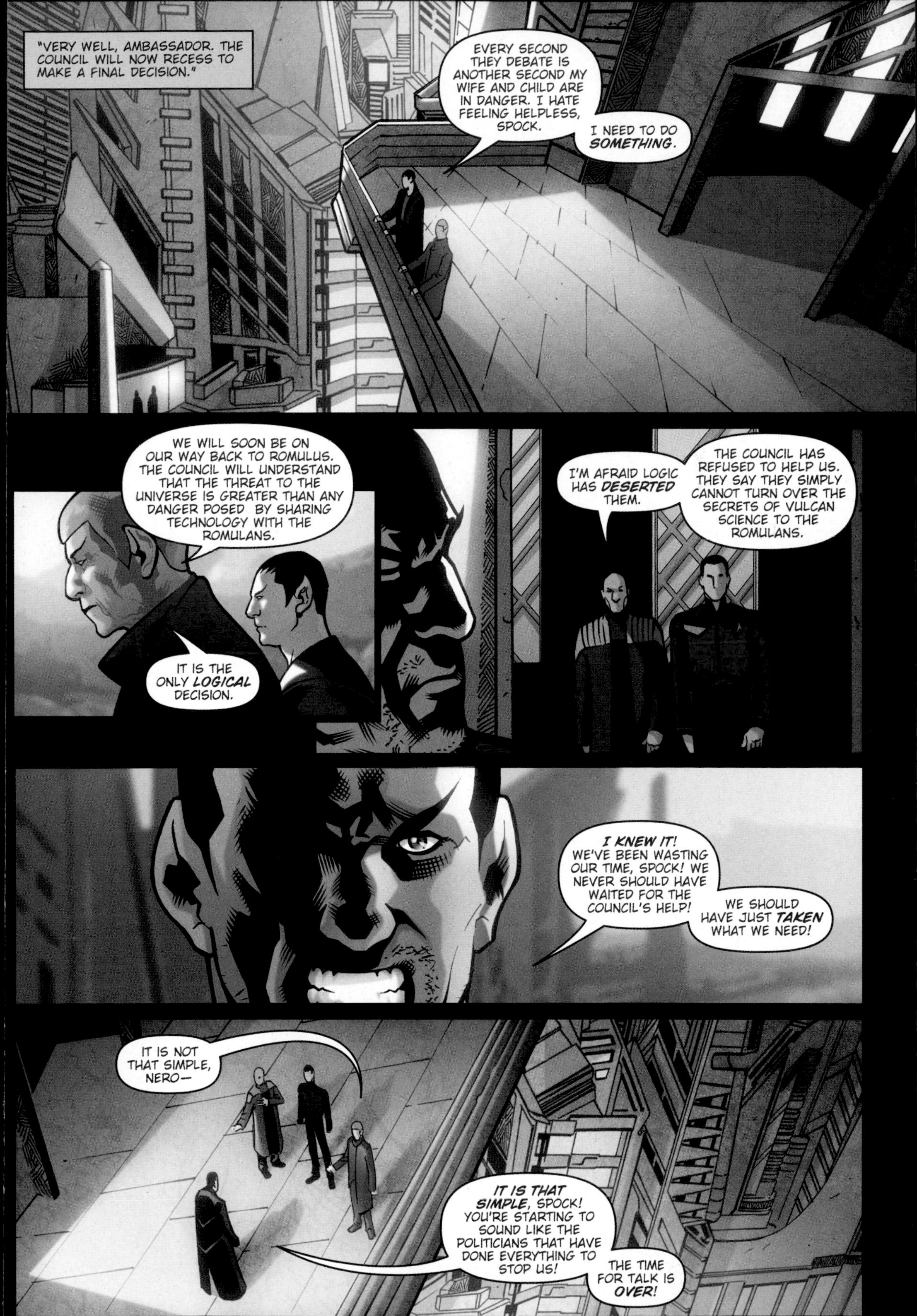
"VERY WELL, AMBASSADOR. THE COUNCIL WILL NOW RECESS TO MAKE A FINAL DECISION."
EVERY SECOND THEY DEBATE IS ANOTHER SECOND MY WIFE AND CHILD ARE IN DANGER. I HATE FEELING HELPLESS, SPOCK.
I NEED TO DO SOMETHING.
WE WILL SOON BE ON OUR WAY BACK TO ROMULUS. THE COUNCIL WILL UNDERSTAND THAT THE THREAT TO THE UNIVERSE IS GREATER THAN ANY DANGER POSED BY SHARING TECHNOLOGY WITH THE ROMULANS.
IT IS THE ONLY LOGICAL DECISION.
I'M AFRAID LOGIC HAS DESERTED THEM.
THE COUNCIL HAS REFUSED TO HELP US. THEY SAY THEY SIMPLY CANNOT TURN OVER THE SECRETS OF VULCAN SCIENCE TO THE ROMULANS.
I KNEW IT! WE'VE BEEN WASTING OUR TIME, SPOCK! WE NEVER SHOULD HAVE WAITED FOR THE COUNCIL'S HELP!
WE SHOULD HAVE JUST TAKEN WHAT WE NEED!
IT IS NOT THAT SIMPLE, NERO—
IT IS THAT SIMPLE, SPOCK! YOU'RE STARTING TO SOUND LIKE THE POLITICIANS THAT HAVE DONE EVERYTHING TO STOP US!
THE TIME FOR TALK IS OVER!

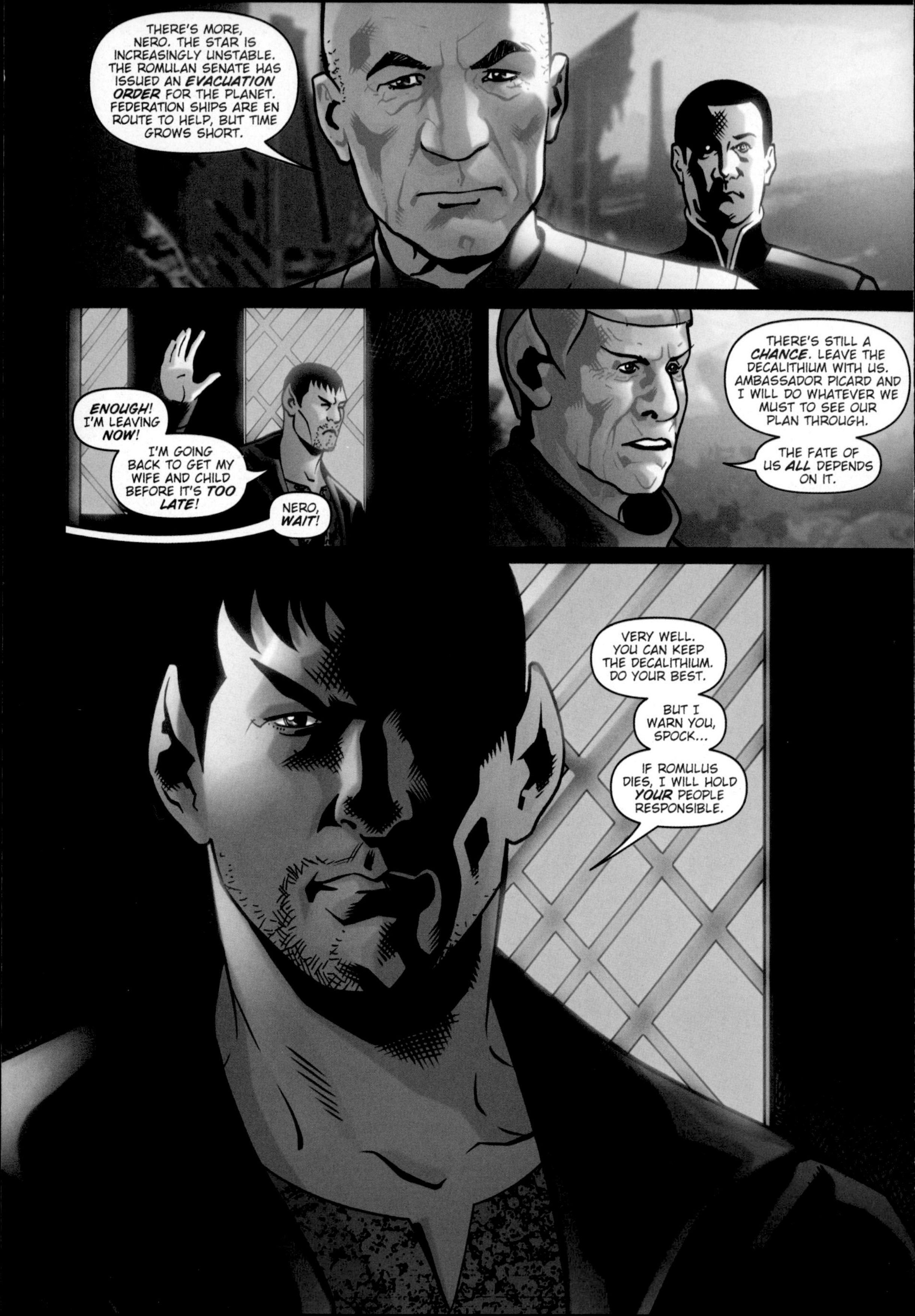
THERE'S MORE, NERO. THE STAR IS INCREASINGLY UNSTABLE. THE ROMULAN SENATE HAS ISSUED AN EVACUATION ORDER FOR THE PLANET. FEDERATION SHIPS ARE EN ROUTE TO HELP, BUT TIME GROWS SHORT.
ENOUGH! I'M LEAVING NOW!
I'M GOING BACK TO GET MY WIFE AND CHILD BEFORE IT'S TOO LATE!
NERO, WAIT!
THERE'S STILL A CHANCE. LEAVE THE DECALITHIUM WITH US. AMBASSADOR PICARD AND I WILL DO WHATEVER WE MUST TO SEE OUR PLAN THROUGH.
THE FATE OF US ALL DEPENDS ON IT.
VERY WELL. YOU CAN KEEP THE DECALITHIUM. DO YOUR BEST.
BUT I WARN YOU, SPOCK...
IF ROMULUS DIES, I WILL HOLD YOUR PEOPLE RESPONSIBLE.

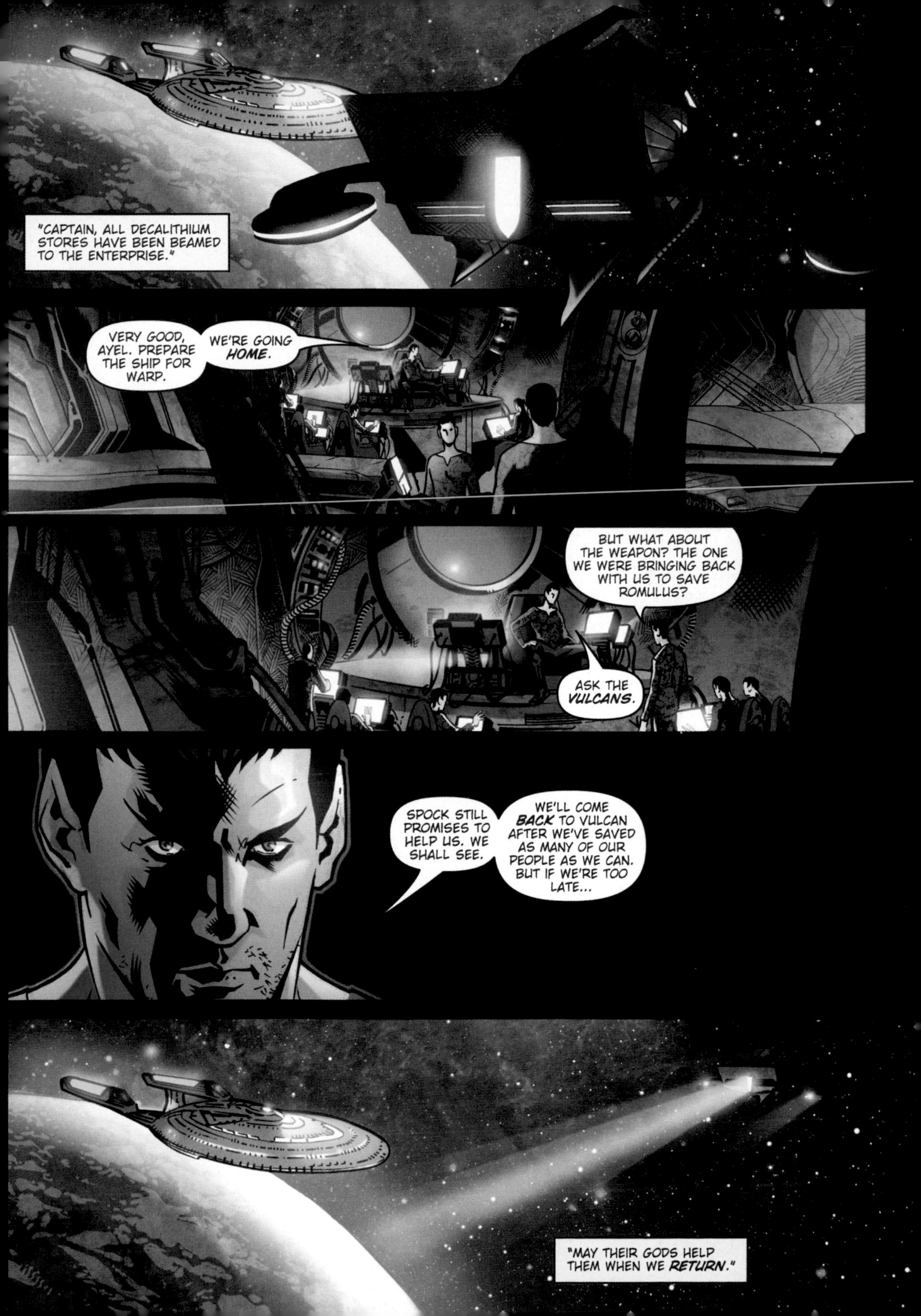
"CAPTAIN, ALL DECALITHIUM STORES HAVE BEEN BEAMED TO THE ENTERPRISE."
VERY GOOD, AYEL. PREPARE THE SHIP FOR WARP.
WE'RE GOING HOME.
BUT WHAT ABOUT THE WEAPON? THE ONE WE WERE BRINGING BACK WITH US TO SAVE ROMULUS?
ASK THE VULCANS.
SPOCK STILL PROMISES TO HELP US. WE SHALL SEE.
WE'LL COME BACK TO VULCAN AFTER WE'VE SAVED AS MANY OF OUR PEOPLE AS WE CAN. BUT IF WE'RE TOO LATE...
"MAY THEIR GODS HELP THEM WHEN WE RETURN."

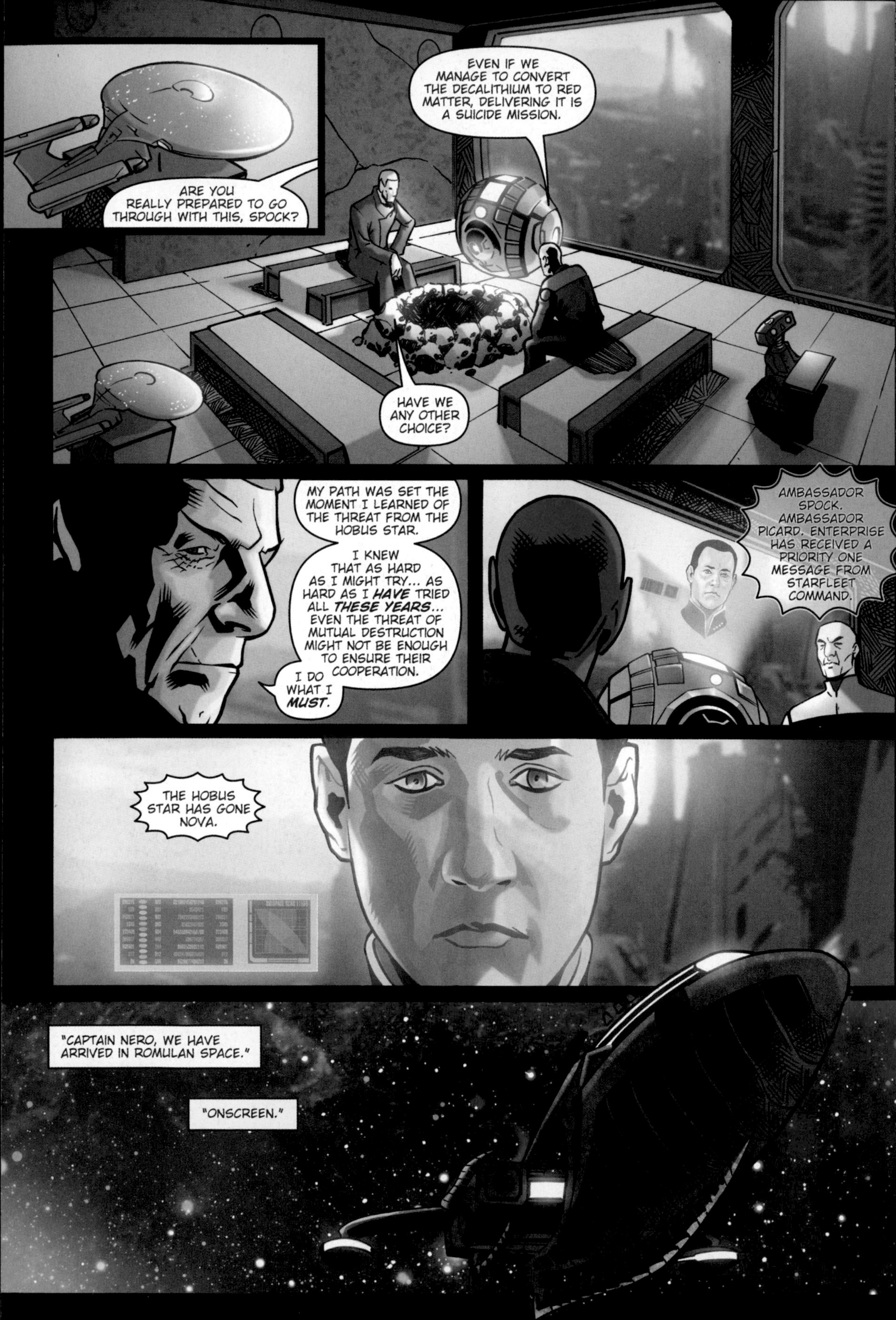
ARE YOU REALLY PREPARED TO GO THROUGH WITH THIS, SPOCK?
EVEN IF WE MANAGE TO CONVERT THE DECALITHIUM TO RED MATTER, DELIVERING IT IS A SUICIDE MISSION.
HAVE WE ANY OTHER CHOICE?
MY PATH WAS SET THE MOMENT I LEARNED OF THE THREAT FROM THE HOBUS STAR.
I KNEW THAT AS HARD AS I MIGHT TRY... AS HARD AS I HAVE TRIED ALL THESE YEARS... EVEN THE THREAT OF MUTUAL DESTRUCTION MIGHT NOT BE ENOUGH TO ENSURE THEIR COOPERATION.
I DO WHAT I MUST.
AMBASSADOR SPOCK. AMBASSADOR PICARD. ENTERPRISE HAS RECEIVED A PRIORITY ONE MESSAGE FROM STARFLEET COMMAND.
THE HOBUS STAR HAS GONE NOVA.
"CAPTAIN NERO, WE HAVE ARRIVED IN ROMULAN SPACE."
"ONSCREEN."

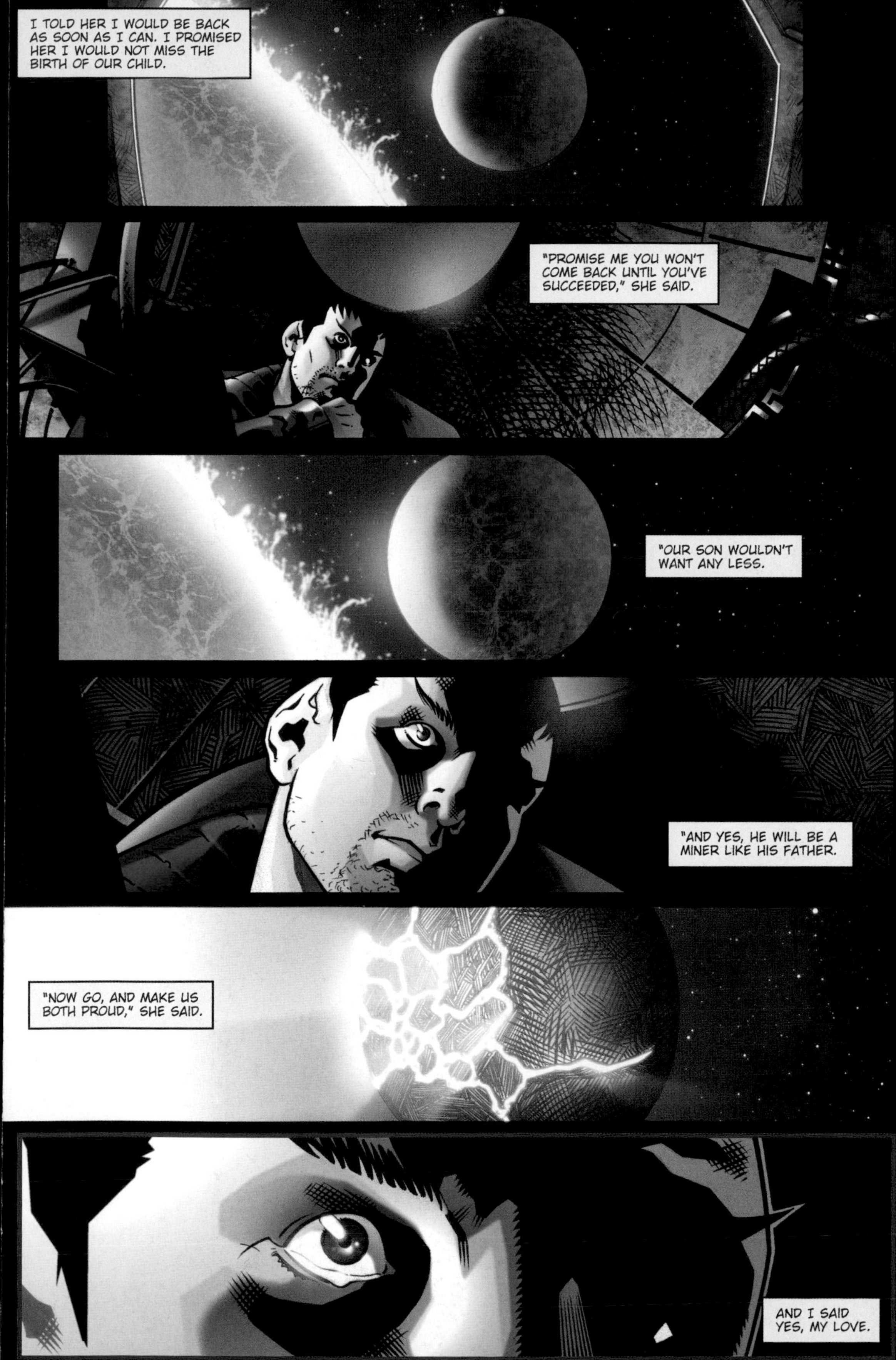
I TOLD HER I WOULD BE BACK AS SOON AS I CAN. I PROMISED HER I WOULD NOT MISS THE BIRTH OF OUR CHILD.
"PROMISE ME YOU WON'T COME BACK UNTIL YOU'VE SUCCEEDED," SHE SAID.
"OUR SON WOULDN'T WANT ANY LESS.
"AND YES, HE WILL BE A MINER LIKE HIS FATHER.
"NOW GO, AND MAKE US BOTH PROUD," SHE SAID.
AND I SAID YES, MY LOVE.

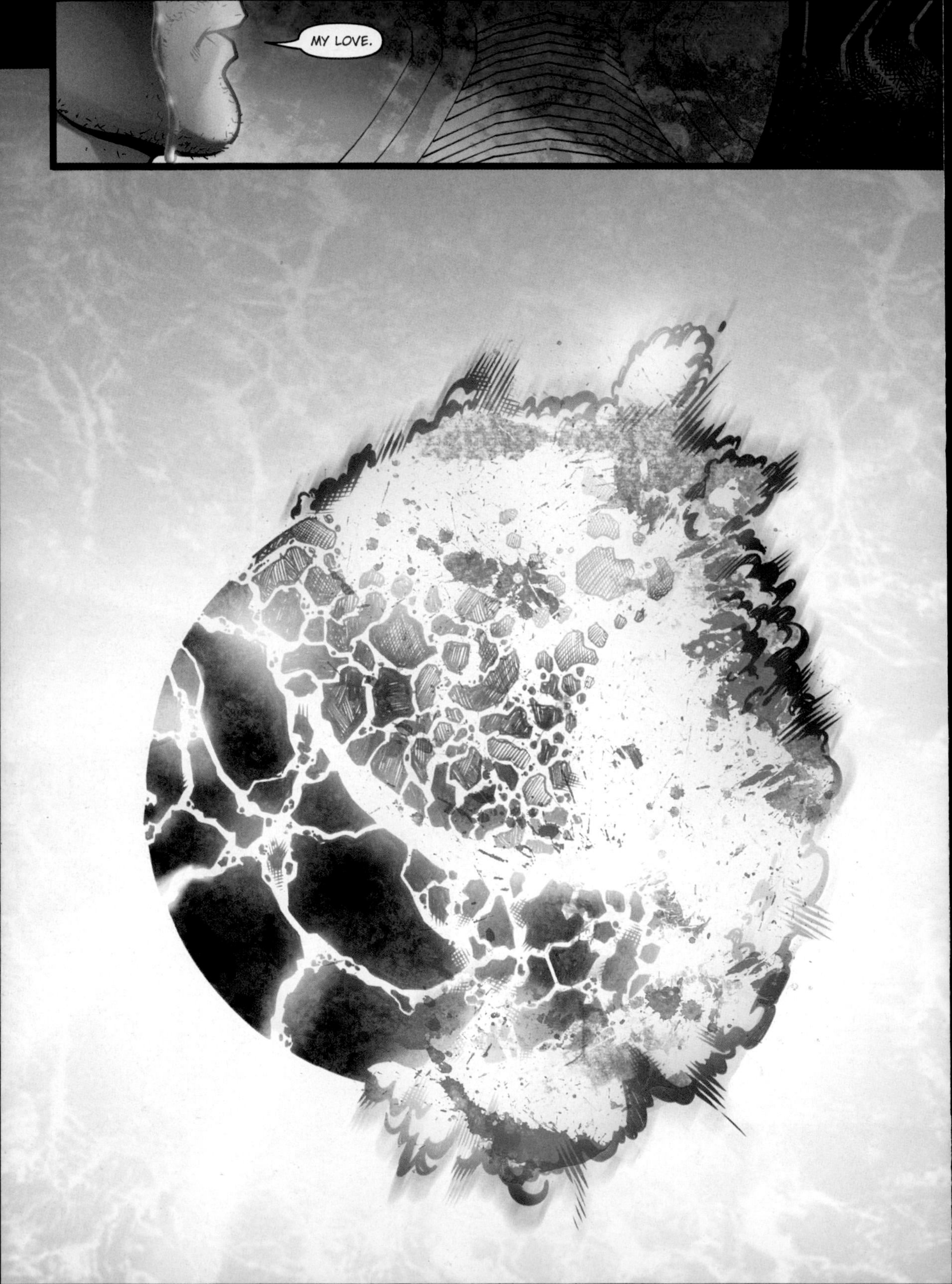
MY LOVE.

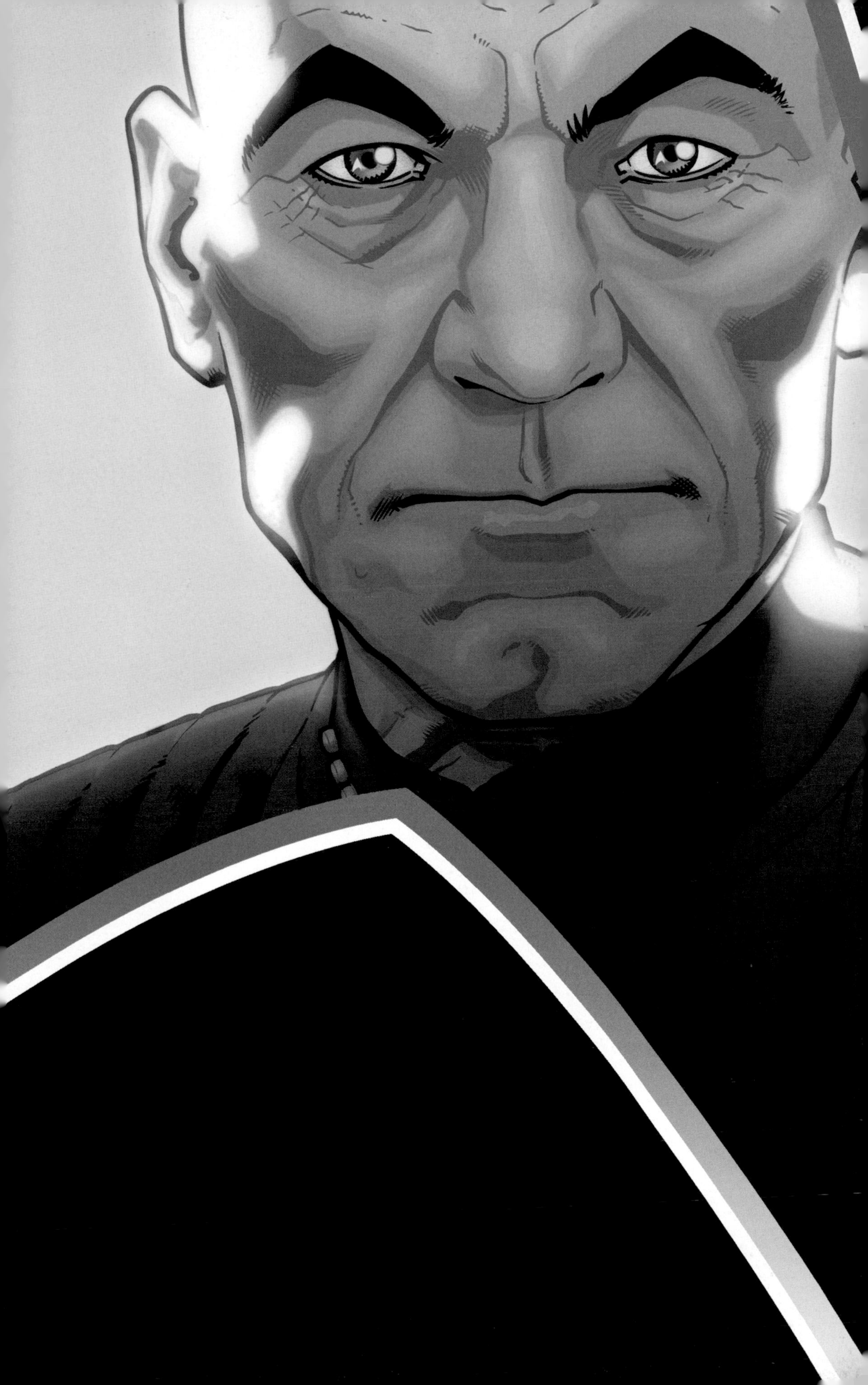

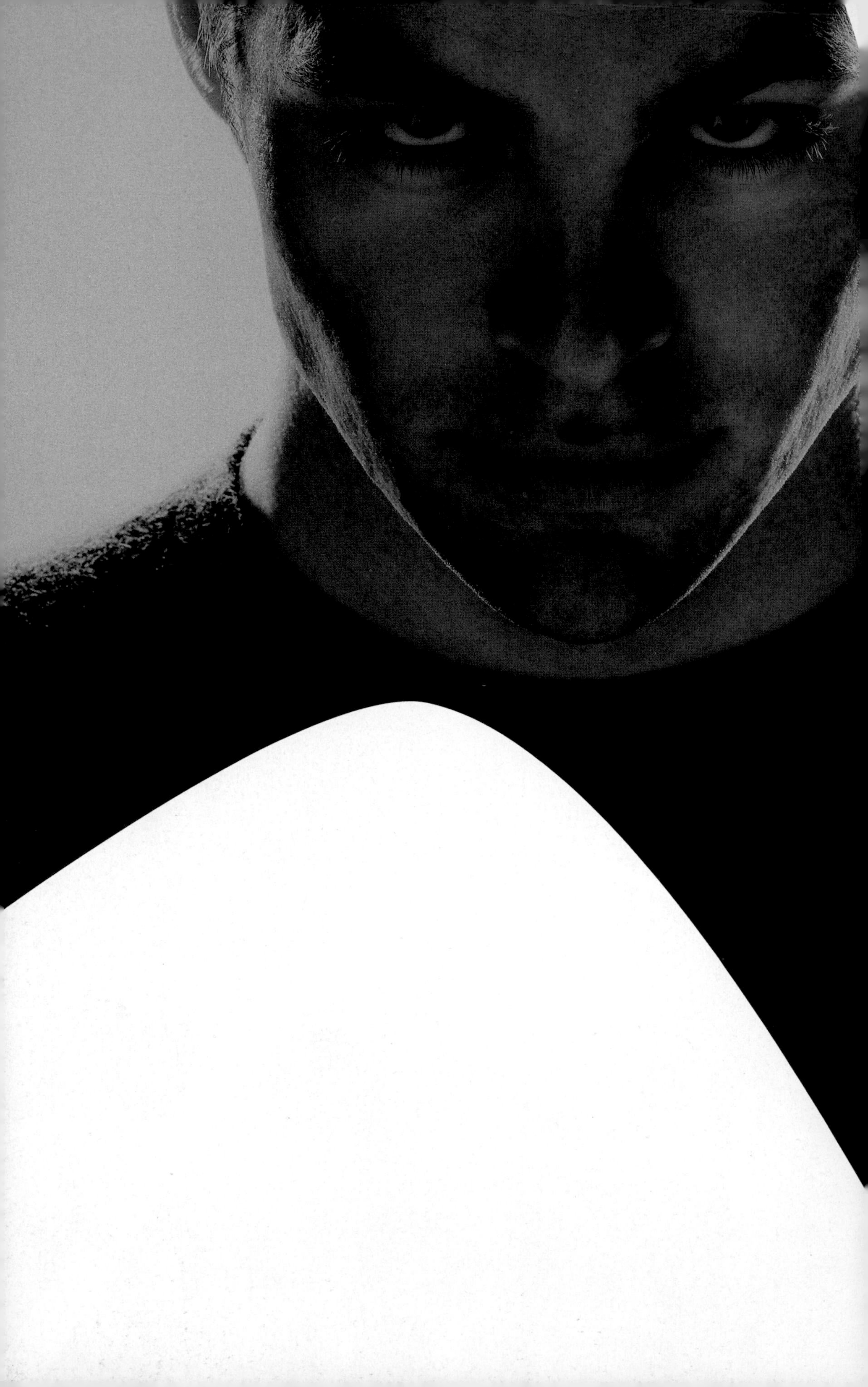

ROMULUS IS DEAD.

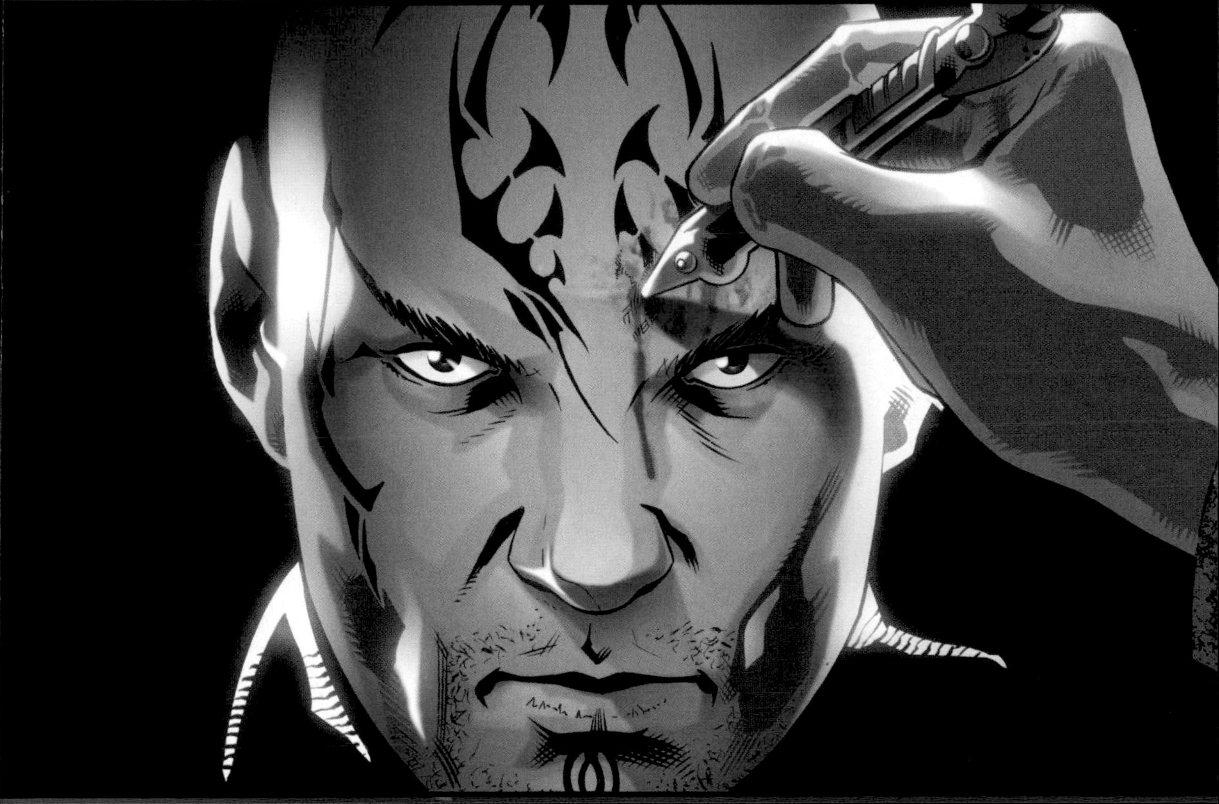

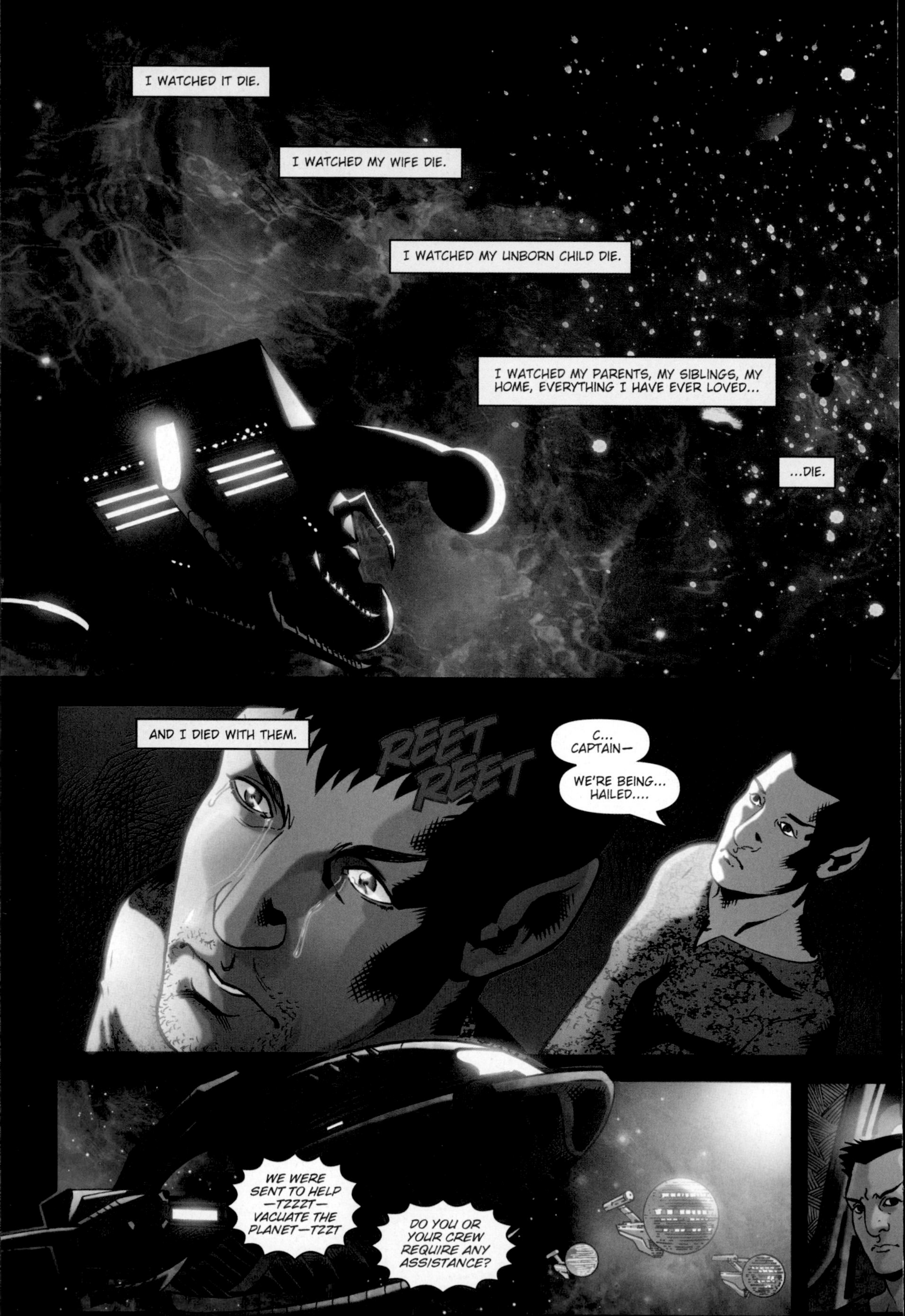
I WATCHED IT DIE.
I WATCHED MY WIFE DIE.
I WATCHED MY UNBORN CHILD DIE.
I WATCHED MY PARENTS, MY SIBLINGS, MY HOME, EVERYTHING I HAVE EVER LOVED...
...DIE.
AND I DIED WITH THEM.
REET REET
C... CAPTAIN—
WE'RE BEING... HAILED....
WE WERE SENT TO HELP —TZZZT— VACUATE THE PLANET—TZZT
DO YOU OR YOUR CREW REQUIRE ANY ASSISTANCE?

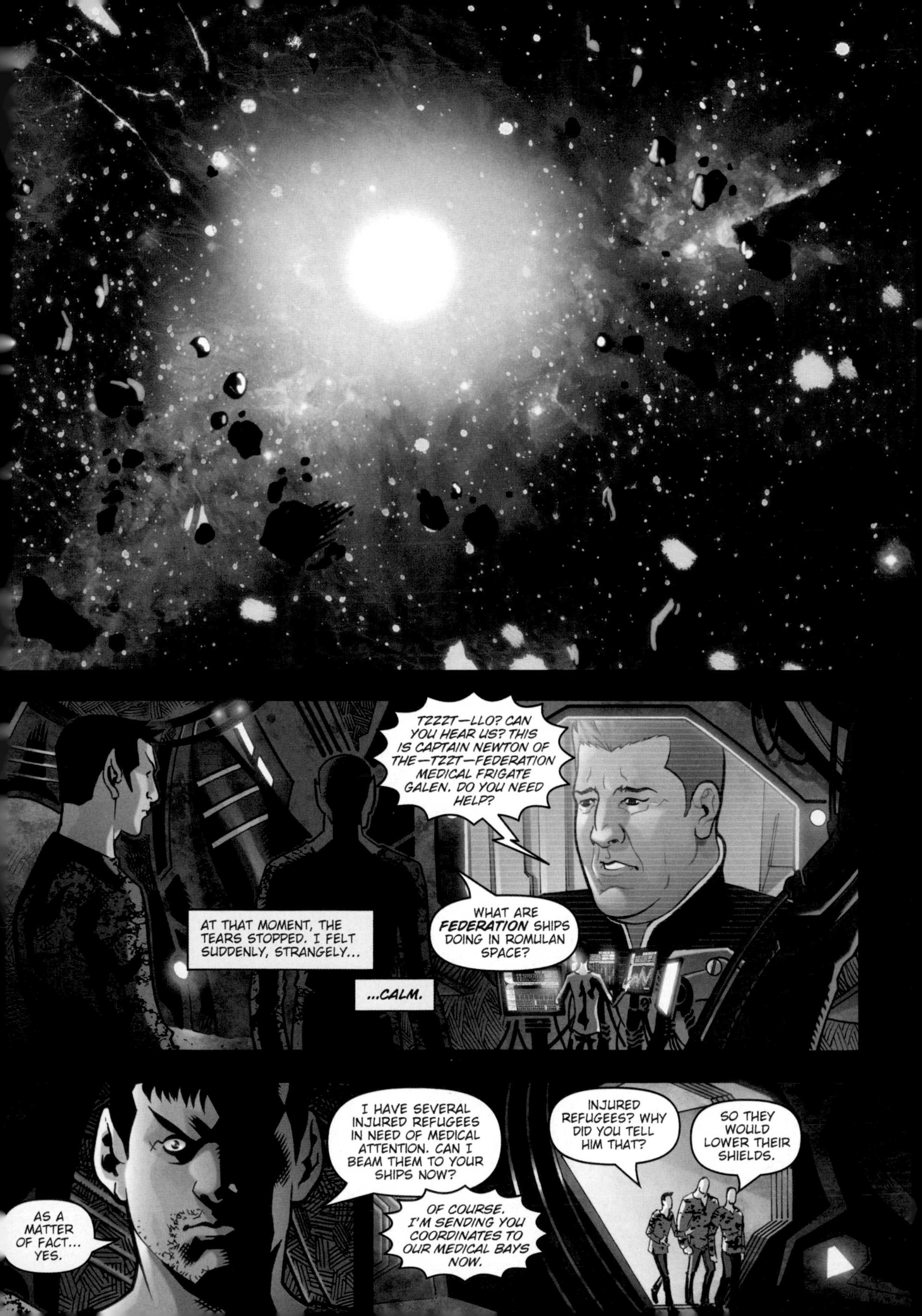
TZZZT—LLO? CAN YOU HEAR US? THIS IS CAPTAIN NEWTON OF THE—TZZT—FEDERATION MEDICAL FRIGATE GALEN. DO YOU NEED HELP?
WHAT ARE FEDERATION SHIPS DOING IN ROMULAN SPACE?
AT THAT MOMENT, THE TEARS STOPPED. I FELT SUDDENLY, STRANGELY...
...CALM.
AS A MATTER OF FACT... YES.
I HAVE SEVERAL INJURED REFUGEES IN NEED OF MEDICAL ATTENTION. CAN I BEAM THEM TO YOUR SHIPS NOW?
OF COURSE. I'M SENDING YOU COORDINATES TO OUR MEDICAL BAYS NOW.
INJURED REFUGEES? WHY DID YOU TELL HIM THAT?
SO THEY WOULD LOWER THEIR SHIELDS.

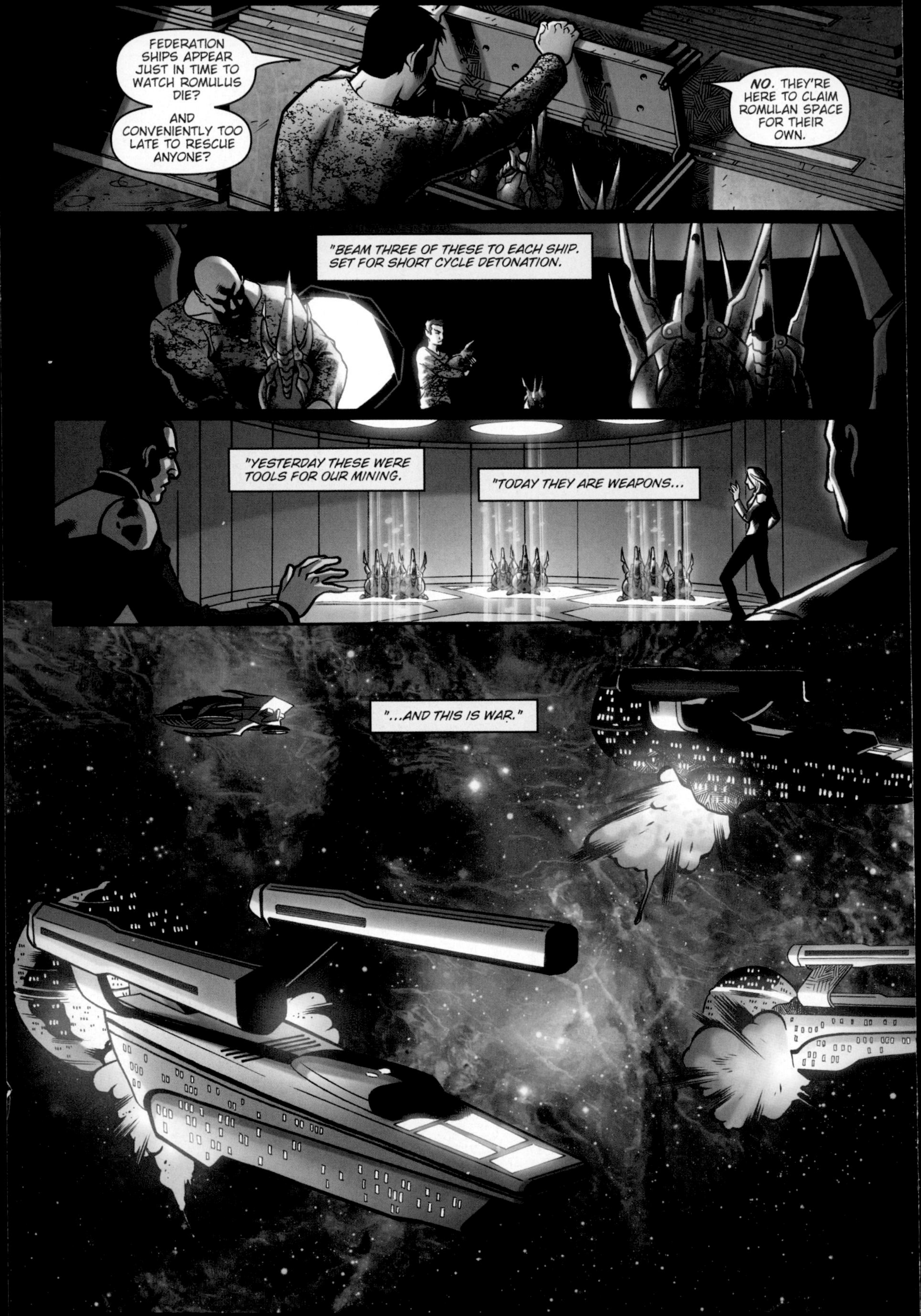

FEDERATION SHIPS APPEAR JUST IN TIME TO WATCH ROMULUS DIE?
AND CONVENIENTLY TOO LATE TO RESCUE ANYONE?
NO. THEY'RE HERE TO CLAIM ROMULAN SPACE FOR THEIR OWN.
"BEAM THREE OF THESE TO EACH SHIP. SET FOR SHORT CYCLE DETONATION.
"YESTERDAY THESE WERE TOOLS FOR OUR MINING.
"TODAY THEY ARE WEAPONS...
"...AND THIS IS WAR."

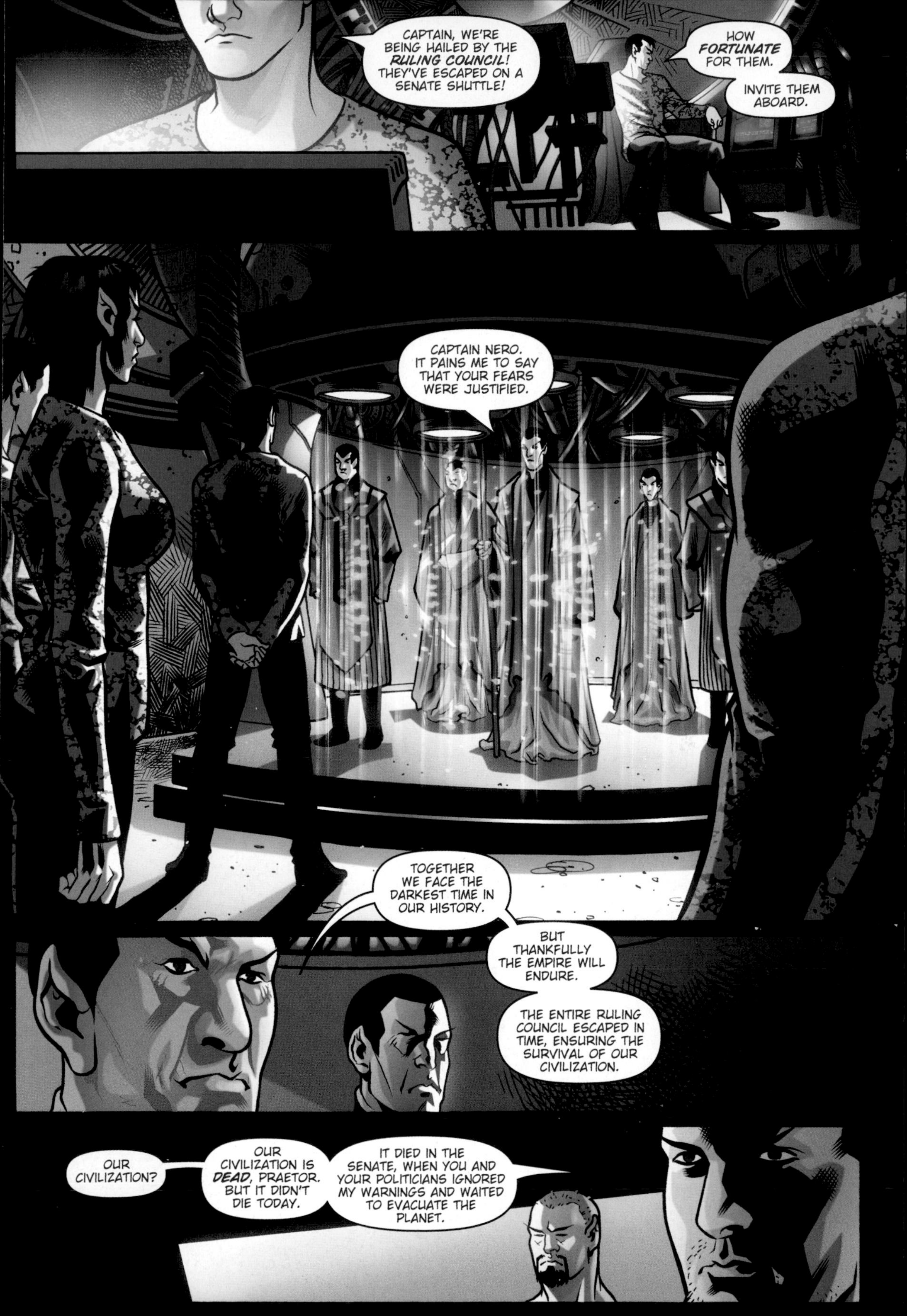
CAPTAIN, WE'RE BEING HAILED BY THE *RULING COUNCIL*! THEY'VE ESCAPED ON A SENATE SHUTTLE!
HOW *FORTUNATE* FOR THEM.
INVITE THEM ABOARD.
CAPTAIN NERO. IT PAINS ME TO SAY THAT YOUR FEARS WERE JUSTIFIED.
TOGETHER WE FACE THE DARKEST TIME IN OUR HISTORY.
BUT THANKFULLY THE EMPIRE WILL ENDURE.
THE ENTIRE RULING COUNCIL ESCAPED IN TIME, ENSURING THE SURVIVAL OF OUR CIVILIZATION.
OUR CIVILIZATION?
OUR CIVILIZATION IS *DEAD*, PRAETOR. BUT IT DIDN'T DIE TODAY.
IT DIED IN THE SENATE, WHEN YOU AND YOUR POLITICIANS IGNORED MY WARNINGS AND WAITED TO EVACUATE THE PLANET.

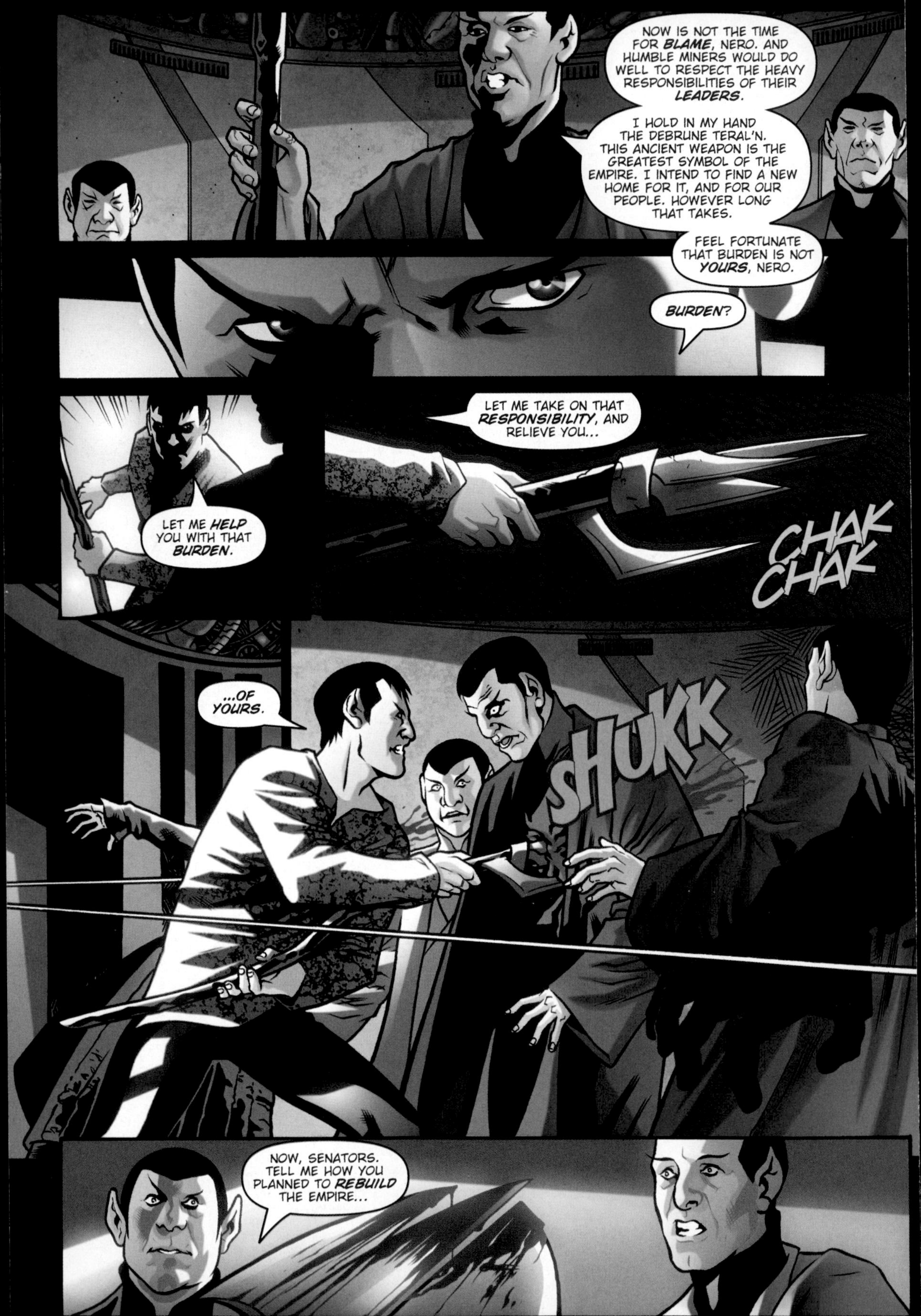
NOW IS NOT THE TIME FOR BLAME, NERO. AND HUMBLE MINERS WOULD DO WELL TO RESPECT THE HEAVY RESPONSIBILITIES OF THEIR LEADERS.
I HOLD IN MY HAND THE DEBRUNE TERAL'N. THIS ANCIENT WEAPON IS THE GREATEST SYMBOL OF THE EMPIRE. I INTEND TO FIND A NEW HOME FOR IT, AND FOR OUR PEOPLE. HOWEVER LONG THAT TAKES.
FEEL FORTUNATE THAT BURDEN IS NOT YOURS, NERO.
BURDEN?
LET ME TAKE ON THAT RESPONSIBILITY, AND RELIEVE YOU...
LET ME HELP YOU WITH THAT BURDEN.
CHAK CHAK
...OF YOURS.
SHUKK
NOW, SENATORS. TELL ME HOW YOU PLANNED TO REBUILD THE EMPIRE...

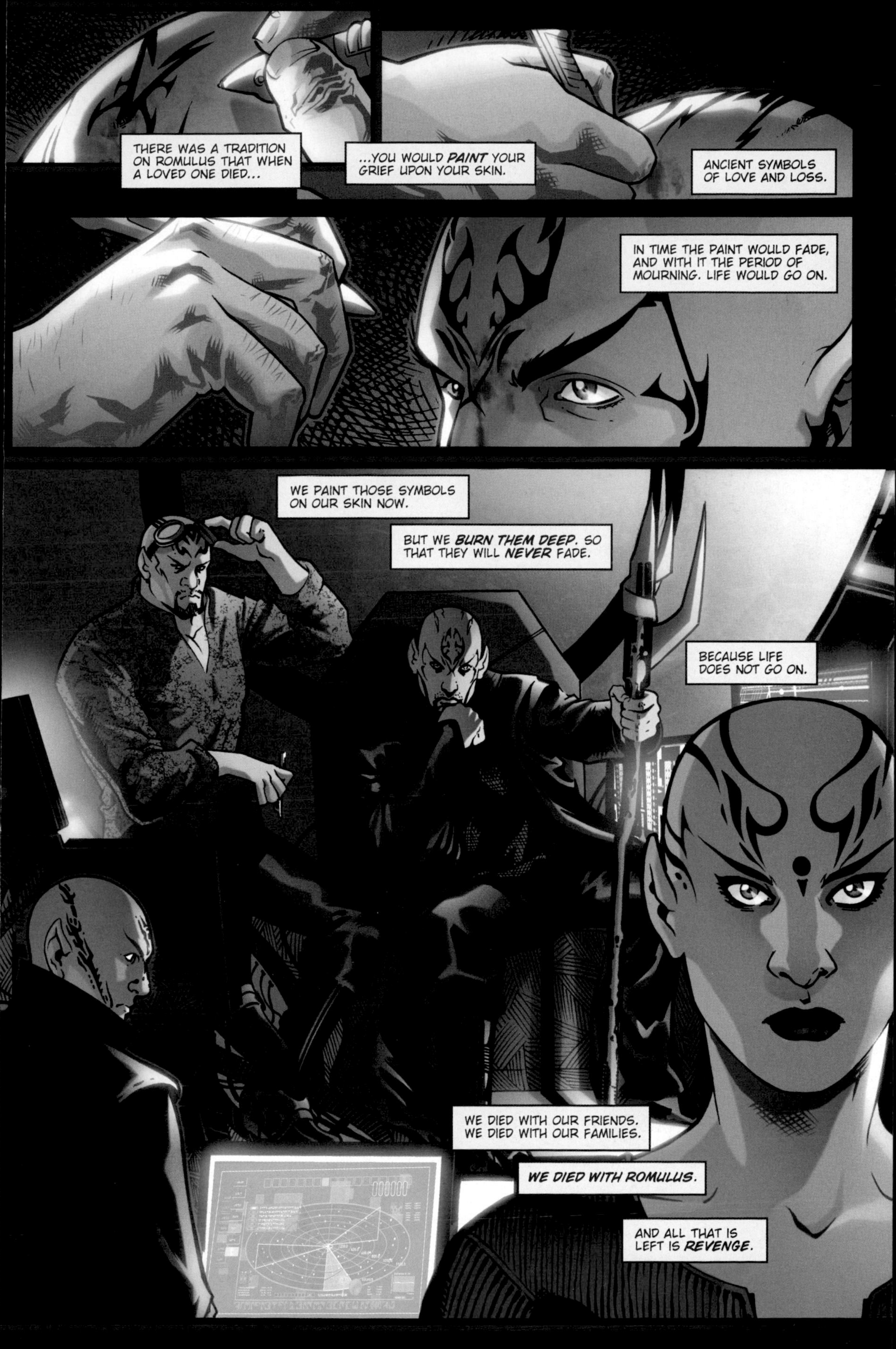
THERE WAS A TRADITION ON ROMULUS THAT WHEN A LOVED ONE DIED...
...YOU WOULD *PAINT* YOUR GRIEF UPON YOUR SKIN.
ANCIENT SYMBOLS OF LOVE AND LOSS.
IN TIME THE PAINT WOULD FADE, AND WITH IT THE PERIOD OF MOURNING. LIFE WOULD GO ON.
WE PAINT THOSE SYMBOLS ON OUR SKIN NOW.
BUT WE *BURN THEM DEEP*. SO THAT THEY WILL *NEVER* FADE.
BECAUSE LIFE DOES NOT GO ON.
WE DIED WITH OUR FRIENDS. WE DIED WITH OUR FAMILIES.
WE DIED WITH ROMULUS.
AND ALL THAT IS LEFT IS *REVENGE*.

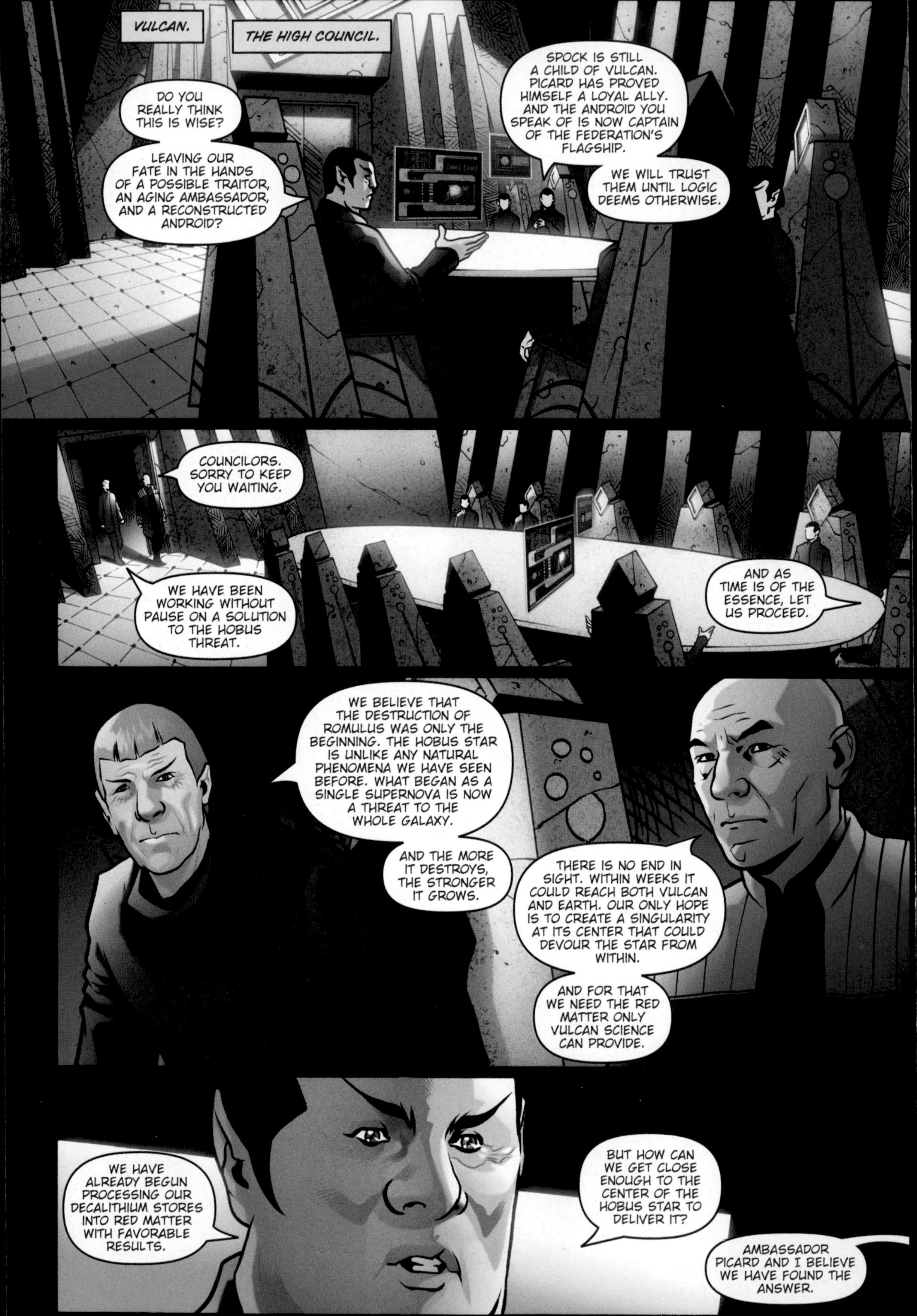
VULCAN.
THE HIGH COUNCIL.
DO YOU REALLY THINK THIS IS WISE?
LEAVING OUR FATE IN THE HANDS OF A POSSIBLE TRAITOR, AN AGING AMBASSADOR, AND A RECONSTRUCTED ANDROID?
SPOCK IS STILL A CHILD OF VULCAN. PICARD HAS PROVED HIMSELF A LOYAL ALLY. AND THE ANDROID YOU SPEAK OF IS NOW CAPTAIN OF THE FEDERATION'S FLAGSHIP.
WE WILL TRUST THEM UNTIL LOGIC DEEMS OTHERWISE.
COUNCILORS. SORRY TO KEEP YOU WAITING.
WE HAVE BEEN WORKING WITHOUT PAUSE ON A SOLUTION TO THE HOBUS THREAT.
AND AS TIME IS OF THE ESSENCE, LET US PROCEED.
WE BELIEVE THAT THE DESTRUCTION OF ROMULUS WAS ONLY THE BEGINNING. THE HOBUS STAR IS UNLIKE ANY NATURAL PHENOMENA WE HAVE SEEN BEFORE. WHAT BEGAN AS A SINGLE SUPERNOVA IS NOW A THREAT TO THE WHOLE GALAXY.
AND THE MORE IT DESTROYS, THE STRONGER IT GROWS.
THERE IS NO END IN SIGHT. WITHIN WEEKS IT COULD REACH BOTH VULCAN AND EARTH. OUR ONLY HOPE IS TO CREATE A SINGULARITY AT ITS CENTER THAT COULD DEVOUR THE STAR FROM WITHIN.
AND FOR THAT WE NEED THE RED MATTER ONLY VULCAN SCIENCE CAN PROVIDE.
WE HAVE ALREADY BEGUN PROCESSING OUR DECALITHIUM STORES INTO RED MATTER WITH FAVORABLE RESULTS.
BUT HOW CAN WE GET CLOSE ENOUGH TO THE CENTER OF THE HOBUS STAR TO DELIVER IT?
AMBASSADOR PICARD AND I BELIEVE WE HAVE FOUND THE ANSWER.

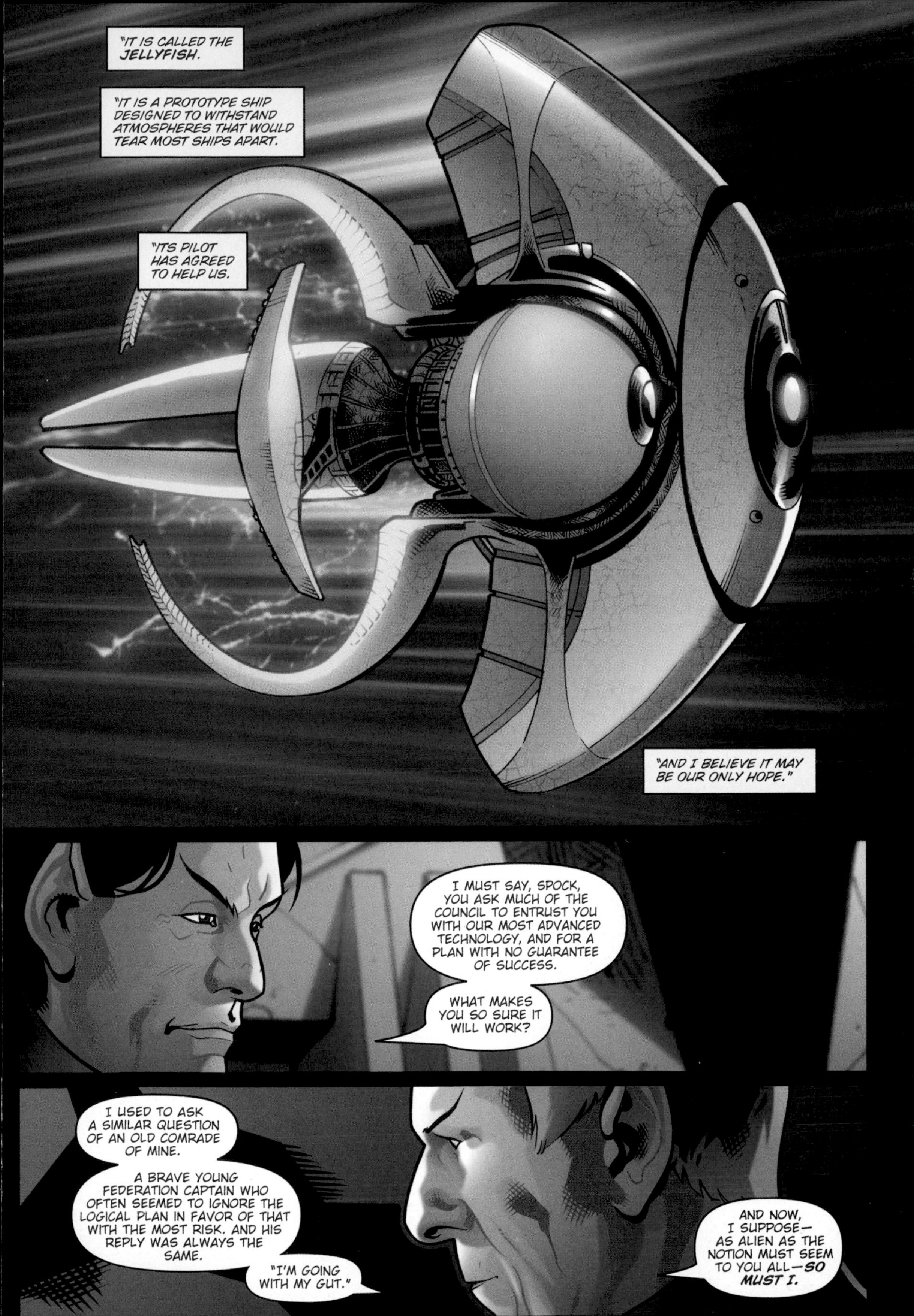
"IT IS CALLED THE JELLYFISH.
"IT IS A PROTOTYPE SHIP DESIGNED TO WITHSTAND ATMOSPHERES THAT WOULD TEAR MOST SHIPS APART.
"ITS PILOT HAS AGREED TO HELP US.
"AND I BELIEVE IT MAY BE OUR ONLY HOPE."
I MUST SAY, SPOCK, YOU ASK MUCH OF THE COUNCIL TO ENTRUST YOU WITH OUR MOST ADVANCED TECHNOLOGY, AND FOR A PLAN WITH NO GUARANTEE OF SUCCESS.
WHAT MAKES YOU SO SURE IT WILL WORK?
I USED TO ASK A SIMILAR QUESTION OF AN OLD COMRADE OF MINE.
A BRAVE YOUNG FEDERATION CAPTAIN WHO OFTEN SEEMED TO IGNORE THE LOGICAL PLAN IN FAVOR OF THAT WITH THE MOST RISK. AND HIS REPLY WAS ALWAYS THE SAME.
"I'M GOING WITH MY GUT."
AND NOW, I SUPPOSE— AS ALIEN AS THE NOTION MUST SEEM TO YOU ALL—SO MUST I.

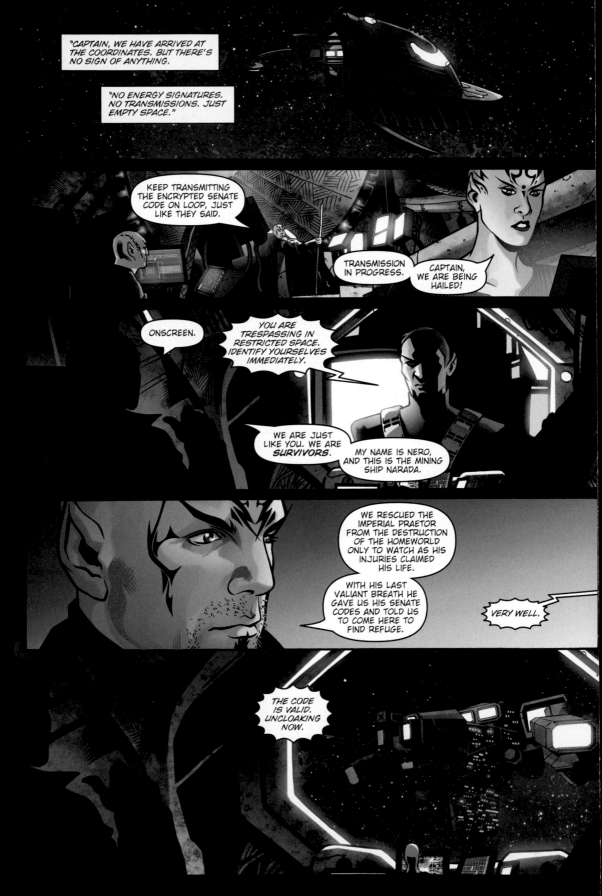

"CAPTAIN, WE HAVE ARRIVED AT THE COORDINATES. BUT THERE'S NO SIGN OF ANYTHING.

"NO ENERGY SIGNATURES. NO TRANSMISSIONS. JUST EMPTY SPACE."

KEEP TRANSMITTING THE ENCRYPTED SENATE CODE ON LOOP, JUST LIKE THEY SAID.

TRANSMISSION IN PROGRESS.

CAPTAIN, WE ARE BEING HAILED!

ONSCREEN.

YOU ARE TRESPASSING IN RESTRICTED SPACE. IDENTIFY YOURSELVES IMMEDIATELY.

WE ARE JUST LIKE YOU. WE ARE SURVIVORS.

MY NAME IS NERO, AND THIS IS THE MINING SHIP NARADA.

WE RESCUED THE IMPERIAL PRAETOR FROM THE DESTRUCTION OF THE HOMEWORLD ONLY TO WATCH AS HIS INJURIES CLAIMED HIS LIFE.

WITH HIS LAST VALIANT BREATH HE GAVE US HIS SENATE CODES AND TOLD US TO COME HERE TO FIND REFUGE.

VERY WELL.

THE CODE IS VALID. UNCLOAKING NOW.

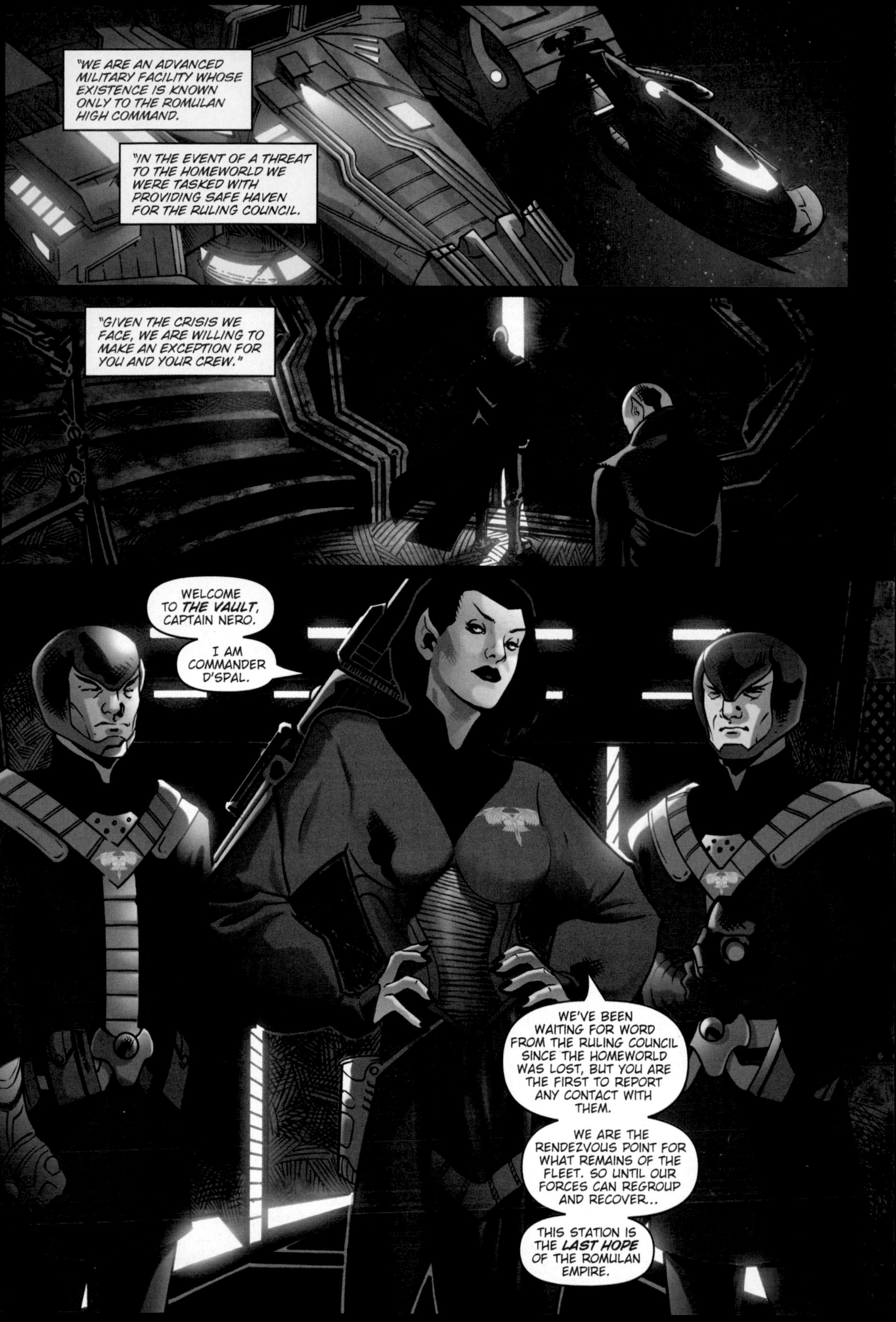
"WE ARE AN ADVANCED MILITARY FACILITY WHOSE EXISTENCE IS KNOWN ONLY TO THE ROMULAN HIGH COMMAND.
"IN THE EVENT OF A THREAT TO THE HOMEWORLD WE WERE TASKED WITH PROVIDING SAFE HAVEN FOR THE RULING COUNCIL.
"GIVEN THE CRISIS WE FACE, WE ARE WILLING TO MAKE AN EXCEPTION FOR YOU AND YOUR CREW."
WELCOME TO **THE VAULT**, CAPTAIN NERO.
I AM COMMANDER D'SPAL.
WE'VE BEEN WAITING FOR WORD FROM THE RULING COUNCIL SINCE THE HOMEWORLD WAS LOST, BUT YOU ARE THE FIRST TO REPORT ANY CONTACT WITH THEM.
WE ARE THE RENDEZVOUS POINT FOR WHAT REMAINS OF THE FLEET. SO UNTIL OUR FORCES CAN REGROUP AND RECOVER...
THIS STATION IS THE **LAST HOPE** OF THE ROMULAN EMPIRE.

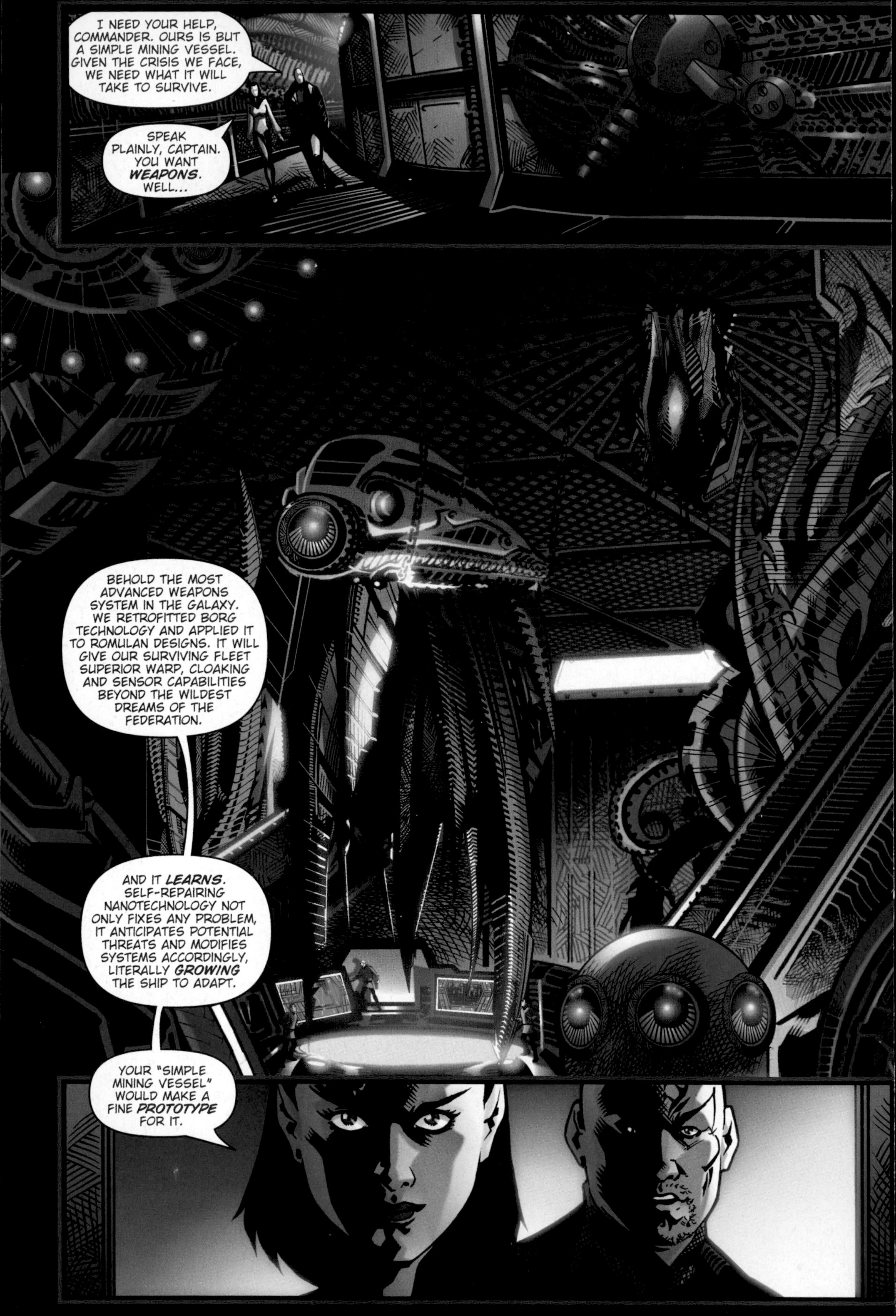
I NEED YOUR HELP, COMMANDER. OURS IS BUT A SIMPLE MINING VESSEL. GIVEN THE CRISIS WE FACE, WE NEED WHAT IT WILL TAKE TO SURVIVE.
SPEAK PLAINLY, CAPTAIN. YOU WANT WEAPONS. WELL...
BEHOLD THE MOST ADVANCED WEAPONS SYSTEM IN THE GALAXY. WE RETROFITTED BORG TECHNOLOGY AND APPLIED IT TO ROMULAN DESIGNS. IT WILL GIVE OUR SURVIVING FLEET SUPERIOR WARP, CLOAKING AND SENSOR CAPABILITIES BEYOND THE WILDEST DREAMS OF THE FEDERATION.
AND IT LEARNS. SELF-REPAIRING NANOTECHNOLOGY NOT ONLY FIXES ANY PROBLEM, IT ANTICIPATES POTENTIAL THREATS AND MODIFIES SYSTEMS ACCORDINGLY, LITERALLY GROWING THE SHIP TO ADAPT.
YOUR "SIMPLE MINING VESSEL" WOULD MAKE A FINE PROTOTYPE FOR IT.

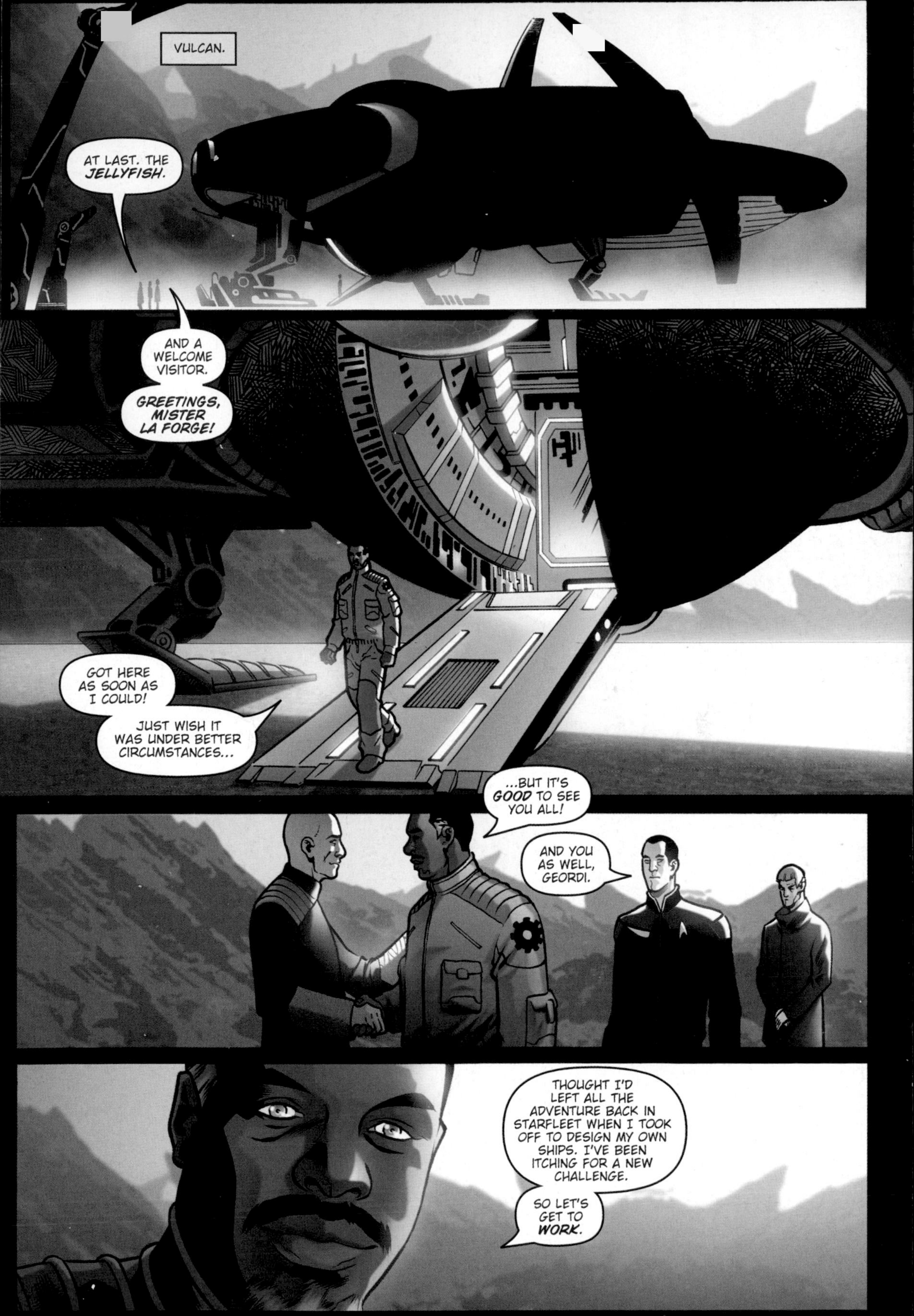
VULCAN.
AT LAST. THE *JELLYFISH*.
AND A WELCOME VISITOR.
GREETINGS, MISTER LA FORGE!
GOT HERE AS SOON AS I COULD!
JUST WISH IT WAS UNDER BETTER CIRCUMSTANCES...
...BUT IT'S *GOOD* TO SEE YOU ALL!
AND YOU AS WELL, GEORDI.
THOUGHT I'D LEFT ALL THE ADVENTURE BACK IN STARFLEET WHEN I TOOK OFF TO DESIGN MY OWN SHIPS. I'VE BEEN ITCHING FOR A NEW CHALLENGE.
SO LET'S GET TO *WORK*.

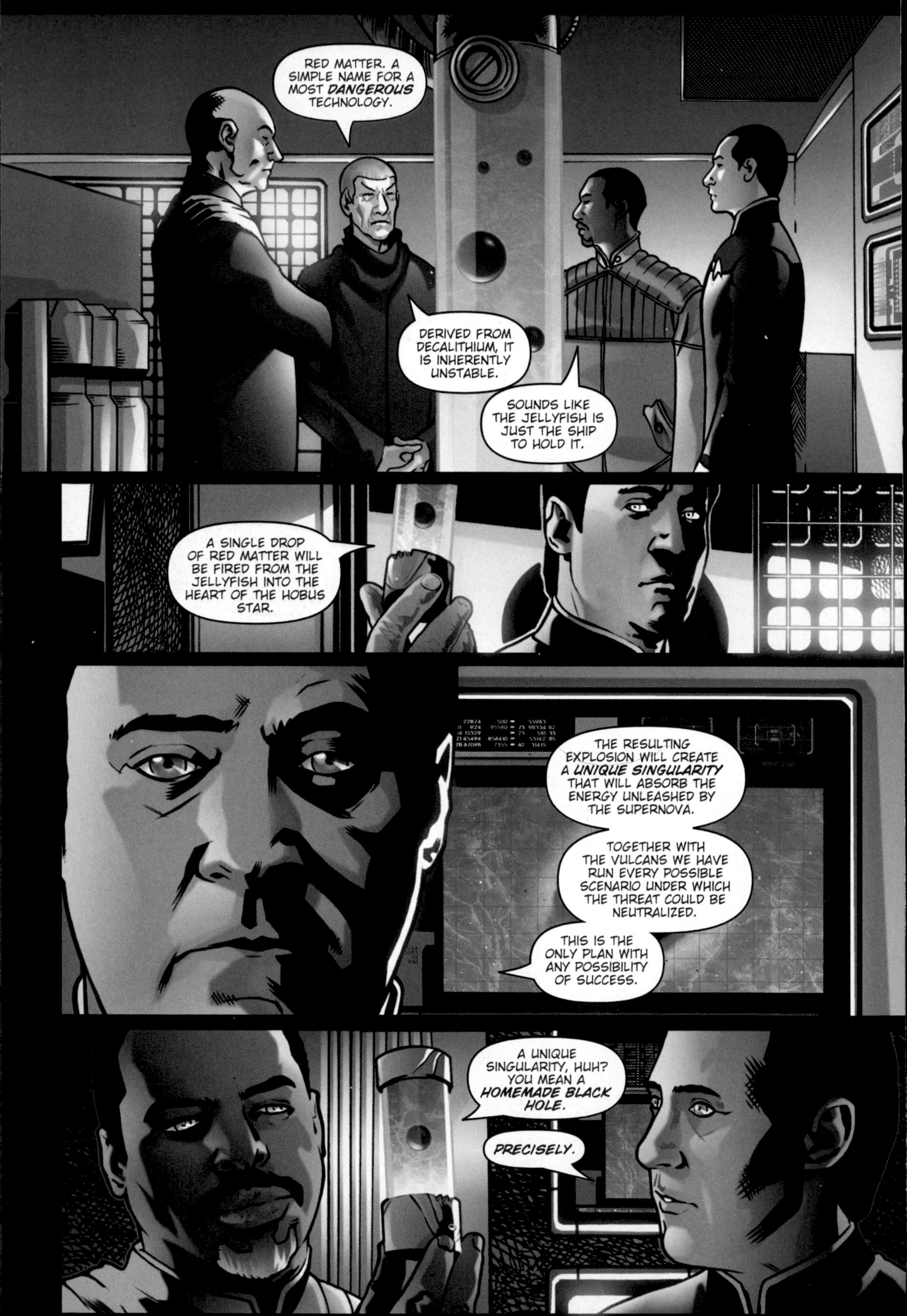
RED MATTER. A SIMPLE NAME FOR A MOST DANGEROUS TECHNOLOGY.
DERIVED FROM DECALITHIUM, IT IS INHERENTLY UNSTABLE.
SOUNDS LIKE THE JELLYFISH IS JUST THE SHIP TO HOLD IT.
A SINGLE DROP OF RED MATTER WILL BE FIRED FROM THE JELLYFISH INTO THE HEART OF THE HOBUS STAR.
THE RESULTING EXPLOSION WILL CREATE A UNIQUE SINGULARITY THAT WILL ABSORB THE ENERGY UNLEASHED BY THE SUPERNOVA.
TOGETHER WITH THE VULCANS WE HAVE RUN EVERY POSSIBLE SCENARIO UNDER WHICH THE THREAT COULD BE NEUTRALIZED.
THIS IS THE ONLY PLAN WITH ANY POSSIBILITY OF SUCCESS.
A UNIQUE SINGULARITY, HUH? YOU MEAN A HOMEMADE BLACK HOLE.
PRECISELY.

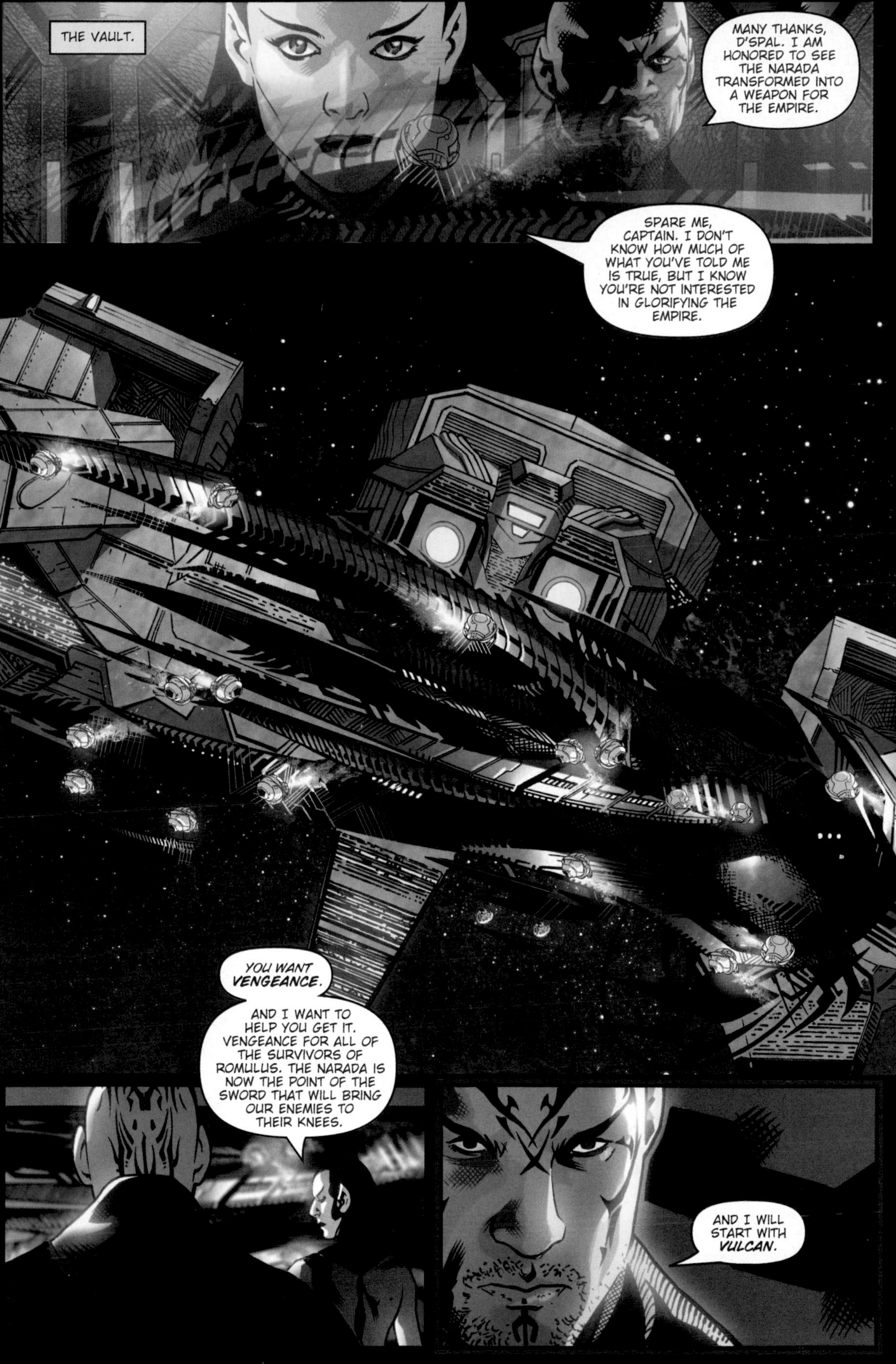
THE VAULT.
MANY THANKS, D'SPAL. I AM HONORED TO SEE THE NARADA TRANSFORMED INTO A WEAPON FOR THE EMPIRE.
SPARE ME, CAPTAIN. I DON'T KNOW HOW MUCH OF WHAT YOU'VE TOLD ME IS TRUE, BUT I KNOW YOU'RE NOT INTERESTED IN GLORIFYING THE EMPIRE.
YOU WANT **VENGEANCE**.
AND I WANT TO HELP YOU GET IT. VENGEANCE FOR ALL OF THE SURVIVORS OF ROMULUS. THE NARADA IS NOW THE POINT OF THE SWORD THAT WILL BRING OUR ENEMIES TO THEIR KNEES.
AND I WILL START WITH **VULCAN**.

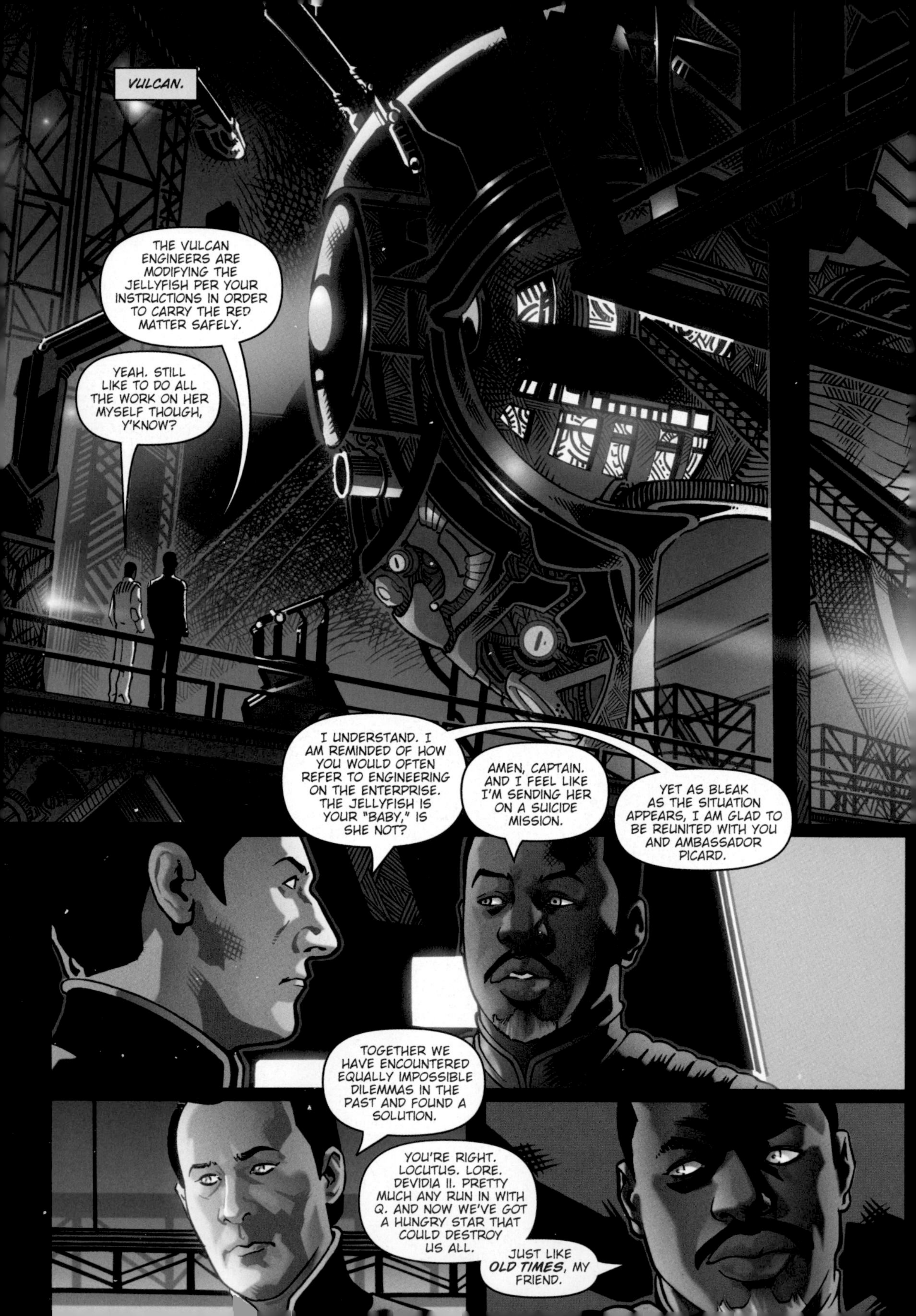
VULCAN.
THE VULCAN ENGINEERS ARE MODIFYING THE JELLYFISH PER YOUR INSTRUCTIONS IN ORDER TO CARRY THE RED MATTER SAFELY.
YEAH. STILL LIKE TO DO ALL THE WORK ON HER MYSELF THOUGH, Y'KNOW?
I UNDERSTAND. I AM REMINDED OF HOW YOU WOULD OFTEN REFER TO ENGINEERING ON THE ENTERPRISE. THE JELLYFISH IS YOUR "BABY," IS SHE NOT?
AMEN, CAPTAIN. AND I FEEL LIKE I'M SENDING HER ON A SUICIDE MISSION.
YET AS BLEAK AS THE SITUATION APPEARS, I AM GLAD TO BE REUNITED WITH YOU AND AMBASSADOR PICARD.
TOGETHER WE HAVE ENCOUNTERED EQUALLY IMPOSSIBLE DILEMMAS IN THE PAST AND FOUND A SOLUTION.
YOU'RE RIGHT. LOCUTUS. LORE. DEVIDIA II. PRETTY MUCH ANY RUN IN WITH Q. AND NOW WE'VE GOT A HUNGRY STAR THAT COULD DESTROY US ALL.
JUST LIKE OLD TIMES, MY FRIEND.

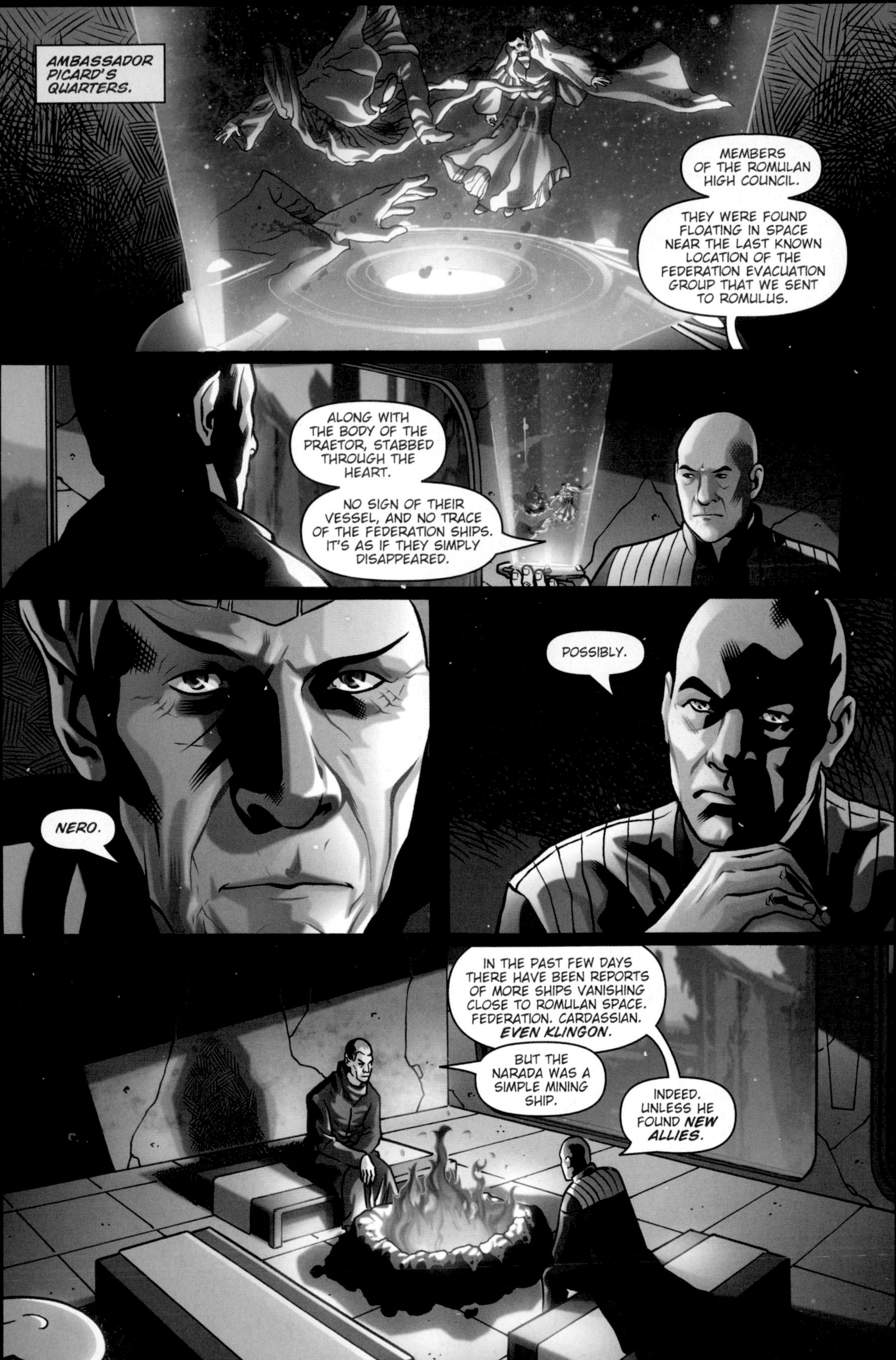

AMBASSADOR PICARD'S QUARTERS.
MEMBERS OF THE ROMULAN HIGH COUNCIL.
THEY WERE FOUND FLOATING IN SPACE NEAR THE LAST KNOWN LOCATION OF THE FEDERATION EVACUATION GROUP THAT WE SENT TO ROMULUS.
ALONG WITH THE BODY OF THE PRAETOR, STABBED THROUGH THE HEART.
NO SIGN OF THEIR VESSEL, AND NO TRACE OF THE FEDERATION SHIPS. IT'S AS IF THEY SIMPLY DISAPPEARED.
NERO.
POSSIBLY.
IN THE PAST FEW DAYS THERE HAVE BEEN REPORTS OF MORE SHIPS VANISHING CLOSE TO ROMULAN SPACE. FEDERATION. CARDASSIAN. EVEN KLINGON.
BUT THE NARADA WAS A SIMPLE MINING SHIP.
INDEED. UNLESS HE FOUND NEW ALLIES.

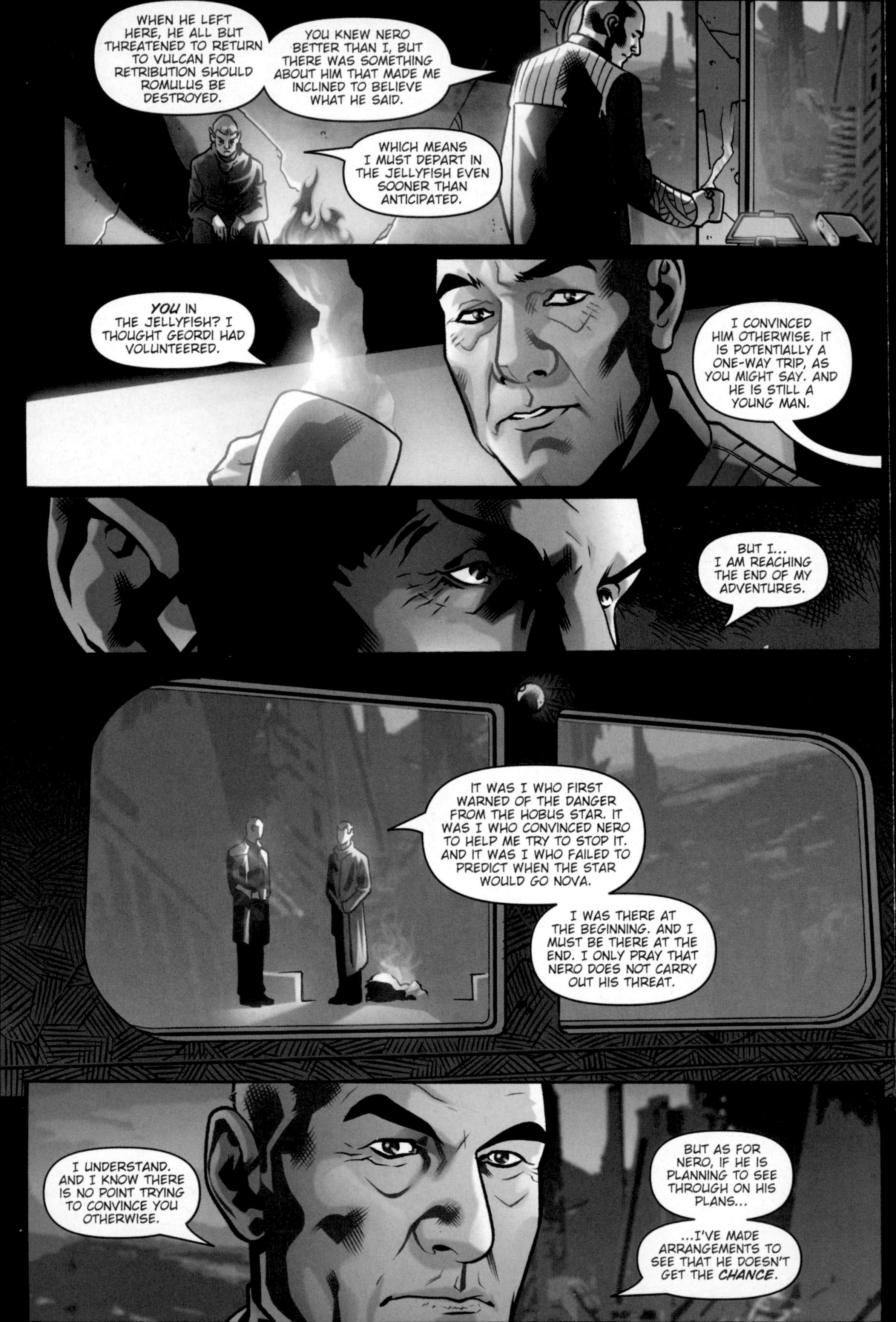
WHEN HE LEFT HERE, HE ALL BUT THREATENED TO RETURN TO VULCAN FOR RETRIBUTION SHOULD ROMULUS BE DESTROYED.
YOU KNEW NERO BETTER THAN I, BUT THERE WAS SOMETHING ABOUT HIM THAT MADE ME INCLINED TO BELIEVE WHAT HE SAID.
WHICH MEANS I MUST DEPART IN THE JELLYFISH EVEN SOONER THAN ANTICIPATED.
YOU IN THE JELLYFISH? I THOUGHT GEORDI HAD VOLUNTEERED.
I CONVINCED HIM OTHERWISE. IT IS POTENTIALLY A ONE-WAY TRIP, AS YOU MIGHT SAY. AND HE IS STILL A YOUNG MAN.
BUT I... I AM REACHING THE END OF MY ADVENTURES.
IT WAS I WHO FIRST WARNED OF THE DANGER FROM THE HOBUS STAR. IT WAS I WHO CONVINCED NERO TO HELP ME TRY TO STOP IT. AND IT WAS I WHO FAILED TO PREDICT WHEN THE STAR WOULD GO NOVA.
I WAS THERE AT THE BEGINNING. AND I MUST BE THERE AT THE END. I ONLY PRAY THAT NERO DOES NOT CARRY OUT HIS THREAT.
I UNDERSTAND. AND I KNOW THERE IS NO POINT TRYING TO CONVINCE YOU OTHERWISE.
BUT AS FOR NERO, IF HE IS PLANNING TO SEE THROUGH ON HIS PLANS...
...I'VE MADE ARRANGEMENTS TO SEE THAT HE DOESN'T GET THE *CHANCE*.

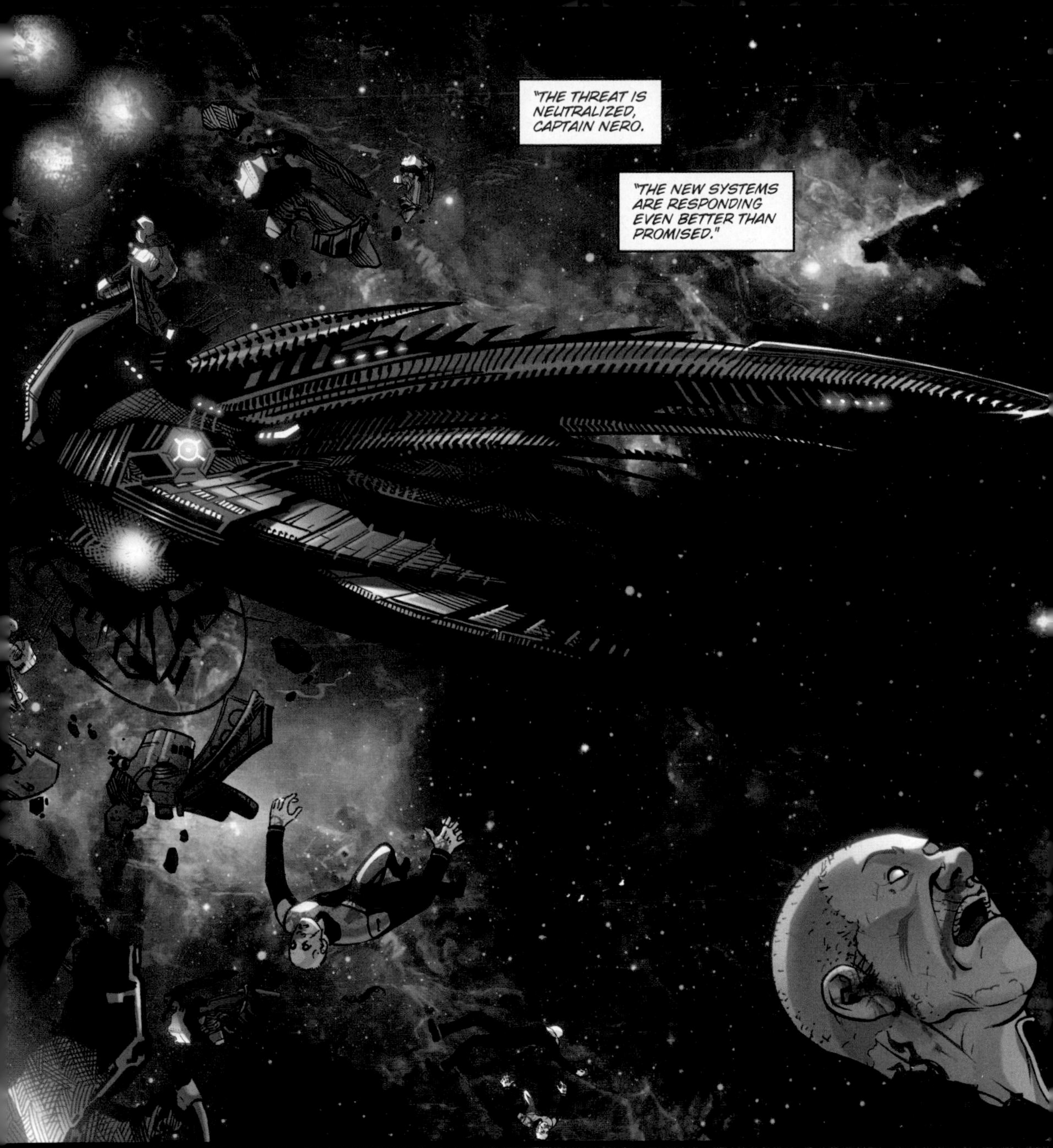
"THE THREAT IS NEUTRALIZED, CAPTAIN NERO.
"THE NEW SYSTEMS ARE RESPONDING EVEN BETTER THAN PROMISED."

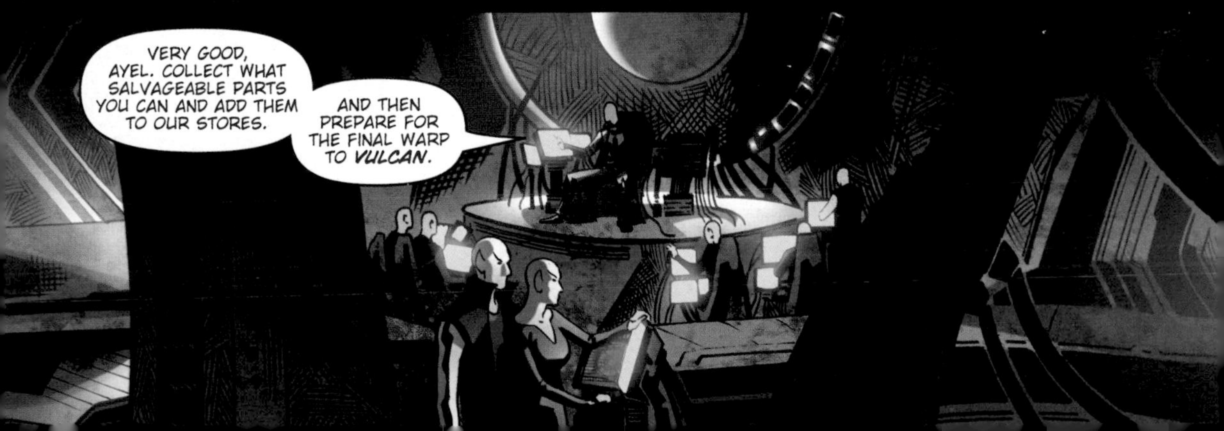
VERY GOOD, AYEL. COLLECT WHAT SALVAGEABLE PARTS YOU CAN AND ADD THEM TO OUR STORES.
AND THEN PREPARE FOR THE FINAL WARP TO VULCAN.

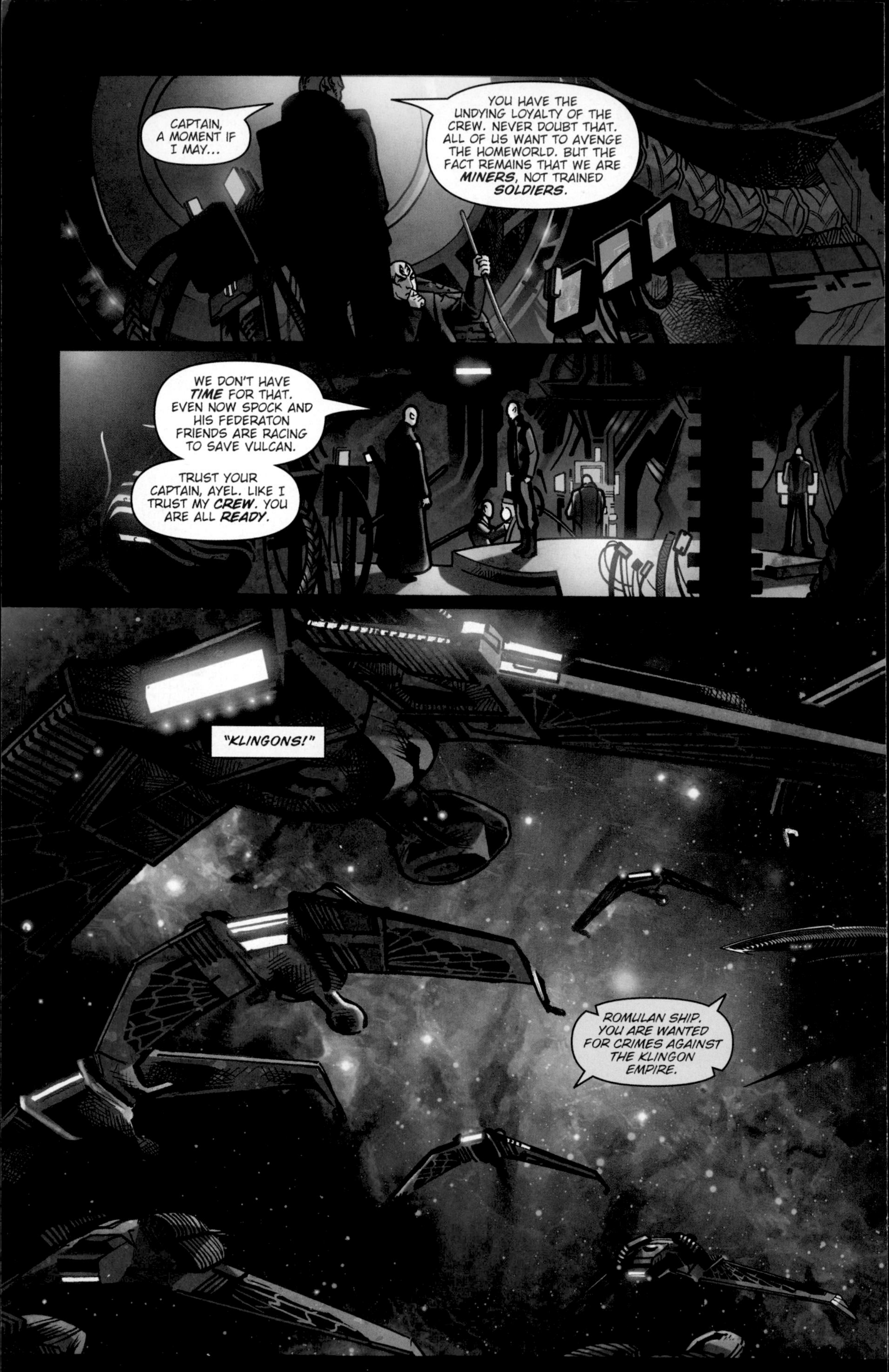
CAPTAIN, A MOMENT IF I MAY...
YOU HAVE THE UNDYING LOYALTY OF THE CREW. NEVER DOUBT THAT. ALL OF US WANT TO AVENGE THE HOMEWORLD. BUT THE FACT REMAINS THAT WE ARE MINERS, NOT TRAINED SOLDIERS.
WE DON'T HAVE TIME FOR THAT. EVEN NOW SPOCK AND HIS FEDERATON FRIENDS ARE RACING TO SAVE VULCAN.
TRUST YOUR CAPTAIN, AYEL. LIKE I TRUST MY CREW. YOU ARE ALL READY.
"KLINGONS!"
ROMULAN SHIP. YOU ARE WANTED FOR CRIMES AGAINST THE KLINGON EMPIRE.

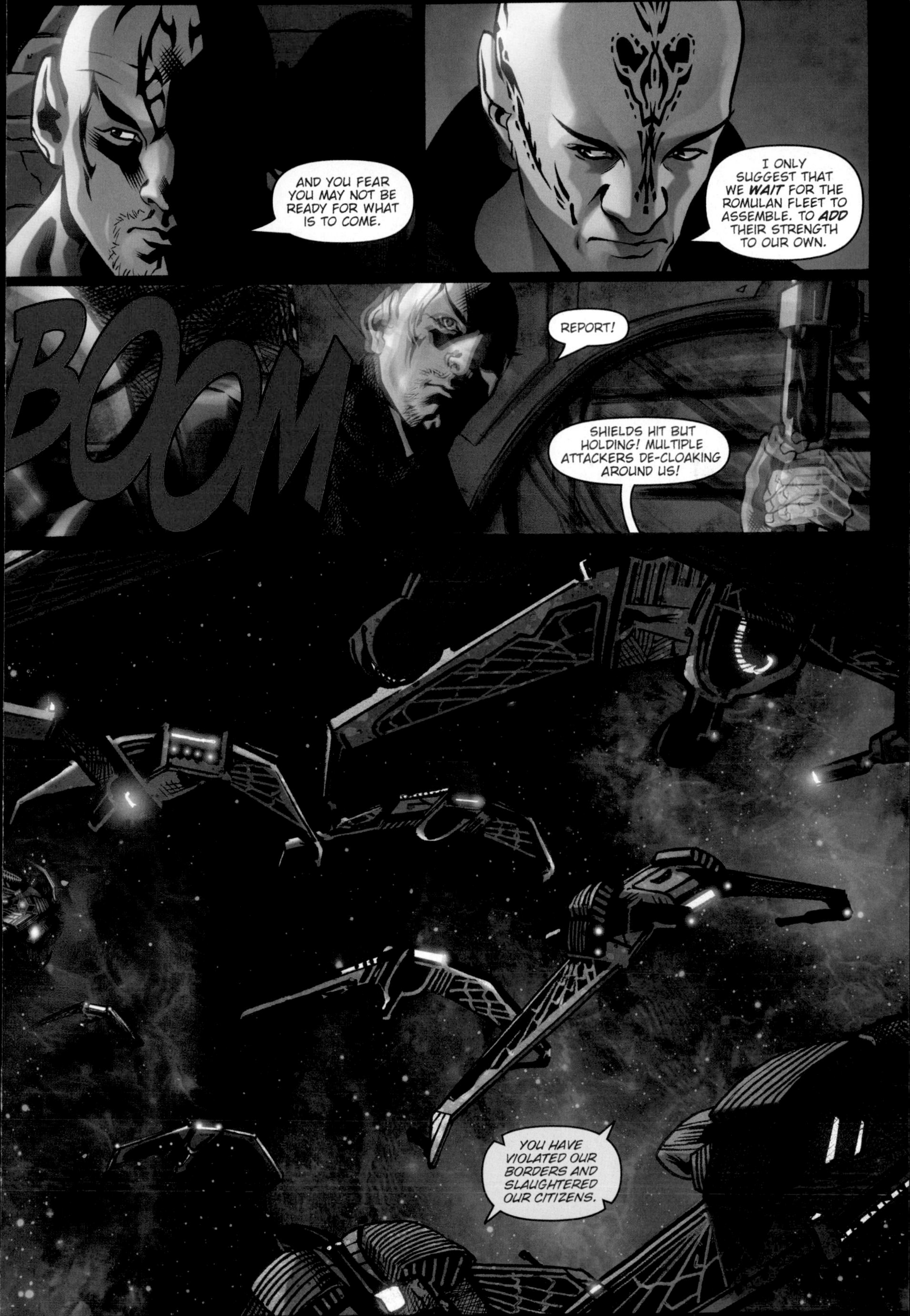
AND YOU FEAR YOU MAY NOT BE READY FOR WHAT IS TO COME.
I ONLY SUGGEST THAT WE *WAIT* FOR THE ROMULAN FLEET TO ASSEMBLE. TO *ADD* THEIR STRENGTH TO OUR OWN.
BOOM
REPORT!
SHIELDS HIT BUT HOLDING! MULTIPLE ATTACKERS DE-CLOAKING AROUND US!
YOU HAVE VIOLATED OUR BORDERS AND SLAUGHTERED OUR CITIZENS.

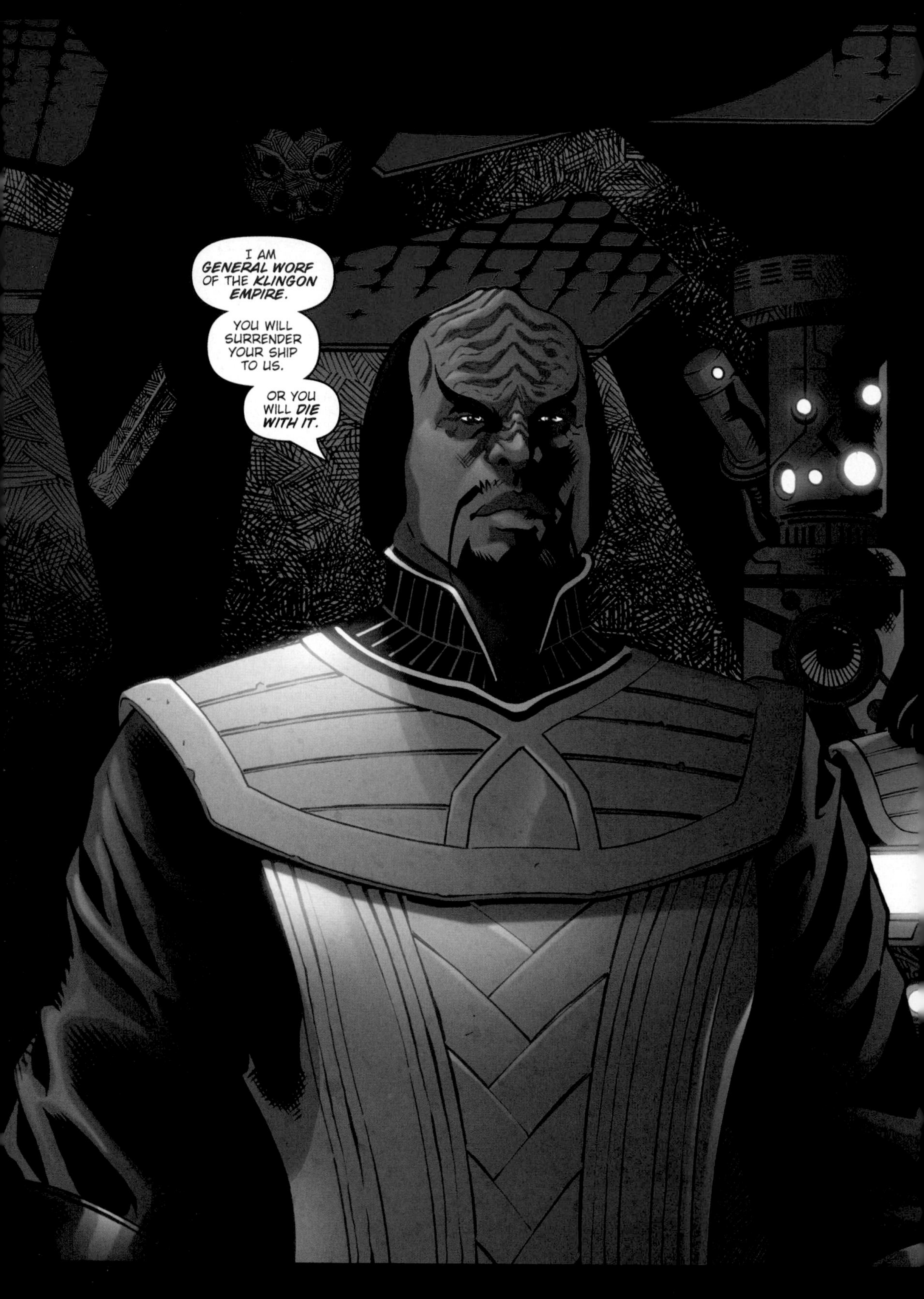
I AM GENERAL WORF OF THE KLINGON EMPIRE.
YOU WILL SURRENDER YOUR SHIP TO US.
OR YOU WILL DIE WITH IT.

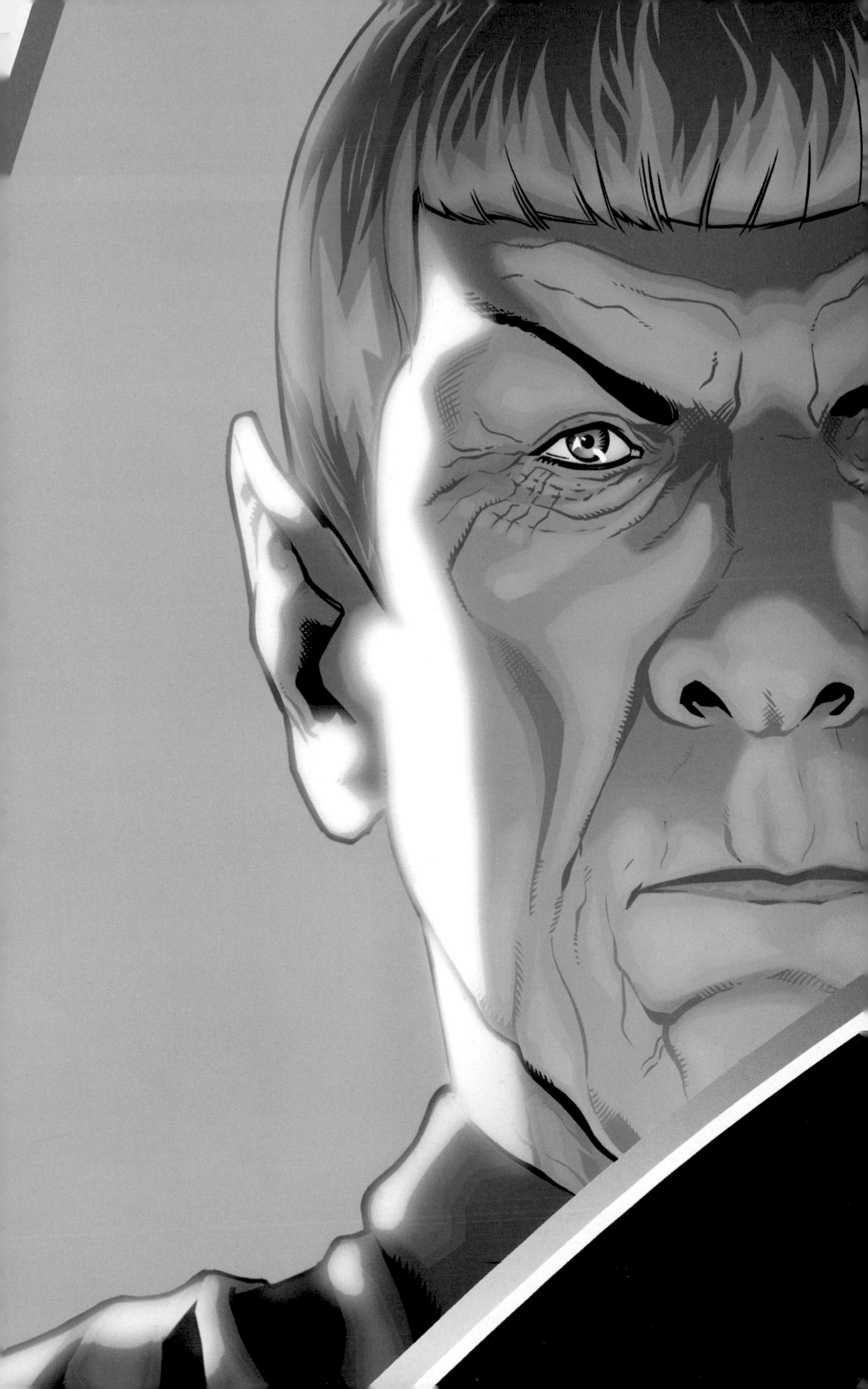

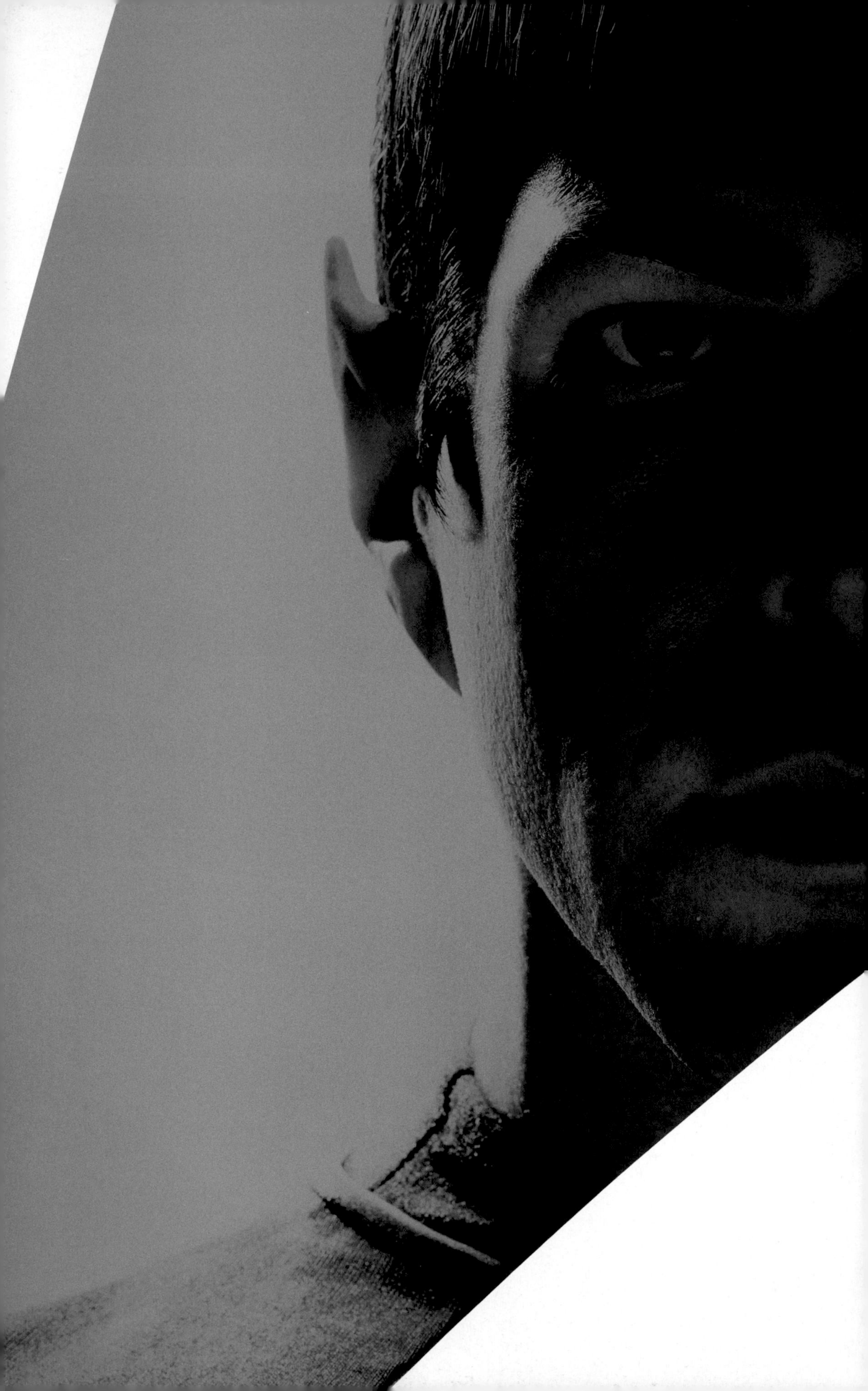

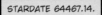

STARDATE 64467.14.

THE BORDER OF THE ROMULAN AND KLINGON EMPIRES.

STAR TREK
COUNTDOWN
NUMBER FOUR

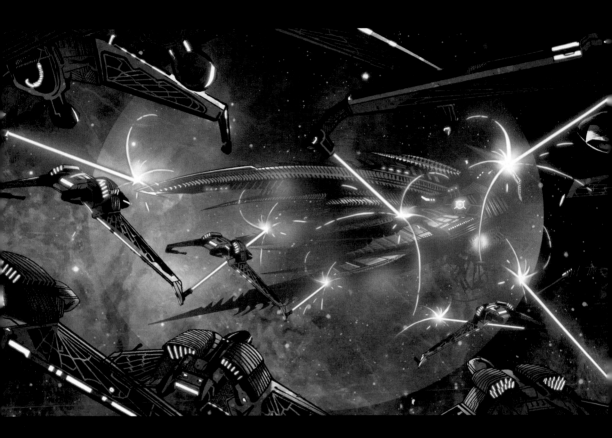

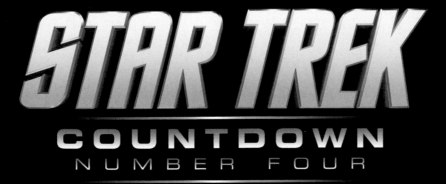

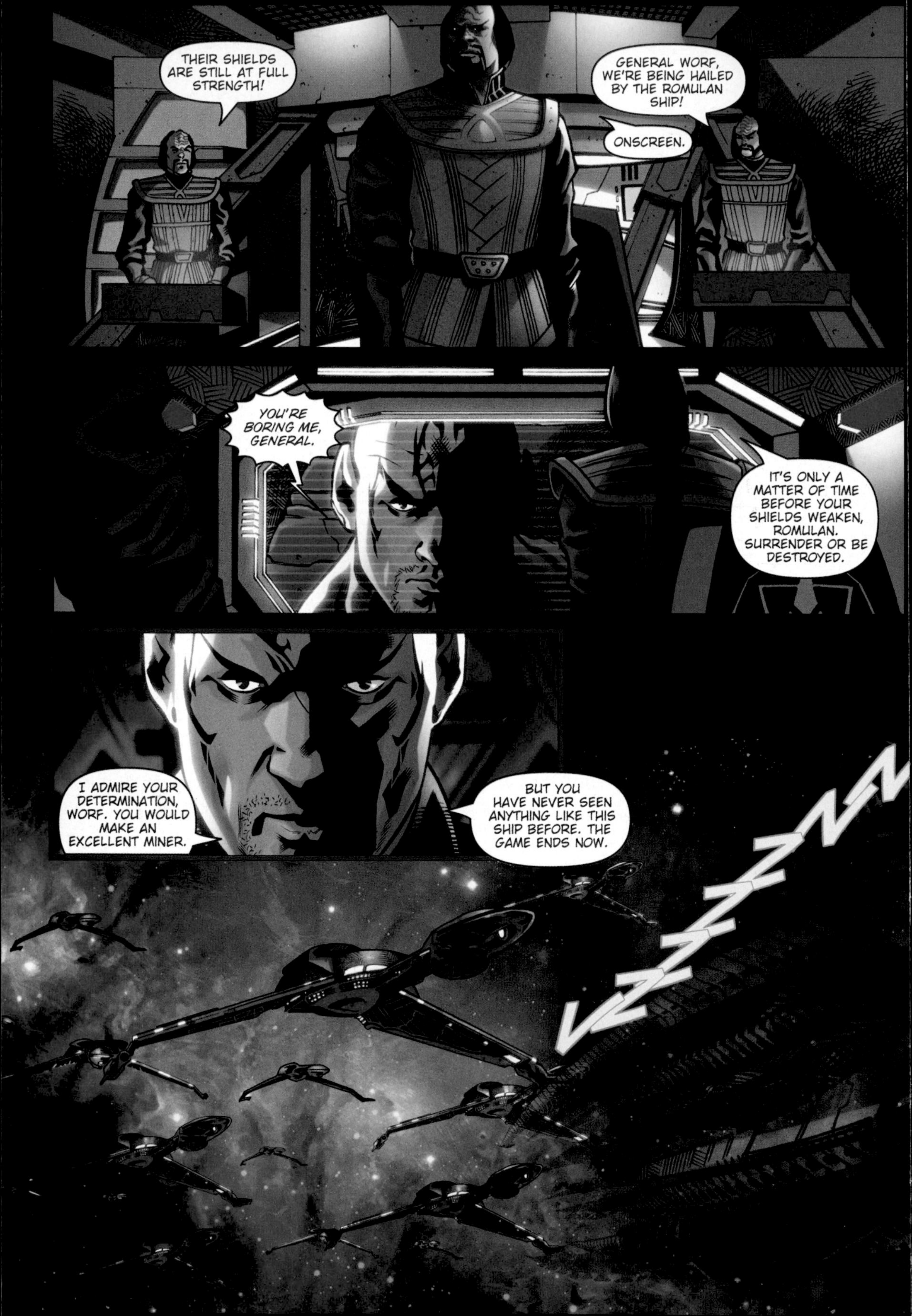
THEIR SHIELDS ARE STILL AT FULL STRENGTH!
GENERAL WORF, WE'RE BEING HAILED BY THE ROMULAN SHIP!
ONSCREEN.
YOU'RE BORING ME, GENERAL.
IT'S ONLY A MATTER OF TIME BEFORE YOUR SHIELDS WEAKEN, ROMULAN. SURRENDER OR BE DESTROYED.
I ADMIRE YOUR DETERMINATION, WORF. YOU WOULD MAKE AN EXCELLENT MINER.
BUT YOU HAVE NEVER SEEN ANYTHING LIKE THIS SHIP BEFORE. THE GAME ENDS NOW.

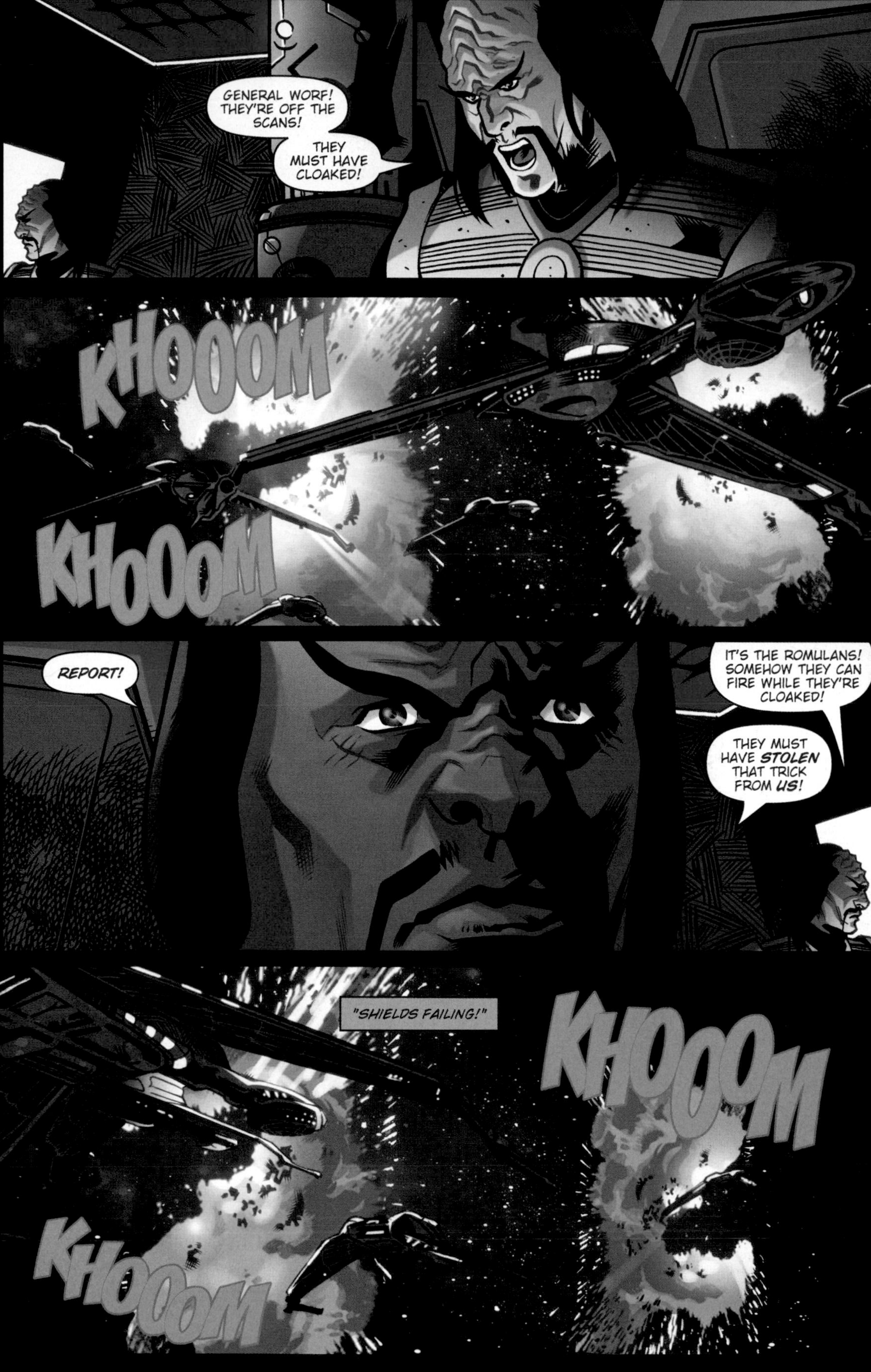
GENERAL WORF! THEY'RE OFF THE SCANS!
THEY MUST HAVE CLOAKED!
KHOOOM
KHOOOM
REPORT!
IT'S THE ROMULANS! SOMEHOW THEY CAN FIRE WHILE THEY'RE CLOAKED!
THEY MUST HAVE STOLEN THAT TRICK FROM US!
"SHIELDS FAILING!"
KHOOOM
KHOOOM

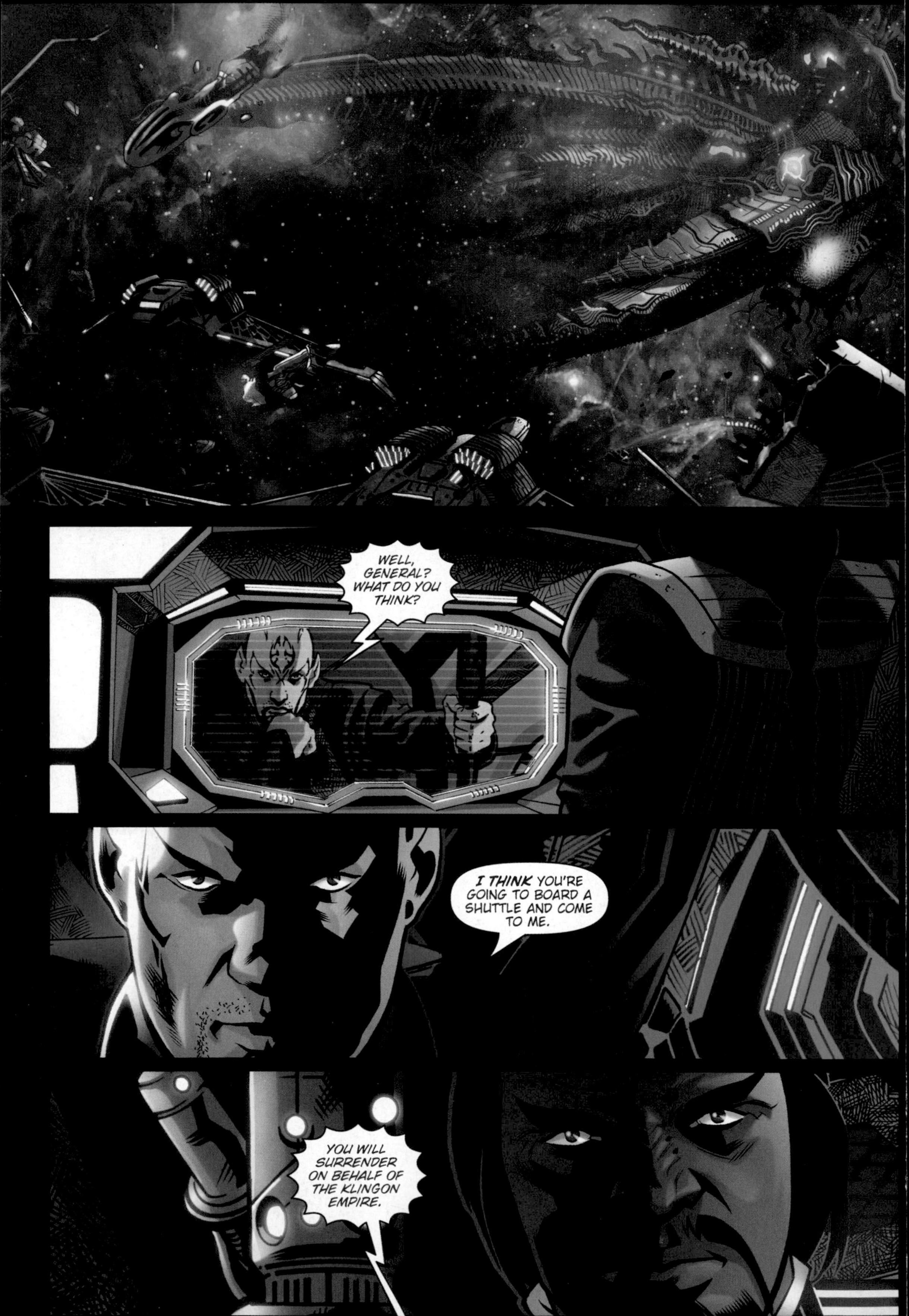
WELL, GENERAL? WHAT DO YOU THINK?
I THINK YOU'RE GOING TO BOARD A SHUTTLE AND COME TO ME.
YOU WILL SURRENDER ON BEHALF OF THE KLINGON EMPIRE.

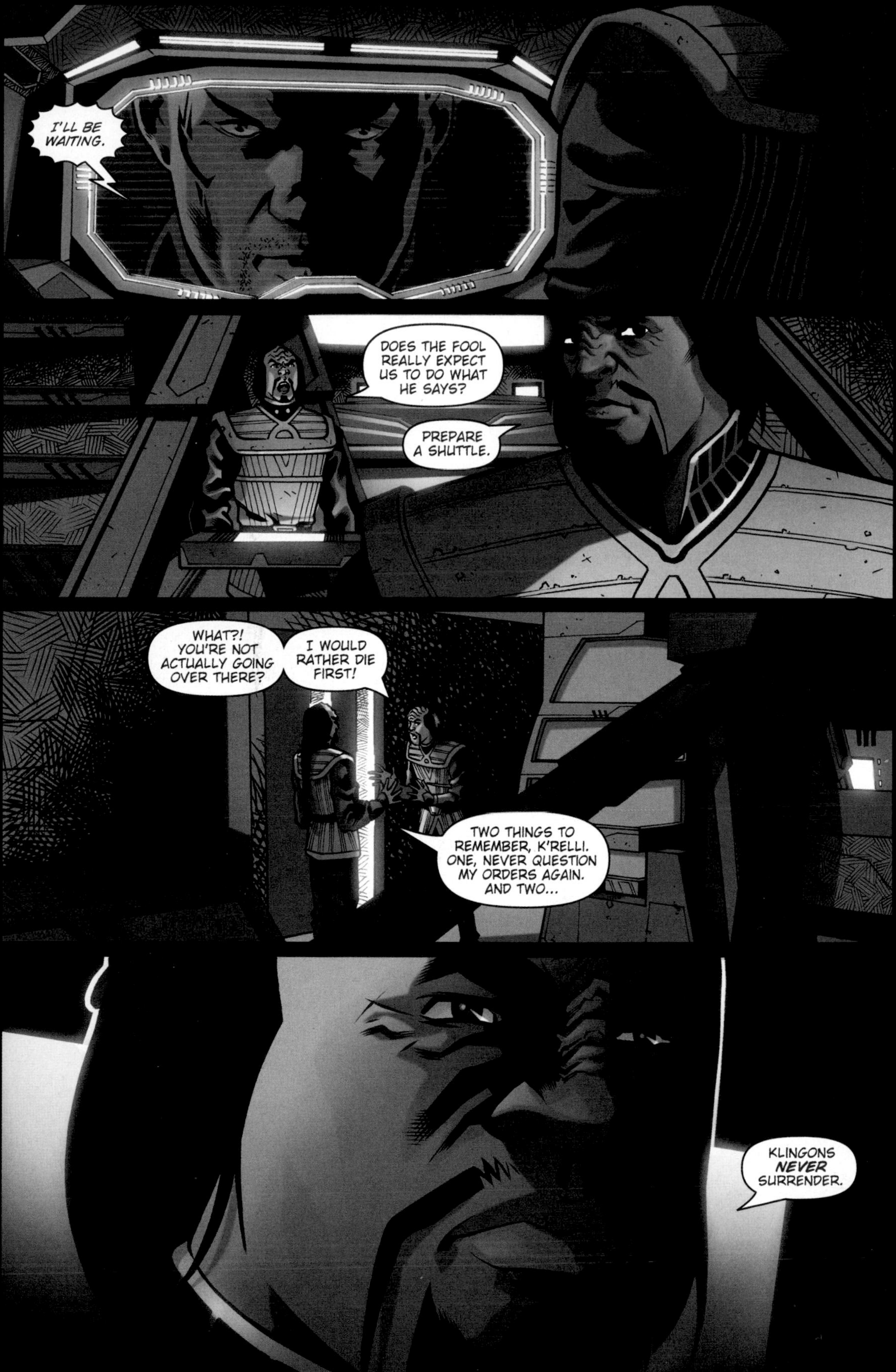
I'LL BE WAITING.
DOES THE FOOL REALLY EXPECT US TO DO WHAT HE SAYS?
PREPARE A SHUTTLE.
WHAT?! YOU'RE NOT ACTUALLY GOING OVER THERE?
I WOULD RATHER DIE FIRST!
TWO THINGS TO REMEMBER, K'RELLI. ONE, NEVER QUESTION MY ORDERS AGAIN. AND TWO...
KLINGONS NEVER SURRENDER.

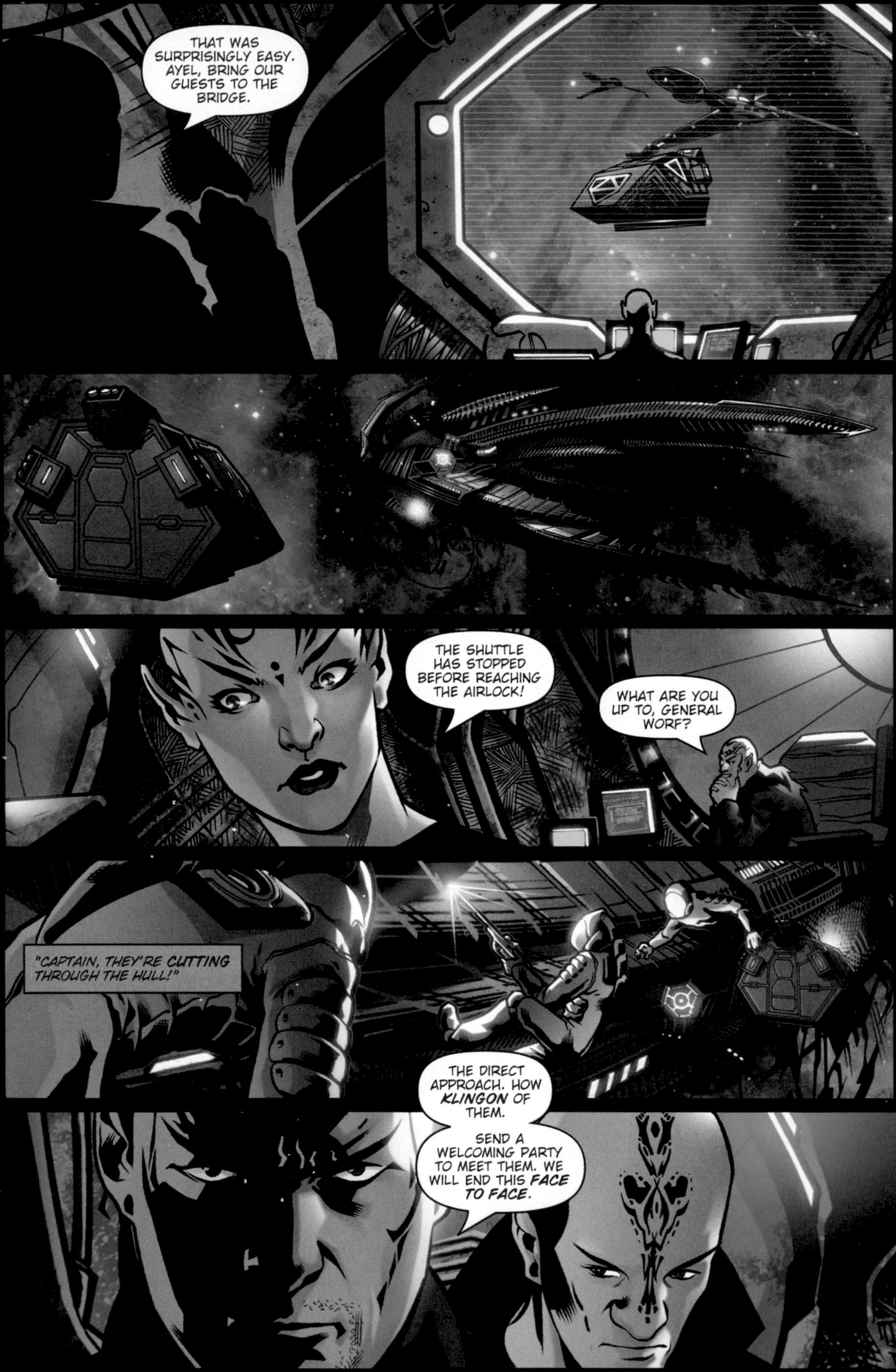
THAT WAS SURPRISINGLY EASY. AYEL, BRING OUR GUESTS TO THE BRIDGE.
THE SHUTTLE HAS STOPPED BEFORE REACHING THE AIRLOCK!
WHAT ARE YOU UP TO, GENERAL WORF?
"CAPTAIN, THEY'RE CUTTING THROUGH THE HULL!"
THE DIRECT APPROACH. HOW KLINGON OF THEM.
SEND A WELCOMING PARTY TO MEET THEM. WE WILL END THIS FACE TO FACE.

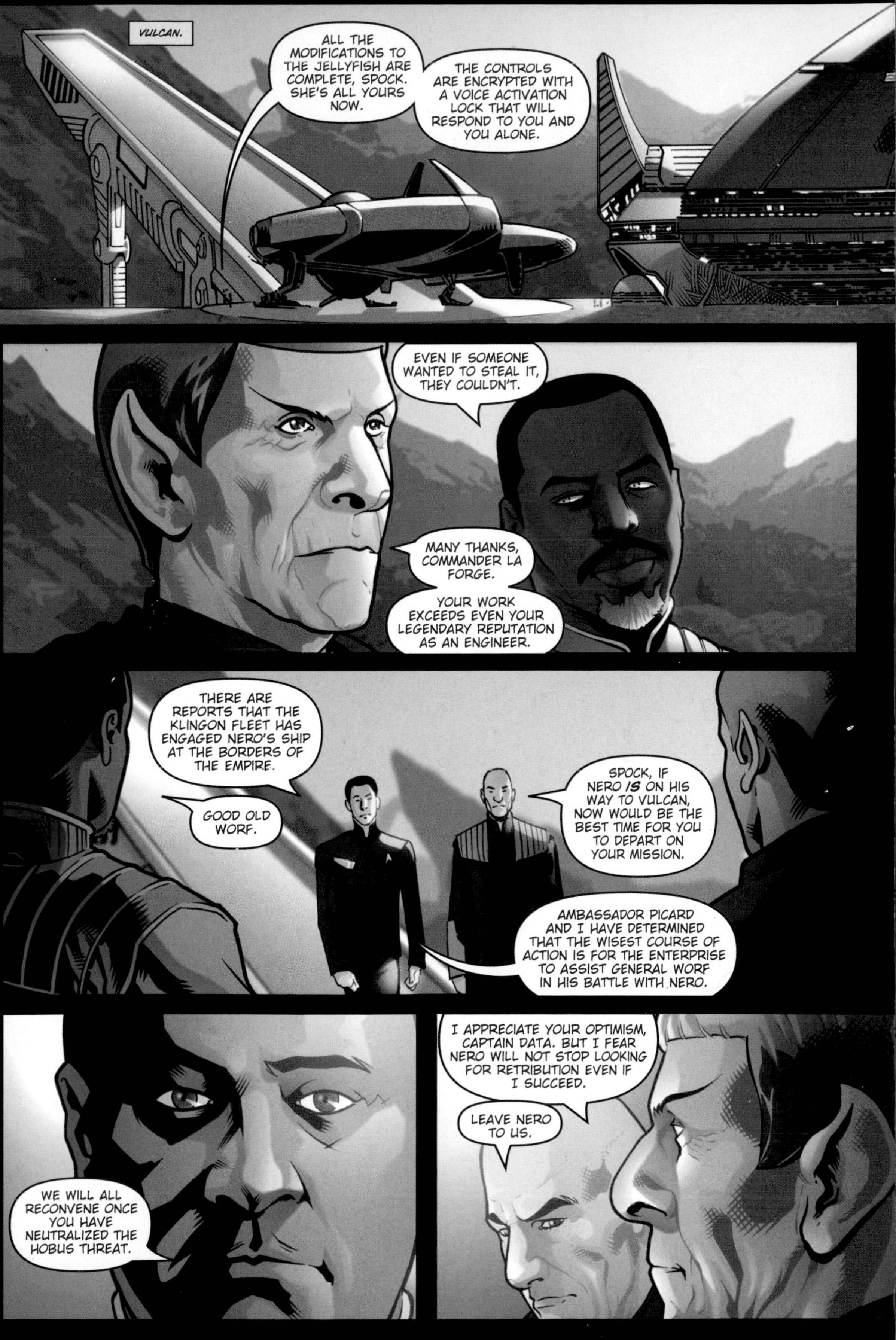
VULCAN.
ALL THE MODIFICATIONS TO THE JELLYFISH ARE COMPLETE, SPOCK. SHE'S ALL YOURS NOW.
THE CONTROLS ARE ENCRYPTED WITH A VOICE ACTIVATION LOCK THAT WILL RESPOND TO YOU AND YOU ALONE.
EVEN IF SOMEONE WANTED TO STEAL IT, THEY COULDN'T.
MANY THANKS, COMMANDER LA FORGE.
YOUR WORK EXCEEDS EVEN YOUR LEGENDARY REPUTATION AS AN ENGINEER.
THERE ARE REPORTS THAT THE KLINGON FLEET HAS ENGAGED NERO'S SHIP AT THE BORDERS OF THE EMPIRE.
GOOD OLD WORF.
SPOCK, IF NERO *IS* ON HIS WAY TO VULCAN, NOW WOULD BE THE BEST TIME FOR YOU TO DEPART ON YOUR MISSION.
AMBASSADOR PICARD AND I HAVE DETERMINED THAT THE WISEST COURSE OF ACTION IS FOR THE ENTERPRISE TO ASSIST GENERAL WORF IN HIS BATTLE WITH NERO.
WE WILL ALL RECONVENE ONCE YOU HAVE NEUTRALIZED THE HOBUS THREAT.
I APPRECIATE YOUR OPTIMISM, CAPTAIN DATA. BUT I FEAR NERO WILL NOT STOP LOOKING FOR RETRIBUTION EVEN IF I SUCCEED.
LEAVE NERO TO US.

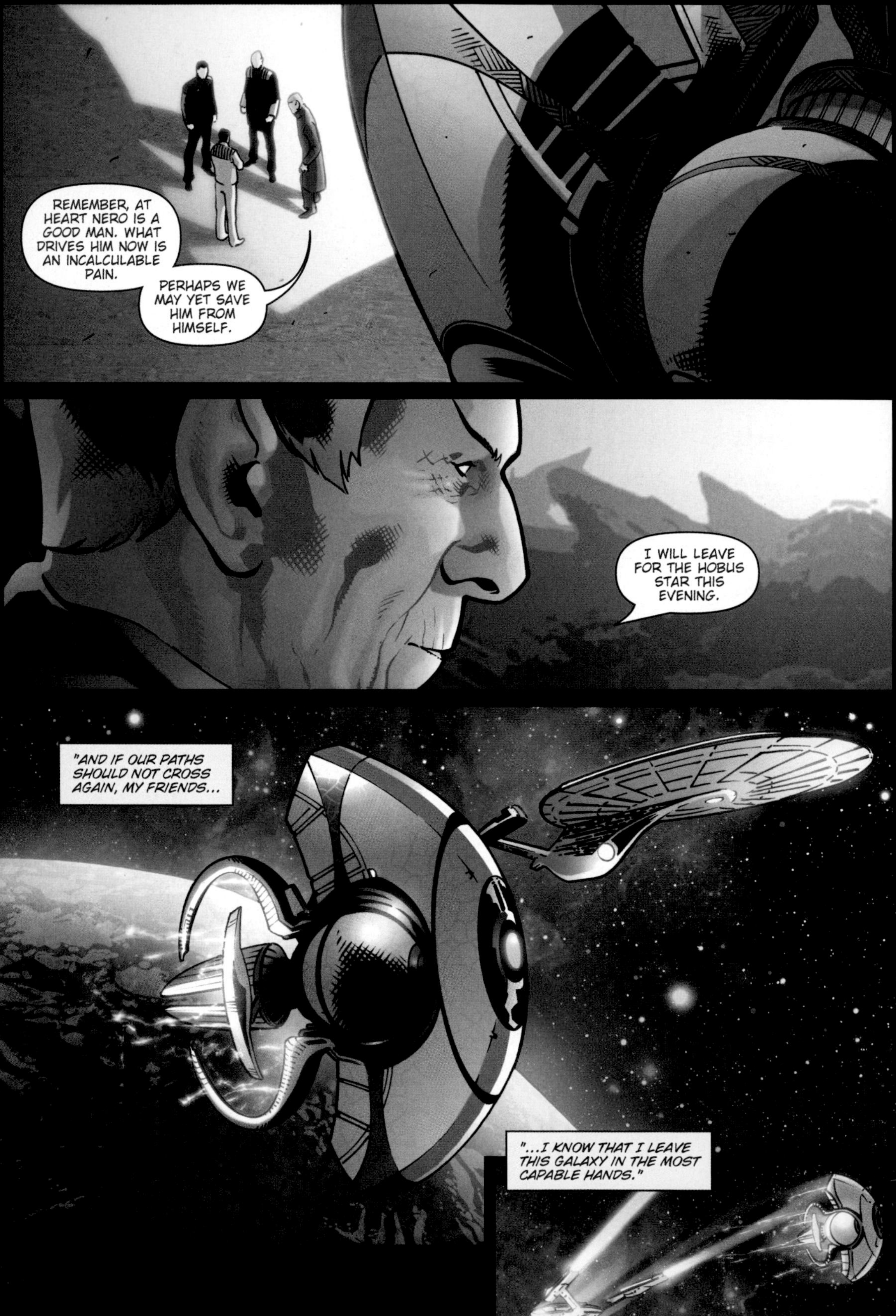
REMEMBER, AT HEART NERO IS A GOOD MAN. WHAT DRIVES HIM NOW IS AN INCALCULABLE PAIN.
PERHAPS WE MAY YET SAVE HIM FROM HIMSELF.
I WILL LEAVE FOR THE HOBUS STAR THIS EVENING.
"AND IF OUR PATHS SHOULD NOT CROSS AGAIN, MY FRIENDS...
"...I KNOW THAT I LEAVE THIS GALAXY IN THE MOST CAPABLE HANDS."

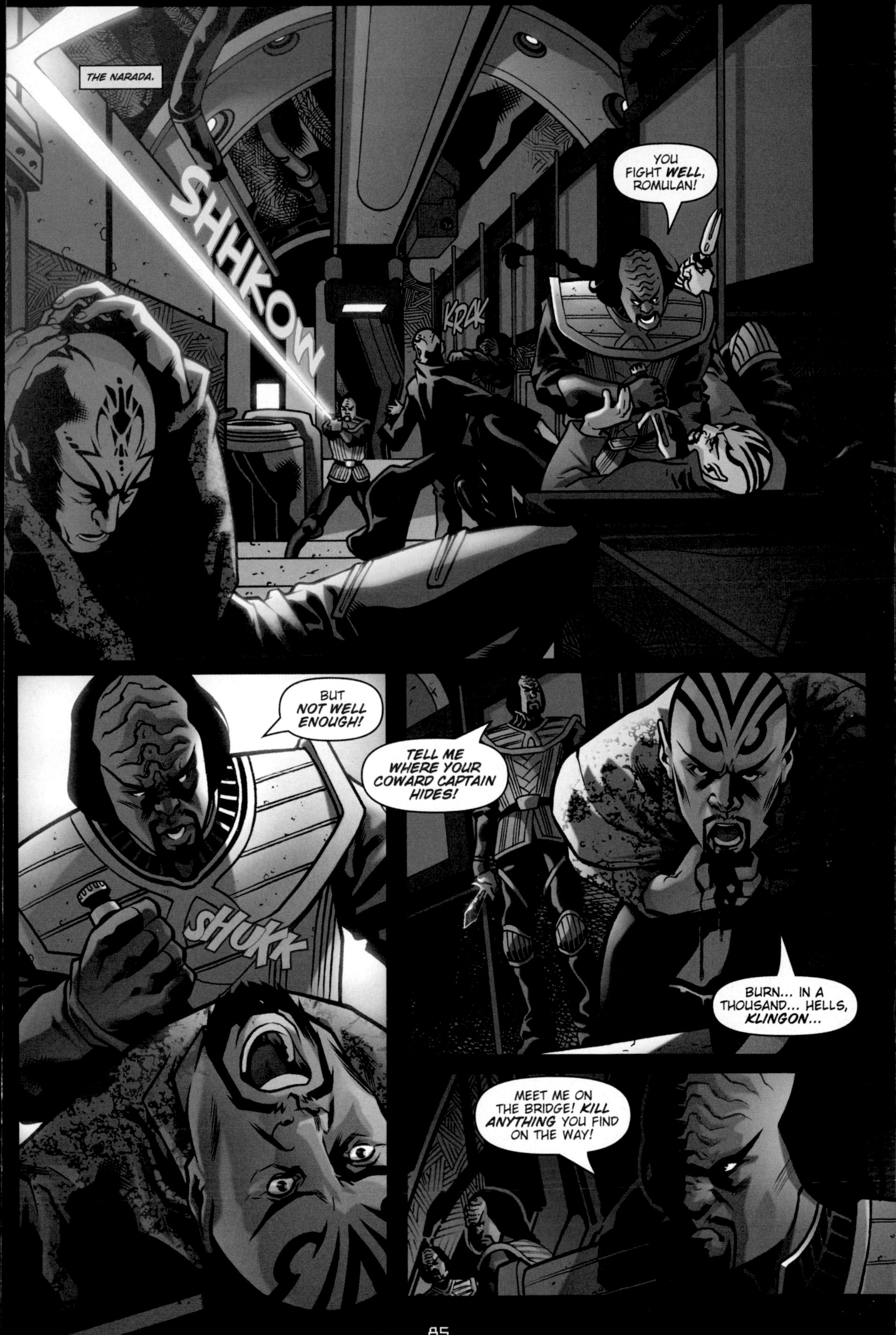
THE NARADA.
SHHKOW
KRAK
YOU FIGHT WELL, ROMULAN!
BUT NOT WELL ENOUGH!
SHUKK
TELL ME WHERE YOUR COWARD CAPTAIN HIDES!
BURN... IN A THOUSAND... HELLS, KLINGON...
MEET ME ON THE BRIDGE! KILL ANYTHING YOU FIND ON THE WAY!

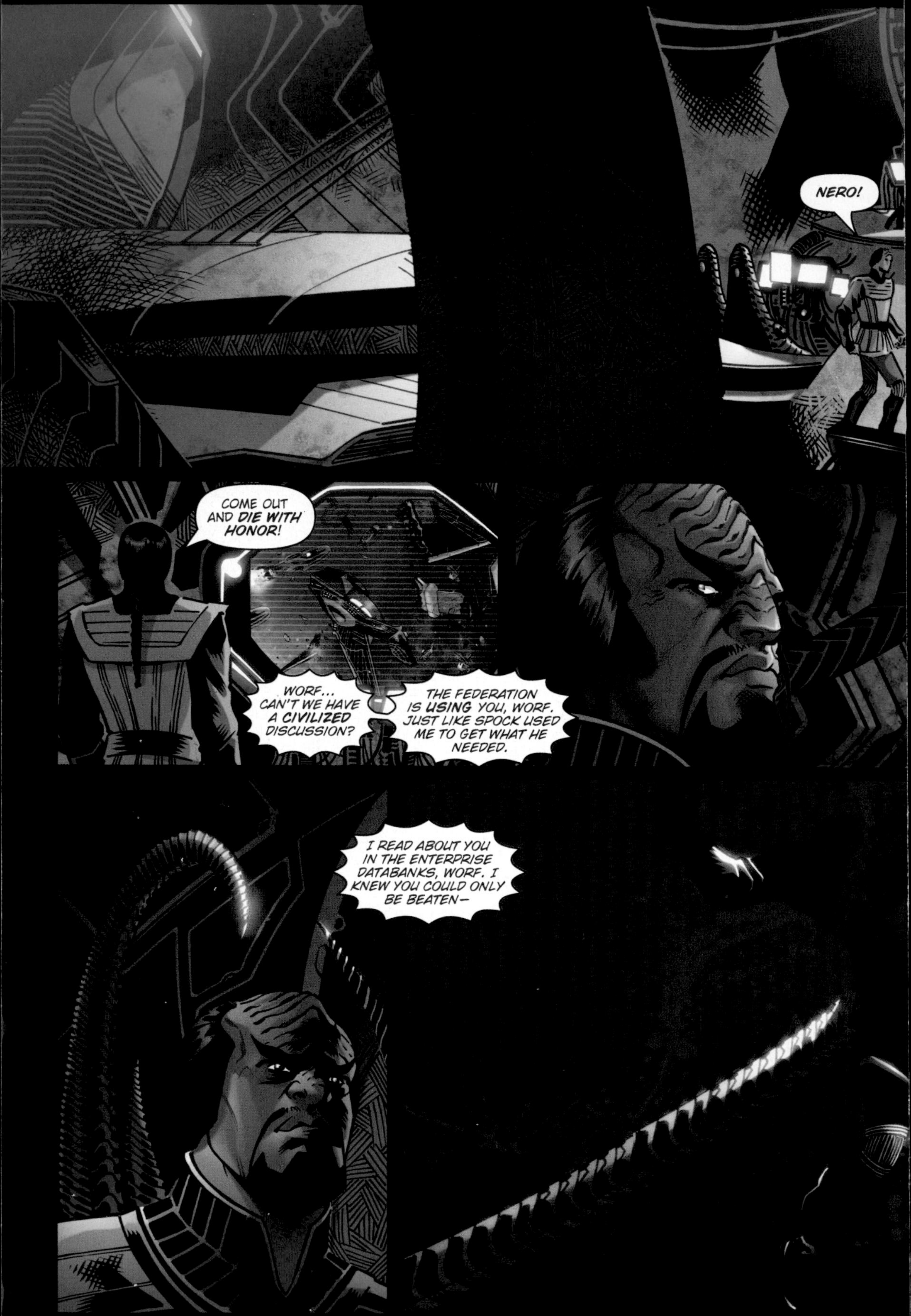
NERO!
COME OUT AND DIE WITH HONOR!
WORF... CAN'T WE HAVE A CIVILIZED DISCUSSION?
THE FEDERATION IS USING YOU, WORF. JUST LIKE SPOCK USED ME TO GET WHAT HE NEEDED.
I READ ABOUT YOU IN THE ENTERPRISE DATABANKS, WORF. I KNEW YOU COULD ONLY BE BEATEN—

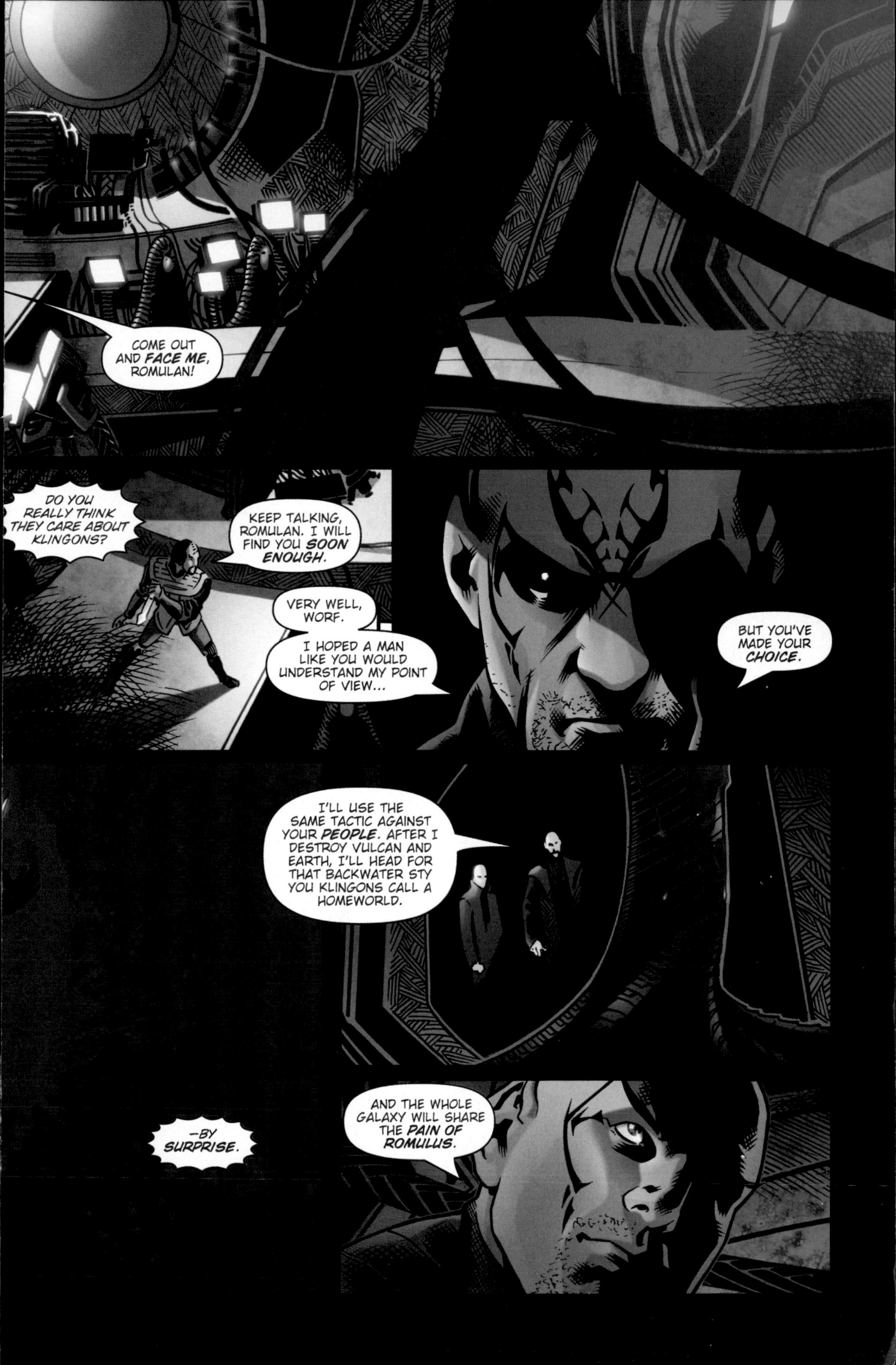
COME OUT AND FACE ME, ROMULAN!
DO YOU REALLY THINK THEY CARE ABOUT KLINGONS?
KEEP TALKING, ROMULAN. I WILL FIND YOU SOON ENOUGH.
VERY WELL, WORF.
I HOPED A MAN LIKE YOU WOULD UNDERSTAND MY POINT OF VIEW...
BUT YOU'VE MADE YOUR CHOICE.
I'LL USE THE SAME TACTIC AGAINST YOUR PEOPLE. AFTER I DESTROY VULCAN AND EARTH, I'LL HEAD FOR THAT BACKWATER STY YOU KLINGONS CALL A HOMEWORLD.
AND THE WHOLE GALAXY WILL SHARE THE PAIN OF ROMULUS.
—BY SURPRISE.

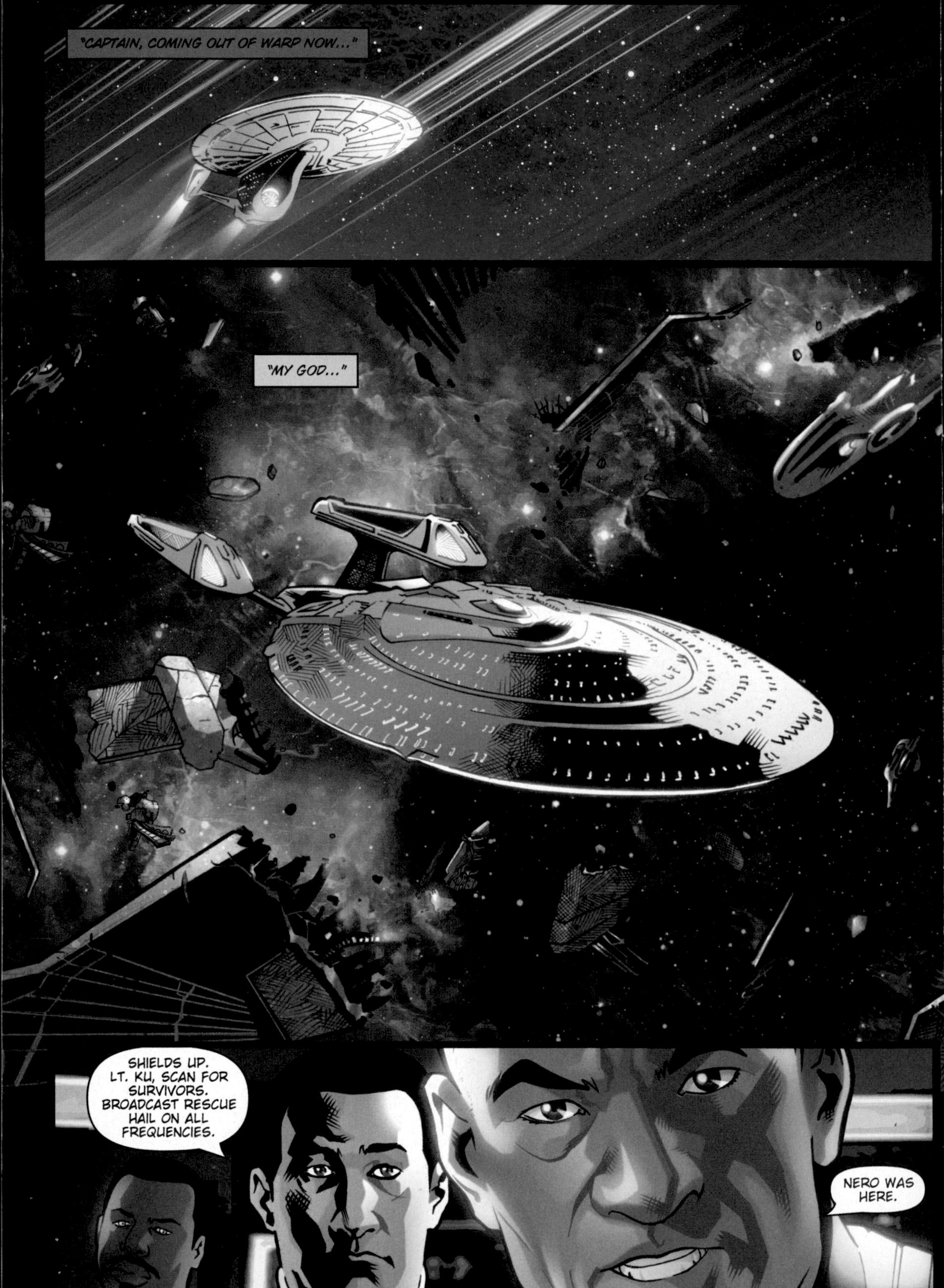
"CAPTAIN, COMING OUT OF WARP NOW..."
"MY GOD..."
SHIELDS UP. LT. KU, SCAN FOR SURVIVORS. BROADCAST RESCUE HAIL ON ALL FREQUENCIES.
NERO WAS HERE.

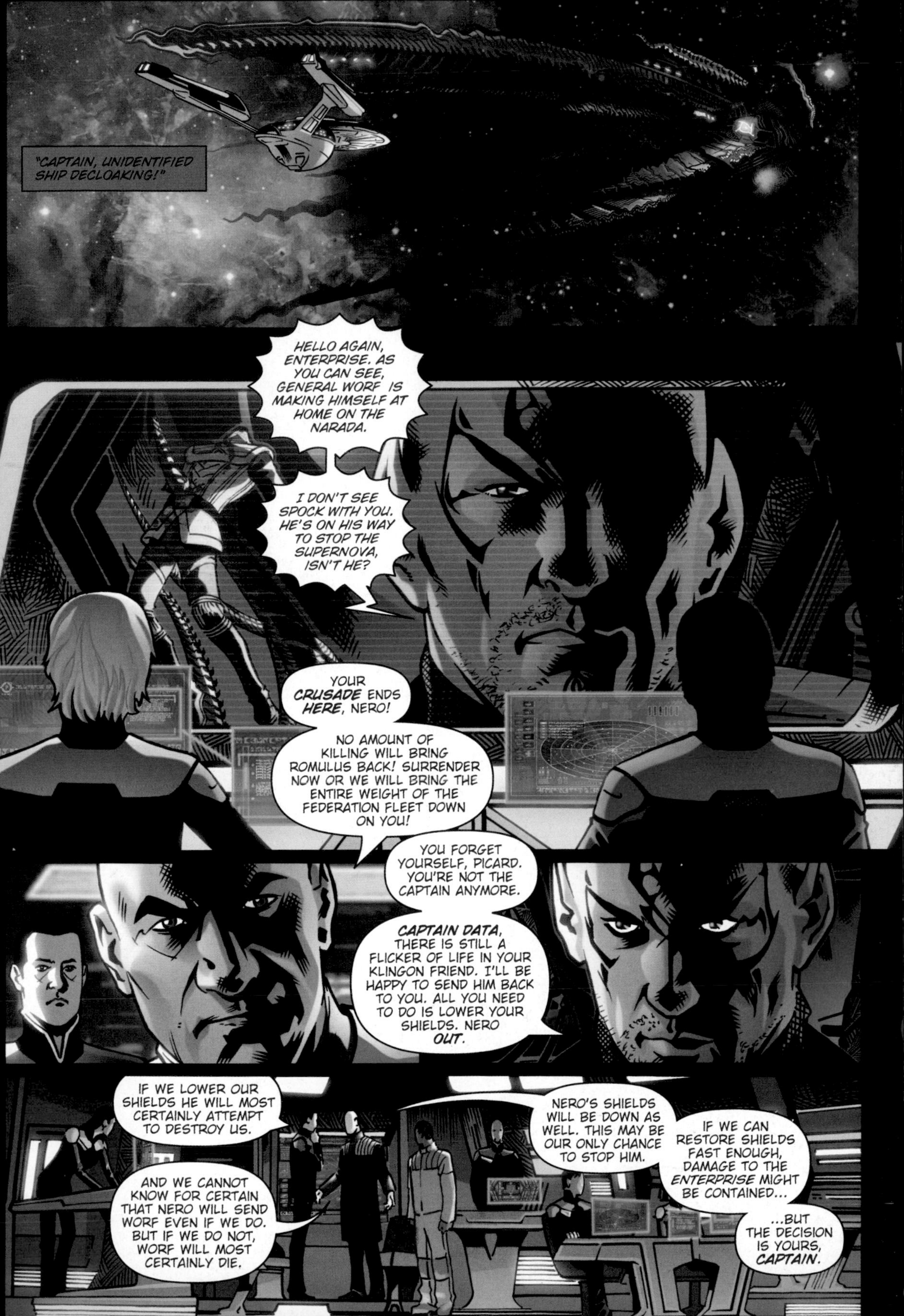
"CAPTAIN, UNIDENTIFIED SHIP DECLOAKING!"
HELLO AGAIN, ENTERPRISE. AS YOU CAN SEE, GENERAL WORF IS MAKING HIMSELF AT HOME ON THE NARADA.
I DON'T SEE SPOCK WITH YOU. HE'S ON HIS WAY TO STOP THE SUPERNOVA, ISN'T HE?
YOUR **CRUSADE** ENDS **HERE**, NERO!
NO AMOUNT OF KILLING WILL BRING ROMULUS BACK! SURRENDER NOW OR WE WILL BRING THE ENTIRE WEIGHT OF THE FEDERATION FLEET DOWN ON YOU!
YOU FORGET YOURSELF, PICARD. YOU'RE NOT THE CAPTAIN ANYMORE.
CAPTAIN DATA, THERE IS STILL A FLICKER OF LIFE IN YOUR KLINGON FRIEND. I'LL BE HAPPY TO SEND HIM BACK TO YOU. ALL YOU NEED TO DO IS LOWER YOUR SHIELDS. NERO **OUT**.
IF WE LOWER OUR SHIELDS HE WILL MOST CERTAINLY ATTEMPT TO DESTROY US.
AND WE CANNOT KNOW FOR CERTAIN THAT NERO WILL SEND WORF EVEN IF WE DO. BUT IF WE DO NOT, WORF WILL MOST CERTAINLY DIE.
NERO'S SHIELDS WILL BE DOWN AS WELL. THIS MAY BE OUR ONLY CHANCE TO STOP HIM.
IF WE CAN RESTORE SHIELDS FAST ENOUGH, DAMAGE TO THE *ENTERPRISE* MIGHT BE CONTAINED...
...BUT THE DECISION IS YOURS, **CAPTAIN**.

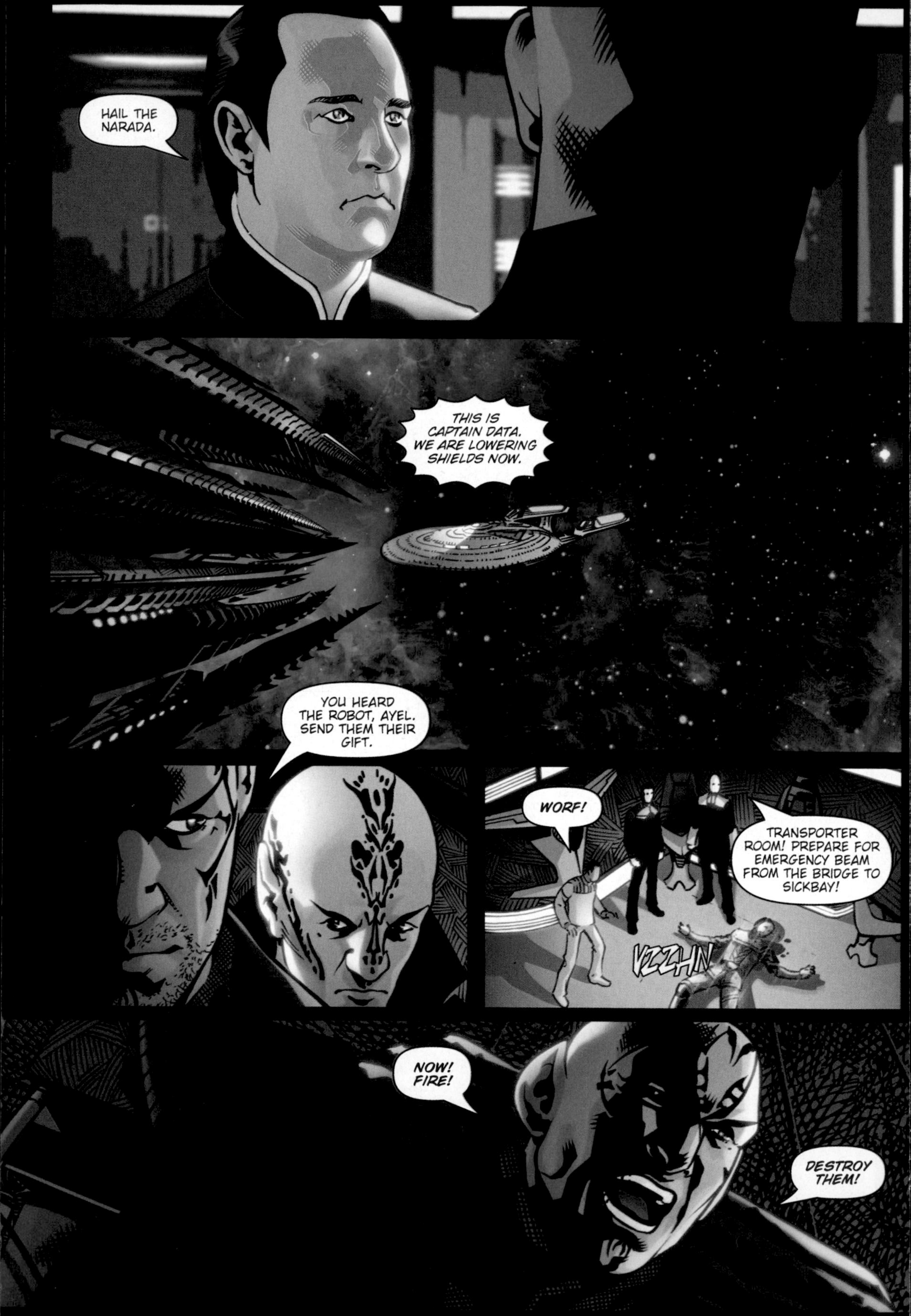
HAIL THE NARADA.
THIS IS CAPTAIN DATA. WE ARE LOWERING SHIELDS NOW.
YOU HEARD THE ROBOT, AYEL. SEND THEM THEIR GIFT.
WORF!
TRANSPORTER ROOM! PREPARE FOR EMERGENCY BEAM FROM THE BRIDGE TO SICKBAY!
VZZHN
NOW! FIRE!
DESTROY THEM!

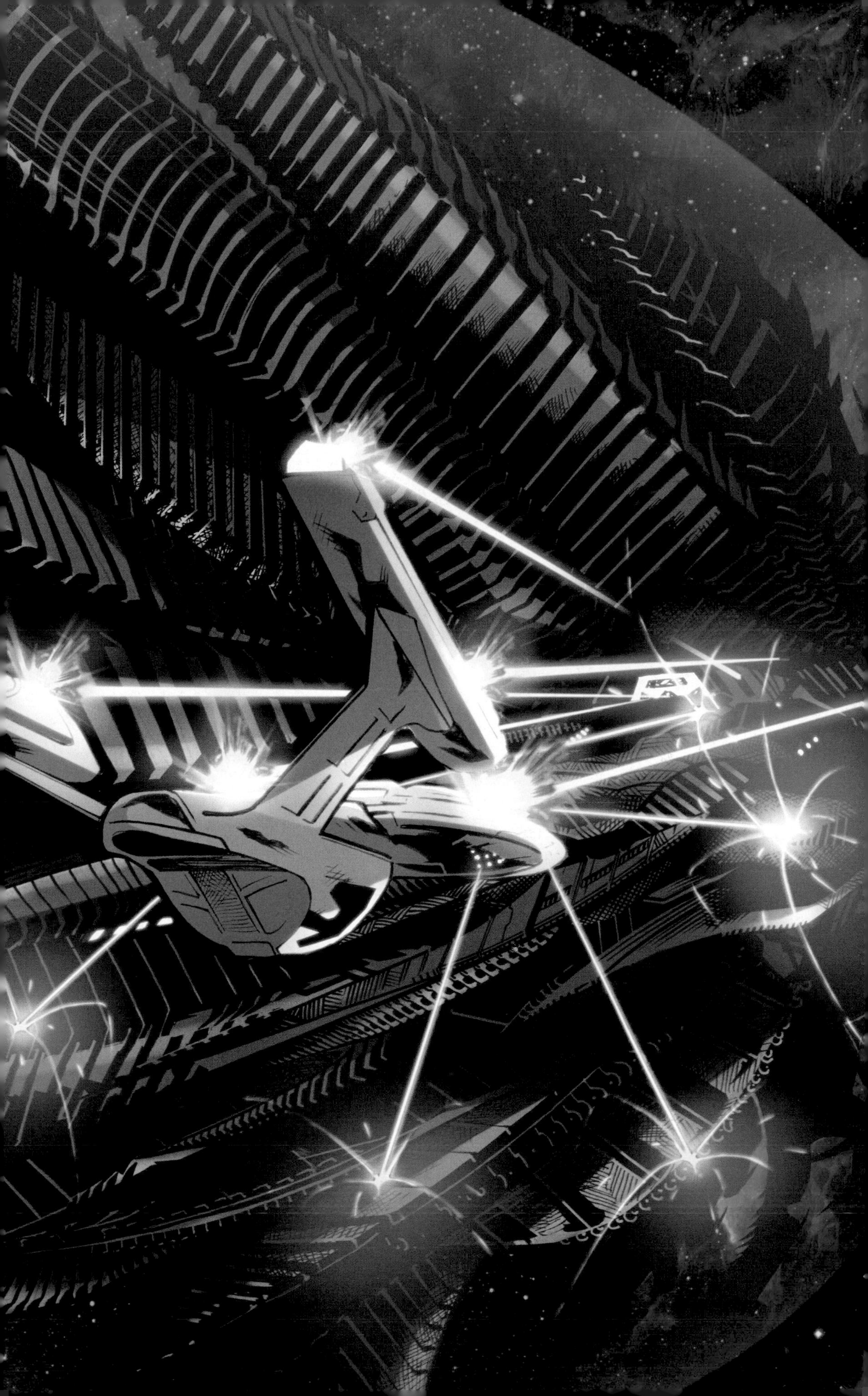

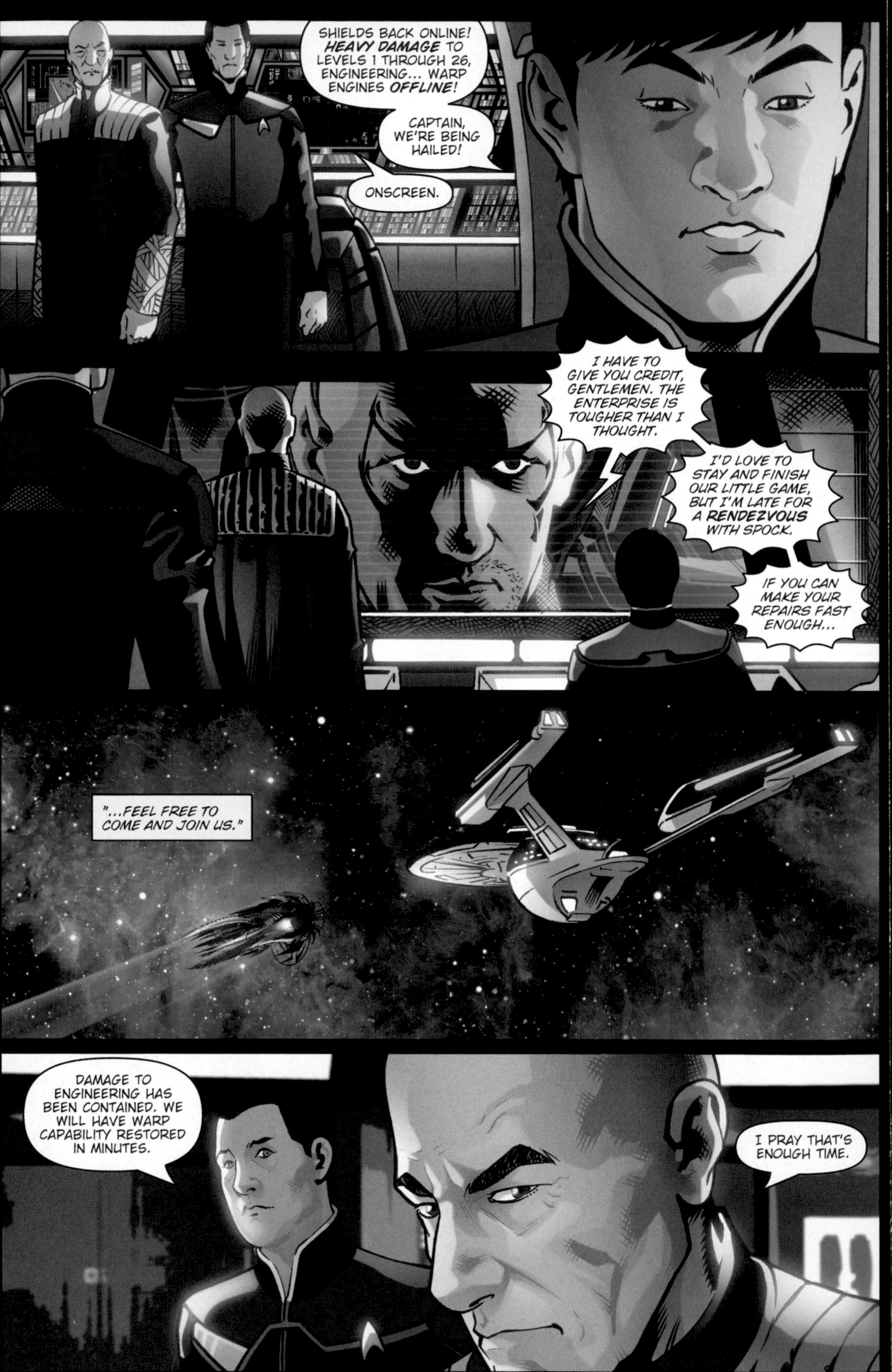

SHIELDS BACK ONLINE! HEAVY DAMAGE TO LEVELS 1 THROUGH 26, ENGINEERING... WARP ENGINES OFFLINE!
CAPTAIN, WE'RE BEING HAILED!
ONSCREEN.
I HAVE TO GIVE YOU CREDIT, GENTLEMEN. THE ENTERPRISE IS TOUGHER THAN I THOUGHT.
I'D LOVE TO STAY AND FINISH OUR LITTLE GAME, BUT I'M LATE FOR A RENDEZVOUS WITH SPOCK.
IF YOU CAN MAKE YOUR REPAIRS FAST ENOUGH...
"...FEEL FREE TO COME AND JOIN US."
DAMAGE TO ENGINEERING HAS BEEN CONTAINED. WE WILL HAVE WARP CAPABILITY RESTORED IN MINUTES.
I PRAY THAT'S ENOUGH TIME.

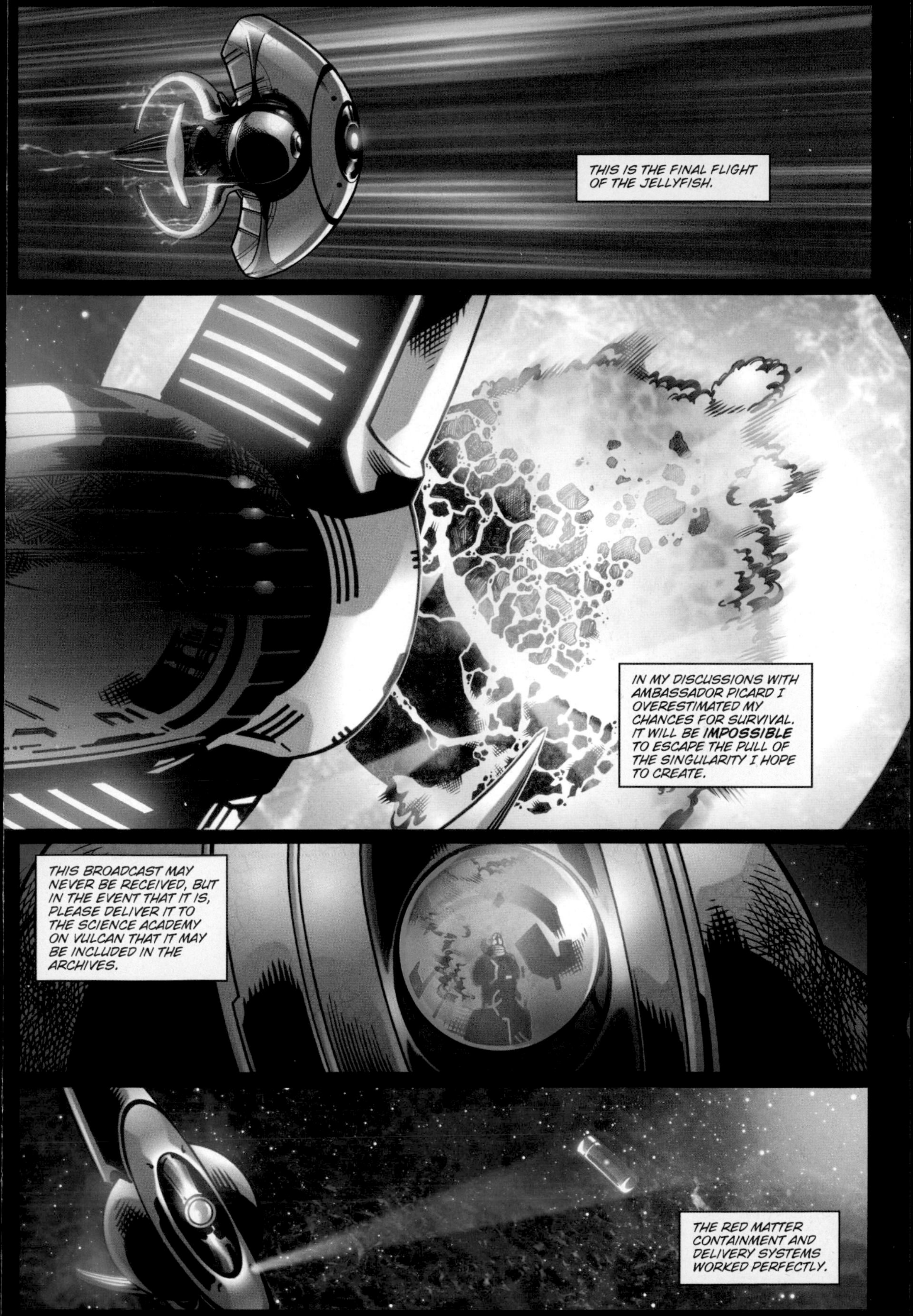
THIS IS THE FINAL FLIGHT OF THE JELLYFISH.
IN MY DISCUSSIONS WITH AMBASSADOR PICARD I OVERESTIMATED MY CHANCES FOR SURVIVAL. IT WILL BE **IMPOSSIBLE** TO ESCAPE THE PULL OF THE SINGULARITY I HOPE TO CREATE.
THIS BROADCAST MAY NEVER BE RECEIVED, BUT IN THE EVENT THAT IT IS, PLEASE DELIVER IT TO THE SCIENCE ACADEMY ON VULCAN THAT IT MAY BE INCLUDED IN THE ARCHIVES.
THE RED MATTER CONTAINMENT AND DELIVERY SYSTEMS WORKED PERFECTLY.

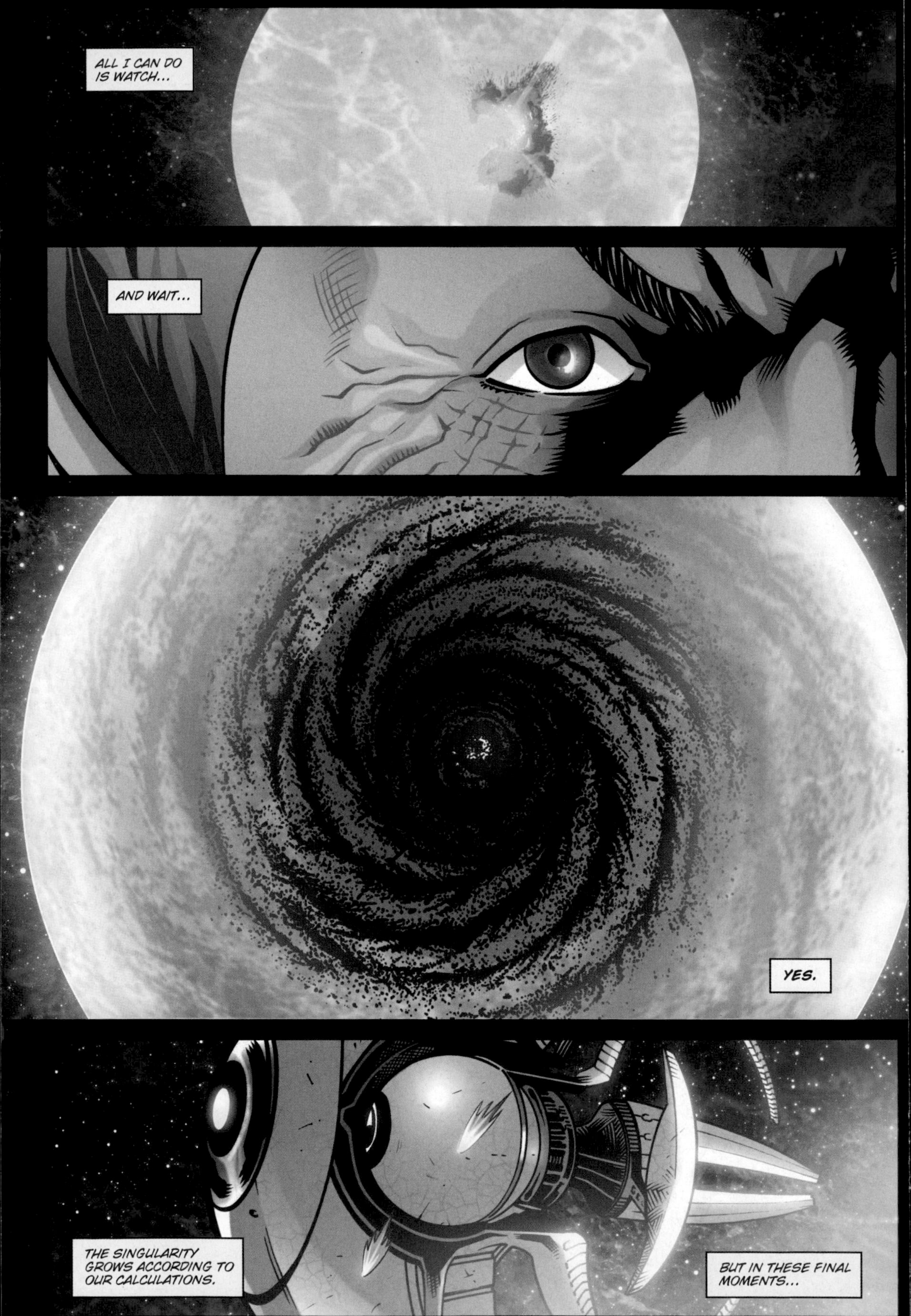
ALL I CAN DO IS WATCH...
AND WAIT...
YES.
THE SINGULARITY GROWS ACCORDING TO OUR CALCULATIONS.
BUT IN THESE FINAL MOMENTS...

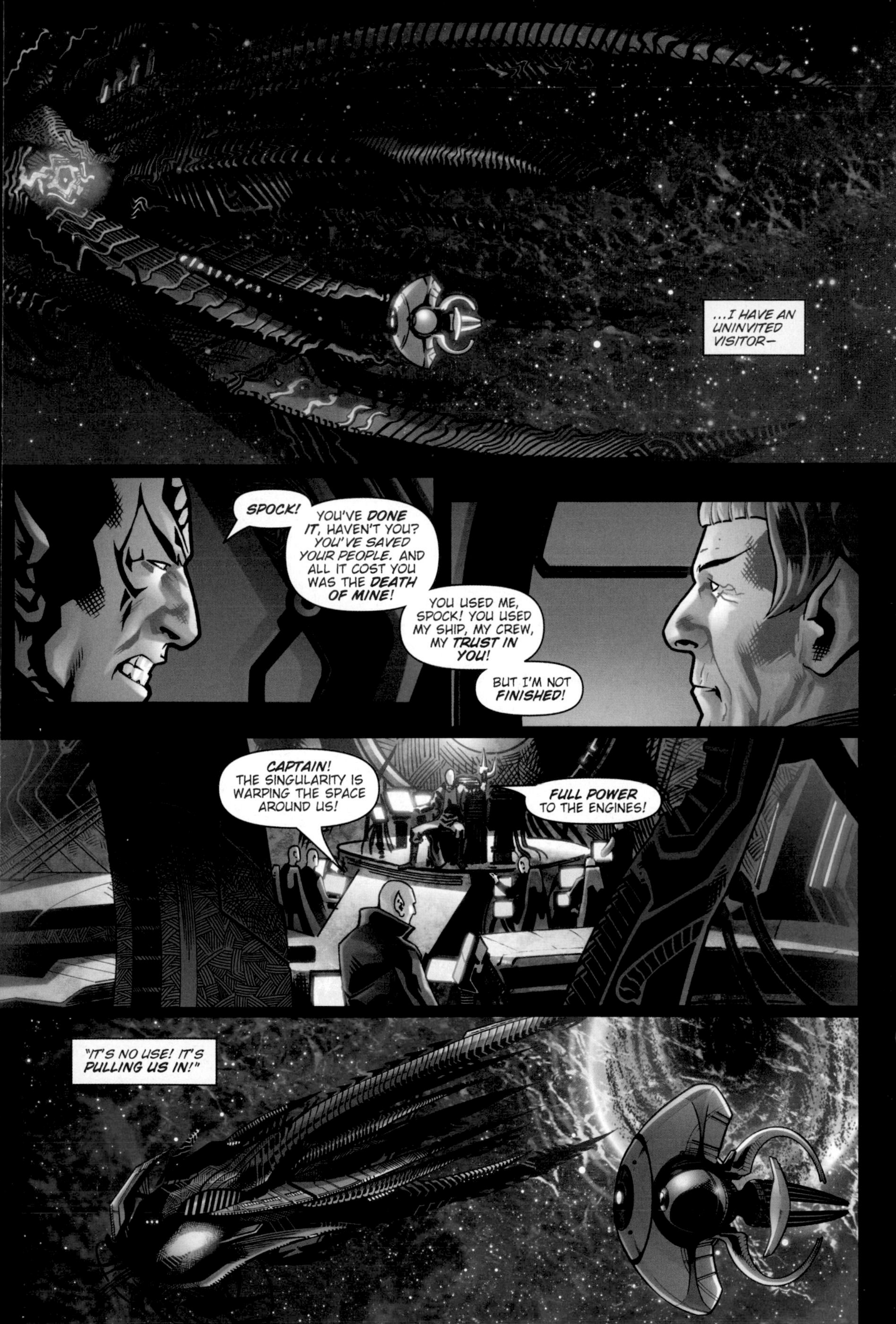
...I HAVE AN UNINVITED VISITOR—
SPOCK!
YOU'VE DONE IT, HAVEN'T YOU? YOU'VE SAVED YOUR PEOPLE. AND ALL IT COST YOU WAS THE DEATH OF MINE!
YOU USED ME, SPOCK! YOU USED MY SHIP, MY CREW, MY TRUST IN YOU!
BUT I'M NOT FINISHED!
CAPTAIN! THE SINGULARITY IS WARPING THE SPACE AROUND US!
FULL POWER TO THE ENGINES!
"IT'S NO USE! IT'S PULLING US IN!"

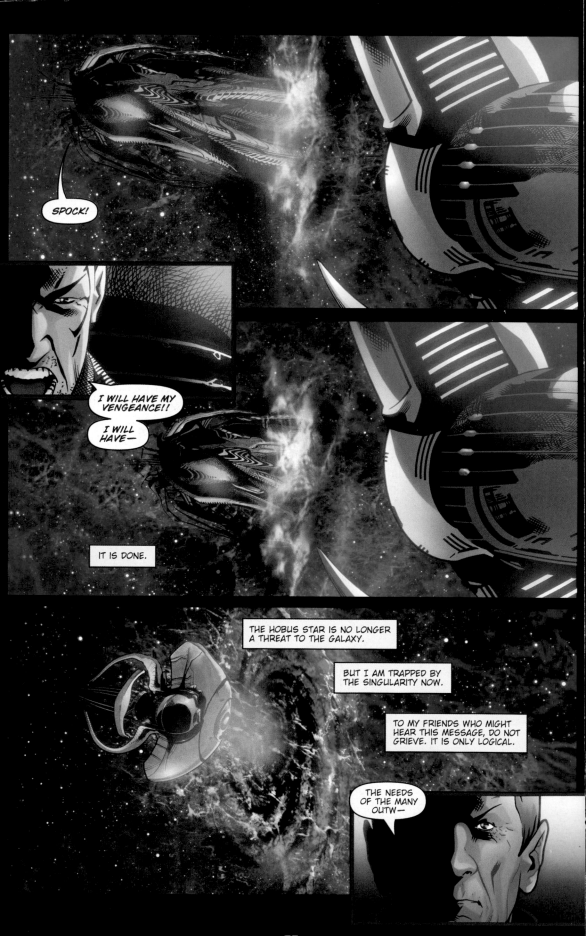

SPOCK!

I WILL HAVE MY VENGEANCE!!

I WILL HAVE—

IT IS DONE.

THE HOBUS STAR IS NO LONGER A THREAT TO THE GALAXY.

BUT I AM TRAPPED BY THE SINGULARITY NOW.

TO MY FRIENDS WHO MIGHT HEAR THIS MESSAGE, DO NOT GRIEVE. IT IS ONLY LOGICAL.

THE NEEDS OF THE MANY OUTW—

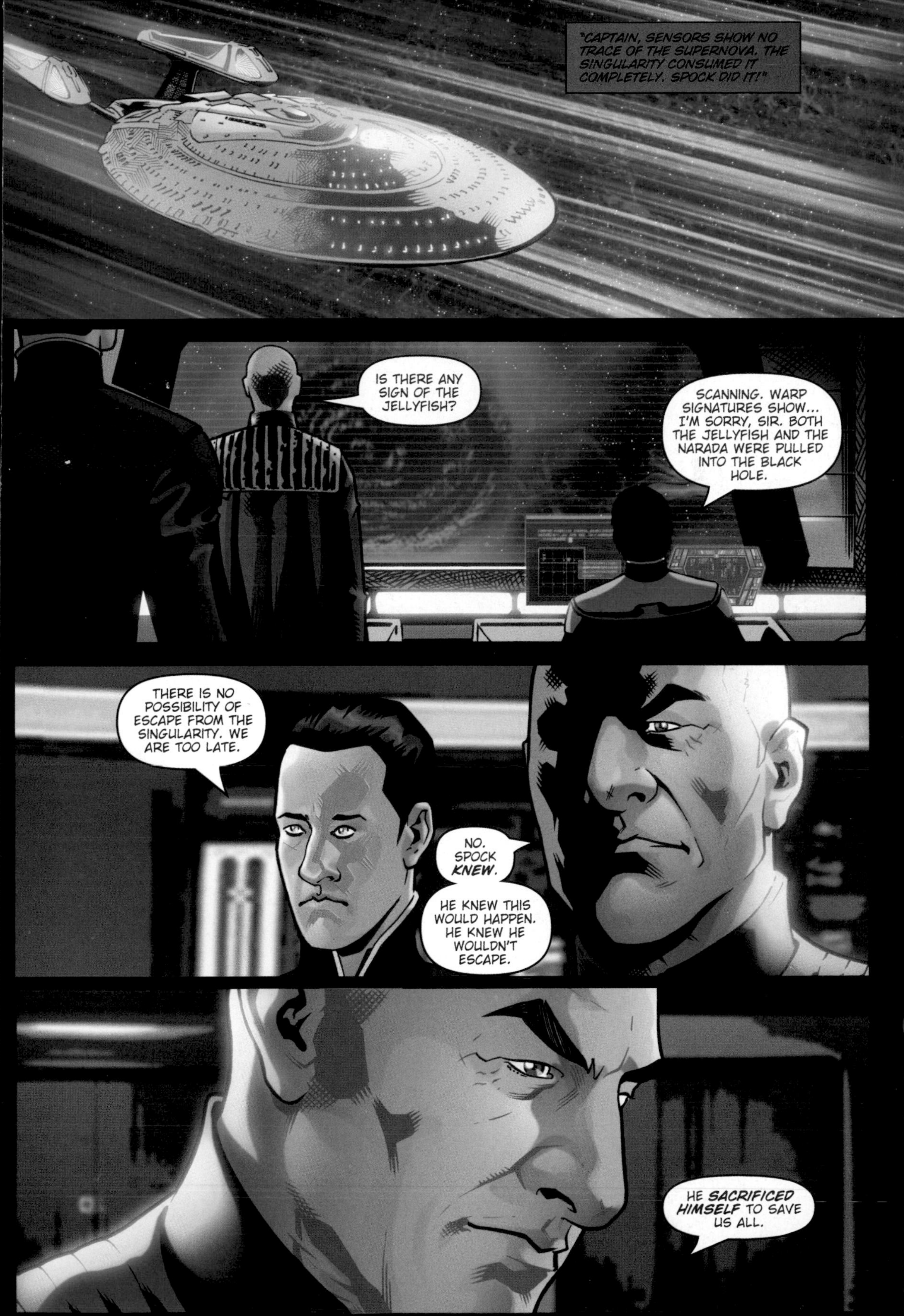
"CAPTAIN, SENSORS SHOW NO TRACE OF THE SUPERNOVA. THE SINGULARITY CONSUMED IT COMPLETELY. SPOCK DID IT!"
IS THERE ANY SIGN OF THE JELLYFISH?
SCANNING. WARP SIGNATURES SHOW... I'M SORRY, SIR. BOTH THE JELLYFISH AND THE NARADA WERE PULLED INTO THE BLACK HOLE.
THERE IS NO POSSIBILITY OF ESCAPE FROM THE SINGULARITY. WE ARE TOO LATE.
NO. SPOCK *KNEW*.
HE KNEW THIS WOULD HAPPEN. HE KNEW HE WOULDN'T ESCAPE.
HE *SACRIFICED HIMSELF* TO SAVE US ALL.

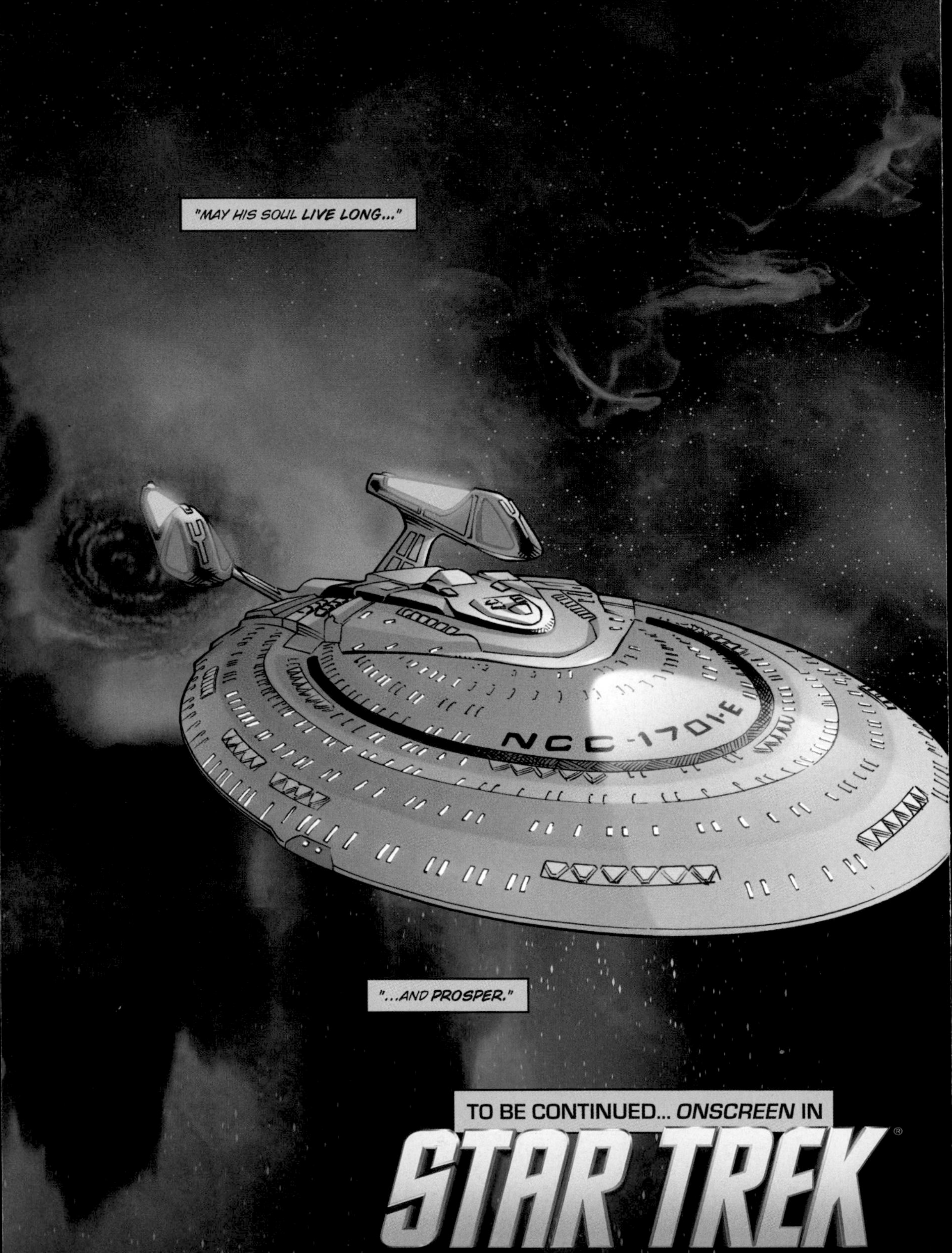
"MAY HIS SOUL LIVE LONG..."
NCC-1701-E
"...AND PROSPER."
TO BE CONTINUED... ONSCREEN IN
STAR TREK®

AFTERWORD

The notion that we'd be called to serve *STAR TREK* in any form is something we never dared dream. This book has had particular meaning for us in that we fell in love with *STAR TREK* through the characters of *THE NEXT GENERATION*. The longest summer of our lives was spent waiting to find out how Captain Riker and the amazing crew of the Enterprise were going to defeat their former Captain, Jean-Luc Picard, after his transformation into Locutus of Borg.

We don't expect to ever feel the same anticipation again, but perhaps we can create some for new fans. That is the intention of this book... to take a ride with a beloved crew that no one believed could ever match the original, and to pay homage to their stewardship of a thing called *STAR TREK*. Their journey now takes us back to the beginning...

Roberto Orci & Alex Kurtzman

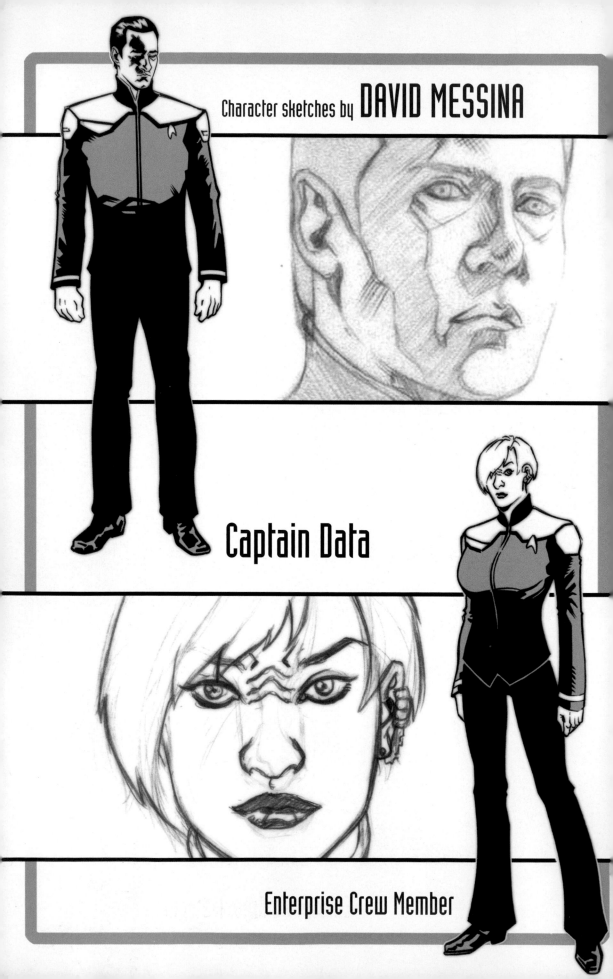

Character sketches by **DAVID MESSINA**

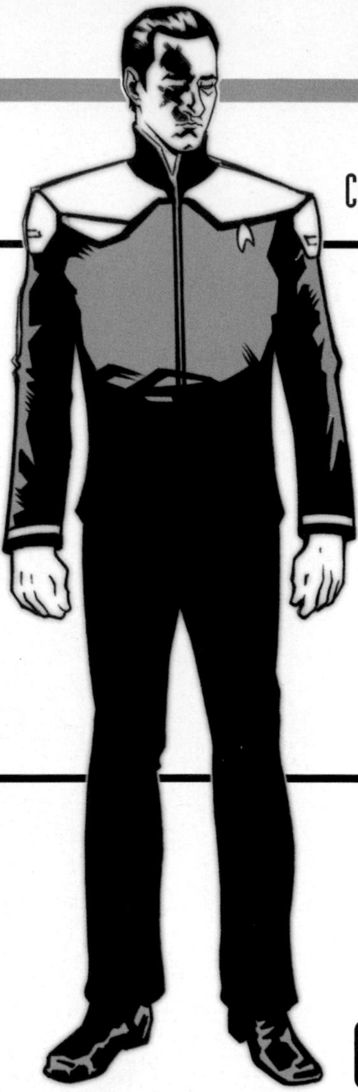

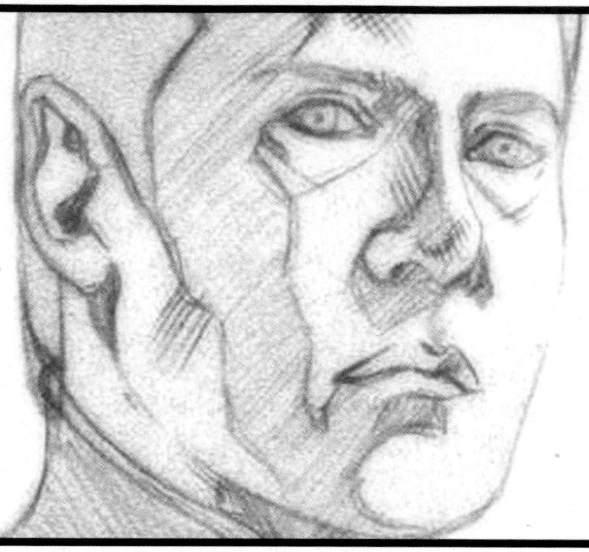

Captain Data

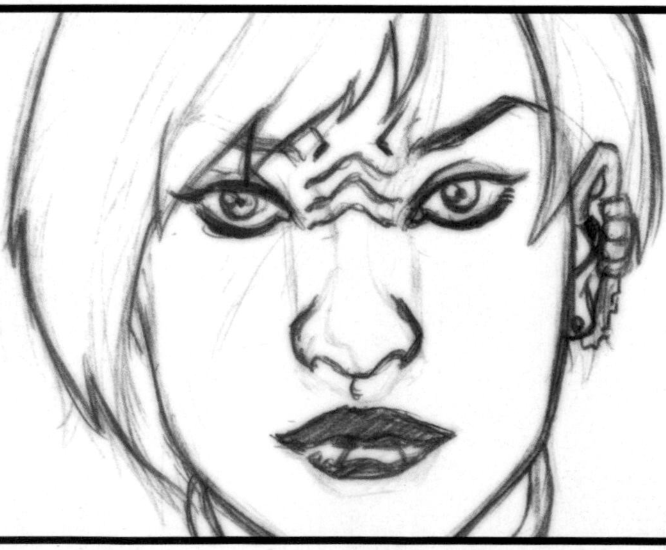

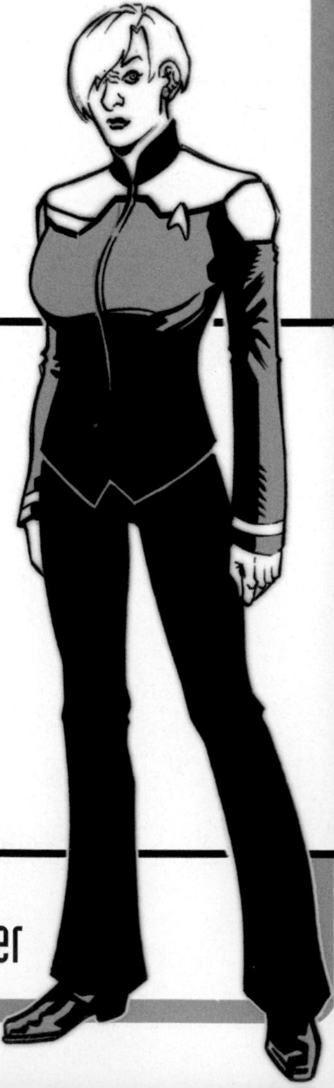

Enterprise Crew Member

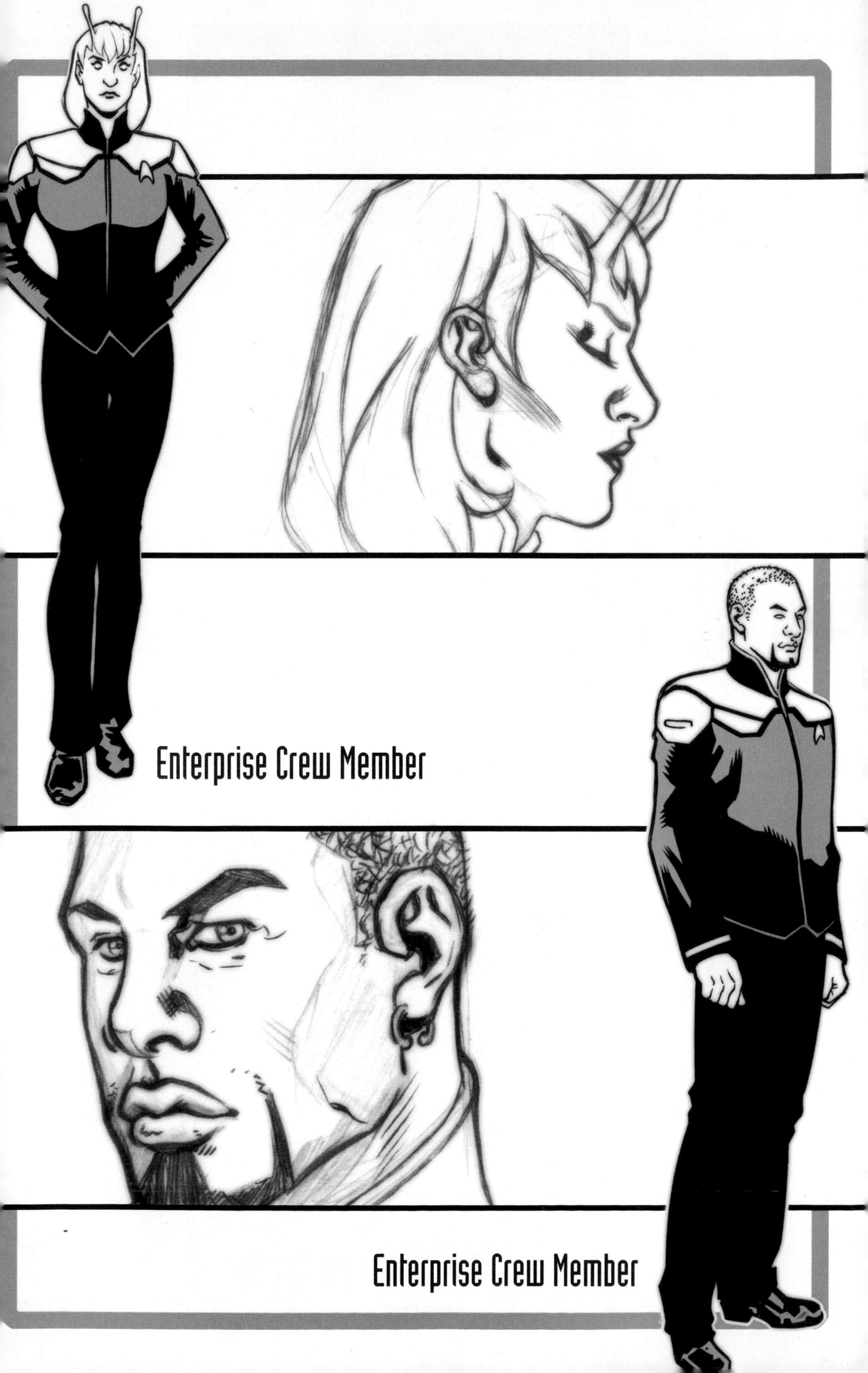

Enterprise Crew Member

Enterprise Crew Member

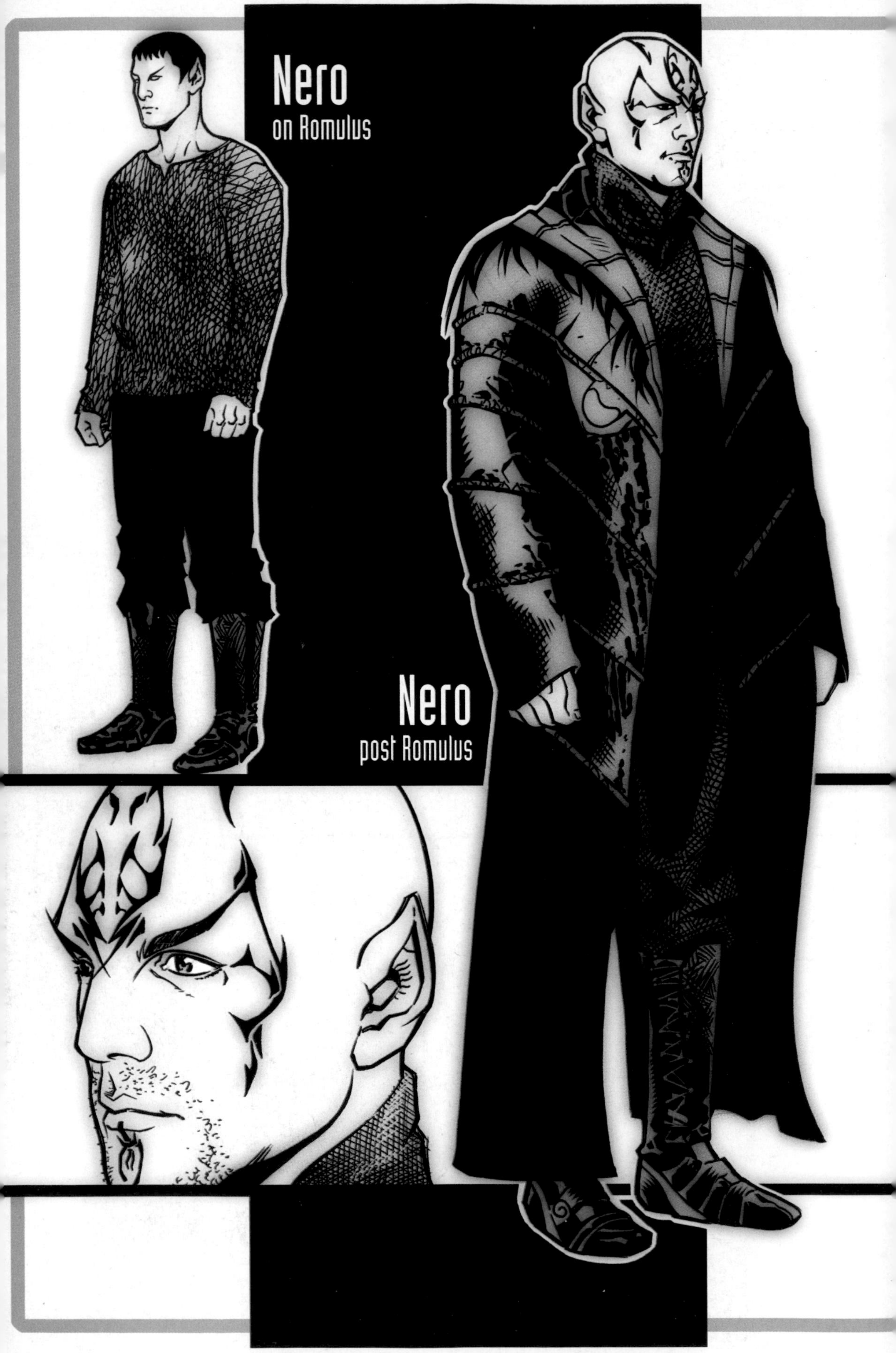
Nero
on Romulus
Nero
post Romulus

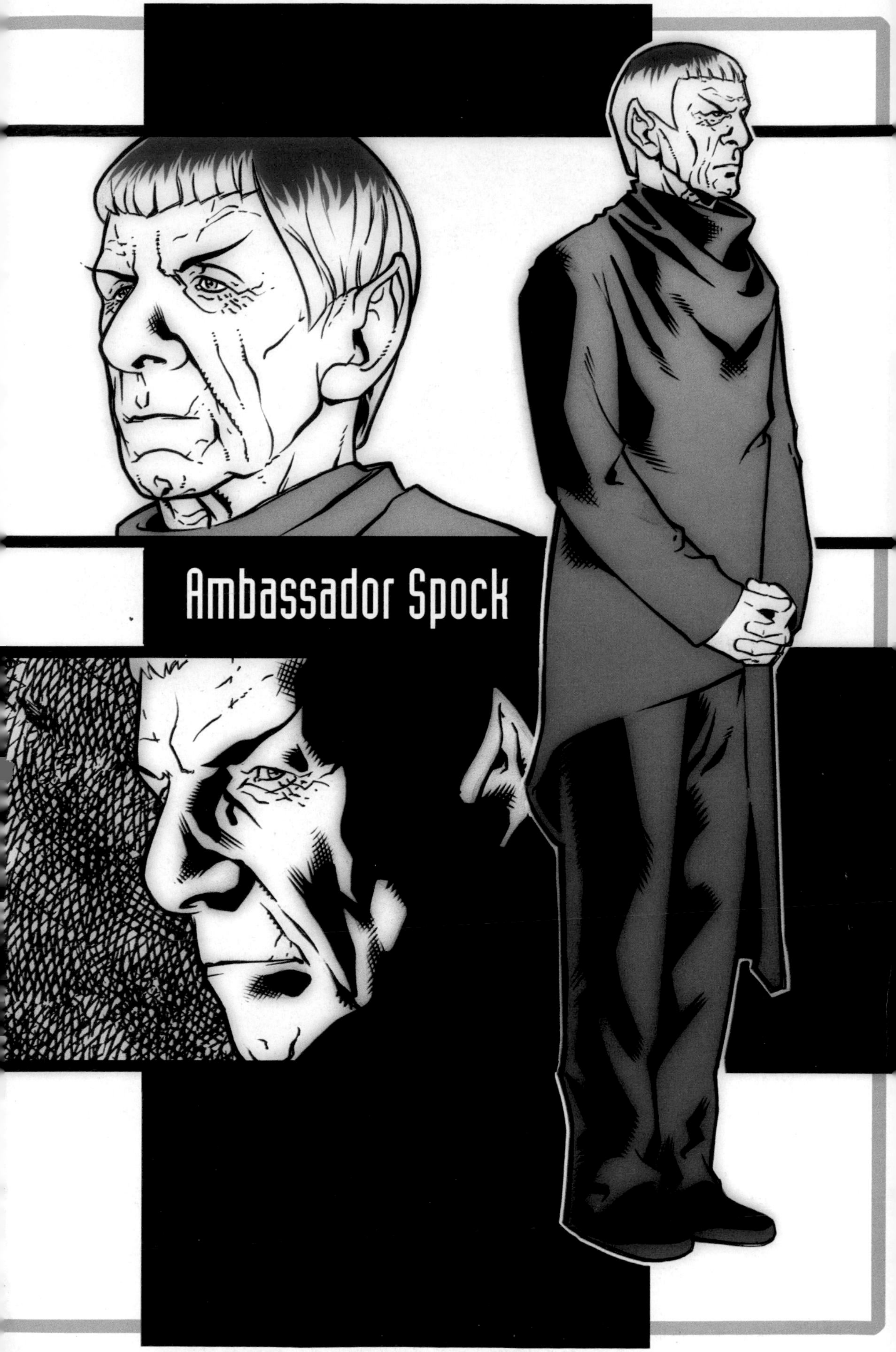
Ambassador Spock

Captain Data and Enterprise Crew

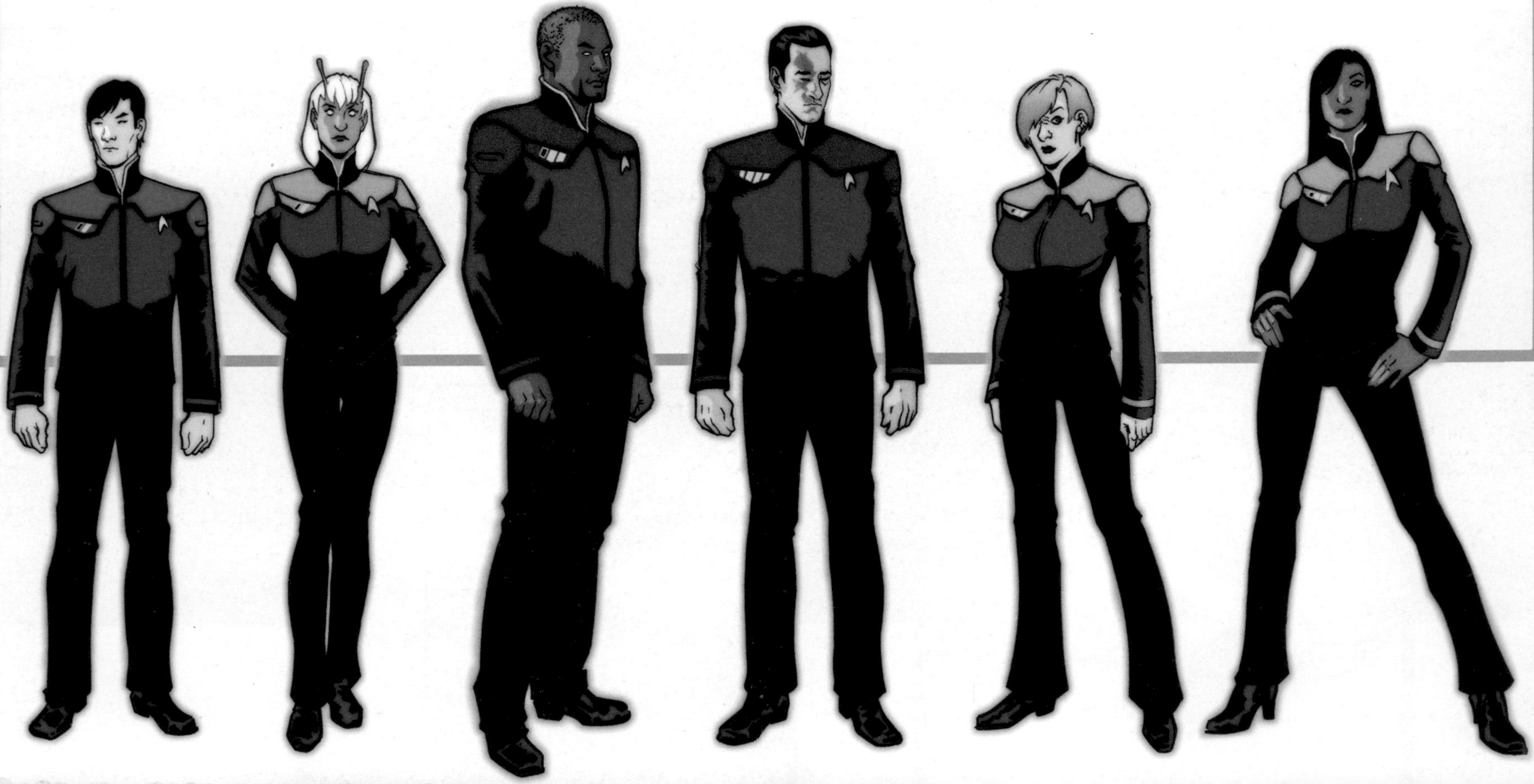